Rapture and]

For Love of a Horse

by Jemma Spark

© 2019

Epona Publishing

Table of Contents

List of Characters

Rafael Pisano – Twenty-two-year-old Uruguayan stable boy working at Melilla Polo Club in the riding school. Orphaned at the age of ten he was unofficially adopted by Carina, an elderly British woman.

Carina – Eccentric immigrant from Britain who went into exile in Uruguay when she was twenty-five years old. She settled in a shanty town on the outskirts of Montevideo. A skilled horsewoman who adopted Rafael as a ten-year-old orphan, and taught him all he knows about horses. She died when he was eighteen years old.

Facundo – The riding instructor at Melilla Polo Club, handsome, arrogant and totally immoral.

Tomas – An acolyte of Facundo, also a member of staff at the Melilla Polo Club.

Marianela – Wanton seventeen-year-old schoolgirl with her sights set on Facundo. The only daughter of Claudia.

Viviana- Marianela's best friend.

Claudia – Sexy thirty-five-year-old divorcée, mother of Marianela, on the hunt for a second husband to finance her lifestyle when the generous child support paid by her first husband ceases when her daughter, Marianela turns eighteen.

Emilio Rodriguez Ortiz – Ex-husband of Claudia, father of Marianela, rich businessman living in Columbia with contacts in one of the powerful drug cartels.

Pablo – Best show jumping rider in Uruguay, fifty-seven-year-old charming, handsome and lover of Florencia, thirty years his junior.

Florencia – Show jumping rider from a rich Paraguayan family, ugly but sexy, rampantly ambitious girlfriend of much older Pablo.

Valentino – The second-best show jumper in Uruguay with ten show jumping horses stabled at Melilla Polo Club.

David Lester-Blythe – Recently appointed forty-five-year-old member of staff at the British Embassy. Handsome, charming, amoral and from lower class background married to Grace.

Grace Lester-Blythe – Aristocratic, dowdy, wealthy, forty-five-year-old wife of David. Her family home is Kiss Wood in Oxfordshire.

Phoebe Lester-Blythe –Seventeen-year-old daughter of David and Grace, overweight, brainy, shy and lacking in self-confidence in her last year of school. Does not like riding as she is too fat.

Poppy Lester-Blythe – Fifteen-year-old daughter of David and Grace, pony-mad and has lessons at the riding school three times a week.

Tate Wade – Nineteen-year-old daughter of Verena Wade. A socialite who works as a model, has a serious taste for cocaine.

Penelope ('Loppy') Wade - Fifteen-year-old daughter of Verena Wade, best friends with Poppy.

Verena Wade – Grace's childhood friend, lives in Oxfordshire near Grace's family home, has a glamorous daughter Tate, and also a younger daughter 'Loppy'.

Angela – one of the grooms at Blythe Star Stables.

Ruby – Another of the grooms at Blythe Star Stables.

Oliver Soames - Sixty-year-old widower, charming, well-off and owner of Tall Chimneys and one thousand acres in Oxfordshire. An old friend of Grace Lester-Blyth.

Hector Soames – Eighteen-year-old only son of Oliver Soames, lives with his father at Tall Chimneys and plays polo.

Jamie Landon - Forty-year-old stable manager who works for Grace at the Blythe Star Stables.

Jerome Bradley - Nineteen-year-old groom, aspiring eventing rider, works at Blythe Star Stables.

Panda – Young married woman who lives in Oxfordshire, Phoebe's friend.

Charles – Husband of Panda.

Tinker Stourton – Young self-published writer, friend of Tate.

Thomas Morton – Traditional show jumping coach who remembers Grace as a girl.

Nic – One of the London crew who hangs around with Tinker, moody, writes biographies and histories.

Maddie – One of the London crew who hangs around with Tinker, thick long hair draped around a pale Madonna face, writes about Chinese art.

David – One of the London crew who hangs around with Tinker, smart, likeable, a gifted musician who produces musicals.

Georgia – One of the London crew who hangs around with Tinker, an aspiring writer who has to date only had textbooks published for a training organisation in Dubai.

Stiggy – One of the London crew who hangs around with Tinker, a Romanian émigré who thinks of himself as a poet.

Shea – One of the London crew who hangs around with Tinker, a tiny bird-like girl with a high-pitched voice. She is twenty-years-old but looks like a twelve-year-old.

Mason and Maddox – Heavenly twins who turn up at the Kiss Wood house party.

Chapter One

Rafael slept uneasily the night before the show jumping event at the riding school at Melilla Polo Club. His dream world had been a tumbling kaleidoscope of monstrous, scary scenarios. He woke with a start, cold sweat beading his forehead, staring at the thin stream of moonlight that shone through the flimsy curtains of the ugly window. He looked at his mobile phone. It was only four o'clock, the alarm was set for six, another two hours to go.

He lay there, breathing heavily, he knew he was awake, but he felt as if he were still in the nightmare. First, it had been Facundo, the riding instructor, mocking him while he cowered naked in front of half a dozen of the young female students who were seated on the tiered benches that ran down the long side of the indoor riding school. There was Carina, looking like a haggard old woman offering him a poisoned chalice studded with blood-red rubies and topaz gems. Then he was watching helplessly as Tomas was crashing Estrella, over the brick wall. The beautiful black mare, with a shiny coat like a raven's wing, fell to the ground, maimed, with broken legs and Tomas and Facundo were laughing, standing over her heaving dark hulk, while Rafael. tears streaming down his face, tried to wipe away the hot, salty blood that was staining the mare's thin, white blaze.

The nightmare took root in his mind; it seemed more real than his waking reality. Still sweating and gasping for air, he fumbled clumsily for the pack of cigarettes that lay on the splintered, wooden box that served as a bedside table. The first lungful of acrid tobacco smoke soothed him. He forced himself to relive the nightmare and tried to reason his way back into some semblance of rational calm.

The first part of the dream about Facundo, the riding instructor was real enough. Facundo lived to make spiteful fun of those he considered his inferiors, and Rafael as a lowly stable boy had absolutely no defences against him. He was expected to bow his head and not answer back. He knew that nakedness in a dream symbolised defencelessness and vulnerability.

The second part of his dream about Carina was harder to understand. Carina had been the only good person in his life - an eccentric, older woman, an immigrant from England, who had gone native and lived amongst the poor people in a pig-stinking shanty town on the outskirts of Montevideo, the sprawling capital city of Uruguay. To her people back home, she would have been considered a misfit, an outlaw or a woman who had fallen into degradation. For Rafael, who was orphaned at the age of ten, she was a guardian angel who had cared for him as if he were her own. He had lived with her for eight years until her sudden and inexplicable death a few years ago. She was the only person who had ever shown him kindness, not the evil witch who had loomed threateningly in his dream. Her goodness had been palpable. She had encouraged him to attend school and at home had taught him English: and most importantly of all, she had shared her knowledge of horses with him. They had owned a number of horses, rescued from other people in the shanty town who used them to pull the carts. Ugly, marked with fresh wounds and old scars, the horses would collapse in despair after long days being driven into the city to haul back recyclable materials found in rubbish bins.

Rafael had learned to ride on the horses that they had nursed back to health. Carina had taught him how to look after them and to treat them when they were ill or injured. Sometimes they would purchase a foal and nurture it and train it according to the principles of good horsemanship. Later they would sell it - only to the best of homes, to the rich people who owned *estancias*.

Carina had died one night, without warning she had simply stopped breathing. Rafael had woken to find her stiff and cold in the bed in the next room After the funeral he had taken the small metal box containing her few paltry possessions, including one precious reference book on dressage, and his own tatty clothes, and left the two-room shack. He wasn't stealing. There was no-one else to inherit her belongings. He knew that she had no family in South America. She had left England many years ago and lived in exile. He could have stayed on in the shack, but he could not bear to be there without her.

He had managed to get himself a job at the Melilla Polo Club, employed as a stable boy. He had hoped that he might one day become a riding instructor. He knew more about equestrian theory and could ride better than any of them. But now, after four years, he had bitterly come to the realisation that there would never be an opportunity for promotion. There was no chance for the upwardly mobile in the Polo Club. Rich Uruguayans were probably more class conscious and more pretentious than British people and carefully kept to their own type, knowing that it was too easy to tumble back down the precarious social ladder.

The worst part of his nightmare had been about Estrella, the beautiful black mare that was one of the ten horses that were in his charge. He had no difficulty in understanding its significance. Today she was to be ridden by Facundo, rather than Tomas, in the 130 cm jumping event. This filled Rafael with black dread. It was going to be an utter disaster, and he was doomed to watch helplessly from the ringside. Facundo considered himself one of the best riders in the world, which he certainly was not. He was young, handsome, arrogant and careless of the lives of the people and horses around him. Rafael knew that the mare was not yet ready to compete at that level and certainly not while being ridden by Facundo. But no-one was going to listen to him, and if he said anything at all, then Facundo and Tomas would make his life even more of a misery.

He decided not to try and go back to sleep. Grinding out the cigarette in a cracked saucer that served as an ashtray, he sat up on the sagging, iron bedstead. The floor of his room was beaten earth, a couple of hooks on the wall served as somewhere to hang his clothes. There was a naked bulb swinging from the ceiling.

Now, on the morning of the show jumping competition he didn't want to go over to the stable block where his horses would still be asleep. Horses were creatures of habit, and they thrived on an unvaried schedule. If he woke them earlier than usual, they would be anxious. So, he went outside and headed down towards the indoor riding school that loomed in the predawn light, like a large domed spaceship. They had set up the jumps the night before, and unlike English horse shows which began with the lowest classes here, it was the other way around. The first event was the 160 cm. There would only be a handful of horses and riders competing at this level; the great Pablo Rusoni on his stallion, Tontino, and his girlfriend, Florencia Pancino mounted on one of the horses that her rich parents had bought her. She was more than thirty years younger than Pablo but utterly devoted to him and their horses, and rampantly ambitious. The only other possible local competitor was Valentino who had represented Uruguay in several international competitions.

There were also two Brazilian riders who had brought six horses from across the border. They were hoping to sell them for exorbitant prices to the rich parents of the young girls who rode at the riding school. The

Brazilians were flashy young men, with long, glossy black hair, broad shoulders and slim hips, ready to flatter and persuade the parents into spending at least thirty thousand US dollars on each horse. They made a practice of bringing across their second-rate horses that were never going to make the grade at Grand Prix, but who would be more than adequate for the spoilt children of the wealthy Uruguayans who, like rich people the world over, loved to show off to their peers. They would make reasonable mounts competing in the lower levels of show jumping, the 80 cm and the one metre, and possibly even the 130 cm.

Rafael had sniggered to himself to see Facundo and Tomas upstaged by the Brazilians. It would be interesting to see how they fared in the competitions. If only Facundo hadn't been entered in the 130 cm on Estrella, he could have enjoyed the day, having a break from the endless routine of feeding, cleaning and grooming. Rafael had watched the way that Facundo had wooed Georgina, the owner of Estrella. She was a tall, shy girl with long brown hair, a good rider but lacking in self-confidence, certainly not one of the popular group, and had been flattered when Facundo had singled her out, complimented her and shown her attention. That had been how he had persuaded her that he should jump the mare in the 130 cm competition.

Rafael had understood the English expression about 'blood boiling', Carina had explained it and many other idiomatic expressions to him. She had also trained him to speak in an upper-class accent, rounding his vowels and not dropping his 'aitches'. If he had displayed his ability to speak English at the riding school it would not have gone down well, so he just played the dumb Uruguayan from the shanty town.

Even so, Georgina had always been kind to him, talking to him as if he were a person, not merely a lowly employee who was far beneath her. He had even wondered if he might talk to her about Estrella and help her to train the mare, but Facundo had stepped in and managed to charm and persuade the young girl to allow him to ride the mare.

Rafael lit another cigarette and looked at the layout of the course. He knew the track perfectly and had measured out the distances between each jump the previous day when he had helped to build the course. He drifted off into a daydream where he was wearing a brand-new outfit, perfectly fitting breeches, long leather brown boots and a stylish riding jacket, slapping his whip against his boots walking around the course with the other riders.

Then he imagined riding the course on Estrella. He had never ridden the mare in the arena, but he had managed to sneak a few rides on her bareback. In his spare time, he would lead out some of his horses, so they could graze on the lush grass on the edge of the polo field. During the lunchtime break, if there was no-one around, he would go down to the far side where the thick trees screened the view from the stables and would vault onto the mare and ride her bareback in a headcollar. He controlled her with his weight and a slight pull on the rope, and she was divine to ride. He adored her more than any human or horse he had ever known, except of course Carina, but she was dead.

He walked slowly back to the stables, still in his dream world. There was no-one else around, and he went into the staff kitchen area, roofed with corrugated iron, furnished with a dirty table, an old fridge, and a gas element for cooking and heating water. He put the kettle half-full of water on the gas and when it had heated poured it into his maté cup. Maté is a South American herbal drink that has a stimulatory effect like coffee and depressed one's appetite. He helped himself to the dried-up pizza in the fridge. Then it was six o'clock, and he made his way over to the stable block, knocking on the doors of the other staff on the way, so they would be up in plenty of time, there would be a lot to do today.

His horses all neighed and whickered when they saw him. They banged on their half-doors, hanging their heads out for a glimpse of him. He looked up the row to make sure they were all bright-eyed and happy. Estrella was on the end of the row, and he stopped and patted her gently, murmuring nonsense into her ears, his usual sullen expression lit up with a smile full of love.

It didn't take him long to do the feeds, he knew each amount off by heart and scooped out crushed oats and barley and pellets from the metal bins and hurried down the row tipping the mixtures into each of the feed bowls. Then he started cleaning the loose boxes, expertly picking up the lumps of manure with a fork, digging out wet patches with a small broken-handled shovel, then topping up the rice husk bedding from the huge pile around the back of the stable block, where flocks of pigeons, white and grey and mottled, cooed and strutted, flapping their wings.

He had just finished when he saw Pablo and Florencia arrive in their clapped-out old Fiat sedan. In spite of Florencia's rich parents, who lived on a big *estancia* in Paraguay, they were chronically short of money. Pablo was charming and handsome, but Florencia was short-tempered and tactless, and the rich clients often went off in a huff when she offended them. They had run the riding school at Melilla for several years. Still, Florencia had argued with the staff at the Polo Club, and they had had to leave, setting up a riding school without an indoor arena over near the coast, too far from Montevideo to attract many of the former clients, who were now taught by Facundo.

The first event didn't begin until ten o'clock, but Pablo and Florencia's four horses arrived early in a beat-up old truck. Florencia leapt up the ramp and led down the first of them, a small bay mare with loppy ears. She was not beautiful but fit and sleek and shining. Rafael hovered nearby and moved forward to hold her lead rope while Florencia peeled off her rug and travelling bandages. She went back for the next horse, and he led the mare around.

"You, bring that horse back," shouted Florencia in her rasping, ugly voice.

"*Gracias*," said Pablo graciously when Rafael handed over the lead rope. "We appreciate your help."

"Humph," grunted Florencia, carrying out the leather jumping saddles and bridles that were gleaming and smelled of saddle soap.

Rafael didn't care when Florencia was rude. She was like that with everyone, whether it was a lowly stable boy or a rich bitch who was flirting with Pablo. One wondered what he saw in his much younger, ugly girlfriend. He had had a beautiful, soft-spoken wife with two young children and he had left her to hook up with Florencia. Obviously, Florencia's rich parents would have been in her favour, and perhaps he would hang in until she got her inheritance. Or perhaps she was a miracle when it came to sex. She was that sort of girl, probably eager to do anything in bed, with a raw sexuality that glittered from her squinty eyes.

Relationships were always a mystery to Rafael. He watched men and women and wondered what it was that kept people together, obviously children and mutual dependence, but he couldn't imagine himself sustaining any sort of emotional relationship with another human. When he had been a teenager in the shanty town, he had had sex with several of the girls with whom he had grown up. But there had been no thrill of intimacy for him; it was only with horses that he felt a deep connection.

The riding school students, mainly girls, just a couple of boys, were arriving in dribs and drabs. The girls were dressed up in their best jodhpurs, with pockets trimmed with pretty, pink floral designs, pristine white shirts and polished boots. The girls had, almost without exception, long brown hair with smooth olive skin and brown eyes. But one of them, perhaps the bitchiest of them all, Marianela stood out with her dark green-blonde hair which matched her strange light-green eyes, highlighted with light-coloured eyeshadow. She had the longest legs and the most magnificent breasts and was the leader of the popular group, stalking around bitching and laughing, tossing back her hair, clinking the inappropriate chunky gold bracelets on her wrists.

Rafael saw that Georgina, Estrella's owner, had arrived and had gone straight over to see her horse. She was probably the only one of the rich girls who groomed her own horse, fussing over the mare, kissing her soft neck, secretly licking the salty, black, satin coat, and then feeding her pieces of carrot and apple from an open palm. Rafael went down to the tack room and brought back her saddle and bridle and helped her to saddle up. Then Facundo stalked up, smiling at Georgina, crinkling his rather small brown eyes attractively, totally ignoring Rafael as if he didn't exist.

"Hurry up and saddle her, I'll warm her up now, then the boy can lead her around until the event."

"I have to help with the jumps in the 160 cm," said Rafael, unable to quite disguise his dislike, curling his nostrils at the smell of after-shave that Facundo splashed himself with every morning.

"Whatever," said Facundo off-handedly.

"I'll lead her around," said Georgina quickly. She was a kind-hearted girl and didn't like the way that they treated Rafael. She knew how well he cared for her horse and liked him with his huge, dark, slanting, sad eyes hidden beneath the too-long, black, glossy hair.

Facundo vaulted onto the mare, picking up the reins and pulling them short kicking her into a semblance of collection that was all wrong. Rafael lowered his eyes, remembering the way that Carina had always taught him the textbook principles of warming up horses; riding them first on a long rein, gently taking up contact and pushing them into a more shortened frame, maintaining suppleness and relaxation. He despised the way that Facundo rode - but there was absolutely nothing he could do about it.

Georgina trotted after him, her long gangly legs awkward as she rushed to keep up. Facundo didn't look back, nor wait for her. He was in a hurry. The beautiful black mare stretched out her stride and seemed to float across the ground, pointing her toes like a ballerina. They entered the practice arena, and Facundo kicked her into a canter, and after only one circle he jumped her over the practice jump standing at 140 cm, ready for the Grand Prix horses to warm up.

Rafael didn't want to watch. It hurt too much to see Facundo riding his favourite horse. He went back to his other charges. As well as Estrella, there were three other horses owned by students, who were riding in the 80 cm competition after lunch. He needed to give them a thorough grooming before he was due to help with the first event. He was burning with resentment at the injustice of the situation and haunted with a horrible feeling of doom that Estrella would fall and be maimed for life. And he was utterly helpless and could not intervene.

Rafael hoped that Facundo wouldn't take sexual advantage of Georgina - that she might be spared. She was one of the kindest girls at the riding school, lanky and somewhat plain, lacking in self-confidence, not at all flirtatious although she did look at Facundo, shyly and longingly. Rafael knew that if the riding instructor chose, he could take her as casually and carelessly as he fucked the others. Hopefully, all he was after was the ride on Estrella. And besides, Georgina's father was very rich and influential, and if he felt that his daughter had been badly treated, he would make sure that Facundo would get the sack, or worse.

Over the last few months, it had become clear that Facundo was losing favour with Valentino, who was perhaps the second-best show jump rider in Uruguay. Previously, Facundo had exercised some of his horses and would jump them under supervision, but now Tomas rode two of them. It looked like Facundo's star might be on the wane. Rafael had wondered if there had been some way for Valentino to see himself ride then perhaps, he might have his chance. Today Facundo needed some wins on the board to re-establish his ascendancy. He seemed sure that riding Estrella in the 130 cm would put him back in the limelight.

Chapter Two

Most of the parents would not roll up until after lunch when their progeny was competing in the lower classes, but Marianela's mother, Claudia, had arrived early. She had dragged her ungracious teenage daughter out of bed and insisted that she accompany her. Today she was on a mission and wanted to make sure that everything went to plan.

They were some of the first to arrive at the Polo Club, parking in the shade of the huge eucalyptus trees that grew around the stables. Claudia checked her appearance in the rear vision mirror of her smart silver Audi convertible. Then she climbed out, flashing her long slim brown legs. She was wearing a tiny little pale pink skirt and a white singlet top that showed off her wonderful tan and her amazingly slim, shapely arms. Tottering off towards the arena on very high-heeled sandal shoes with silver studs and buckles, she would have looked distinctly out of place at any equestrian event in England, but in South America, the women dressed more flamboyantly. Tossing back her thick mane of carefully silver-streaked blonde hair and walking slowly, her hips swayed, and a cloud of heavy sexy perfume wafted around her. She was used to men's heads turning wherever she went.

After prancing around calling '*buenos dias*' to anyone she knew, she settled herself in the front row of the benches that ran the length of the indoor arena in order to watch the first event which commenced in about half an hour. She had told some of her friends that she was thinking of buying Marianela an absolutely top-class horse and wanted to view some of the animals for sale. In reality, there was hardly five thousand US dollars in her bank account, and certainly not the thirty thousand dollars that was the standard minimum price for a good quality horse. She was in desperate need of money to maintain her lavish lifestyle, and, for that, she needed a man, preferably a husband, rather than a married lover. She was hoping that the one she fancied would be here today. Although he was married at this point, she was fairly certain that it would be a small matter to steal him away from his dowdy and undoubtedly boring wife. The plan was to tempt him, seduce him and persuade him that he couldn't live without her. If it was necessary, she was prepared to risk getting pregnant and manipulate him in that way. At the age of thirty-five, she was still young enough to bear another child, but the years were slipping away, like sand through the hourglass.

She arranged herself artfully on the bench. Her short pink skirt hiked up around her hips. Her back straight, her neck held at an advantageous angle, so there was no hint of a widow's hump. She had buxom silicone breasts with a glorious cleavage and a tight little arse that got exercised at the gym every day. She was a high-class cat, but her days were numbered. Carefully botoxed, there was not a line on her face, and her huge green eyes, just like her daughter's, were lined with sparkling white eye shadow that made them look larger. Her pouting bee-stung mouth was painted bright pink. Her last lover had loved her mouth. He said that it looked just like her pretty pink vagina.

She knew that by the time she was forty, it was going to be harder and harder to maintain her looks on a low budget. Marianela was in her last year of school, and this meant that the lucrative child support payments would be coming to an end. She had always looked after herself, subsisting on fresh fruit and salad and yoghurt, eschewing carbohydrates. Her voluptuous body was toned all over, not to mention the twenty minutes a day of pelvic floor exercises to keep the walls of her vagina tight.

Divorced from Marianela's father for fifteen years now, she had been involved with countless married men, and also young single men but now was the time to get serious. She regretted all those wasted years on men who would not support her into her old age. The warning bells were ringing loud and clear. Soon she would be in the twilight zone, regarded as a mature woman. This made her very nervous. She had to pull this one off and would then be set for life, leave Uruguay and go and live in the first world. She had fucked too many men in this small country with a population of just over three million and her reputation as a man-eater was becoming a distinct disadvantage. She was beginning to notice the women's eyes sliding away from her during society events. It was the men who talked to her, but increasingly they were pleasant for a few minutes then trotted back regretfully to their wives.

Last week she had met David Lester-Blythe, the man upon whom she had set her sights. He had recently arrived at the British High Commission, a diplomat who had enrolled his daughters at the British School. The summer holidays were almost over, and the academic year commenced in February. David had mentioned that his thirteen-year-old daughter, Poppy, was getting riding lessons with Facundo. This English man was tall, handsome and exuded that wonderful understated British charm. His younger daughter, barely a teenager, was cute and adored horses. She was

16

getting three riding lessons a week, usually chaperoned by her mother, but hopefully, David would be attending the event today as she was due to jump in the 80 cm competition after lunch. There was another daughter as well, Phoebe; a fat, pale slug of a girl, in Marianela's school year. Apparently, she didn't ride but was very good at schoolwork and aiming to return to England to attend Oxford University in the following year. The wife, Grace, was the epitome of dowdy - as far as Claudia could tell. Surely, she could manage to seduce the husband away from that frumpy woman. Claudia, not understanding the way that British diplomats were supposed to behave, was sure that she would be viewed as a social asset, a trophy wife who could attend events on David's arm. Leaving his present wife and marrying her would help to boost his career and with any luck they would get a brilliant posting in the States, or somewhere in Europe, perhaps Spain.

Had Claudia troubled herself to research the nature of the relationship of this married couple, she might not have decided on this course of action. Not only did she misunderstand the unspoken rules of the diplomatic world, nor the even more mysterious class system of the British, she assumed that the financial power lay in the husband's hands. She didn't know that Grace's family trust fund was the solid basis of their financial comfort, and had they had to live on David's salary alone there would be no riding lessons and barely one meal out a week.

The 160 cm show jumping event was set up ready to go and, as Rafael had predicted, there were only six entries: Pablo on Tontino, Florencia on Batatino, Valentino on three horses that were probably not quite ready for such a challenging course, and one of the Brazilians on a seasoned show jumper that had already seen its best days. Claudia gave the appearance of watching intently. The colossal jumps hardly registered, she was absorbed in her plan for the day. Pablo entered the arena on Tontino, a magnificent grey stallion, with a wide chest, long clean legs and a powerful rump. The thin crowd clapped enthusiastically, as they went clear. The Uruguayans loved an Uruguayan rider to win, resenting the higher-class entries that came across the border from Brazil. When Florencia had only four faults, there was no clapping at all. She was bad-tempered and had burned too many bridges with her sharp tongue to be popular. The Brazilian rider had eight faults and the three horses ridden by Valentino all knocked down poles all over the place.

Rafael stood at the edge of the arena and ran in with one of the other stable boys and put up the jumps whenever the poles were knocked down. He was spellbound during Pablo's round. He worshipped the older man and would have laid down his life for him. He had even considered offering his services for nothing, living on air just to work for him and Florencia, but was too shy to approach them. They rode up to get their rosettes, and Florencia's horse was hotted up, throwing its head around and snorting, and when they cantered a victory lap, it threw its head in the air and overtook Pablo, sweeping out of the arena ahead of the others, Florencia's ugly face flushed with irritation that she had not won, but at least it had been Pablo who had beaten her. Driven by ambition winning was everything to her.

The next competition was the 130 cm, and the Brazilians had entered six horses, each rider having two entries. Pablo was riding two horses and Florencia one, Facundo was on Estrella. Rafael hurried into the arena and went around with the head groundsman, who had the measuring stick. All the jumps were lowered, but the layout was unchanged. The course was not designed with any originality, just plain jumps in a predictable pattern. Pablo was riding a huge bay gelding that they had purchased in Brazil a few months before and a thin raking grey gelding that had come off the racetrack and had been rushed through his jumping training. Florencia was riding a compact little bay mare that had competed all last year winning one metre competitions and was now judged ready to step up. They were hoping to sell her and wanted to make sure that she beat the Brazilians' horses. The parents at the Polo Club were only really impressed with winning; they had no concept of good horsemanship. The black mare, Estrella, was easily the most impressive of all the horses. She had perfect conformation, straight movement, a well-developed rump and a broad chest that housed the biggest heart. Her head was small and delicate, huge gleaming dark eyes and the thinnest of white stripes down her face.

The riders were walking the course, and Marianela was with Facundo, cavorting around beside him, trying to catch his attention while he was concentrating on the distances between the jumps. Then, she tossed her dark-blonde mane back and turned to the Brazilians who were walking behind them, wiggling her bottom to catch their attention. They smiled back, eyeing her up appreciatively and cried out flirtatious comments.

Like her mother, Marianela was determined when she set her sights on a conquest, and she had decided that Facundo as a boyfriend would mean

18

huge social success at the Polo Club. Her mother had discouraged her in this, suggesting instead that she should focus on one of the young boys of the rich families. Facundo was middle class, but only just, his family had lost their fortune a couple of generations ago, and he was now forced to live off his meagre salary, supplemented by his parents who were surviving on his father's salary as a civil servant and the scant remains of the family fortune. But Marianela didn't care. She assumed that her father would always look after her and was hoping that when she turned eighteen, he would set her up in her own apartment, that way she could get away from her mother and run her own life.

Contrary to Rafael's nightmare, Estrella and Facundo jumped a perfect clear round, and then the fastest in the jump-off by three whole seconds. Rafael was smouldering on the sidelines and didn't know whether to cry with relief, or pain at the idea that this meant Facundo would ride the mare again and again. He kept his feelings shut in, and narrowed his eyes and set his lips in a straight line.

Claudia sat up and clapped a little too loudly, bored with watching the horses. She had no appreciation of the science of show jumping. There was no sign of the Lester-Blythe family, and it was hot, her hair was dusty from sitting beside the arena, which was always inadequately watered. She felt cheated, having wasted the whole morning, and now she was not looking her best. Getting up, she smoothed her skirt and hurried over to the bathroom next to the riding school office and freshened up, carefully wiping the dirt from her face and reapplying a subtle layer of makeup, then brushing out her hair that was a little tangled. She noticed that her white top had a smudge of dirt down the front.

She was feeling distinctly annoyed, and the harsh light showed the beginnings of tiny crows' feet at the corner of her eyes. Her resolve hardened. She had to pull this one-off, or she would be faced with a future where she would have to actually get a job, and salaries were notoriously low in Uruguay, and she had no skills. Working in a boutique on the lowest of wages was about all she could hope for. The thought of this black future filled her with horror. She had been so sure that the whole Lester-Blythe family would come and watch the younger daughter, but perhaps she had miscalculated. Carefully she made her way over to the dining room in the main hall. They were serving fresh salmon and salad, and the inevitable pasta with a tasteless cheese sauce or chorizos on bread.

Then she saw them. Like a mirage on the horizon, four Lester-Blythes walking over from the carpark. David was just as attractive as she had first thought, tall, long-limbed and elegant in a beige linen suit. His younger daughter, Poppy, the horse rider was wearing jodhpurs and a white shirt that had obviously been purchased in England, not from the only equestrian store in Montevideo. She was holding her father's hand and chattering away to him, leaping up and down at his side like a little monkey. She looked much younger than fifteen-years-old. He smiled down at her fondly. The mother and the fat teenage girl walked behind them. Both of them looked like absolute frights, Claudia noted with satisfaction, suddenly filled with hope and certainty.

She stood back and waited to see where they were heading, and sure enough, they were going into lunch. She timed her entrance to coincide with them and smiling, she greeted them, making sure that she was particularly friendly and attentive towards the wife. It was a token effort to appear to be a genuine potential family friend, rather than a husband-snatcher.

"Let's all sit here?" she said airily, her voice low and husky, her smile as sweet as sticky honey.

"Of course," said David, smiling back, and she knew that he was taking in every detail of her appearance. He could smell sweet pussy. The wife's thin lips tightened a little, and there was a distinct *froideur* in her manner. She was wearing a crumpled linen beige skirt and a blouse of white cotton, done up nearly to her neck. The elder daughter looked as boring as her mother, very overweight in a long, dark-blue skirt with a baggy matching top. Grace did not seem to be fazed by the glamorous appearance of their newfound best friend and conversed politely across the table. She had seen it all before. Twenty years as the wife of a diplomat had inured her to meeting all sorts of foreign people. She knew what was expected of her and good breeding dictated no expression of negative emotions.

"You've only just joined the Club?" asked Claudia.

"Yes, we're new in town," replied David boyishly.

"I'm so pleased to meet you again, you know that I have a daughter Phoebe's age, her name is Marianela, and she is also in her final year at school," tooted Claudia, her laugh tinkling out around the dining room.

Grace looked at her evenly, not reacting to the mincing, flirtatious undertone. Suddenly she felt unutterably weary. This woman would undoubtedly manage to seduce David, who viewed life through a veil of sex. In fact, it would take a lot less effort than Claudia was currently making. He was prone to jump anything remotely attractive and female that came across his path. There was no need for the rather obvious too tight and too short skirt, nor the heavy cloud of perfume. They had been through this scenario so many times throughout their married life. Other diplomats joked that they were the Bill and Hilary Clinton of the diplomatic circle and it was one of the reasons that David had not advanced significantly in his career and they were now stuck in this backwater for the next three years. Grace had come to watch Poppy riding during the last week and felt depressed at the low standard of equitation here. She had imagined that in a South American country, there would be a much higher level of knowledge and skill when it came to horses. For a moment, she thought about her childhood of grey misty mornings out hunting, leaping huge obstacles and the cameraderie of the hunting field. She experienced an extraordinary longing for her own country and her own horses.

"So, Poppy, you look like the rider in the family," said Claudia, who knew perfectly well that Facundo was giving the young girl lessons three times a week. The jodhpurs were another clue!

"I've been riding for years," said Poppy, "at our last posting we were in Spain, and I rode a lot there."

"Well, that must be useful with speaking Spanish," said Claudia.

"Yes, but they speak Spanish here with such a strange pronunciation," said Poppy.

"Perhaps we would say the same about them," said Claudia, "they sound as if they're lisping all the time."

Thus, the conversation went around in predictable circles, the usual polite patter that Grace had suffered through so many times. She didn't bother to contribute much. Mainly she left it to David, who was all lit up the way he was whenever he was first imagining an affair. She wondered when she had become so unutterably bored with him; he was so predictable. Phoebe was also quiet. She was usually shy, not outgoing and bright like Poppy. This was really not a suitable life for her thought Grace. Perhaps it was not a suitable life for any of them. Claudia was suggesting that Phoebe might want to pal up with her daughter. If the daughter was anything like her mother, Grace could not imagine a more unsuitable friend for Phoebe.

Then they trooped over to the indoor arena to watch the one-metre competition together. David strode lightly and comfortably, Claudia tottered beside him, Grace stepped neatly and economically, and Phoebe trudged, her wide feet kicking up clouds of dust. Poppy had dashed off to find Tibbet, the pony she was to ride in the 80 cm competition. Claudia introduced them to some of her friends, and they sat in a large group. Grace found herself sidelined next to a woman whose son was riding in the 80 cm event. Somehow David and Claudia were sitting together in the row behind them. She listened to the woman's voice tinkling away, making an effort to enrapture David.

Claudia gave David a running commentary of each rider and flashed her legs about, flung back her hair and batted her eyelashes. He responded very appreciatively, and she knew that he wanted her. She was determined, that this time, he was going to fall in love, not just treat her as a meaningless diversion. She knew that she had him on the hook, but she had to play him artfully, to reel him in and make sure he didn't wriggle away after she had put out. She would think of a suitable strategy before the actual seduction.

Claudia wanted Marianela to befriend Phoebe so that they could sidle in as friends of the family, but she wasn't sure that her daughter would go along with it. Lately, Marianela had been increasingly arrogant, ever since her last visit to Columbia to visit her father. Claudia found herself resenting her daughter, almost as a rival.

The one-metre competition had about fifteen competitors, each horse's hoofs stirring up the dust that settled with unpleasant grittiness on the spectators' faces. Claudia hated this, she would much rather be knocking back champagne in an elegant hotel.

There were only three clear rounds, all by the Brazilians, and the jump-off decided the top three places and the competitors dutifully cantered around the arena with their rosettes on the horses' bridles, flashing their eyes and their white teeth. Everyone clapped. Young girls whispered to their doting fathers that they wanted the chestnut, or the grey, or the black, and the fathers nodded approvingly. Winning was everything in this world.

Before the 80 cm competition, a crowd of more parents trooped in to watch their offspring. Claudia sat there with a wide, fixed smile, she could feel David's desire washing over her, and she wriggled a little in her seat. Pondering the problem, she wondered whether she should get pregnant and have his son. Every man wanted a son. It was the perfect solution. She smiled to herself and purred, just like a cat who had a foolproof plan to get the cream. She didn't relish the thought of an uncomfortable pregnancy, stretching her skin, making her waddle, she would have to be sure before she risked it.

Marianela was riding one of the school horses in the 80 cm, and Claudia preened herself and twittered on about it to David who was watching for Poppy on the fat, little, round pony called Tibbet. Claudia was enjoying a fantasy, one day she and David would be watching their son in the show jumping, only he would be riding something a lot better than the very common-looking pony on which Poppy was mounted. Her imagination ran into the future, she would be a serene Madonna. David's daughters could go back to gloomy England with the frumpy mother who smelled of stale wool, and she would be the perfect diplomatic wife.

Facundo was on the ground supervising the young girls, checking their stirrup lengths and that the girths were tightened. Then he stood next to the practice jumps shouting out instructions and encouragement. It was important that his students did well, he didn't want them drifting back to Pablo and Florencia. Marianela was wearing a pair of diamante spurs and a diamante-studded whip which she flourished to great effect.

Rafael was busy in the ring, helping to lower the jumps. The course stayed the same; there was no-one in the whole country who was capable of innovative course design. Then he went to help in the collecting ring, dashing in to put up the practice pole whenever one of the horses knocked it. He noticed that at least half of the riding school horses were stiff and not moving forward in straight lines. This was probably due to the fact that when Facundo exercised them, he lounged in the saddle, in what he assumed was an elegant position, collapsing one hip causing them to not move forward in a straight line.

There was a clutch of students from the Military School who had arrived in a large truck at lunchtime. They were taught by one of the old military men, and they rode very correctly and carefully. There was none of the careless, lounging, pretentious elegance of Facundo's students.

One of them stood out, she was the acknowledged star pupil, if an unlikely one; a small girl with black pigtails tied with pink ribbons trotting around on a bouncy little piebald pony. It had short legs and a big horse head and moved with a jerky stride, legs flashing up and down inelegantly. She had plaited its mane with an intertwined pink ribbon that matched the amateurish exercise bandages. After circling the practice ring a couple of times, she turned to the first jump and as the pony rose over the bars a little shriek burst from her throat. But the pony jumped neatly, tucking up its feet, ears pricked.

"She always goes clear," said Marianela to her best friend Viviana, a spiteful note in her voice.

"She's from the Military School," said Viviana disdainfully. "She won the 80 cm in the last three competitions," she added. The two girls sat on their horses watching, with sly, mean eyes.

"The pink ribbons are so awful, and she shrieks over every jump as if she's seen a mouse."

Rafael stood nearby silently. He was essentially invisible, being a stable boy. He hoped that the young girl with pigtails would win again today, she was a good rider, and the ugly pony jumped like a bird. The pair of them cleared the practice jump three times then quietly trotted off on a loose rein to walk around the edge of the polo field away from the other horses.

Rafael watched Marianela with narrowed eyes as she began to warm up for the event. She was riding one of the best of the riding school's horses, a big, raking, chestnut gelding. It pulled against her dead hands on the reins that held on relentlessly. It tucked its chin to its chest, overbent and desperate to get away from the cruel straight bar curb bit with the tightened twisted curb chain, needled by the rider's sharp spurs, white flecks of froth foamed from its mouth. The spoilt bitch was heedless of her horse's discomfort and pushed her chest out, her breasts like over-ripe pomegranates, laughing as Facundo strolled over and familiarly put his hand high on her thigh.

"Very good Marianela, I have taught you well," he crooned, his enormous ego evident, his eyes on her tits, not her face. She had been flirting with him for months now, and he was considering taking her round the back of the stables later and pushing her up against the wall and taking her like a bitch on heat, what she had been begging for. He wondered if he might be able to persuade her friend Viviana to be in it too. He would have liked to have both of them, see which one could suck his dick the best, make them compete against each other instead of whispering maliciously together.

Rafael could read Facundo's mind. He despised him probably more than any other human he had ever met. He was sure that Facundo was a closet homosexual. He and Tomas were inseparable, always draping their arms around each other and engaging in very physical horseplay. Tomas openly admired and adored Facundo. Facundo's sexual arrogance, and lack of respect, indicated that, in fact, he disliked women, and that was why he treated them like sluts. But as far as Rafael could see the stupid bitches lapped it up, falling for his cheap charm every time.

Poor Phoebe was sitting on the other side of her father. She shifted uncomfortably in the mid-afternoon stuffy heat, sweat running down between her large floppy breasts. It didn't matter how many diets she attempted, or half-hearted attempts to exercise at the gym, she just couldn't manage to lose weight. This made her even more depressed, and she would sneak down in the middle of the night and secretly binge on ice-cream and butter-shortbread biscuits that were specially sent over from England. She knew that she was probably working her way towards an eating disorder and had wanted to try laxatives but just couldn't quite face it. She was sweating now in the heat, and her baggy shirt over the long skirt made her look even bigger than she was. She longed to be back in England in the cooler weather, wearing jumpers and tweeds and blending in with the tubby population.

She was uncomfortably aware of that frightful woman Claudia, dressed up like a high-class hooker who was unashamedly flirting with her father, who seemed to be enjoying it all too much. She looked down at her mother and wondered why she didn't seem to mind or react. She would have hated it if her own husband behaved in such a way. Not that she was ever going to have a husband, she couldn't imagine any man ever being interested in her.

She sensed that things were changing in her family, it was her last year of school and then presumably she would be an adult, but at the moment she felt more childish than Poppy who was always merry and chattering and happy, the epitome of a well-balanced child. Phoebe was also aware that this posting to Uruguay had been a step backwards for her father, he'd been passed over when he had applied to go to more attractive and important countries. Usually, her mother would talk to her uncle who worked in the Foreign Office, but she had overheard them arguing and her mother had declared that this time David could get his next posting on his own merits. There had been a coolness in her mother's voice that boded ill for the future of the family, and Phoebe wondered if after all these years they might get a divorce. She remembered her mother saying to one of her friends, "Of course people like us don't get divorced, we just find that we spend less time in each other's company". It had seemed a strange old-fashioned thing to say, but then her mother was old-fashioned, born and bred aristocracy while her father for all his smooth manners and charm came from a lower middle-class background.

There was a strange tension in the air during meals, and her mother seemed more reserved than ever. Phoebe felt afraid as if her world were about to come crashing around her ears. She would finish this school year, taking her Baccalaureate and then there were eight months before university in September. The plan was that she would go to Oxford. She was an A star student and only really happy when immersed in her books. English Literature was her favourite subject. Her mother had suggested that she could travel if she wanted, although it was not as if she hadn't spent her childhood bouncing around the world from one place to another. Perhaps she would go back and live at Kiss Wood, the family home in Oxfordshire.

It was only recently that Phoebe had noticed her father's attitude to other women before she had been blissfully unaware. She looked at her mother, hoping that somehow, she would intervene, but her mother was opaque as always, her face set impassively, betraying neither emotion nor thought. She seemed so cold, in comparison to Phoebe, who felt she would drown in the surging mass of inexplicable emotions that plagued her. It was as if she was doomed to feel every feeling that her mother refused to entertain. She wished she was like Poppy, who was such an adorable little livewire, jumping up and down, entering into every experience with such finesse.

When Marianela jumped around the course, Claudia leaned forward, her hand casually brushing against David's thigh, and happily suggested that Phoebe and Marianela would become the best of friends. Phoebe smiled politely and couldn't think of a thing to say. She turned away, staring fixedly at the ring, trying not to notice the way Claudia was touching her father. It made her feel physically ill. She jumped up like a fat elephant, and stumbled along the bench, tripping over everyone's feet, on her way

26

to the refuge of the bathroom. She found a cubicle to lock herself in. She sat on the toilet and pulled her top over her head, like an ostrich burying its head in the sand, somehow it felt comforting.

She knew she had to go back to watch Poppy jumping, but couldn't bear the thought of watching Claudia and her father dancing around each other flirtatiously. She got up and washed her hands and splashed her face with the cool water. She would go down to the collecting ring and wish Poppy good luck. It was the hottest part of the afternoon, and the smell of the eucalyptus trees was dry and sharp. A haze of dust was rising from the hoofbeats of the horses, who had all jumped too many practice jumps and just wanted to go back to their cool, peaceful stables.

Poppy was quietly walking Tibbet up and down the green strip that bordered the clubhouse. Knowing that her pony had already jumped the metre class with a rough-riding boy called Michel, she was giving him a chance to relax, cropping on the carefully tended short green turf. She waved happily to Phoebe as her big sister lumbered over towards her.

"Are you alright?" asked Phoebe, projecting her own angst.

"Yes, I'm fine," said Poppy. "Tibbet is such a brave little fellow. I'm sure he'll do his best for me."

Phoebe reached out tentatively to pat the little pony's neck.

"He's very friendly, you know, he loves people," Poppy said encouragingly. "It must be boring for you, just watching, and it's so hot."

"That absolutely ghastly woman Claudia," sighed Phoebe.

"Her daughter Marianela is just like a mini-me," said Poppy, "she's great friends with Facundo."

"He's your riding school teacher, isn't he?" said Phoebe.

"Yes, but Mummy says he doesn't know what he's talking about. He tells me to lean forward as I ride into the jumps, which is all wrong; it puts weight over the pony's shoulders just as they have to lift into the air."

"Well, I think Mummy knows what she is talking about, she is rather an expert at horses," said Phoebe.

"Walk with me. It should be my turn soon," said Poppy. "Once I've jumped, we can go home."

Ten minutes later, Poppy went into the arena and rode very well, her back was straight, her seat perfect and Tibbet soared with a correct bascule over every jump, but on the last upright he just tipped the rail, and they had four faults. Poppy patted him gently.

"You're such a good boy."

"Well done," said Rafael, quietly in English, as she rode past. Poppy looked at him in surprise and smiled sweetly.

"It was my fault we had a pole down," she replied.

"That boy, the dark one with the black hair, he spoke to you in such a posh English accent," said Phoebe, in astonishment.

"His name is Rafael. He's one of the stable boys. I had no idea he could speak English," said Poppy.

Phoebe looked over at him. He had turned away. He had a beautiful profile, dark eyes and a straight nose and full lips, smooth olive skin and glossy black hair.

"Well done, Poppy," said David, striding towards her, Grace two steps behind him stiff and uncomfortable, with Claudia tottering along in her spangly sandals.

"I'll take Tibbet back to his stable, it's the last event," said Poppy. "Phoebe can you come with me, and we'll meet you back at the car."

She dismounted and loosened the girths. They walked together to the long line of stables.

"That stable boy, Rafael, he looks after Tibbet," said Poppy. "He loves the horses, I can tell."

Phoebe walked on, she thought he was beautiful, like a man in a classical painting. She sighed, she could only ever look on from afar, no man would ever be interested in her.

Chapter Three

After Facundo won the show jumping competition on Estrella, Rafael's feelings deepened towards him into a dark, all-consuming, primaeval loathing that he knew would obsess him until he had destroyed that fucking Facundo, as he thought of him.

That morning, as he fed the horses and groomed them, he found that he no longer felt any joy in his tasks with his equine friends, it was if he had been poisoned. He almost blamed Estrella for carrying the hateful Facundo to victory. He knew that her character was such that she did her best no matter who rode her, but he also felt, perhaps illogically, that she had betrayed him, in the same way, that Carina had betrayed him by dying.

Mondays were traditionally a day off for the riding school, but the horses still had to be fed and exercised, and the stables mucked out. Rafael was in such a devil-may-care, black mood that he decided that instead of lungeing Estrella in the round yard, he would ride her. At midday, after he had finished his usual jobs, he tacked her up and mounted. There was no-one around. He was unobserved when he rode her down to the indoor riding school. It was the first time he had ridden her with a saddle and bridle, and he was amazed at how smooth and flowing were her paces. She held the bit delicately in her mouth, her neck arched correctly, responding to the slightest pressure of his calves. He walked her in a circle and gradually took up contact and rode her in a curving snail shell pattern, leg yielding, moving slightly sideways, on a circle that became smaller and smaller. She curved her spine perfectly, and then he gave her the aids to leg yield back out onto a larger circle. Pushing her into a trot he rose in time to the movement then sat deep in the saddle and pushing with his seat bones she trotted smoothly, her hind legs deep under her body, her back relaxed, haunches lowered, poll raised. Rafael felt as if he had been transported into his own private dream world. It was exactly as described in Carina's books. She must be the only perfectly-schooled, obedient horse in Uruguay.

After several minutes at the trot he pushed her into a canter and it was the most divine rocking-horse movement, as soft as sweet-pink fluffy marshmallows. He brought her back to the walk and then asked her to canter on the other leg, and she smoothly executed the transitions. No wonder she had jumped so well for that fucker Facundo he thought to himself. Somehow in this backward country, she had been broken and trained by an expert.

Momentarily, he considered riding her away along the motorway, then down by the side roads, deep into the country so that they could both disappear into oblivion. But reason asserted itself. He looked around, and the place was deserted. It appeared that no-one had seen him. He was tempted to jump her but decided she had had enough yesterday. He slid off and untacked her, putting the saddle under one of the benches and led her out to the polo field. He let her graze with the bit in her mouth, just this once it didn't matter. She deserved some time out in the open. It was one of the huge disadvantages at the Polo Club, there was nowhere to turn out the horses during the day, just a few small yards under the trees but nowhere for the horses to relax and graze and roll.

He stood watching her mouth delicately cropping at the sweet, green grass. Her eyes were huge, luminous, her black coat sleek and shining. She seemed to have suffered no ill-effects after yesterday's exertions. She was the most perfect being that he had ever encountered. He pondered the way in which horses were such marvellous creatures whose responses and instincts worked in a way totally different to people. His insight into their consciousness was like an open door into a wonderful world. He was always straining toward that perfect telepathy which would give him a one-ness with his horse and with Estrella he felt as if he had almost achieved it.

He began to dream; one day, he would ride this mare and compete at the highest level. He would go to Brazil with Pablo and Florencia and win a Grand Prix competition. Of course, it was a hopeless plan for someone of his lowly status, but somehow, he had to bring it about. Perhaps Georgina was the key. He had to win her trust. At this point, ultimately it was up to her parents who rode the mare, but even if he pulled it off, such would be Facundo's rage that he would revenge himself upon the lowly stable boy who had usurped him. Still, it was worth a try, all he had to lose was his job, and if that happened, he would go up to Brazil and get a job there. The joy of riding Estrella had given him hope, and he became reckless. Four years here and he knew he would never be more than a stable boy.

He then fell to thinking about Georgina. She was so lacking in self-confidence that it seemed almost hopeless to think that she would champion his cause, even if he did manage to persuade her that he was a better rider than Facundo. And at the moment, she seemed rather enchanted by Facundo, like all the other teenage girls who rode here. He had to think of a way in which to gain her confidence. The more he thought about it, the more he brooded, the more impossible it seemed. He would never have the slick charm and manners of Facundo.

He let Estrella graze for an hour and slowly led her back to the stable, putting her in the loose box with an extra ration of fresh green alfalfa that was delivered to the stables every day from a farm in Canelones. He decided that he would wait until Georgina next came to the stables then talk to her. He couldn't quite imagine how they might become friends, crossing the great social divide between members of the Polo Club and lowly employees was probably impossible. But he reasoned that Georgina loved Estrella nearly as much as he did and perhaps that mutual passion might be a bridge between them.

It was another three days before Rafael got a chance to talk to Georgina about Estrella. He was used to staying silent, head bowed in servile, sullen submission, now he looked her in the eye and tried a smile, his lips curved and his eyes lightened, but it felt strange. Georgina was her usual sweet self.

"She jumped well at the show," said Rafael.

"I absolutely adore her," said Georgina, "but I don't suppose I'll ever be able to ride as well as Facundo."

Rafael managed not to retort at this fatuous comment.

"It's very important that she moves in a straight line, doesn't start crabbing sideways," he said, wondering if Georgina understood the technicality of this issue.

Her sweet brown eyes clouded over.

"She has to move in a true straight line as she approaches the jump."

"I didn't realise that," said Georgina, a little breathlessly.

Rafael then decided it was now or never.

"Are you riding today?" he asked.

"Yes, I thought I would just trot her around the edge of the polo field a few times, out in the sunshine. She must get sick of being cooped up in the stable all day."

"I wondered if you would like me to show you, I could school her a bit in the arena with you, perhaps give you some pointers," said Rafael.

"You! But you're only .. " her voice trailed off, realising that she was going to say something offensive.

"I can ride quite well, I was trained by a British equestrian expert. She was my adopted mother," explained Rafael.

"Alright, do you think we need to check with Facundo?"

"She's your mare you're entitled to decide who rides her."

Georgina stood there, puzzled. Her brain was clicking over. He was quite right, but somehow, she thought Facundo wouldn't like it. But Rafael was such a sweet man, and he really did seem to care about Estrella. He looked after her in such a loving fashion.

"Yes, why not," she said, smiling at him. Everybody deserved a chance.

Rafael prayed that Facundo wouldn't suddenly decide to come in as he was about to ride. He would be certain to object. This might be his only chance. He walked quickly to the tack room and brought out the saddle and bridle and tacked up. Then he let Georgina lead her out.

"Do you want to trot her around the polo field a few times, to warm her up?" he suggested. He looked around, and there was nobody there. There were no students booked in for this afternoon. He watched Georgina ride. She had potential; lovely long legs that curved around the mare's sides, which were a decided advantage to any rider. She rode on a very loose rein which was better than the stranglehold that Facundo and Tomas used. The mare was relaxed, almost too relaxed, slopping along, but that was better than stirring her up, to overbend, and sidle.

After three circuits of the polo field, Georgina rode back, and Rafael walked beside her to the undercover arena. She slid down to the ground, and Rafael stepped forward to adjust the stirrup leathers. Then he vaulted on and sitting lightly, he trotted the mare once around the arena, gradually taking up the contact through the reins he pushed her into a canter. Her hoofs thudded with a soft echo on the sand-covered surface. She has beautiful natural balance and rhythm; she is easy to ride, thought Rafael. The jumps were set at 120 cm, and he turned her, and she flew over the first one, cantered a small circle at the top and he set her straight down the middle over the double, just two neat strides between the elements.

"Gosh!" said Georgina, "you ride so well, I had no idea. I would love you to train her and perhaps you could help me as well."

Rafael smiled at her, and for the first time, she noticed the classic beauty of his face. He wasn't sure how to proceed from this. The minute Facundo found out he would be on the warpath. On the other hand, he couldn't embroil Georgina in any sort of deception, or even suggest keeping quiet about it.

"I would love to help you, perhaps just every Wednesday we do this again. If I put the jumps down would you like to try her over them."

"Oh yes, I am quite confident at 60 cm or 80 cm."

Rafael felt safer that way, as a stable boy, it was perfectly acceptable for him to put the jumps up and down for clients.

"Perhaps if you took up a little more contact through the reins. Don't lean forward as you approach the jump, stay upright and then lean forward as she goes up in the air."

He watched them both carefully, and the mare rose perfectly at the jumps. Georgina just sat there, and Estrella found the perfect stride. Georgina rode over to him a wide smile on her face.

"Let's meet up every Wednesday then. I get off early from school every week."

"That's a plan then," said Rafael, carefully the avoiding the word 'date'.

He was feeling jubilant but also worried. This could cause him a lot of trouble, and stable boys were a dime a dozen, but he had to do something. He somehow had to move forward in his life otherwise, he could try going up to Brazil, although the Brazilians were just as class conscious as the Uruguayans, and they looked down on the Uruguayans as well.

Facundo was there on Thursday, strutting around arrogantly and fortunately was too busy to ride Estrella, he had several adults who came for lessons. They were well-off middle-aged women, and Facundo enjoyed the banter and flirtation. He would correct their leg positions, sliding his hands up and down their lower legs and smiling up at them meaningfully while they tittered.

Marianela turned up that evening and walked in on one particularly suggestive exchange between Facundo and an extremely overweight woman with huge amounts of glittery gold jewellery, who was having a sedate walk and trot lesson on the most cobby of the riding school horses. Marianela tossed her hair back and flounced around huffing and puffing and fluttering her eyelashes at Tomas in retaliation. Facundo ignored her. They were more or less an item now, but not quite as firmly paired up as Marianela would like.

On Friday evening, Poppy arrived for her lesson. Phoebe was chaperoning her, and at the last minute, David had announced that he would accompany them. Phoebe felt uncomfortable; she suspected her father of having a pre-arranged meeting with Claudia. David was wearing his second-best suit, and he looked extremely elegant, with a knotted colourful tie and his hair freshly cut and swept back in two wings from his face. He walked over to the indoor arena with Phoebe. She looked at him sideways, and his eyes were sweeping around, possibly looking for Claudia. They sat on the top tier of the benches and watched Poppy riding Tibbet.

"Your mother can't bear to come, she thinks that the standards here are abysmally low," said David.

She probably can't stand to watch you slavering over Claudia, thought Phoebe, but she said nothing out loud. Sure enough, ten minutes later, Claudia arrived in a cloud of fresh perfume and make-up. Phoebe smelled her before she saw her.

"Oh, Claudia, what a pleasant surprise," said David, giving her a knowing smile. She came and sat next to them.

"Oh, your little girl, she is such a promising rider," fluttered Claudia, sugary sycophancy dripping from her meaningless compliment.

"I cannot believe that Marianela is your daughter. You look like sisters," replied David.

Phoebe groaned. Such clichés! Such inanity! She wondered how people could even be bothered to go through these boring and ridiculous exchanges. Perhaps they should just have sex and get it over with.

"Phoebe, I'm sure you and Marianela should get together, perhaps you could have a little study group. Apparently, you're frightfully clever."

As opposed to glamorous, thought Phoebe sourly.

"Perhaps," she replied noncommittally, with only the shadow of a smile. She's her mother's daughter, thought David.

Phoebe couldn't imagine anything worse than spending a minute with Marianela who had clearly showed her how much she despised her. In fact, Marianela and her mother had had a furious row that morning over their breakfast of black coffee and egg-white and fresh herb omelettes. Marianela had point-blank refused to have anything to do with Phoebe.

"She's an utter frump, I can't stand her and no-one in my group would be seen dead with her!" she had declared flouncing out of the room, sweeping her long green-blonde tresses back from her face. It was annoying that Phoebe was loved by their teachers, she was such a brain, perhaps it was too easy to make fun of her.

Phoebe hated sitting with her father and Claudia. She felt like a chaperone and an unwelcome one at that. She opened her book and started reading again. She may as well live up to her reputation as a brainy student. Claudia was leaning in and whispering in David's ear, and he was murmuring back.

"Facundo, Facundo," shouted Poppy shrilly. "He seems to run at the jumps with his head in the air. It doesn't feel right, how can I make him curve his neck more?"

"You need to pull on the reins, keep a tighter grip," said Facundo authoritatively, unprofessionally smoking a cigarette. A knowledgeable riding instructor would have explained that horses need to look through the top half of their eyes to judge distances and that to do that, their heads would be held high. They had another twenty minutes to go, and Poppy was astute, she wouldn't let him get away with not giving her sufficient time.

"Heels down, and keep your eyes on the centre of the jump. When you land, I want three strides and then circle to the right and down the long side," he called out.

She was probably one of the best riders at the school, and Facundo was congratulating himself on his teaching. When Poppy's lesson had finished, Phoebe thumped down the steps and followed her back to the stables. She couldn't bear to sit with her father and Claudia another minute. She knew that Poppy would lead the pony back and unsaddle it and spend some time fussing over it in the stable. Phoebe saw Facundo walk over to the riding school office where Marianela was loitering, waiting for him.

"I see that stupid fat bitch is here again," said Marianela in English, her voice carried over on the wind, so Phoebe could hear her. "My mother is sweet on her father, and his tongue is hanging out. Huh! You should see the British mother, what an ugly old woman!"

Phoebe blushed, her round pale face went an unattractive tomato-red colour. She was all too well aware that her father was planning, or had, in fact, already, established a sexual relationship with Claudia. But now Claudia and Marianela went to great lengths to flaunt the liaison as if in some way they were legitimising their claim on him as if it were a public relations exercise. Phoebe hated it, she felt so stupid, as if her father were being unfaithful to all of them, not just her mother.

David and Claudia's relationship was like a streetcar sliding down a hill without brakes. They graduated to intimate lunches in hidden-away restaurants where Grace or the other staff at the Consulate would never venture. There was a lot of soft touching of hands over lunch, and within a week they were driving off together to the *Alta Rotividad*, a high rotation motel on Ruta 5, a few kilometres beyond Melilla Polo Club. They drove up to the gate, and Claudia didn't admit that she had been here before with many other married lovers. She wasn't pretending to be a virgin, but she didn't want David to know just how many men, and also women, she had entertained over the years.

She leant over and spoke into the intercom system, using rapid Spanish that David, for all his facility with foreign languages, couldn't quite follow. He still had not adjusted to the thick Uruguayan accent. Claudia's heavy breasts pressed against his bare arm and he felt an irrepressible surge of sexual excitement. The woman on the other end of the intercom pressed the button, and the boom swung up. They drove through and around the curved driveway that encircled the motel, and the automatic door of the garage of number 12 slid up, and the car purred in and came to a stop. Then the door slid down behind them. It was all designed for total discretion. The car was now out of sight, and if perhaps David's wife was in the next room with her lover, unless they were unlucky enough to leave at exactly the same moment, there was no way of recognising a car parked in plain sight.

This was a building that had seen countless adulterers arriving with all the excitement of a secret and hidden sexual liaison, and leaving with their desires sated. There were revolving coloured lights in the shower that might be seen as tacky to outsiders, but to those who frequented the place they were the symbol of that artificial paradise of sexual delight. Standing under the shower, with the magic lights revolving above, the delicate sluice of needles of warm water hitting one's skin that would soon be caressed by passionate hands. Children were not conceived here; this was the antithesis of happy, family life; this was sheer self-gratification.

Claudia did a slow striptease that she had practised many years ago in front of her mirror. Turning this way and that, exhibiting her full breasts, with large brown nipples to their best advantage, and then bending over to slide her lacy knickers over her feet she flashed her gaping gash in a tantalising movement. David sat on the edge of the bed and slipped his slim feet out of his cream loafers. He could feel himself hardening, ready to plunge into that orgy of swollen pink flesh that promised to tighten and grasp him with a very practised pelvic floor movement. This was a woman of experience; he was enough of a man of the world to know that. They would have had at least a hundred lovers between them but still the dance of attraction, the mutual compliments, the light of lust set their senses on fire.

But to Claudia, this was not a casual act; she was determined that this fish would not get away. She wanted David perhaps a little too desperately, and she had to be careful that she acted as the soul of nonchalance. A man can smell desperation a mile away. She flaunted herself for just the right number of moments and then slid into the shower to make sure that no stale vaginal odour remained, to present her pussy in its most edible and delicious state. She came out wrapped in a towel that slid right down to the end of her nipples, just brushing across her toned thighs with a glimpse of her fully bare pubic area that had been painfully waxed the preceding day. She knelt down in front of David, who had opened his flies and gently

37

took his cock in her mouth. It was long and thin, rather British, she thought, an expert of all the different nationalities of penises.

It smelt very English as if he were using Badedas in the bath, she remembered that scent when she had had an English woman who had liked to be stroked and fondled and then watched while her husband fucked Claudia's arse. Really, the English were the most perverted race that Claudia had ever known. In this case, it was of advantage to her; she could tease and shock David with every trick in her extensive repertoire until he could think of nothing but her.

If it came to it, she would use Marianela. Her daughter would be the bait, and then they would have evidence, and if David wouldn't leave that drab little wife, he would be charged with sexual abuse. Marianela was still only seventeen, under the legal age in Uruguay and how would it look for a British diplomat to be disporting himself with a girl the same age as his daughter.

There were no boundaries with Claudia, and she had raised her daughter to be a high-class whore. Like Mrs Castaway, she had sent her elderly lover into her young daughter's bedroom one night, whispering in his ear that she had fantasised that he should be her daughter's first lover. He had been particularly repulsive but very, very rich and he had paid her handsomely for the privilege of deflowering Marianela. The poor girl had cried out in terror when she had felt him lowering himself onto her slim body. He had a huge hairy belly, and his cock smelled strongly of old cheese. He was so excited that night that he had forced himself inside her without any attempt at foreplay and she had been rubbed red and raw the next morning. His gnarled old fingers had grabbed hold of her prominent buds of breasts, hardly formed in puberty yet and he had pinched and twisted them until she screamed in pain, then he had sucked her like a calf on a teat with his toothless gums, and run his disgusting slimy tongue over her fresh, young skin.

Marianela had been richly rewarded by her mother the next day. She had fed her strawberry ice-cream and then taken her to MacDonalds, which was all the fashion with the thirteen-year-olds. She had explained that they needed to please old Signor Gaviria because they were months behind with the rent, but now thanks to Marianela and her co-operation they could stay in their penthouse flat.

Marianela had looked at her wide-eyed and scared. But her mother had explained that it was a family secret and she must never, never, ever tell anyone. There was enough money now to buy her that expensive pair of jeans that all her friends were talking about. She would look the sexiest in them and then she had taken her to the hairdresser and had her hair cut in a fashionable style and streaked white blonde. Marianela had made herself forget the horrors of the night and delighted in parading before her friends. She was definitely the prettiest girl in her class, and now she had the very latest in designer jeans she whizzed to the top of the schoolgirl hierarchy.

Since then Claudia had kept a strict watch over her. She had been absolutely forbidden to have any boyfriends of her own age. That would not have suited Claudia's plans at all. She was allowed to flirt with whatever boyfriends Claudia was entertaining. She would sit on their knees and squirm innocently until she felt them aroused. She would brush her breasts that were developing rapidly against them and kiss them full on the lips then Claudia would send her off to bed, the door fitted with a secure lock so that no lover could stray into her bedroom in the middle of the night. If they wanted to have sex with her daughter, then they had to pay dearly for it.

Inevitably, people became aware of the mother and daughter who stood out with their blatant sexuality and their beauty. Women's eyes would slide over them uncomfortably, and men would look for too long. Claudia knew that she was running the gauntlet whenever they appeared in polite society. She needed fresh pastures, and Uruguay was too small a country. David Lester-Blythe, a newcomer, was just the answer, and in his way, he was rather handsome. Not that she hadn't been fucked by the ugliest men in the land, but she liked the idea of a handsome husband on her arm. This one was going to be a keeper.

David had no idea about the extent of Claudia's whoring. He would have been genuinely shocked at the idea of her selling the sexual services of her daughter when she had been just thirteen-years-old. Although he was promiscuous, he also shared the old-fashioned values of Grace as far as Phoebe and Poppy went. In fact, the idea of his own daughters' sexuality was abhorrent to him, and it also reminded him of his own inevitable ageing.

Claudia made sure that she bought him a series of expensive small gifts. Some of them she had shoplifted from expensive stores. It was another of her secret vices; it somehow assuaged her feeling that she had been deprived. She had been married to a very important and rich Columbian businessman, Marianela's father, well almost certainly he was the father, although there were two other men who were vague possibilities. He had had an affair with her best friend when they had lived in Bogota and when Claudia had found out, she had made the momentous mistake of kicking up a fuss and leaving him. Had she known what her future was she would have stayed put. She could have played the game, had her own discreet affairs and enjoyed her social and financial position. She forever regretted this and somehow felt that in having sex with other women's husbands, she was in some way redressing the balance.

The affair with David flourished with Claudia's careful nurturing. She never let it go stale. There was always a hint of uncertainty; she would express some feelings that it 'wasn't right' and then let David persuade her that anything that felt so good had to be right. They only went occasionally now to the high rotation motel, and more often than not, he would come to her house for lunch. She lavished delicious treats upon him and scented the house with exotic ylang-ylang oil and tried different little sexual tricks. She was drawing him into her web. She made sure not to embarrass him in public.

She didn't quite know how to stage him leaving his wife. It would be death to their sexual affair if she actually suggested it. It had to be made such an attractive option that he couldn't resist. Public embarrassment had to be avoided at all costs. She pondered the issue for hours and hours and even surfed the internet to see if there were any helpful suggestions. There were plenty of articles on how to spot if your husband was being unfaithful, but not a lot about luring a faithless husband away from a loyal wife.

David, in his turn, had no intention of leaving Grace. He knew who buttered his bread, and it was his wife, with all her lovely 'old money'. When it came to Claudia, he never paid for anything with a credit card but would withdraw cash, usually from Grace and his joint account which she always obligingly topped up. His wage barely paid for the essentials and certainly not meals in restaurants or riding lessons and the gym which he went to religiously five times a week, to keep himself looking trim and attractive.

He had not heard the whispers about Claudia, and even if he did, he would write it off as typical jealous gossip. She was the sexiest woman on the scene and would undoubtedly attract the wrong sort of attention.

Marianela had not been drawn into Claudia's affair with David. She had grown up a lot, and she realised that she could play her own sexual games, not just be an accessory for an ageing mother. Resenting her mother more each day, money was tight, and she was limited to only one riding lesson a week, and her mother was resisting all her pleading for some new clothes. Her best friend, Viviana was from a very rich family. Every weekend her parents went off to their *estancia* which was just five kilometres from Punta del'Este, the most expensive and upmarket real estate in Uruguay, full of rich Argentinians who brought over bundles of cash every summer which they kept in strong boxes cemented inside their penthouse apartments.

Viviana and Marianela had been best friends for three years now and although Viviana was rich, she was also generous, and Marianela was more beautiful, attracted lots of attention and knew so many intriguing things about sex that Viviana was always entranced by her. Marianela never really admitted to her own personal experience but made out that it was her mother's friends who talked about sex when they thought she was out of earshot.

They often dated boys of about their own age and loved to tease them but Marianela had always made sure to insist that she was still a virgin. Putatively Facundo was to be her 'first' although it would probably be obvious to him that she was no virgin. Hopefully, Facundo was so self-centred that it would barely register, he would be concentrating on his own performance.

When Viviana had her first sexual experience of serious kissing and touching, she had rushed to Marianela to tell her. She spoke in breathless hushed tones, stumbling over the words. Marianela listened intently and acted out her part, like a good friend. Marianela knew that if it ever got out that she had been prostituted by her mother at the age of thirteen, she would be a social pariah. If her father ever found out, he would undoubtedly kill her mother and lock her up forever, never to be let out until a suitable husband was bought for her. She visited her father twice a year, and he watched her like a hawk. His old mother would come to stay, and they never let Marianela out of the house without an escort. She understood how Muslim women must feel in the Middle East, not allowed out of the house without a male relative. Her father had bodyguards in Bogota. Although it was much safer these days, her father had lived through the bad old days and was determined never to take any risks until the day he died. He would give Marianela some money but never huge amounts. His generous child support payments to Claudia would come to an end soon.

Facundo was essentially Marianela's first serious and public relationship. She liked him because he was hugely popular amongst all the girls at the Polo Club who swarmed around him like flies. She knew that it would be an enormous social cachet to be his proper girlfriend, and that was her aim. She went so far as to admit this to Viviana who said that she preferred Tomas - so this settled the matter between them. They planned to be the 'Awesome Foursome'. They would not become competitors for the same man but rather co-conspirators. They spent hours and hours together discussing them and often they would go to the Polo Club and sit up at the back of the stands and watch the two young men riding horses and giving lessons. They would giggle and flick their long hair back, and stretch their legs out over the back of the seats and arrange themselves in attractive and tempting postures.

They went out a few times in a group and Marianela and Viviana made sure not to try and monopolise the young men's attention, instead they would link arms and lean against each other. It had been Viviana who had first kissed Tomas and then Marianela and Facundo gave in. Each had wanted the other to make the first move, but they drew together and feasted on each other's lips, and the electricity between them had crackled. Marianela found herself pushing her hips up against him in perhaps her first-ever spontaneous sexual move, not orchestrated by her mother, and then they went back to the Polo Club and had it off on the couch in the office. Viviana and Tomas continued to fool around nearby. Facundo was tempted to make the whole thing a proper foursome but restrained himself. He had the beginnings of a plan for Marianela – the little slut, pretending she was a virgin!

Chapter Four

While David and Claudia were preening each other and Facundo and Marianela spat and hissed and made love, Rafael was secretly riding Estrella. Although Georgina had agreed that he should ride the mare, he knew that it was better not to do so in front of the others. In a fair and just world his superior riding ability would be recognised, fêted and encouraged with the reward of the best horses in the land, but unfortunately, he - like the rest of us - lived in a world with the upside-down values of the scum rising to the top.

The person he needed to impress was Valentino who had so much experience and knowledge and was now getting older and wanted to bring on a younger rider. Valentino had chosen Facundo because he was the best of a bad lot. Rafael was often seconded to help with the training sessions run by Valentino when Facundo would be put up on his horses. The whole exercise was utter hell for him. Watching Facundo slouching and riding in such a way as to ruin the horses made him grind his teeth in anguish. He had noticed the way that Valentino would narrow his eyes and squint at Facundo's rough hands, and lack of consideration for the horses. Rafael longed to run to Valentino and shout, "Let me ride, let me show you what I can do!" but he knew that this approach would never work.

He would rise every morning at five and go down and feed the horses early and then take Estrella out and walk her around, letting her stretch her legs and sniff the fresh morning air, before the sound of traffic and the smell of car exhausts crept over the polo field. He would let her crop at the grass and have half an hour to let her breakfast digest. Instinctively he knew that horses digested best with their heads lowered to the ground, it was more natural for them.

He would saddle up the mare after this and ride her around the indoor arena. He daren't work her for too long, first suppling exercises, practising long straight lines, trying to stop her moving unevenly. He felt as if he were trying to hold back the waves with his hands, correcting the bad habits that she was learning from being ridden by Facundo. He set up the show jumps in straight lines, two strides, one stride and then a bounce apart, to help her to learn to round her back and use all the impulsion of her hindquarters.

She would be brilliant one day, focusing on the next fence as she landed, he could almost feel her calculating the distances. On other days she would throw her head in the air and jump all over the place as if she were frightened. Rafael wanted to kill Facundo for the way that he rode that put the beautiful mare in such a state. He knew this couldn't go on, a continuous see-saw of improvement, then two steps back.

He varied the jumps and then put them one stride and a right-angle turn, another stride and over the jump. He focused on turning her in an even curve, vibrating the inside rein and guiding her hindquarters with his outside leg. He even tried jumping her 160 cm and found that the higher the jumps, the better she performed. She was brave and kind. He adored her and would have lain down his life to protect her. He felt as if he and Georgina were her only hope. But Georgina was just a kid and a timid child who lacked confidence, dominated by a brute of a father who wanted to show off to his mates.

Rafael had never ridden such a well-trained horse, and he asked Georgina where they had purchased her. She mentioned that there was an Australian woman who had a farm near Los Castillos up near the Brazilian border. Rafael had perhaps unrealistic hopes that he was going to be able to compete on the mare and somehow win here on home territory and then go up to Brazil where the big competitions were. It was Georgina, sweet, artless and not realising the effect it would have, who told her father about Rafael riding the mare and how well she was going. Her father frowned, a stable boy, that wasn't what he was paying for. He went straight to Facundo and began to remonstrate with him. Facundo's face became very still and expressionless.

"Don't worry, I'll make sure this won't happen again," he reassured Georgina's father, whose body was broad and powerful, with a bristled face and shrewd eyes.

"That stable boy is not to ride the mare again, I've sorted it," he told his daughter brusquely, then hurrumphed impressively.

"Oh Daddy, I can't believe that you've done this. I told you Rafael is absolutely marvellous with her. Why don't you give him a chance and watch? We'll get him to jump her around a course, and then Facundo can jump her, and we can judge who is the better rider."

Georgina had set up an unwinnable situation for Rafael. If Estrella went better for him, he would qualify for Facundo's undying hatred and undoubtedly an act of cruel revenge. If Estrella went better for Facundo, then he would never get another chance, and would probably get the sack anyway. He shrugged, he had to go through with it.

"I'm going to ask Valentino to be the judge. He can assess them on style as well as whether or not they clear the jumps," said Georgina, thinking that this would be Rafael's chance to prove himself.

Facundo didn't look at all thrilled at this new arrangement. He felt as if his supremacy was in question. He shouldn't have to prove himself. He stiffly agreed, but his small, brown eyes were an arctic gold, narrowed and glinting with rage.

"Alright, let's do it today," said Georgina, suddenly feeling doubtful, wondering whether this was really a good idea. "I'll go and ask Valentino, the jumps are already set up, I'm not sure how high they should be, perhaps 130 cm, and we can toss a coin to see who rides her first."

Rafael went and saddled the mare. He vaulted on and trotted off around the polo ground. She felt good. He had become accustomed to her stride now, and she knew his voice and responded well. He hoped that he would get to ride her first. If Facundo rode her first, she might well become unsettled, and it would be difficult to calm her down.

He rode her into the arena.

"Look lad, you're on her now, you may as well go around, and then we'll see how much better Facundo rides her," said Georgina's father. He didn't look at all like his daughter, with a big belly sticking out in front and hanging over his belt. His thick features were rubbery and swollen, his eyebrows bristling above mean little eyes. How did such an ugly monster father the sweet, delightful Georgina?

Rafael nodded at him. His mouth set in a straight line. He was swallowing back down the urge to retch. He could taste the acid in the back of his throat. He had to pull himself together. If he wanted a successful competitive career, then he couldn't succumb to nerves. He pushed the mare into a steady canter, and the smooth rocking motion of her pace calmed him. The show jumps were set up in the usual design. There wasn't a lot of scope for variation.

Facundo stood a little apart from the others. There was Valentino, Georgina, her father, and one of the other stable boys who was to run in and put up any jumps that fell. Facundo had his long legs set wide apart, his arms folded across his chest, an evil glint in his eye as he watched Rafael riding.

Valentino was chatting amiably to Georgina's father, trying to dispel the murderous tension in the air. Georgina now realised that she had caused this very awkward situation and she was hopping from one foot to another, biting her lip with nervousness. It wasn't what she intended at all. She had just been so surprised and happy about the way that Estrella was going. Now all her happiness had drained away, and she knew that she was making trouble for Rafael, and she felt terribly guilty.

Rafael pushed the big mare into a canter and gathered her up delicately, his hands playing the reins as if they were spider webs, his seat pushing but no nagging legs. She dropped her hindquarters, and he kept up the pressure until she was bouncing like a rubber ball, with lots of impulsion coming from her back end. He turned for the first jump which was set diagonally across the centre of the arena. It was an upright, with no spread at all and they bounced right up to it, and she sprang as if her legs were coiled springs. He rose out of the saddle and went with her; it felt like flying. As they landed, he settled back into the saddle as light as a feather. He turned her left across the top of the arena and then slightly lengthening her stride they headed towards the two spreads, just three strides apart. She stretched her neck out over the first, and he increased her pace through the three non-jumping strides, and she took off over the second jump and cleared it, not by miles, but economically, just as much as was needed without wasting effort. He cantered across the short side, and he could see the faces of the group as they watched him intently. Georgina's father was frowning, Georgina, biting her lips but eyes shining, Facundo looking like thunder, but it was Valentino that mattered. He was smiling broadly, like someone who had just discovered that they had won the lottery when they had forgotten they had bought a ticket.

The last fence was the highest, the red brick wall and it was actually 160 cm, and lots of the horses hated it. He gathered her up again and applied a little pressure with his legs as he felt an almost imperceptible hesitation, and they cantered the last stride, and he told her to take off. It was a perfect parabolic jump. They landed, and he smoothly gave her the aids for a complete stop. She almost propped, and he sat still in the saddle. They stood for three whole seconds, immobile, her legs four-square and then he asked her to canter from a standstill, and they performed a volte, a circle just five metres in diameter and came to a halt in front of the small group of people. He dropped his hand and bowed his head and then patted her gently along the neck. Georgina was the only spectator who clapped, 'Bravo!' she called and flapped her hands together. Her father looked determinedly unimpressed.

"Anyone can jump a trained horse," he said brusquely, "and we paid a lot of money for this horse, you would expect her to jump like this."

"Well, let's put that to the test," said Valentino with a tight smile, "Facundo let's see how you go with her over these heights."

Facundo was strung uptight as a string on a bow. Rafael sprang off and landed two feet together on the sand. He moved away so that Facundo didn't touch him as he stepped forward to mount. He made no attempt to adjust the stirrup leathers as a stable boy would. He went and stood a small distance from the others. He hated watching Facundo riding Estrella.

Facundo knew that he had to do better, not just as well, but better.

"Hey you, put those spreads up to 160 cm and widen them," he said to Rafael, making sure the others realised that he was just a stable boy. Rafael stood there obstinately, for it to be a fair comparison, the jumps should be the same.

Facundo vaulted onto the mare, thrust his feet through the stirrup irons and flicked her, quite unnecessarily with his long riding crop. She swished her tail, and her ears went back, half-flattened along her head, making her look a little demonic. Rafael absolutely hated this. He knew that Estrella didn't need a whip. Facundo was flourishing it around trying to make himself look like he was master of the situation. Estrella could feel Facundo's pent-up anger, and she stiffened her back and set her jaw against him. She began to run forward, her head high. He tightened his hold on the reins and pulled her head as hard as he could. She changed tactics and tucked her head in towards her chest, which made her look like a warhorse.

"Now that boy can ride!" exclaimed Georgina's father. Valentino was tempted to say that she was overbent and evading the action of the bit, but he said nothing. In his mind, he was replaying the sight of Rafael jumping that last jump. The boy was a miracle. He knew he was quiet and shy and seemed to care for the horses exceptionally well, but beyond that, he had known nothing about him. No matter how Facundo performed, Georgina's father was going to think it was marvellous, which was just fine. He wanted Rafael for himself. What a find, and right under his nose all the time!

Rafael had no idea that he had made such an impression on Valentino. He imagined that his fate hung in the balance, dependent on how Estrella went for that fucker Facundo. The black mare was clearly unsettled, but Facundo didn't try to calm her. He tapped her with the whip again and pulled on her mouth. Then, he decided to follow the same course that Rafael had taken. He pushed her towards the upright jump in the centre of the ring. She was anxious and rushed with no rhythm in her stride and no attention focused on the jump ahead of her. She jumped high and wildly, cleared it but landed awkwardly on all four legs. Facundo was jarred in the saddle, and it took him five strides to get himself organised again. They turned left down the long side of the arena, and he pushed her on strongly but kept a tight hold of her head, so she would be unable to stretch out over the spread jump.

Valiantly she stretched as far as she was able. She was such an honest mare who always tried. He hit her with the whip on each of the three intervening strides but kept an iron grasp on her mouth. She just couldn't make the distance, and her hindlegs hit the last bar. As she landed, Facundo's face contorted with rage and spite. He hit her behind the saddle, a stinging thwack and she skittled sideways, and arrived in front of the wall and had no chance to prepare herself for a leap. She made a desperate effort to launch herself but landed in the middle of it. The painted-red wooden blocks splintered as they crashed. She fell heavily, and Facundo went down beside her. As she flailed and struggled to get up her metal-shod shoes kicked him. Rafael ran in and grabbed the reins of the mare and quietened her down, looking at her legs, thinking they would have to carefully pick out all the splinters.

"This is your fault, you fucking little shit," hissed Facundo, nursing his arm where the mare had kicked him, it felt like it was broken.

"It was a level playing field," said Rafael mockingly, using his high-class English accent that Carina had taught him as a child.

"Where did you learn to talk like that?" asked Facundo. "You're not who you make out you are!"

"I'm just a stable boy!" sneered Rafael. "But unlike you, I can actually ride."

By now, Georgina had rushed over, and her father bumbled along behind her.

"That's a valuable mare you pair of idiots have been messing around with," roared her father, purple and swollen like a bullfrog. "She cost $30,000."

"I'll take her back to the stable, you might want to call the vet just to check her over," said Rafael. He wanted to wash her carefully with antiseptic and water.

"I'll come with you," said Valentino, "I'll help you."

As they walked, he spoke to Rafael quietly.

"You rode her brilliantly. I want you to work for me. I'll talk to the manager, get him to release you to look after my horses. And ride them, train them."

"Won't Facundo make trouble for me?" asked Rafael.

"Don't worry. I'll make sure he has no chance to interfere," said Valentino. "It's a shame about the mare. She's wasted on that young girl. But the father won't sell her for less than he paid and I don't pay those silly prices."

"She's very honest. She always tries her hardest."

"I know lad, but there are hundreds of horses, they come, they go - you can't get too fond of them," said Valentino thinking that Rafael's kind heart might hold him back in the future. He would never sacrifice a horse for his career.

Rafael spent several hours with Estrella. Georgina hovered anxiously, feeding her treats. The mare didn't seem to have suffered any serious injury.

"My father is furious. He says it is your fault and Facundo's, and he blames me as well," she said despondently.

"At least she is not injured. What do you think he'll do, will he let Facundo continue to compete on her."

"He's threatening to sell her. He says that I don't deserve such an expensive horse."

"That's too bad," said Rafael sympathetically. He knew that Georgina loved her as much as he did. "Perhaps when he calms down, he'll think about it more logically."

"He's not really that sort of person," Georgina.

Perhaps she takes after her mother, who must be an angel, thought Rafael.

"What did Valentino say?" asked Georgina.

"He wants me to work for him," said Rafael, smiling shyly.

"I don't think I've ever seen you smiling before."

"Perhaps there hasn't been much to smile about," said Rafael.

"Well, at least that is one good thing that's come out of it," said Georgina. "You deserve it. You're so good with the horses."

Rafael was feeling elated, although a little cautious. These sorts of things didn't happen to people like him. Orphans from a shanty town didn't usually rise to the top of the equestrian élite in such a class-conscious society.

That night he went to his room and lit some of the candles. He had bought himself a couple of bottles of beer, and he set them down on the packing case. He would drink to the future, drink to his career with Valentino.

The next day he did his usual horses and then went over to Valentino's area of the stables where he kept his eight horses in a line of stables, with his own feed shed and tack room.

"Valentino told us you are coming to work here," said old Eddie.

"Yes, that's right, just got to organise it with the manager."

"Good," said Eddie, "there is plenty of work here."

"Good morning Rafael," said Valentino, emerging from the tack room. "I want you to ride Tormenta this morning. She has not been jumping well lately. I want you to work out what is wrong with her."

Rafael smiled. He had begun to wonder if it was all just a dream. They led Tormenta out. She was an ugly grey mare with a strange shambling gait, but she could jump - she had cleared 170 cm in a competition in Brazil, but that had been a few years ago. She was looking a little moth-eaten these days. Could it be age, arthritis, slowing down, or was there a specific reason for her lack of form?

He mounted, marvelling at the saddle. It was a European design, beautiful soft leather, and so easy to sit in the correct position. He let her walk out on a long rein.

"Shall I ride her around the polo grounds a few times to warm her up and get the feel of her?" he asked.

"Yes, good idea," said Valentino, smiling with satisfaction, every minute he liked this boy more. Rafael was beginning to enjoy himself. He loved a puzzle, working out what was going on with a horse, helping to bring it back to the way it should be. He wanted to impress Valentino, and this was a second chance.

She had a strange wobble in her walk, but she wasn't actually lame, her steps were even. He pushed her into a trot. It was as if she had a weakness in her back. Perhaps she had gone over backwards, or fallen and needed some sort of chiropractic treatment. He remembered a trick that Carina had shown him once, she had learnt it from an old man who worked as a farrier but did a bit of bone-crunching, as he called it, on the side.

He pushed her into a canter, and she had a lovely, soft stride, even with the funny wiggle in it. He pulled her to a stop and led her back. It would be a huge risk, performing the chiropractic move that Carina had shown him. He had seen her use it twice and both times the horse had been miraculously healed, but if it didn't work and Tormenta wasn't healed, perhaps even got worse, then he was sacrificing his only chance to have a job where he could jump top quality horses. If he got it right, it would seal his sudden new promotion, and he would rise even further in Valentino's eyes. He led her slowly back to the stables and unsaddled her.

51

"What are you doing?" asked Valentino. "I wanted to watch you schooling her in the arena."

"I think that she has had a fall," said Rafael.

"Yes, some time ago she went over backwards, but she's not sore or lame. The vet looked her over."

"I want to try something," said Rafael. "It is a treatment that I have seen done twice, but it is quite . . . ," he paused, searching for the correct word, "drastic."

"I'll trust you, see if you can fix her. What is this treatment?"

Rafael remembered that Carina had told him that ideally, they would use a rubber hammer. As long as you got the right spot, one crack, the horse's back would collapse under itself and then it would be fine. He didn't have a rubber hammer. He got a bucket, turned it upside down and stood on it next to the mare. He felt carefully down her spine until he came to a point behind the saddle, before the rump. He carefully placed one hand over the place, and then with the other, he pushed down hard and fast. Tormenta dipped her back, not quite in the same melodramatic way that the horse had all those years ago with Carina, but she did dip.

"What have you done?" asked Valentino.

"It's a way of doing chiropractoring. Perhaps it didn't work, can someone trot her up so we can watch."

He held his breath as he watched. The wobble was gone. He couldn't quite believe it.

"She's lost that strange movement," said Valentino. "Boy, you're a miracle worker!"

Rafael took a long deep breath. He didn't know why he had risked everything. Perhaps he just wanted to show off? Now, all he had to do was ride to the very best of his ability, and, hopefully, there would be no disasters. He felt a weight lift from him. He hadn't been this happy since before Carina had died.

Facundo had come into the riding school much earlier than usual that morning. He was if it was possible, angrier than he had been the day before. He was consumed with rage. His complexion was a rather patchy yellow beneath his tan. That little fucker, he thought over and over again, who would have thought he could ride like that, it was just chance, and now both he and Tomas were out, as far as Valentino was concerned. Rafael would be Valentino's boy, and he would have nothing to do with the riding school horses, and there would be no way to put Rafael back in his box. He would have to do something. He went down the line of horses and abused one of the other stable boys for no good reason; then he shut himself in the office. He had to think, one way or the other, that little shit was going to be taught a lesson.

His mind ran like a rodent down the sewers sniffing out the possibilities. He had to get rid of that guttersnipe, that piece of rubbish from the shanty town. Perhaps Marianela could accuse him of rape, but there would have to be some physical evidence. But then again, there was something in this. Perhaps the little shit could steal some jewellery, which would be found in his room, that would have to be at least banishment from the Polo Club, working for Valentino or not, and charged with theft it would mean prison. He would talk to Marianela this evening and see what she could come up with, undoubtedly her slut of a mother, who was always dripping with glittering, showy pieces would have something suitable to be 'stolen'. There was a party at the club on Friday night. This might give them a chance, an excuse for Marianela to borrow her mother's jewellery.

Usually, Rafael wouldn't even be invited to such a party but perhaps now, if he was Valentino's rider, then he might, especially if his little friend Georgina asked him. He could tell her that it would smooth things over, get rid of any ill-will that she might have unwittingly created. Marianela would have to take one of her mother's special pieces. He would go down and see his cousin, who worked at the local police station. He needed to make sure that they would be prompt in attending the complaint and make sure that they would arrest Rafael. It was a good plan, and perhaps then Valentino would see that he had been wrong.

Chapter Five

Poppy was sitting at the dining room table with her mother, father and Phoebe.

"There's a party at the Polo Club this Friday night, and I do so want to go. I do think it is important to make friends with people of my own sort."

"Poppy," said David with an indulgent paternal smile. "You sound just like your mother, people 'of our own sort'. It's like something out of a Mitford novel, the Hons and the Counter-Hons."

"Unlike you, David, you're quite happy to mix with anyone from the highest to the very lowest," said Grace with a meaningful, darting look.

Phoebe shifted uncomfortably in her seat. She knew what her mother was thinking, her father's self-indulgence with sluttish women like Claudia. She had been putting up with Marianela at school, making snipey little comments, laughing at her behind her back, and undoubtedly entertaining her friends with all sorts of stories. It had been overwhelmingly embarrassing.

Grace was all too well aware of David's latest flirtation. It was only one in a long line of casual adulteries. In fact, Grace was making plans. Her stock of tolerance and patience as far as her husband went, had suddenly run dry. She didn't want to put up with this. It was a combination of too many years and too many indiscretions, and the fact that she hated Uruguay. It had to be the most boring country she had ever known. There was no Latino charm here, nothing to do, nowhere to go. Melilla Polo Club was the epitome of dull and it was where the rich and pretentious Uruguayans clustered. Most of all, she hated the abysmal way in which they treated their horses. It appeared that no-one was capable of shoeing a horse correctly, every single hoof she had looked at was set up high on the heels, not at the correct 45° angle, the shoe slapped on, and then the toes trimmed to fit the shoe, not the other way around. The horses pulling the carts and being ridden around the streets all sported the most savage, rusty curb bits and the ill-fitting saddles were made even more uncomfortable by the riders jogging and bouncing, incapable of any type of rising trot. Grace had wanted to start riding again, but the sight of the horses at the riding school and the so-called instructors had put her off. This had prompted her to make the huge decision to leave her husband.

After more than twenty years of sticking to a marriage that was increasingly unsatisfactory, she had decided that enough was enough. Not that bolting was unusual these days, in fact getting divorced was so commonplace that no-one lifted an eyebrow. She only had to look at David to feel intensely irritated. She would take Poppy back to England with her but thought perhaps that Phoebe could stay until the end of the year. The British School here did have a good reputation, and Phoebe was predicted to do very well with her Baccalaureate in November.

Grace was going home to Kiss Wood, where she had grown up. It was a beautiful Georgian house set in spacious grounds, a garden once designed by Capability Brown, a park for the horses with white painted railings, a stable block with a clock tower and an indoor riding arena. The estate was located in the neighbourhood of Burford, not far from the famous and idyllic village of Swinbrook. It was situated in an area of outstanding natural beauty and resembled a Rousseau-like green jungle, through which ran the Windrush trout stream. Grace remembered childhood picnics beside the stream with swirling, green, river grass edging the banks. There were deer, hedgehogs, ducks and ducklings, a 'veritable haven of sylvan joy'.

It was also horse-riding heaven, and that was what Grace loved. She had big plans for Poppy, who she believed was destined to get to the top of the junior show jumping scene in England, perhaps one day she might even ride for Britain, win a gold medal at the World Equestrian Games or the Olympics.

As soon as Phoebe had done her exams, she could come home, and they would make arrangements for her to go to university, perhaps with a gap year so she could settle back into English life, find her feet, and establish a satisfactory social life.

Best of all, she would leave David in a very awkward position. While ever she remained firmly ensconced in the family home, he was protected from the aspirations of his mistresses. This time he would have to fend off Claudia's determined advances, and he would have to do it on his own. Of course, Claudia would have no idea that all the wealth of their family was solely down to Grace's private income. David's paltry wage from the Consulate would barely take them out to dinner once a week. Her family lawyers had set up a watertight trust when she had married the lower middle-class and rather bumptious young David, and in the event of a divorce, he would have absolutely no claim on her millions. It was distributed in such a way that both Phoebe and Poppy would come into substantial lump sums on their eighteenth birthdays, and significantly more money when they turned twenty-five. No divorce settlement could ever touch the money in the bank. For this reason, David had had no intention of ever divorcing Grace and her millions, and he assumed that she would care more about keeping up appearances and maintaining a nuclear family for her daughters. He was sexually entranced by the voluptuous Claudia but beyond that he found her company rather silly. Claudia certainly over-estimated her sexual appeal and assumed that she could trap him.

Grace was very quiet that evening, her mouth was set in a straight line. Poppy chattered on about Tibbet and how well he jumped. In a lull in the conversation Grace spoke.

"David, I think I might go back to England for a visit. There are some issues with the estate that I must attend to personally."

David looked at her with a half-smile. Grace knew what he was thinking; this was the green light to go ahead with an affair with Claudia.

"I'm going to take Poppy with me. I don't want you to have to look after her. It will do her good to go back to England for a while. We will leave on Saturday morning."

"But Mummy, you didn't say this before, I'm meant to be riding Tibbet on Sunday," said Poppy, her mouth in a round 'o'. Phoebe looked at her mother, whose expression was inscrutable.

"Poppy, there is no problem, there are a number of very good riding schools in Oxfordshire, of a far higher standard than the Polo Club. I am not at all impressed with what I have seen there."

"But how long are you going for?" asked David.

"I don't know as long as it takes. I'm sure that you'll survive without me around," said Grace crisply. "Phoebe, you should be alright, you can drive yourself to school and back and Greta will look after the house and supervise the cleaners."

"Yes, Mummy," said Phoebe looking down at her plate. She felt like crying. There was something about this arrangement that wasn't right. Her mother wasn't prone to spontaneous trips halfway around the world. She felt that there was something quite definitive about this. Should she ask if she could go? But her subjects had been chosen, and it was her final year. Perhaps her instincts were wrong, and they would only be gone for a month or two and then be back. She felt sad, home without Poppy wouldn't be the same, her little sister was like a sunbeam lighting up all their lives.

Poppy was sitting there pouting a little, also puzzled. They had only just arrived, and this wasn't at all like her mother. On the other hand, the sound of riding schools in Oxford sounded good. She had a tremendous ambition to be a professional showjumper, and she knew that wonderful as Tibbet was, the riding schools in England would be a thousand times better than Melilla Polo Club. She could get some new riding clothes too, the latest fashion, a new riding coat that would match the most beautiful shiny electric-blue boots that she'd seen on the internet.

"I've booked us on a flight on Saturday morning," said Grace.

"This is all a little sudden," said David. "We've only just arrived. How am I going to manage without you?" He smiled at her.

"I'm sure you will manage admirably," replied Grace wryly.

David didn't reply. His brain was working overtime. Grace couldn't have timed it better, it would give him plenty of opportunities to enjoy Claudia. Obviously, she was common, 'dead common' really. But that was the way he liked his bits on the side, slutty was great! He smiled indulgently at Grace.

"Well, my dear - Phoebe and I will just have to struggle along together until you get back." He couldn't have sounded more insincere if he tried thought Grace with a grimace. She had endured more than twenty years of the vicissitudes and vagaries of marriage, and she had learnt through experience that marriage took more from you than it gave back. She had been careful not to become embittered, just cynical. So very cynical about the nature of men in general, and her own husband in particular.

It was her best friend in Oxfordshire, Verena Wade, who had stirred her up. They had a phone date once a week and were able to talk about everything going on in their lives. Verena was flighty, often enjoying a flirtation with a younger man, sometimes going too far but always sticking to her stodgy husband, Christopher. Now Verena, who was fearing the onset of menopause, was striking out - not on her own - but with her latest younger man, a thirty-two-year old lawyer, Justin, who she had met in Oxford. She was utterly convinced that this was the 'real thing' and she was divorcing Christopher. She bubbled away to Grace on the phone, mentioning Justin's name every few minutes, as if it were a magic spell.

Grace knew all about Verena's various flirtations and affairs and reserved judgement. Now, she felt very uneasy; something was stirring within herself. Instinctively she knew that there was a sea change coming. She had realised that all the putting up with, that she had done in her marriage, had been a miscalculation. Subconsciously she had thought that being a martyr would tip the scales in her favour and there would be some sort of reward at the end of it. But as the old saying went, life is not a dress rehearsal, you don't get another one at the end of it, this was it, and she was five years off fifty, if she didn't take her chance now then there might be no more chances.

She had put up with a lot, not even for the sake of the children, but mostly for the sake of appearances. But now Phoebe was obviously squirming with embarrassment at David's latest flirtation, and Marianela would probably be gossiping at school. Phoebe had adored her father when she was younger, even if Poppy had always been his obvious favourite. Now it was as if she were the jilted lover. It didn't help that Marianela was a rather sophisticated Lolita, the power of her sexuality wielded carelessly and destructively. In fact, Grace wouldn't have been surprised if David didn't find himself embroiled in a mother and daughter situation that would be worthy of the very worst of the Sunday newspapers!

She was going to leave him. She felt unutterably lighter from the moment she made this decision. At night her dreams had become vivid and real, always back at Kiss Wood, just as she had left it, all organised and ticking over with a skeleton staff, dreaming in the streaming golden sunshine of an Oxford afternoon. On other nights it was an alternative scenario, that it had been left neglected and fallen down, the roof collapsing, grass and weeds running rampant over the ruins. The horses were in the field with their hoofs so long and overgrown that they were walking on their heels. Sometimes when she awoke, she felt terribly anxious, and other times a great excitement.

She booked their tickets, first-class, one way and with extra baggage. Her lawyers in England had been told of her plans. They confirmed that all was in order and they would look over her file and expect a visit shortly. Grace ran with the plan that David was not to know what she intended. This would also entail deceiving Phoebe, as she didn't want to burden her elder daughter with a secret that would have to be hidden from her father. She wanted to give Phoebe the best chance of passing her Baccalaureate.

That Friday night Poppy was madly insistent that she should go to the party at the Polo Club. She had begged and pleaded and whined, and, finally, Phoebe had agreed to accompany her. Although it was the very last place she wished to go, she consoled herself with the thought that this would be her last visit and she wanted to do something for Poppy before she went away.

"I'll take you, but I'm not staying beyond eleven," Phoebe said firmly, thinking she would find a quiet corner to settle in with her Kindle. She absolutely hated parties, she always had, and she was sure she always would.

"I'm going to wear my new jeans and that pretty top I found at Punta Carretas last week," said Poppy, leaping up and down. "I've got some mascara too, and a lipstick, but it's not very dark, Mummy made me choose the closest colour to my own lips, which is rather pointless." She pranced around the room, pirouetting and snorting, shaking her head.

"Poppy, are you pretending to be a pony?" asked Phoebe. Poppy neighed at her and galloped down the passage to her bedroom.

On Friday afternoon Phoebe looked in her wardrobe. The best she could do was black so that she melted into the darkness and it hid her far too-opulent curves. She could brighten it up with a pair of hooped silver earrings and a simple silver chain with her lucky medallion. She was hoping to read over Wuthering Heights again and highlight some quotes that she needed to learn, putting them together with her character and theme summaries. She would sit in the shadows and read in peace.

Poppy was bouncing around like a rubber ball.

"Come on, Phoebe! Let's go! Let's go!"

59

"You know it's much more cool to arrive at a party late rather than early," said Phoebe, not really speaking from experience.

"I don't care, I want to go down and pat the horses, and give them some apples, I especially want some time with Tibbet. It'll be ages til I see him again."

"Alright, alright," said Phoebe, smearing on a few strokes of bright lipstick and a couple of swipes of blusher to try and give her face a slightly sculptured look, rather than a large circle of cheese.

Grace stood in the driveway, waving them off. She felt like a cat on a hot tin roof, thinking that something was going to happen to prevent her from getting on that plane with Poppy tomorrow morning. Her dreams had been taking on the quality of hallucinations and she was terrified that she might talk in her sleep.

Phoebe drove ultra-carefully to the Polo Club. The traffic in Montevideo was a nightmare, and she hated it.

"How do you feel about going back to England?" she asked, wondering how much Poppy knew about their father and that horrid woman.

"Well, of course, it's strange to miss school when I've barely started, but the best thing is that I can see Loppy, and she's got a marvellous new pony that she wants me to see." Loppy was the younger daughter, actually named Penelope, of Verena Wade. At this stage, neither Poppy nor Phoebe knew that Aunt Verena and her husband were going to be divorced.

"He's a skewbald, you know we're both mad on skewbalds, and he's the best jumper, but a bit unreliable. One of his eyes is ringed with white, and it makes him look a little sinister. Sometimes he's brilliant and sometimes he tries to cart her out of the ring."

"You're both absolutely pony-mad!" said Phoebe, thinking how lucky it was for Poppy to have a best friend in England. There was Tate of course, Verena's elder daughter, a couple of years older than Phoebe. Although they had known each other since they were tiny, they didn't share the same interests in life. Tate was glamorous, stick thin with the most sculptured facial structure, a part-time model and a full-time party girl who loved - above all things – cocaine!

"Yes, we're planning on running a show jumping yard when we leave school, probably at Kiss Wood."

"What does Mummy think about that?" asked Phoebe, wondering if her mother would approve of Poppy devoting herself to an equestrian career and not go to university.

"Oh Pheebs, you know I'm not like you, I like action, to be out and about, not sitting with my head in a book," replied Poppy. "You're the one who is going to have the fabulous career using your brain, and I'm going to be a top showjumper."

"I suppose Mummy approves. She's pretty keen on the horses too," said Phoebe.

"That's right," said Poppy, smiling, imagining a benign future of horses leaping coloured jumps, and rows of beautiful Thoroughbred heads hanging over stable doors, gorgeous long-legged foals frolicking in the park during the summer.

"You've got it all mapped out, haven't you," said Phoebe laughing. She was pleased that Poppy was so emotionally stable, so cheerful and full to the brim with optimism.

"Yes, well, you know you're going to be the best writer in the world," said Poppy.

"How do you know I'm going to be a writer," said Phoebe, blushing a little.

"You're got it written across your forehead," laughed Poppy. "I'm not stupid you know, even if I don't read a million books a week."

"You're a wise little cracker," said Phoebe. "Now all we've got to do is get through this evening and then there will be no more South American social events to suffer.

Poppy went zipping down the stables until she reached Tibbet's stall. As far as she knew, this was going to be the last time that she saw him for weeks and weeks. Her mother had been very vague about how long they would be in the UK. She slipped inside and stuffed him with apple quarters and sliced up carrots.

"My lovely, lovely Tibbet," she said, giving him a huge hug. He whiffled and snorted and nosed around trying to find more titbits.

Phoebe stood around outside the stable. She felt uneasy tonight. Change was in the air. Discoloured clouds were gathering high in the sky, a strange dark purple light diffused the setting sun, and a light, ghostly wind whined through the high branches of the eucalypts. Finally, Poppy was finished with her protracted farewell. They walked back to the clubhouse together.

"Are you going to be alright without me and Mummy?" asked Poppy.

"I might feel a bit lonely, but obviously Daddy will be around."

"Come on, let's go inside, there are some eats, but they won't last long, and I'm desperate for a coke," said Poppy. Phoebe sighed the last thing she needed was to eat more. She'd already had dinner followed by ice-cream, every minute she felt more and more like a blownup balloon about to burst. When she lay in bed, there were rolls of fat around her back and even on her arms. She hated herself more every minute. She would find a seat hidden away and read. She settled at a small table at the back of the room and moved the seat back into the dark corner. She could look out and see Poppy who had faithfully promised not to go back outside without telling her.

She settled down to read. She loved the classics, although she also read contemporary novels she was always drawn back to the classics. She saw Marianela on the other side of the room and found it hard to suppress a shudder. That girl really had it in for her, and now that her mother was going away, it would be even worse, her father and Claudia carrying on more obviously. She wished she had Poppy's innocence and didn't see the depressingly carnal side of life.

Marianela was hanging out with her friend, Viviana giggling maliciously about the other girls. Facundo and Tomas were standing at the end of the table, and the girls drifted down towards them. They all moved as a group and sat not far from Phoebe. She shrank back into the shadows, glad that she had chosen to wear black. Hopefully, they wouldn't notice her. They were rattling away in Spanish, but she could understand them. She had a good grasp of the language which she had learnt when they had been in Madrid. Then Marianela said in a clear, ringing voice, 'Don't worry she won't understand what we're talking about, the fat English cow,' and they had all laughed.

Unfortunately, she did understand what they were saying. Marianela was now speaking in dramatic tones, "So the plan is in place. I'll get Georgina to invite that little bastard Rafael to come over, and when he's here, I'll go into his room and plant my mother's necklace. Then at the end of the night, we'll call the police and say that we saw him take it out of my bag. He'll never ride Valentino's horses again, and he'll go to prison."

Phoebe gasped. She had heard every word and understood perfectly. They were going to set up that nice dark-haired stable boy, Poppy's favourite, with a piece of stolen jewellery. She sat very, very still - hardly daring to breathe. They didn't seem to notice her. They were cackling with glee at their nasty little plan. Facundo was secretly gently massaging Viviana's bottom, and she squirmed with delight, she loved Marianela, but she also loved stealing a march on her. They drifted off to the bar where the staff were giving the two boys alcohol, which they shared with Marianela and Viviana.

Phoebe stood up, she knew she had to do something, but she wasn't sure what. She had to save the poor hapless Rafael. She had to foil their nasty, despicable little plan. She didn't know which was Rafael's room, but if she waited until he came in, then she would follow Marianela, who was the one who was going to plant the necklace. She would retrieve the necklace from his room and warn him. She wondered if she should find Poppy and tell her what was happening, then there would be two of them to keep watch. She wasn't sure which was Georgina, but it might be that gawky girl who was standing beside Viviana now, who was whispering in her ear. If she followed Georgina to Rafael's room, then she would know where he lived, rather than risk following Marianela later, and being spotted.

She watched as Georgina was walking across towards the exit. Phoebe walked around the outside of the room on the opposite side, trying to look nonchalant and natural, trying not to slink. No-one seemed to take any notice of her. It was strange how being overweight seemed to make you invisible.

Georgina was loping along, so Phoebe had to quicken her step to keep up. If she lost her in the dark then she was missing a very good opportunity to find out where Rafael lived. They walked around past the indoor arena and then she saw Georgina disappear down an alleyway. She hurried after her and saw a thin stream of light coming from an open door. A dark figure was standing in the doorway. She could faintly hear Georgina's voice, light and high-pitched rattling away in Spanish. She couldn't hear Rafael speaking. Then Georgina turned away and hurried back down towards her. Quickly she stepped into the shadows and tried to melt away into the darkness. Georgina tap-tapped past in her high heels.

Phoebe stepped out and made her way towards the doorway. This was an ideal chance to tell Rafael what was happening. She tapped on the closed door.

"*Un momento,*" said Rafael, probably thinking that Georgina was returning.

"*Buenos noches,*" said Phoebe in her very correct but stilted Spanish.

He stood there staring at her silently, his face closed and unfriendly.

"*Puedo entrar?*" asked Phoebe, hoping he would let her in.

She spoke to him quickly in Spanish, every now and then correcting her grammar self-consciously, telling him of the dastardly plan and how she wanted to help him. He replied that even if they removed the necklace that wouldn't be the end of it. Just Marianela, saying that she had seen him steal it might be sufficient for him to be charged. Phoebe said to him that he had to run away to be safe, and she would help him. He asked, but where, where could he go? Then it came to Phoebe. It was like one of the exciting, dramatic moments out of the books that she read. She declared that if he packed his belongings, she would drive him away and find a safe house where no-one could find him. He looked at her in amazement, and she wondered if he had understood her Spanish.

She started again, using more words and phrases, explaining that as soon as she saw Marianela plant the necklace and leave, she would go in pack up his things and grab the necklace. He would then disappear into the night. She would give him her mobile phone and tell him only to answer if he received a call from Poppy. She would have Poppy's phone and ring him in the morning and pick him up, and they would drive over to the coast. She suggested Punta del Diablo because she had been there, and it was a lovely little village, the most picturesque in Uruguay.

64

Rafael was reluctant to agree, and she was hopping up and down impatiently. If they were found here together, then Facundo and his crew would know that something was happening. Finally, he agreed to her plan. She gave him her phone and told him to go to the clubhouse as if going along Georgina's invitation. Phoebe pulled back the thin dusty fabric curtain and left the light on so hopefully she would be able to see where Marianela put the necklace. He showed her the few possessions that he wanted to take, two pairs of riding trousers, called *bombachas*, three T-shirts, a white cotton shirt and a large book in a plastic bag with some trinkets.

They came out and locked his door, and Phoebe carefully pocketed the key. There must be a spare key that Marianela would use to enter his room. Phoebe hid across the alleyway in an empty stable and watched. After he had been over to the clubhouse, he would make his way into the maze of streets in a slummy part of the town and hide until morning. She told him she would drive back to pick him up at about nine o'clock and she would arrange to rent a house in Punta del Diablo unless he wanted to go anywhere else. He looked dazed, barely understanding what was happening and helplessly shrugged his shoulders. His future freedom lay in the hands of this woman who was Poppy's big sister. He had never even noticed her before. He wasn't so sure why she wanted to save him, and he hoped she wasn't in cahoots with the hated Facundo and Marianela and this wasn't part of an even more elaborate plan to make him run away and lose his chance with Valentino.

He walked slowly over to the clubhouse. It was the last place he wanted to go. Perhaps if he stayed just for a moment and then dashed back, he could catch Marianela in the act of hiding the necklace and shame her into giving up her dastardly plan. But then she was just as likely to throw herself to the ground screaming and claim that he had attacked her. His word was never going to be believed against hers.

He ran a comb through his hair, squared his shoulders and walked into the club room feeling as if he were a French aristocrat going to the guillotine. He couldn't believe it, in a single moment, his whole life was in pieces, and he would be on the run, perhaps it was all a ruse to make him run away, or perhaps she had misunderstood what she had heard? Why should he trust this strange fat, white English woman?

He was trying to think. If it were true and Facundo and Marianela wanted him in prison, then he was quite powerless to stop them, if they went to such lengths and they found the necklace in his room, then he would go to prison. And even if they foiled the plan this time, then it could happen again at any moment. If only Valentino would move his horses to another stable, then he would be safe. If he ran away now, he would never have another chance like this.

He felt filled with anger, bitter black bile. It would be so easy for those four to destroy his life, such a small and unimportant life, he couldn't understand what pleasure they would get from this, like snapping their fingers in his face. He got to the clubhouse entrance and looked around. There was the filthy foursome, laughing together. Was he just imagining it or were they laughing at him? Georgina came forward holding a drink for him. She was smiling shyly, she wanted to make up for the way her father had treated him, but she was glad that it had worked out so well with Valentino.

He sipped his drink and watched Marianela saunter across the room. She smiled at him malevolently, and he knew beyond any doubt that she was out to destroy him. He had made a fool of her beloved Facundo. He felt a huge desire to go after her, catch her in the act and punch her in the face, but that wouldn't solve the problem. The only thing to do was go along with Phoebe's plan at least he would retain his freedom, and he could take his few precious belongings.

He stood there sipping on the coke that Georgina had given him. He turned to her and smiled, a tight insincere smile, more of a grimace. Marianela walked straight up to him and asked him to buy her a drink. She pushed herself up against him, and he felt her full breasts straining against the tight fabric of her dress. He felt sick. He was tempted to vomit all over her. Tactfully, he moved away. He guessed that this was an act and that later she would say that he had gone through her bag. He hated her with such vicious fury that he had to clench his fists inside his pockets. She shrugged when he didn't respond and walked with swinging hips towards the door. Obviously, she was going to his room now to plant the necklace.

Facundo was smiling. Rafael watched him. Thank God for the English girl, he couldn't even remember her name. He would have to trust her, tempting as it was to go back to his room and get his belongings. He waited until Marianela returned and he walked out. He had his wallet with his *cedula* (identity card), and his birth certificate was lodged in the Central Civil Register. He had Phoebe's mobile phone. She had told him to only answer a call from Poppy. He could do that. He walked in the opposite direction to his room, across the rugby field, the tennis courts and out onto the narrow road that led down to the central avenue that ran through the main street of town. He turned off into the streets that led through the slums, hugging the shadows he made for a small park where he would settle down into the bushes and wait for morning.

If Phoebe changed her mind and didn't come for him, then he would go back to the shanty town and start again. He had some friends there that would take him in. In a few months, he would go over to Pablo and Florencia's riding school on the coast and ask them to let him work there in return for his keep. He really didn't expect Phoebe to ring him in the morning. His main regret was his one memento of Carina, a book called 'Dressage' by Henry Wynmalen. She had brought it from England. It had been a present from her brother. He had wanted to ask her about her family in England, but her face had all closed up, and he knew it was a forbidden topic.

He settled on the ground, shrouded by a bush. It was a beautiful night, late summer and still warm, with just a promise of chill to come in the forthcoming months. He considered walking up to the Ruta 5 highway so it would be easier for Phoebe to find him, but he would be too exposed up there. He pulled the mobile phone out of his pocket and saw that it was 11 pm. There was plenty of charge on the phone, so at least it wouldn't be dead by morning, then he would have no way of ever contacting Phoebe again.

Very soon they would be staging their little melodrama and calling the police who would be shown to his room. If Phoebe had carried out her part of the plan, there would be a few things left behind, so it wouldn't be immediately obvious that he had left. They would search the grounds perhaps. He wondered what Phoebe would do with the necklace. Presumably, she would leave it somewhere in the clubhouse, and it could be 'found' later.

Phoebe had stood inside the stable peeping out around the corner for ages. It felt like an eternity, and she began to wonder if she had dreamed up the whole thing – which would be inordinately embarrassing and disastrous for Rafael. Finally, she could hear the tip-tap of high heels on the ground.

Marianela hurried up, and she could see something glittering in her hand. It looked like Marianela had been drinking as she fumbled with the key and finally let herself into the room. Through the thin curtain, Phoebe could see her moving around. She seemed to go towards the bed. The obvious place where one would hide something was under the mattress and Marianela was at least predictable, not a young woman of much imagination, thought Phoebe with a hot rush of hate. She watched her leave, locking the door behind her. Phoebe waited, counting slowly to twenty before she moved out of the shadows.

She had the key in her hand, and she went inside. The light was still on; she began to gather the belongings that Rafael had indicated. It was a hardback book with a very tattered dust jacket as if it had been carried halfway around the world. She picked up his pairs of pants, t-shirts, and a towel. The towel was so thin and grimy that she decided she would leave it, she would buy him a new towel, or just take one out of the linen cupboard at home. She had checked his pockets, and there was no necklace. She went to the bed and lifted up the mattress. There was the necklace glittering in the dim light. It looked like cubic zirconia, not even valuable!

Phoebe thrust it in her pocket and hurried out. She carried the bags around to her car and put them in the boot. She didn't want Poppy to see them. She hurried back to the clubhouse and was relieved to see Poppy dancing on the little disco floor with her friends. She smiled at her and felt the bulk of the necklace in her pocket. She stood there for a while. It was going to be hard to persuade Poppy to leave early, and it might be interesting to watch the police search which would occur in an hour or so. She hoped that Rafael was well away and wouldn't be picked up wandering around in the night. She could feel adrenalin running through her veins; she didn't feel like eating at all. Obviously, intrigue was an antidote for food cravings. Tomorrow promised to be even more exciting driving Rafael up the coast. She thought about him. He really was extraordinarily good-looking, but he looked so sad.

Finally, she saw Marianela start to squawk, looking through her bag frantically.

"Oh my God, someone has stolen my necklace," she cried at the top of her voice. The security guard who had been quietly drinking beer out in the kitchen lumbered out. She turned to him.

"My necklace has been stolen, call the police!"

He looked at her in a daze, his hand on his pistol, and then turned to the barman and asked him to ring the police. Everyone was staring at Marianela now. She was over-acting like a bimbo who was trying to get into the movies. Facundo raced protectively to her side and Tomas and Viviana drew closer to support her.

"I know, it was that stable boy, he pushed himself up against me, that one called Rafael!" she cried melodramatically.

"Oh my God, this is so unbelievable," murmured Phoebe.

"Call the police! Call the police!" cried Facundo, like a man taking charge in an emergency situation.

The police arrived very swiftly, and they set off in a posse to Rafael's room. Facundo quickly produced the spare key, and they stormed in. The crowd from the club room trooped after them and watched from a distance. Phoebe grabbed hold of Poppy's hand; she didn't want to lose her in the excitement. She imagined how awful it would have been for Rafael if he had slunk back to his room and gone to sleep, to be awakened in this manner.

The room was bare. A quick search revealed nothing. Marianela stood there, a frown on her face. Something had gone wrong. The police continued to search, and still, nothing was found, no culprit and no stolen necklace. Phoebe found herself smiling broadly. It was good to see Marianela and Facundo shown up as total fools.

"He must have run away with my jewellery," said Marianela melodramatically.

"Do you mean this necklace, it was in the toilets, I'm sorry," said Phoebe, stepping forward and speaking in loud, clear Spanish. "I didn't realise it was this, this is not valuable, it is just cubic zirconia, costume jewellery, surely?" she said, addressing herself to the head policeman.

Marianela looked at her with narrowed eyes, glinting with malice. She hissed and spat in her rage.

"Well, where is he? This Rafael?" asked Facundo, trying to retrieve the situation.

"Do stable staff have to remain in their rooms when they're not at work?" asked Phoebe very clearly.

There was a general shuffling of feet.

"Let's go back to dance," shouted Poppy, instinctively joining in as if she had divined the whole plan. She had always been a smart little cookie.

Marianela and Facundo lost their audience. The police looked annoyed that they had been summoned on a wild goose chase. Everyone else lost interest. Phoebe took Poppy by the hand.

"It's home time for us," she said. "Too much excitement on your last night."

They got into the car.

"Where did you really get that necklace?" asked Poppy.

"I told you I found it in the bathroom," said Phoebe grinning at her little sister.

"Yeah right," said Poppy. "One day, you can tell me the whole story."

"I promise," said Phoebe smiling secretly to herself.

Chapter Six

When Phoebe awoke on Saturday morning, she was filled with a strange, wild, unfamiliar happiness, and she didn't feel hungry – her world really was shifting on its axis! Today she was to contact Rafael, pick him up and drive him to safety. Suddenly she had been transported into real life, not just living it through books. She envisaged an intensely romantic adventure. She would leave a note to tell her father she was going away for the weekend, which meant that tonight might be the night. Perhaps by this time tomorrow morning, she would no longer be an awkward virgin, but a young woman introduced to all the sexual delights one could imagine.

She gave herself a strict talking to. At no time had she and Rafael even hinted to each other that there was a sexual dimension to this situation. Her mind was running riot, and she was fairly certain that Rafael did not share her fantasies.

The plan to secrete Rafael out of Montevideo and drive him to safety, so hastily contrived, was to go off amazingly smoothly. After Grace and Poppy had left for the airport in a taxi, Phoebe had rung her own mobile from Poppy's mobile, and Rafael had answered. She told him to stand at the bus stop outside the Supermercado Dorado on Camino Treinta Dos, and she would pick him up within an hour. He was standing there, looking totally Uruguayan with his flask of hot water and his maté cup. She parked beside the kerb five metres beyond the bus stop, and he slouched over and slid into the passenger front seat. Glancing over at him, she smiled shyly.

"Todo es bien?" she asked.

He smiled faintly and nodded. They drove off heading for the highway out of town, around the ring road and across to join the highway that led up the eastern side of the country, towards the Brazilian border. Phoebe had gone on the internet the night before and booked a house in Punta del Diablo for two weeks and would be able to negotiate to lengthen the rental period. Punta, as the locals called it, was the most popular holiday town on the coast, picturesque, miles and miles of golden beaches, old fishing boats pulled up on the sand, fresh fish for sale in a line of huts opposite the beach, brightly painted restaurants selling an Uruguayan version of ethnic food, and a range of attractive hippy-looking locals who sold home-grown weed. In the summer, 30,000 young people descended on the place for six

71

weeks of a wonderful alcohol and drug-fueled fiesta, dancing on the beach and partying, but the rest of the year it was a ghost town. Late autumn and one had one's choice of six- monthly rentals and only a few smiling locals to contend with.

The early morning traffic was sparse, and Phoebe relaxed a little and attempted to talk to Rafael in her rather formal Spanish when she continually forgot to say 'zsh' instead of swallowing the consonant 'll' with a 'y' sound. She had learnt Spanish in Spain and had yet to pick up the distinctly different South American pronunciation. She stumbled along politely asking him questions. He nodded and replied monosyllabically. Finally, she gave up and switched on the music, hoping that the silence between them was in some way companionable.

Rafael slumped in the passenger seat, turned away from Phoebe watching out the window sightlessly, feeling as if he was being taken away from any hope of a life. These last few weeks riding Valentino's horses had been the pinnacle of his small dreams, and now he was denied even this chance, solely because of Facundo's spiteful jealousy. The bitterness in him swelled. He couldn't imagine what this fat, white whale of an English girl could possibly want with him. It was a mystery to him, but the all-consuming hatred of Facundo flooded his mind and any speculation about Phoebe's motivation was swamped.

He leapt into the old familiar furrow of obsessive hatred. Now it was augmented by an equal hatred for Marianela. As far as he could see, they were two of a kind. He knew that the malice that he was nursing would poison him, but there was no way he could stop it. He was an empty vessel consumed with seething evil emotions.

Phoebe also hated Marianela; the emotion was like a sharp, intense knife stabbing her in the chest. The girl's beauty and wanton, blatant sexuality made her feel even fatter and uglier than ever. She wondered how God had decided to endow such ineffable beauty on such an ugly soul.

"Facundo was going to do anything he had to, in order to stop me riding Valentino's horses," said Rafael, in Spanish.

"Facundo is not a nice person, but it is Marianela that I absolutely hate," said Phoebe in her accurate Spanish. She was finding it hard to understand

72

Rafael's idiomatic shanty-town language. She was frowning trying to concentrate. "I'm sorry my Spanish isn't brilliant," she apologised.

"Perhaps we should speak in English," replied Rafael in faultless, beautifully accented English. Phoebe looked across at him in astonishment. He was not exactly smiling, but there was a mischievous glint in his beautiful almond-shaped black eyes, fringed with the thickest lashes.

"You speak English?" she exclaimed in astonishment. She was confused, perhaps she had imagined it, she was feeling light-headed, she hadn't slept much last night. Then she remembered how he had said 'well done' to Poppy after she had jumped Tibbet.

"Yes, I do," said Rafael.

"Your accent, it is very plum pudding!" she exclaimed and then giggled.

"I was taught by my guardian, her name was Carina, she was from England," he replied a little haughtily

"I had no idea," said Phoebe, stricken that he might think she was laughing at him.

"You speak English very well," she said, trying to make amends. One minute she was performing an act of charity, saving someone from gross injustice, albeit a beautiful-looking young man who she was rather hoping would seduce her because he was grateful. But now he could speak perfect English that would be acceptable in the grandest of English drawing-rooms.

"I hate that fucker Facundo!" exclaimed Rafael, the anger and hatred spilling over like a torrent down a dirty gutter. Apparently, he could swear in English as well!

"It's Marianela that I really hate," said Phoebe, entering into this orgy of negativity.

"Her too!" said Rafael.

"You know her mother is having it off with my father and they don't even try to hide it! She flaunts it in front of me at school. It is so embarrassing, I can't tell you."

"Her mother looks as much of a slut as her daughter, the apple didn't fall far from the tree," said Rafael cattily. Phoebe wondered at his grasp of idiom.

"It's not just that, it's weird, but Marianela also flirts with my father who seems to dote on her," said Phoebe, "I really don't understand how people can behave like that."

Now they bonded with mutual hatred over their enemies and talked themselves around to smugly discussing the various reactions that Phoebe had witnessed when the police had arrived at the Polo Club last night. Phoebe described with relish, how she had produced the necklace like a rabbit out of a hat. In itself, this might be a little suspicious, but Facundo and Marianela could hardly make a move against her, she was no lowly stable boy without status in the world.

They congratulated themselves on the way that the wicked plan had fallen flat on its face. They carefully skirted the issue that Rafael was now effectively homeless and had forfeited the best job he had ever had, nor was likely to have in Uruguay.

"You know you would be much better off in England, you're so good with the horses. My mother says that the standard of horsemanship here in Uruguay is appalling."

"England?" said Rafael.

"By all accounts, you're a very good rider, well Valentino thinks so, and he's the top rider in Uruguay, and you speak wonderful English, why not go and work in England. I'm sure one of the top stables would snap you up," said Phoebe, building shining castles in the air, thinking he would be her special friend and they could meet up and go for a drink and she could show off this gorgeous young man.

"But what about a visa, they absolutely hate South Americans in immigration, they think we're all *narco-trafficantes*," said Rafael, remembering stories that he had overheard.

"I know, but with the EU, I know a lot of Uruguayans with Italian grandparents can get an Italian passport. Or you could get a job in Spain, Italy or France, you know."

"My father did have an Italian name, you might be right, he might have been Italian, or perhaps his parents were. I have my birth certificate. I can go and check."

"And if you're not you could always marry someone and get a passport that way," said Phoebe airily, unable to resist the vision of walking down the aisle, slim in a creamy wedding dress that would set off Rafael's skin tone beautifully. She realised what she was saying and went bright tomato-red.

It was a long drive first across towards the east coast and then up towards Brazil, following the signs to the frontier town of Chuy. They returned to the much safer topic of their mutual hatred and drove on thinking of every single insult they could hurl towards Facundo and Marianela, and then there was Tomas and Viviana as well. In the comfortable silences that fell between them, Phoebe began to daydream, she and Rafael would fall in love, get married and then she would take him home to Kiss Wood.

Eventually, they saw the sign that pointed off to the right, Punta del Diablo and they turned off the main road and headed along the narrow tarmac road that led to the small holiday village.

Phoebe, who liked to be organised, had downloaded a map of the area and printed it out. She looked at it carefully and then shyly asked Rafael if he could direct her to the wooden house that she had marked on it. He pointed here and there, and they criss-crossed a network of dirt roads until they came to a cottage, with the signpost 'Luna'. Phoebe telephoned the number and spoke briefly to the caretaker. They waited for him to arrive to let them in. It was a cute little dwelling; natural wood finish, a wide verandah that looked towards the sea which they could hear but not see. There was a straggling bunch of dark green trees with black bark and no grass, just sand with some large tufty tussocks.

"It looks like we're about four blocks from the beach," said Phoebe, "and we passed that little supermercado on the other road so we'll be able to go down and buy provisions." Then she realised she had said 'we', which was a huge assumption as if they were already together. She went bright red again.

They heard the buzz of a small motorbike, and a jolly black-haired native with merry dancing eyes pulled up beside them. He led them up the rough path and unlocked the front door, fumbling for the electric switch. It smelled musty but was quite clean, much more luxurious than the beaten-earth room that Rafael had left behind at Melilla.

The caretaker rattled away in Spanish, addressing Rafael, who nodded and said "*Si*," at regular intervals. Phoebe didn't even try to understand what he was saying, she let it all flow over her, enjoying the feeling of being part of a couple, with a man to take charge.

Eventually, the caretaker left, and Phoebe busied herself around the house, opening windows and letting the scent of the sea blow in, briny and fresh and reminiscent of her only childhood bucket-and-spade holiday in Cornwall. She felt very nervous. So far, the plan had worked perfectly. She had helped Rafael escape, and now he was safe, but the future yawned ahead, empty of a plan, and neither of them really knew what would happen. Phoebe helped him carry in the bags that were in the boot. She pulled out the battered book.

"Where did you get this?" she asked curiously.

Rafael looked at her for a moment. Then in a burst of confidence, he told her. Perhaps in these circumstances, he could afford to tell someone about himself.

"The woman who adopted me, Carina, it was her book."

"Where is she now?" asked Phoebe.

"She died, and then I went to work at the Polo Club."

"Look there is an inscription, '*To Catherine Broughton, with all my love, your brother, Edward*'. So, you said her name was Carina, in England she would have been Catherine."

Phoebe felt rather embarrassed as she brought in her own bag with a change of clothes and toiletries. She put it down beside the table, too shy to unpack it as if she was presuming that she was staying and spending the night with him. Perhaps, she should say good-bye and head back to Montevideo. There was also the question of funds. The rent was paid for two weeks, but what about food? It would be embarrassing to give him cash as a handout.

"Let's walk back down to the supermercado, and buy some food," she said brightly.

Rafael nodded brusquely, probably the same questions about the immediate future were worrying him as well. As they set off, Phoebe was thinking desperately. They would buy food, plenty of staples so that he could survive during the week and then she could suggest a walk to the beach. Perhaps by then, they would feel more comfortable with each other. She picked out a big back of pasta and another of rice, and butter, milk, cream, ham and vegetables from the shelves. She quickly paid for their purchases hoping that Rafael didn't feel awkward that she was the one with money. Loaded down with plastic bags, they walked back to the cottage and emptied the food into the cupboards and the fridge.

"Let's walk down to the beach," he said to her, his dark eyes large and questioning. He was as unsure as she about what would happen tonight.

"What a good idea," said Phoebe, relieved that they could put off the whole issue of going to bed, separately or together.

The beach was about ten minutes walk away. They were drawn by the sound of the sea. It was late in the afternoon, and already a large full round moon was hanging over the horizon. The scent of pine trees hung in the air. Seagulls soared gracefully above them. Their wings painted pink by the light of the setting sun. They walked across the beach that stretched in front of the huts where they sold fresh fish. The fishermen were dragging their boats out for the night's fishing. They skirted around the rocks at the end of the beach and came out to a very long stretch of pure white sand, a broad crescent that curved around the bay for several miles. They walked and walked, with the waves rippling in around their ankles, the water was very cold in the autumn air. The sun dipped below the western horizon, and the moonlight was reflected on a shiny fragmented path across the sea. It was pure romance, and Phoebe felt that if nothing happened tonight, then it never would – she would be an awkward, unwanted virgin for the rest of her life.

They stood looking out to sea, and she felt him take her hand. It was warm and dry. She was not as tall as him, but she felt so bulky and fat and awkward. He would never want her as a girlfriend, the most she could hope for was they would be friends, and she was willing to do anything to help him. She felt so much love for him as if she were haemorrhaging.

He turned towards her and swooped like a beautiful blackbird, and his lips found hers in a kiss so tender, yet sensuous, beyond anything she had ever imagined. Not that she ever daydreamed much about romance - except in her most private secret moments, it was not something that she thought she deserved. She was not the sort of girl that men liked, that was for young women like Marianela.

Rafael made love to her on the beach, in a way that could only ever have been in books. She was studying *Wuthering Heights,* and it seemed as if her fictional world had merged with the everyday. He was her Heathcliff. She would have liked to be Kathy, but she rather feared that she was the insipid Isabella Linton, and that Rafael only turned to her out of desperation and thankfulness. The passion she felt took her breath away, and finally, her brain stopped running in circles. She could never have asked for a more romantic, first experience.

Afterwards, as the stars speckled the sky, they walked back to the cottage and Phoebe disappeared into the bathroom to have a shower. She wanted to be fresh and fragrant for the night, and now there was no doubt, they would sleep together in the only double bed.

She emerged with her clean clothes and saw that he had cooked pasta, with vegetables, ham and cream – absolutely delicious and better than anything she could have concocted. He ate a huge plateful. Phoebe picked at hers. She had no appetite, but she didn't want to hurt his feelings by rejecting his food. They drank half a bottle of white wine each and then finished with very strong coffee and small sweet biscuits. Then without discussing it, they piled the dishes in the sink and went to bed.

This time the love-making was slow and languorous, not hurried, and Rafael was as good in bed as he was on a horse. Phoebe responded eagerly. Eventually, they fell asleep, curled around each other. It was a perfect end to a perfect day thought Phoebe. She was utterly irretrievably in love. How Rafael felt was a mystery, as much to himself as to anyone else. He had acted instinctively, feeling that in this situation, such a response was expected. He liked Phoebe, she was a good woman, she had looked after him, and he felt under obligation, all he had to offer were his sexual services.

Early the next morning, they got up and went down to the beach. They chose at random, buying a kilo of fresh fish. They fried it up with butter and ate half each. Phoebe had never eaten fish so delicious and so fresh. Reluctantly she got ready to leave. She felt as if she tarried then the miraculous bubble would burst. She casually left some peso notes on the table, and with a perfunctory kiss on the lips, she left. She drove home with her head in the clouds, reliving every exciting moment in her imagination.

She arrived back at the apartment, and no-one was home. It felt very empty, without her mother and Poppy. Suddenly desolate and alone, she thought this must be how Rafael felt when Carina had died. He seemed such a solitary person. Undoubtedly her father was with Claudia. She hated the way he was behaving. She was restless, worried and very tempted to drive to Melilla Polo Club just to find out how things stood now that Rafael had disappeared, but she realised that would be a bad idea. Already, the fact that she had produced the necklace had implicated her in some fashion, and she had no excuse to go there. If she showed up and said that she wanted some riding lessons, then it would look very odd. Perhaps her father might have some news. She waited and waited, but by ten o'clock he still hadn't come home, so she went to bed. She fell asleep dreaming of Rafael, the texture of his skin, the feeling of his lips, his hands on her. She ate nothing; she felt as if she need never eat again.

In the morning, her father was at the breakfast table, looking a little sheepish. Phoebe smiled brightly at him. Obviously, he didn't care at all where she had been. Her mother would have been eagle-eyed and have immediately spotted that something had happened.

The days dragged by. She kept her eye out for Marianela, wondering if perhaps the evil little bitch might try to pay her back for producing the necklace. Nothing happened. Even Marianela's usual catty remarks about her mother's relationship with Phoebe's father had stopped. This, in itself, was suspicious. Phoebe put her head down and tried to concentrate on her school work. But she could only dream of Rafael, wondering what he might be doing at Punta, perhaps long walks along the beach, getting to know the locals, or even looking for a job. She had told him that she would return late on Friday evening and she found it very hard to get through the long, boring days until then. She went to the shopping mall at Punta Carretas to buy some new clothes. Already she had dropped a dress size. She had absolutely no desire to eat. She bought a warm fuzzy jumper that felt lovely to touch, imagining Rafael running his hands up and down her arms.

She felt so different. This was being in love. It was as if a phosphorescent trail swept behind her. She was brimful of ecstasy and adoration, her body thrumming with desire whenever she thought of him. Of course, she knew he didn't really love her. Probably he was just grateful. But being near him, making love with him, that was enough for her. Perhaps when she was thin, he might truly fall in love with her.

She had packed her bag on Friday morning and planned to leave straight from school, getting changed at the service station along the way. The drive would take at least four hours. She took some food supplies out of the pantry, and also purloined several bottles of rather good wine that her father kept in the drinks cupboard. She took two of the crystal glasses out of the cabinet, wrapping them carefully in tissue paper, so they didn't break. She was planning a rather delicious platter of fresh olives, cold cuts of meat, different cheeses from Tienda Inglesa (the expensive supermarket), and fresh crusty bread. They could snack and drink wine, and perhaps he might have prepared a meal.

Arriving at the cottage, there was just a flickering light in the darkened window. Panic swept through her, what if he had gone, left without leaving a word. She was finding it hard to breathe. She couldn't bear it if she were to lose him now, after a week of dreams and fantasies. She sat in the car and tried to catch her breath. Then the front door opened, and his body was outlined in the doorway. Oh, my God! He had been waiting for her. She felt a rush of pure passion and began to shake.

"Phoebe!" he called.

"Hi," she called back, trying to sound casual and insouciant.

She stumbled as she walked up the path towards him and he stepped forward to help her with her parcels and the little suitcase she was carrying. She looked up at him, his face was hard to discern in the dark, but his white teeth shone as his mouth stretched in a welcoming smile. They went inside, and she could smell onions from a creamy pasta sauce that he had prepared.

"Oh, that smells wonderful," she gushed, producing the wine and the glasses. "Let's have a drink."

She understood for the first time the way that grown-ups 'needed a drink'. The wine ran down her throat and smoothed the sharp angles of anxiety

80

that were twisting in her soul. He asked about her week, but there wasn't much to tell him - tales of school and her humdrum home life were not at all entertaining. She asked him what he had been doing, and he told her that he had been down to the beach and asked the fishermen if there were any work and one night they had taken him out. He was paid in fish and just a few pesos, but it was enough to buy some tobacco to roll his own cigarettes.

He ate the olives, cheese and meat and tore off chunks of fresh bread dipped in olive oil and herbs. Then he jumped up and served her the pasta. It was the most delicious meal she had ever eaten. Then they went to bed and made love passionately, and it was everything that she had ever imagined and so much more. But nothing felt real. If they took their mutual passion out to the real world then it would dissolve into nothingness.

They walked down to the beach the next morning and got some fresh fish for their breakfast. After they had breakfasted, they went for a long walk up the beach. They ran out of conversation, but it didn't seem to matter.

On the way back she asked him about his childhood in the shanty town, and he told her about Carina and the horses and all he had learnt. Then he asked her about her home, and she described Kiss Wood, the only point of stability as they had moved around the world from one diplomatic post to another. The last before Uruguay had been Spain and then at least they had been able to regularly visit their home.

"You would love Kiss Wood," she told him. "There are the most wonderful stables, and my mother has written to say that she has bought Poppy a pony. Which is strange, I mean what will they do with it when they come back. And they're building another indoor arena, even bigger than the one that had been there for years."

"What will you do?" he asked, and she noticed the strain in his voice.

"I'll stay here until I've done my exams in November, then I guess I'll go back to England." She took a deep breath. "You could come with me if you want, I'm sure Poppy and my mother would love you, they are both mad about horses. I would be the odd one out."

He frowned at this, clearly disbelieving that he would be welcomed at Kiss Wood. But Phoebe was dreaming the most enticing vision, she would take Rafael back to Kiss Wood when she came into her money in November, and even if her mother didn't welcome him, she would have the resources to set them up in their own house. Of course, if they married then his stay in England would be assured, as her husband, but she was not going to propose to him. She was far too shy and uncertain for that. She hoped that he would understand and then suggest that they married, but although he brooded, his black eyes staring straight ahead. She doubted it was a picture of them tripping down the aisle together.

The weeks flew past. She couldn't risk driving down during the week. She attended school and forced herself to study every night, doing her homework and revision. She stayed up late drinking coffee and steeping herself in literature and history. She felt as if she had a pact with the gods of love, as long as she studied diligently and conscientiously during the week Rafael would be in Punta del Diablo waiting for her at the weekend. Her target grades had been set high, and she was determined to achieve them. As long as she was doing well at school, she felt that luck was with her. The future beyond her exams was shining with hope. She elaborated on her vision to take Rafael back to England. The equestrian scene in the UK held so many more opportunities for such a talented rider.

As she studied *Wuthering Heights,* she fantasised about Rafael with his dark gipsy looks, an orphan, alone in the world. All his love seemed to go to horses, not people. He showed signs of liking her, and, certainly, he took care not to hurt her, but she existed in an almost breathless hope that her abundant love and passion, was more than enough for both of them.

However, there was one thing that was for certain, Rafael was like Heathcliff in that he was fueled by hatred and dark thoughts of violence. Revenge on Facundo and Tomas, and also Marianela, circled in his mind, like rats running around a treadmill. He and Phoebe were closest when they bitched together about the evil foursome. They bonded on the basis of their mutual hatred. As long as they stayed together on this track, they felt safe. Venturing on to romantic declarations was not easy, and perhaps Rafael never felt that need. Occasionally Phoebe would tentatively try to express affection in an everyday casual way, but he hadn't responded.

However, with early winter nights when the last fingers of sunlight shone through the thin kitchen curtains, they would light candles, put on music and fall into bed and make love. Phoebe was becoming a little more proactive during these love-making sessions. When she took her breaks from studying literature, she googled sex. A plethora of erotic images bombarded her, but it didn't match with her fantasies, it was too mechanical and staged. She studied the different positions, turning her head this way and that, trying to memorise certain movements but she felt embarrassed by her body and she was not nubile like these women, even the so-called 'amateurs' had good figures. She was losing weight. She did walk briskly every morning, sometimes trying to jog a few steps, but years and years of sedentary pursuits meant that she was not naturally athletic.

Rafael was very awkward about taking money off her for food, and then there was the fortnightly rent. She brought food from the pantry at home, which she would put in the kitchen, guessing what he might eat. He did eat whatever she brought. Sometimes she bought a few expensive luxuries from the Tienda Inglese at Carasco, but usually, it was just staples.

On Saturday morning they would walk together down to the beach where the fishermen sold fresh fish, and she would buy kilos of it and leave it in the fridge for the rest of the week. She sensed that he hated being an object of charity, but there was nothing either of them could do about it at this point. She tried to tell him that in England, he would be able to not only earn his own living, but have a wonderful career. He would look at her disbelievingly, and she could see no way forward, not until he agreed to go back to England with her.

Chapter Seven

Even though Rafael hated taking her money and living off her, he was screwing himself up to ask her for $US 400. He was fully aware of the crass paradox, and this was a huge amount of money for him. He wasn't sure how she was placed financially. She seemed to have unlimited funds, but she was still a schoolgirl living in her family's house. He needed the money to rescue a horse that he had found. It was starving, a bony wreck; cruelly and relentlessly driven around in a cart picking up scrap metal. He had talked to the owner and asked him how much he would sell him for and he had summed up Rafael in a glance and seen the pity and the passion in his dark eyes and asked for $US 800.

Everyday Rafael would walk around town until he found the man and the horse. He would stand back and watch the horse being whipped behind a cart overladen with scrap metal, half-starved, dirty, with big feet that had been rasped at different angles, an ugly head with a bump on its profile and ears that were set at odds and flopped at strange angles. The driver of the cart was a mean-looking man with a large stomach and narrow, squinty, darting eyes. He haggled like a cunning trader as if he had seen into Rafael's heart and knew that he would do whatever he had to do to rescue this horse. Rafael considered dragging the bastard off the cart and punching him senseless. He clenched his fists rigidly by his sides. He had followed the man, refusing to sit up on the cart, giving the horse extra weight to pull. They went several miles up the coast towards Brazil and finally came to a clearing on the edge of the National Park and he saw that the man had built a bit of a shack and there was a pile of scrap there.

Finally, they had agreed on $US 400 which was a ridiculously high sum for a horse so close to death, but Rafael was determined to save it, and he would have to put away his pride and ask Phoebe if she could lend the money to him. He would swear to repay it, although how he was ever going to do this, he didn't know. In the end, he just blurted it out when they had sat down for their Saturday breakfast feast of fresh fish.

"There's a horse that goes around the streets, in a cart, he is in terrible condition, but there's something about him, I feel we have to save him, but they want $US 400 for him. Could you lend me that money? Please."

Phoebe raised her head scenting the air, like a gun dog pointing. There was a passion and purpose in Rafael's words that she had only ever heard in their plots of revenge. And with her keen ear for language, she had heard the words 'we have to save him', something that they did together, a mission!

"Of course I can gi.., lend you the money," she stumbled. "We'll have to drive into Los Castillos to the ATM there though. What type of horse is he?"

Rafael smiled his beautiful, soul-wrenching smile.

"He is about 16 hh, poor in condition but not that heavy-set, although he looks old, it might just be his poor condition. He is very gentle, and when I pick fresh grass, he seems very happy to see me. He has funny, loppy ears, like a rabbit I used to have when I was a child until the neighbours ate it."

Phoebe was feeling light and happy. Somehow she interpreted this development as if they were moving forward in their relationship. Rafael felt able to ask her for money. Her idea of a married couple was modelled on her mother and father, and it had always been her mother's money that had financed their lifestyle. She felt they had had a breakthrough in their relationship. He felt confident enough to ask her for money, and she had been pleased to give it to him, it made her feel wanted. She longed for him to be happy. She didn't continue on with the logical progression, that encumbered with the responsibility of an animal he wouldn't be free to fly to England with her. Her heart was filled with joy to see the thankfulness in Rafael's eyes, which she chose to interpret as love.

Rafael marveled at the way that Phoebe immediately agreed to give him the money. He thought of her as a large friendly dog who had blundered in and rescued him. It was like a miracle, a rather unlikely miracle. His mind filled with a vision of Rapture, as he had called the horse, he would take him each day to find grass, wandering as far afield as was necessary and then he would tether him here in the garden at night, even sleeping outside with him, to keep him safe. He would rescue Rapture, as Phoebe had rescued him.

His major preoccupation of revenge against Marianela and Facundo had begun to fade. Instead, his mind filled with love and care and hope for his new horse. He could go back and beat Facundo in a show jumping event, demonstrate that he was not a weakling to be rescued by a female, that he was not helpless. He had never yet hit back at those who wanted to keep him down. Somehow, he wanted his revenge to be more sophisticated than brute violence. He wanted to compete against Facundo and show his superiority in horsemanship in front of all those snobbish, supercilious, arrogant, ignorant members of the Melilla Polo Club. That would be a victory, and he could always return later and then punch Facundo senseless. Perhaps Rapture really would turn out to be an amazing show jumper.

When Phoebe had first driven him here, she had suggested that he might go to England and have a life there. She was always talking about it. He found it too awkward to take her seriously. Although they had sex, there were none of the conventional declarations of mutually exclusive love. He had thought a lot about a life in England, a land where horsemanship was practised at the highest level, where he would have a chance to learn from the best, to be a small fish in a big pond. He wondered if it was a land full of people like Carina, but somehow - he doubted it. Carina had sent herself into exile and had never wanted to return. Obviously, something terrible had happened to her, but she had never spoken about it.

He didn't want to take Phoebe with him to buy the horse. If the man saw her, he would definitely put up the price. He waited until she set out for Montevideo very early on Monday morning and then he went down to the beach, up along the surf line and into the National Park. When he arrived at the hovel, he found Rapture without water or feed standing desolately tied to a tree. There was no sign of life from the hut. Rafael felt tempted to just take the horse and walk away, but he knew that he would never feel secure.

He banged on the door, and the man finally emerged bleary-eyed. He could smell the pigs that were in the pen next to the man's sleeping place. He handed over the money, having crumpled it up and made it look hard-earned and scraped together and not fresh and pristine just out of the ATM. Then without much conversation, he took the old rope halter and led the horse slowly back through the forest towards the beach on the northern side of Punta del Diablo, then across the soft sand to the firm sand on the edge of the land where the waves rolled in. Walking slowly, the soft, frothy line of water washed over his feet. He felt its cool, icy touch. He had to walk slowly as Rapture stumbled along, his coat was eaten away by mange, and one of his eyes was swollen from a recent injury, making him half-blind.

They eventually reached the end of the long beach, and he led the gelding through the labyrinth of dirt roads lined with houses here and there and vacant lots with old *Se Vende* signs. A woman came out of the door of a strange wooden house that was three stories high, with a distinct lean to the left he wondered if it would survive the next high wind. She stared at him. He waved and bid her good morning, and her face split in a smile.

When they arrived at the rented cottage, he tied the halter rope to the silky oak tree in the back garden. He fetched a bucket of clean water. He wanted to go and find some grass, but he had to go back further away from the sandy soil. Rapture seemed anything but rapturous at the moment. He stood with his head drooping to the ground, utterly dispirited. Rafael was loath to leave him, in case he came back to find him dead.

Then a truck pulled into the driveway. Rafael started in shock and fear, like a frightened animal. It was a delivery man from the produce store in Los Castillos arriving with two big sacks of pollard, half a dozen sacks of horse cubes for racehorses, a huge round bale of plain grassy hay, and a smaller bag of cracked corn. Phoebe had thought of everything. He felt a huge gratefulness towards her, his fairy godmother but inexplicably - at the same time – an ignoble hatred of her wealth and generosity.

He dragged the sacks inside and stacked them in the living room. He would have to think about the risk of mice and rats later. Now he ripped open one of the pollard sacks and put just two handfuls in the bucket that was designated for cleaning. He added a little boiling water to damp it down. He couldn't just stuff Rapture full of good food, so he would try pollard to begin with. The horse's stomach needed to adjust slowly and carefully; he had probably not had such good quality feed ever in his life. Rafael carried the bucket out and put it in front of the horse. Again, Rapture turned away listlessly as if he didn't recognise food. Rafael became desperate; he couldn't bear it if the horse died now. He shuddered at the thought of how he would have to dispose of the corpse.

He took some of the food, warm and soft and crumbling and desperately tried to force it into the big gelding's mouth, just so he would get a taste for it. Rapture stood there, unresponsive, almost catatonic. Rafael felt tears coming into his eyes. It was as if everything he touched turned to death and dust. He sat in the dirt in front of the big gelding, praying that he would stay alive and not crumple to the ground and die. If he did Rafael felt that his last hope would also die, and he would lie beside him and let death take him, they could drift into oblivion together.

He felt the cold wind blowing in from the sea. He went inside and took one of the thin woollen blankets off the bed and threw it over the carcass of the horse. He tried again to push some of the food into his mouth. This time Rapture seemed to move his jaws, working them a little in a circular motion. The taste of the warm pollard would be unfamiliar, and he opened his mouth, and it fell out. Rafael took a tiny half-handful and tried again and this time Rapture seemed to taste it, but couldn't swallow.

Rafael went inside and brought out a kettle of warm water and mixed it through so that the feed had a sludgy consistency. He held it up to the horse's head and tried to position it beneath his mouth. Slowly the old horse dipped his muzzle into the slush and seemed to suck some of it into his mouth, and then ground his jaws a little and finally swallowed.

"Yes, yes, that is right, my poor old fellow," crooned Rafael. He was filled with hope, yes, he would save this horse. He sat on the ground with him all day and through the night, wrapping himself in a blanket. Slowly the horse began to chew. Then Rafael became concerned that he had to find him some grass; he couldn't risk shifting him to a different diet so quickly. He hurried away with a bag and searched feverishly about four blocks back where the sand receded and the grass grew. It was hard to find green, sweet grass in the middle of winter. He feared to leave Rapture alone.

Then, Rafael had a thought. It was probably his teeth. Why hadn't he thought of that before? He slid his finger up inside the side of Rapture's mouth, and the edges of his molars were sharp as knives, and he could feel the swelling inside his cheek where they had lacerated the soft tissue on the inside of his mouth. Rafael knew that in England, there would be a professional horse dentist, who would have a metal gag which opened the horse's mouth and then various horse-cheek shaped files to take the edges off the teeth. He thought about it and remembered an old chap at the shanty town who had had a special stone bound on the end of a stick which he would use to do all the horses' teeth. He tried and tried to remember the name of the stone and late that night he awoke suddenly, in the dark it came to him, '*carborundo*'. He could buy it at the hardware store.

First thing on Wednesday morning he walked down to the only ferreteria in Punta - but they didn't have it. He would have to go to Los Castillos, but he had no money for bus fare and only a few pesos to buy the product. He texted Phoebe and asked her to buy some for him before she came next weekend. He hated having to wait, but he was without the resources to get it any earlier. He would also need a rasp, and hoof cutters would be good to try and fix Rapture's feet. He texted Phoebe again. He despised himself for having to ask her to buy him more things, but there was no alternative. He hoped that in the summer when the visitors descended there would be loads of work washing dishes in restaurants, but until then there was nothing he could do to earn money.

Phoebe texted back at lunchtime, telling him she would do her best. She even thought of skipping school the next day to drive over to see him. She wanted to see this new horse and hoped that this meant that they were entering a new phase in their relationship where they would draw closer together bound with a mutual project. Straight after school, she whizzed around the ferreterias and found the items that he wanted. Tomorrow she had two free periods, and it was double English, and she was miles ahead of the class anyway. She would leave the apartment at the normal time as if she were going to school, with a scribbled message for her father that she was going to a friend's house after school to study and would stay the night.

As she set off towards Punta, her heart was singing, so filled with love, it felt as if it would burst. She imagined the gory mess of a burst heart and laughed hysterically. Somehow everything seemed hilarious. Then, she had an appalling thought, what if on her surprise visit, she found that Rafael had another woman and she walked in on them. She almost pulled over to text him that she was coming but then decided if that was to happen, then she would have to bear it. She drove on, taking deep breaths, telling herself to have faith in their relationship. It was her first love and as far as she could tell Rafael's as well, although anything was possible. Besides telling her about Carina, he hadn't confided in her about any past relationships. She drove on, stopping only to stock up on bottles of coke, which she knew that he loved. She got herself diet coke. One good thing was that she was losing weight!

She arrived at the cottage in the middle of the afternoon and saw Rafael sitting in front of a horse that looked an absolute wreck. He had said it was in bad condition, but she hadn't envisaged such a sorry sight. She adjusted her face, wiping away the look of shock.

"Hi Rafael, I've brought you those things, it sounded quite urgent!" she called.

He smiled at her. He is so beautiful, she thought. She chose to believe it wasn't just that she had brought things for him, that he really was happy to see her. She handed over the bags.

"This is brilliant," he said. "Rapture has a problem eating. His teeth are like razors cutting into his gums. Will you help me and I'll try and rasp them down."

"Of course," she said, even though she was very nervous around horses. This horse looked so sick and sorry for himself that her heart went out to him, and she forgot her fear.

Rafael went over to the tree in the garden and with his penknife carefully cut down a thin branch and scraped the leaves off it. Then he took some string and carefully tied the stone at both ends. He had to make sure to leave the surface of the stone in the middle unbound so that he could use it to rasp the teeth.

"If we open his mouth and I'll pull his tongue out to one side, and you hold the lead and then hang onto his tongue. Hopefully, he'll stay still enough so we can do him some good."

The thought of holding a horse's tongue was not attractive to Phoebe. She was just not a hands-on sort of person. But she would do anything for Rafael, so she pulled herself together and held the lead rope. Rapture's tongue was a horrible looking object, pale, slimy and huge. Taking a deep breath, Phoebe grasped it and thought fixedly about her huge love for Rafael and how this would help the poor horse to recover. If he were to die, then that was $US 400 down the drain, not that she cared about the money, but she knew that Rafael would feel honour-bound to pay her back and apparently this horse meant a great deal to him. Rafael reached up and gently rubbed the rock back and forth across the sides of the horse's back teeth. It seemed to go on interminably, and Rapture didn't like it, he threw up his head and pulled away, and Phoebe let his tongue slide out of her clutched fist. Patiently, Rafael began again, giving him a minute then pulling his head down firmly the tickled the corners of his mouth until he opened his jaws and then he slid his hand in and took a fresh grasp of the tongue and pulled it out. Once Phoebe was holding it as tight as she could manage, he began to file again, scrape, scrape, scrape back and forth. Again, Rapture pulled his head away, and his slippery tongue slid out of her grasp.

"Let's just give the old fellow a minute," said Rafael. Then quietly, he slid his finger up inside his cheek, feeling the edges of the teeth.

"That is much better, we'll do a bit of work on the other side, and then I'll try again later."

Phoebe pulled herself together and again grasped the repulsive-looking tongue. This time Rafael seemed to work a lot more quickly, and they managed to finish in one go.

"It'll take a while for the sores on the inside of his mouth to heal, but that should make all the difference," said Rafael smiling shyly. "Thank you for bringing those things to me. I didn't want to interrupt your studies. I know that they're important to you."

Phoebe felt tears coming into her eyes. He really did think about her as a person and care about her and what she wanted. She turned away so he couldn't see how much she was affected. He asked her if she would mind buying a wormer as well, which they could give Rapture when he picked up a bit of condition. Then Rafael began to worry. Presumably, Rapture had never been wormed, and if he was heavily infested, then a wormer might finish him off. He would have to just use a small amount at a time and hope for the best.

Phoebe promised to go to the equestrian shop near the racecourse. She was also secretly planning on buying some smart new tack for the great day when Rapture would be ready to be ridden, or at least a snaffle bridle. His back was so bony and ridged that riding bareback would be a nightmare. That evening they went to bed late, as Rafael insisted on sitting outside with the horse. The bed was cold without the blanket, and Phoebe made a mental note to bring more bedding from home. She set her alarm for three in the morning, and she had to be off to get back in time for school in the morning. She kissed Rafael good-bye. He came out to wave her off and returned to his vigil with Rapture. She felt sad as she drove away, but she would be back tomorrow night. It was fortunate that her father was so tied up with Claudia that he didn't notice the hugely increased mileage on the little car.

Chapter Eight

It was weeks before Rapture began to pick up some condition, but Rafael relentlessly nursed him back to health. They would wander into the National Park and find sweet patches of green grass hidden amongst the trees, and at night he would feast on pollard, horse cubes and cracked corn.

Every weekend Phoebe would tell Rafael that Rapture looked better and it became a ritual. They bonded over the horse in the same way that they might have drawn together over a child. At night when it was dark, they crawled into bed and made touching, sweet love. They never spoke out loud about their love, but Phoebe could feel it gushing out of her, this perfect love that she hoped would make up to him for all the hardships in his life.

Finally, she arrived to find him sitting on Rapture's back with the smart new leather bridle that she had found. She had even managed to buy a rubber snaffle, probably the only one in existence in Uruguay where harsh, rusty, brutal curb bits were the rule. Fortunately, she had picked up some general knowledge from her mother and Poppy's obsession, and she knew that snaffle bits were considered the kindest. When she had produced the rubber snaffle, Rafael had looked at her as if she was an angel sent from heaven.

"How did you get this?" he asked in wonder.

"It was at the bottom of a dusty pile in the produce store in Las Piedras. She smiled in triumph. She had even considered an emergency visit to the UK to buy him a beautiful Prestige jumping saddle but then had decided that it was all too hard. When she got him to England, he could have anything he wanted. She wanted to shower him in gifts, 'horsiana' to the zenith if that could mend his poor cracked heart. She longed to see him smile, as he did so rarely. She would lay down her life for him.

Since she had discovered the feeling of being 'in love' the world had seemed brighter, the air cleaner, and her thoughts flowed with surprising clarity. It was as if she were living on the very edge of the meaning of life.

The next day they went down to the beach to buy fresh fish. Rafael had ridden Rapture. He plodded along quite happily, putting one neatly trimmed hoof in front of the other.

"He looks so much better now!" exclaimed Phoebe.

Rafael smiled at her, his slow, shy smile spreading across his beautiful face like the sun rising. After this, Rapture began to put on weight quickly. He didn't become a beautiful good-looking horse, but he looked less desperate. Rafael would take him down to the beach every day and walk along the edge of the waves. Then he would take him into the water and let the healing seawater wash over him. As Rapture improved, so did Rafael. He began to feel as if he was real again as if the grey horse anchored him to the earth. He was very grateful to Phoebe, but he knew that he was not in love. He saw it shining from her eyes, and he didn't know what to do. How to tell her that he was not going to be able to love her back, not in the same way that she loved him. He doubted if he would ever really love another human, not in the way that he loved Rapture and Estrella.

Over the weeks they graduated to trotting and cantering. Then Phoebe arrived with a saddle. It was English-style, not one of the ghastly enormous, heavy leather pads that the Uruguayans rode in. Scratched and hard, but at least the gullet was narrow, and it fitted over Rapture's prominent wither.

"How did you find it?" he asked.

"I've been searching *Mercado Libre* ever since we bought him," said Phoebe. (This was the Uruguayan equivalent of ebay). "I went up to Durazno late on Wednesday evening." It hadn't been cheap. Somehow Uruguayans believed that second-hand goods were more valuable than new. As if owning it and using it made it more precious.

They saddled Rapture, and Rafael adjusted the stiff uncared-for stirrup leathers. He vaulted lightly up and gathered up the reins, holding them delicately between his beautiful hands.

"You go ahead," said Phoebe, "I'll follow you on down."

Riding with a saddle made all the difference. He sat lightly in the shallow seat. Rapture seemed to be stepping out well. Walk was the hardest pace to establish rhythm and cadence, but he could feel it developing. They got to the dirt road that led to the beach, and he pushed him into a trot, rising lightly up and down and gradually establishing something resembling what English riders called a 'working trot'.

He got to the beach and went down onto the hard sand, and they cantered. He was surprised at how smooth Rapture's pace was: low, long strides with a very definite three-beat. He rode to the end of the small beach and then went into the water to go around the headland to the long beach that ran parallel to the National Park. Punta was a brilliant location for riding, one could go for days, along the beaches, or into the National Park.

Over the next few weeks, he continued to train Rapture, trying some lateral work, trotting forward but then bending the forehand around, so they were proceeding along three tracks. Such work helped to increase flexibility, building up back muscles. It also increased obedience to finely nuanced commands.

The rubber snaffle worked very well, and he was able to vibrate his fingers and feel Rapture responding to the lightest touch. It wasn't what he had expected after seeing him hauling that heavy unbalanced cart. He tried some ten-metre circles, and although the big horse swung his quarters sideways, he felt him beginning to bend around his inner leg.

There was a line of low rocks that lay at the water's edge, and he turned and cantered towards them. Rapture leapt over them joyfully, as if he were an old hand. He seemed to love jumping. Rafael's heart sang. He knew now that he and the grey gelding had a future. He rode back to the fish shop where Phoebe was sitting outside on an upturned bucket. She was huddled in a big woolly cardigan and watching the sea. It was beautiful today, steely grey ripples, frothing white at the edge as the wavelets rolled in. She loved it when it was deserted like this, without crowds of beautiful slim, sexy, brown-skinned young girls laughing and wiggling their bottoms for the benefit of the careless youths that lay around drinking cans of beer. The party-goers loved Punta during the summer, but now it was blissfully desolate.

Rafael rode back towards Phoebe at a walk, the reins dangling, Rapture's head low and relaxed.

"How is the new saddle?" asked Phoebe.

"It's brilliant. It makes all the difference," he replied. "And we jumped a line of rocks, not high but he seemed to love it, pricked his ears and bounded over. He's going to make a show jumper!"

"Jolly good," said Phoebe. Suddenly her heart sank. She saw the future. Rapture would improve beyond their wildest dreams, and Rafael would stay in Uruguay and try to forge his way as a showjumper, and from here he could ride up to the border and slip into Brazil over a small bridge in Barra del Chuy and then go to the proper show jumping competitions without paying the huge fees that were charged to take a horse over the border.

She hung her head, feeling the pain sweep over her. Of course, they could have Rapture shipped to England, but her mother and Poppy would look at him, in comparison to their well-bred glossy mounts and they wouldn't understand what Rafael saw in him. They certainly wouldn't understand the expense of exporting a horse, that was not much more than an old wrecked cart-horse.

They went back to the cottage, and Phoebe took the fish into the kitchen. Lighting the gas ring on the stove, she melted a big knob of butter in the battered frying pan. The fish was divine. The flesh melted in her mouth, and it wasn't fattening. She was losing weight, even purchasing a smaller size of jeans which she was proudly wearing. Not that Rafael seemed to notice, she never caught him looking at her in the way that boys looked at other girls. At some point, they were going to have to talk about the future. She had tried once before, but Rafael's face had closed up as if the subject were forbidden.

"Rafael, I've been thinking, once I've finished my exams, you know that this cottage is already booked up, they make a fortune in the summer, thousands a week. Do you think we could fly to England? I would love you to see some of the big horse shows over there. It would be just like Carina used to describe it. Well maybe not just the same, it had been years since she was living at home."

Rafael sat staring into the distance, his mouth in a straight line.

"Do you want to come to England with me?" asked Phoebe. "Just say it, yes or no."

He sat there silently. Finally, he spoke.

"What about Rapture?"

Phoebe knew then for certain that buying a horse for Rafael had been a mistake.

"Perhaps we could pay someone to look after him."

"I can't trust anyone," said Rafael.

"That's ridiculous. You're not the only person who knows how to look after a horse. You treat that bloody horse as if it were an ancient Greek god, some sort of graven image, come to show us how ordinary and alien are our modern lives. It's not as if it is well-bred or quality, he is hardly a vision of beauty!" She spat the hateful words out at him as if an evil spirit were talking through her mouth.

This was the first time she had disagreed with him, and then to have slagged off his precious horse. She was flooded with fear. He wouldn't love her anymore. Then she thought, he probably never did love me anyway. They had never come close to even using the 'l' word. To distract him from this awkward conversation, she got up and made coffee.

"Shall we go for a walk up to the forest we can take Rapture so he can have some grass," she suggested.

Rafael nodded. He hadn't uttered a word since she had criticised him.

In the end, he took Rapture himself, and she stayed behind in the cottage, with the excuse that she had to study. As soon as he left, she sat down and wept. She knew now. There was no denying it, that the golden future that she had imagined for them in Oxfordshire was just never going to happen. She had rescued him, and he was grateful, but that was it. She picked up the old book that was his most precious possession, and read the dedication on the front page, 'To Catherine Broughton', and wondered who this woman had been and why on earth she had gone to live in a shanty town until she died. It was not unusual for aristocratic families to ship off young men who behaved badly, out to the colonies so that they were out of sight. But a woman with no family connections and no money. That was odd.

Phoebe and Rafael didn't talk much that evening, and when they went to bed, he turned away from her and didn't make love. She was in utter despair and not wanting him to know that she was sobbing she went outside. It was very sharp and cold but there was a full moon. Rapture was standing near the tree wearing a couple of blankets that Rafael had painstakingly sewn together.

"You and me, both washed up, but he loves you so much. He doesn't love me," Phoebe said piteously, and the tears poured down her face. If only he would wake up and come out and put his arms around her and tell her to come back to bed. But the cottage door remained firmly shut. She felt the pain searing through her, like a finger crushed in a vice without release. Above her head was the infinity of space cradling in its void the round, cold disc of the moon. She began to shake as if a constant, repetitive, catatonic movement would somehow soothe her. She was far beyond any ideas of how to pull herself together. She lay down on the cold ground and wished that it would swallow her up and she could slip into oblivion.

The next day driving back to Montevideo, she felt subdued and hopeless. She tried pulling herself together, giving herself a good talking to, but it was a dreary wasted effort. She had to think of something, anything that might make Rafael love her. Perhaps if she went to the riding school and learnt to ride. She could find out about shipping horses back to England. But she knew that wasn't the problem. At the very heart of things, we are alone, she thought, that was the sad truth of it. She had to learn to live within herself and not rely on other people to make her happy.

Phoebe spent the week desperately trying to concentrate on her revision, she tottered into the kitchen, to the freezer in the middle of the night and guzzled ice cream that had been there for months. She would have to ask Greta to buy some more. If Rafael wouldn't come to England and he couldn't stay indefinitely at Punta, then he had to go somewhere. Finally, she came up with a possible solution. They should go to Pablo and Florencia's and see if they would give him a job, or at least a place to live with Rapture, working for his keep. The minute she arrived on Friday night, she suggested the idea to him.

He didn't seem happy. He was discomfited, but he could think of no reason why not, and really the only risk was the fear of rejection and then the cancellation of this possibility which he liked to hang on to as a last resort. Otherwise, he would ride over the border to Brazil like a hobo and look for work, travelling by horseback. But arriving at any reputable equestrian establishment riding a rather ugly horse was not going to secure him a job.

Phoebe went down to buy the fish by herself on Saturday morning. They fried it up and ate. Her appetite had disappeared again but now through despair, rather than love. Rafael wasn't sure of the exact address, but they went to Atlantida and began to ask around. A man in the supermercado gave them some detailed instructions. They headed off inland across the motorway and down various dirt roads. Finally, they arrived, and there was a small makeshift sign, and they drove into the yard. Rafael began to understand why their riding school business might not be booming. It was hardly a convenient location for the clients from Montevideo.

They got out of the car, and they could see Florencia jumping a big brown Thoroughbred-type horse over three post-and-rails set up in a row. She was undoubtedly brave and fearless, and her contorted face was set in grim determination. Rafael and Phoebe walked hesitantly towards the jumping area. Pablo was there, shouting suggestions to Florencia.

"*Buenos tardes*," they called out, and Pablo smiled at them, a big welcoming smile, perhaps he thought they were new clients wanting riding lessons.

Rafael went over and began to talk to him. Phoebe stood there awkwardly, letting the men talk between themselves. If they wouldn't give Rafael a job at least for his board, then she was going to have to jump in and ask if they could keep Rapture there on livery. She had begun to understand the huge Latino macho pride that stood in the way of a desperate foreign female wanting to splash her money around. Eventually, Pablo and Rafael wandered off together. She didn't know what they were saying, then Pablo was on his phone. Rafael came back and explained to her that it was all arranged. Valentino had agreed to employ him, and Rapture could stay here as part of the deal. Valentino was even going to the States in about six months and there was the possibility that he would go with him as his rider, depending on how he went at the next show in Brazil.

"That is absolutely amazing!" said Phoebe, clapping her hands with happiness for him. It was like a fairy tale ending, well at least for Rafael and Rapture. She wasn't a part of it. She was out in the cold, but the kind and decent part of her was genuinely glad for Rafael. In the end, it had all worked out in the same way that it might have if the whole necklace drama hadn't occurred. She had just played a small interim part of it.

They arranged for the truck to go to Punta on the following day and pick up Rapture. She and Rafael would drive back now and pack up the house and return the key. This was to be their last night together. She knew that once he was at Pablo and Florencia's, there was no reason for her to continue to visit. She would be shut out and no longer needed. This thought made her want to break down and sob, walk into the sea until the waves closed over her head and she drowned in unhappiness. It wasn't Rafael's fault; he had had no control over their lives together, and he had played his part as best he could; but it had been a scenario of Phoebe's, her own private rich girl's fantasy that had now come to an end and she was exit stage left.

She had to hold herself together and get through tonight without breaking down. She couldn't show Rafael how devastated she was. She had to be happy for him and continue on with her predetermined life, her exams and back to England.

The night passed uneventfully. They didn't make love; there no longer seemed any point. Rafael held her, he didn't reject her, but it was the end, and, for him, it had never been a deep passion. She put a brave face on it and held back her tears. She knew when she drove away alone to Montevideo. She would pull over and dissolve into a storm of weeping that would have no end. She couldn't bear to even think of her own future, whether or not she was pregnant with his child was a secret that she nursed inside herself. It would be a reason not to lie down and die. It would be proof that they had been together.

She had thought that when she returned, she would be alone, her father over at the ghastly Claudia's. She noticed that he was tired of his latest mistress, but as Grace had not returned and Claudia's pursuit was so relentless, he was trapped. For the first time, Phoebe began to wonder why her mother had not returned. She had been away for more than six months. Up until now, Phoebe had only been thankful that no-one was around to ask where she was disappearing to every weekend; no longer even bothering to leave notes advising her father of her whereabouts, as it was obvious that he had no interest in her. She drove down into the underground carpark, and trudged up the front stairs of the apartment.

Chapter Nine

Tate Wade was sitting on the front step, casually flicking through the glossy pages of a magazine. Phoebe smiled to see a familiar face, one of the few people in the world who cared about her. Tate was the elder daughter of her mother's best friend, Verena. Phoebe had known Tate all her life, and now she stepped forward and flung her arms around the slim, elegant woman. Tate looked mildly astonished. She had never known Phoebe to be so demonstrative. After they had embraced, Tate got to her feet. She was wearing a sloppy cashmere white sweater, tight designer jeans and a beautiful pair of red leather cowboy boots.

"You're always so very elegant," said Phoebe. "No matter where, or how long you've been travelling, and I'm so glad to see you."

"Oh, poor little Pheebs, left for so long, with that father of yours. I'm come to take you home, baby."

Then Phoebe began to weep; it was the mention of 'baby'. At last, she had someone in whom she could confide, and it all poured out. She told Tate that she was almost certain she was pregnant. Tate was astonished; this was not the news she had been expecting.

"I've got my exams this week, and then I'm finished. He doesn't want me. I have to go home and have the baby by myself."

"Darling, let's get inside. We don't want the world to know," said Tate. "I would give you some brandy, but if you're pregnant, it might not be the best idea. How pregnant are you?" It was the obvious question, was an abortion a possibility?

"No, no, no, I'm having the baby, I'm not getting rid of it, it's all I have left!" declared Phoebe.

"What does your father think?" asked Tate.

"He has no idea; he doesn't care about me. I hardly ever see him he is always with Claudia, this awful woman, a total slut and she has a horrible daughter who makes my life at school hell."

"Ah yes, Claudia. Your mother told me about her."

"My mother doesn't seem to care. She hasn't come back, and there's been no-one here, just me and Greta."

"I know darling. Aunt Grace didn't think that your father would abandon you in such a way. She thought he would look after you."

Phoebe howled again. It felt wonderful to finally have someone who understood, someone who cared about her. She had been so alone with her solitary one-sided love of Rafael.

"He only cares about the horse, the wretched horse! I hate horses!"

"What horse?"

"We bought a horse, he was a skeleton, and Rafael wanted to rescue him, he has called him Rapture, doesn't that tell you everything!" she cried.

"Not quite," said Tate. "But I believe I am getting the picture. You have had a boyfriend, and you've bought a horse together, but he doesn't really care about you and the baby."

"He doesn't know about the baby," said Phoebe, shaking her head

"But why haven't you told him, it might make all the difference?"

"Never! He has to love me for myself, not for a baby. Anyway, he's safe now he's gone to live with Pablo and Florencia, and he'll work for Valentino and Rapture is with him."

"So, he has got a job then," said Tate.

"He didn't have a job all winter, he was living in Punta del Diablo, and I went up every weekend, but today he went to work, near Atlantida. He doesn't need me anymore. He never really loved me, he was grateful, but I do love him so," wept Phoebe.

Tate thought she was beginning to understand this twisted tale of unhappiness.

"How did you meet him?" she asked, thinking that Phoebe's sheltered life would have made it hard for some chancer to latch onto her and use her like this.

101

"I can't tell you. No-one must know who he is," said Phoebe.

"Darling, this all sounds rather complicated. Have you been to a doctor yet, to make sure everything is alright? With the baby that is."

"No, no-one must know, you're the only person I have told. You see, I don't have any friends," said Phoebe. She was unaware just how pathetic this sounded. She had been essentially friendless, except for Rafael ever since she had arrived in Uruguay.

"Phoebe, I've come here to take you back to England. But now I'm wondering if perhaps you would be better staying here. Although if the father really doesn't care for you, then you need to go home, I know that Aunt Grace and Poppy will care for you, and the baby," she added. She wasn't entirely certain how Grace was going to react to an illegitimate grandchild, but then she did rather leave Phoebe on her own for six months, and, obviously, Phoebe had not been grown up enough to cope. This had to be down to David and his mindless philandering.

"Why didn't Mummy come back?" asked Phoebe.

"She's not coming back. She's going to divorce your father, but she was waiting until you returned before she tells him. I would have thought that it was obvious that something was in the wind, she's been away for many months now."

Phoebe screwed her face up. She hadn't thought about it much. She had been thankful that her mother wasn't there as she would soon have sniffed out the mystery and demanded to know what was going on.

"Really," she caught her breath. She found it hard to understand. "But why?" she asked. "That's a stupid question, why did she stay with him for so long? Has he always been like this with other women?"

"I'm afraid so. Your mother put up with it for a long time. I guess she thought it was for the best, for you and Poppy and for appearances and all that. But finally, she had enough. You know that my mother got divorced and I think this influenced her. Aunt Grace has had a far more unsatisfactory marriage than Mummy and Daddy. She's got it all ready to go into action as soon as you are away and clear. She wants to make sure that you're not going to give your father any money. She doesn't want him leeching off you."

"Like Rafael did," said Phoebe. "He was the same as Daddy, but he was so sweet and loving. I love him so much," she began to wail again.

"This is not right. You've got to pull yourself together for your exams, after all your work, you can't mess it up. Although I suppose you could take your exams later, you don't have to do them now. We could book you a ticket to fly away tomorrow if you like. All we need to do is pack your things up, and we're one-way first class, back home, back to the people who love you."

Phoebe gulped. She shook her head. "It's all I'm good for, doing exams, I may as well prove myself at that if nothing else."

"Oh darling, this is terrible. We hate you being like this. You know we love you, and we'll love the baby, in spite of the father, and we'll be your family," said Tate. "You have lost weight. You're looking very svelte."

"I thought if I was thin - he would love me," said Phoebe, gulping down more tears

Tate rocked her back and forth with her slim arms wrapped around her.

"I was going to whisk Uncle David off for dinner tonight leave you in peace to do revision or whatever it is that you do before an exam."

"Tate, you got three As for your A levels, you know jolly well what it is to revise. You just pretend to be an air-head, but really you're very bright," said Phoebe, finally showing signs of recovering her poise.

"Now, don't you go telling anyone that. You'll completely ruin my street cred," chided Tate gently.

She went into the kitchen and looked around for the makings of a cup of tea.

"Would you like me to stay with you tonight, or shall I take your father out to dinner and put the cat among the pigeons with the ghastly Claudia. It would be rather fun to upset the apple cart before Grace delivers the *coup de grace*. You know she is planning on cutting the supply of funds, and then your father is going to have to pay the bills out of his salary, and I believe that Claudia is not going to be very happy about that."

"You make me a nice cup of tea, and I'll be fine," said Phoebe bravely. "I can do my revision then and try and recover my composure. It has been rather strange actually having someone to talk to about this. I'll do my exams, and then we can fly back to England and then Daddy will just have to face the music."

"You're a good girl," said Tate, smiling and patting her hand.

They drank a cup of tea together, and then Phoebe took Tate upstairs.

"This definitely looks like Poppy's room. It's nothing but horses and ponies for her and your mother."

Phoebe smiled sadly and left Tate to unpack and shower and change. Her father returned, and she went down to talk to him. He didn't even notice her reddened, swollen eyes.

"Tate has arrived. She wants to take you out to dinner," she told him.

He opened his mouth to protest and then thought better of it. Perhaps Tate would have news of Grace and what was keeping her at Kiss Wood. She had never left him alone for so long, with no real explanation. David insisted that he take her to the best restaurant in Montevideo. He liked to show off, and Tate would be rather a prize on his arm for the glitterati of Montevideo society, such as it was. He sent Claudia a text saying that he had an urgent appointment for work and wouldn't be joining her that evening. He would smooth her over later. In fact, he was happy to be released from her company that was becoming decidedly tedious.

David's evening with Tate was immensely enjoyable. All the men, and also the women, most of whom he was acquainted with, were ogling her and chattering, speculating on how Claudia was going to feel about this. His ego which had been somewhat bruised lately began to inflate. Tate was airy and sophisticated, positively seductive, and he didn't notice that she was not really informative. She had no intention of giving poor old Uncle David any idea of what was really going on. She rattled on about Kiss Wood and Poppy and the horses. This in itself would have indicated that Poppy and Grace were back home for the long-term. But she mentioned something vaguely about flying the horses out later. She purposely lingered over the meal, and she heard his phone buzzing. He glanced down at it a few times but didn't take the calls. Undoubtedly it was the ghastly Claudia checking up on him.

Tate drank a great deal of champagne which David had extravagantly ordered. He used the joint credit card funded by Grace, who surely would not disapprove of him wining and dining Tate. Then they rolled back to the house. Tate kissed him good night and went up to bed. He padded up the stairs hopefully behind her, but she went in to see Phoebe and firmly shut the door in his face. The heedlessness of the man was overwhelming; he was getting to the 'dirty old man' stage without realising it. She wondered whether he had made a move on Claudia's daughter.

The next morning David stumbled down the stairs bleary-eyed. The front doorbell rang, and Greta answered it. Claudia marched in without an invitation. She and Greta hated each other. David was slouched at the end of the table, trying to revive himself with black coffee.

"Oh, Claudia, good morning."

Claudia plonked herself down in the place set for Tate beside him. She helped herself to coffee.

"That ees the place for Signorina Tate," Greta said snakily, smiling at Claudia.

"Who the fuck is Signorina Tate?" asked Claudia, unable to keep the suspicion out of her voice.

Greta stood there smiling cruelly. At this moment, Tate made her entrance. She showed no signs of a hangover, as she was an experienced and accomplished drinker. She was wearing a loose-fitting white vest that showed every outline of her pert breasts and the tiniest pair of lacy knickers. David looked up and couldn't help smiling at this delectable sight, then quickly recovered himself.

"I think you're sitting in my seat," said Tate with a naughty smile.

"Tate, this is Claudia, Tate is the daughter of an old friend, Verena," said David trying to think how he was going to handle this situation.

"I'm not sure that Mummy would like to be described as 'old'," said Tate flashing him a mischievous smile.

Claudia cast her calculating eyes over the young woman who had elegantly and casually sauntered over to David. Her accent was pure cut glass, her body thin and rapaciously sexy. Her very short hair was slicked back from a thin face with the most extraordinary cheekbones, surely they had to be the result of extremely expensive surgery. Claudia was conscious of feeling overblown, too perfumed and blatantly sexual in comparison. She suddenly knew that she could never achieve that essentially European glamour that was understated, but utterly unmistakable.

"Hello, Mr Lester-Blythe," Tate said mockingly.

"I have known Tate since she was a baby," said David trying to adopt an avuncular tone, "she is Grace's god-daughter, her mother Verena is one of Grace's oldest friends."

"I think it is now time for you to call me David, rather than Uncle David," he said playfully, thinking how wonderfully attractive was this grown-up version of Tate. If only Phoebe had a tiny bit of her *sang froid* and elegance. He couldn't quite keep a note of fawning, quavering lust out of his voice when he talked to her.

"We had so much fun last night. David insisted that we drink three bottles of the most expensive champagne. And again, out tonight, I'm thoroughly spoilt," said Tate, knowing exactly how much this would wind up Claudia. David had already told her it was a work-do and it would be awkward to take her along, people would talk. Tate saw Claudia jittering, a look of hot fury shooting out of her somewhat puffy eyes. Claudia had suspected David was lying when he had made an excuse but, now - she knew the truth. She was inchoate with rage.

"Dinner?" she spat, unable to hide her fury, "You told me that it was a work thing?"

"Oh, David, how terribly naughty of you," said Tate teasingly. David smiled at both of them, but he was fidgeting a little. He didn't like being caught out in a lie. Claudia opened her mouth with a quick, furious retort, then shut it again. She was experienced enough to know that she had to appear cool. Men absolutely hated displays of jealousy.

"Tate this is Claudia, erh, her daughter is at school with Phoebe."

Claudia lowered her eyelids. She didn't want to show just how angry she was, it made her sound like a matron who he had met at a parent-teacher night.

106

"Hello," said Tate perfunctorily, as if Claudia was of absolutely no social interest to her. "So darling David, as you like to be called, are you going to show me around the sights of this little backwater?"

Claudia felt that this was a sly dig at her, a matron living in an uncultured backwater, of absolutely no account. She was seething and didn't trust herself to say another word; her voice would come out shrill as young Poppy's when she was excited. She suddenly wondered if Grace had organised this. Perhaps she had underestimated the dowdy Grace who had so conveniently taken herself off so many months ago. This girl was pure class and unutterably sexy, and an old family friend apparently. David was a fool and couldn't see the trap that was being laid, if any man was led by the dick, it was him, and that she knew from her own experience.

"You know I was at Kiss Wood just the other week. Grace has been redecorating the upstairs drawing-room. It looks absolutely magnificent! She's bought some new paintings by the painter, Klaus that everyone in London is raving about, and the backlighting has been done by a professional. She's got rid of all those fussy ornaments that sat in the glass-windowed cabinets, sent them to her favourite charity shop. She seems to be streamlining everything, getting rid of those priceless antiques."

Claudia couldn't stop herself shooting a sharp and baleful glance towards David. She hated to think of Grace at this Kiss Wood, and what a ridiculous name. How was she financing such expensive improvements when David didn't seem to have the funds to even buy her a new dress, and he continually made excuses not to go out and eat. It was costing her a fortune to supply him with meals. She didn't know what was wrong with him. If his wife could afford to spend thousands on the house that sounded suspiciously like a stately home and donate antiques to charity, then you would think he could splash out a bit of cash on his mistress.

"Apparently, there's a Polo Club where I can go riding. I've got a photoshoot next week in Miami, you know riding up the beach bareback, splashing in the sea, hardly original I know. I thought I might brush up my equestrian skills."

Claudia smiled tightly. Tate lingered over breakfast. She had no intention of going upstairs to get dressed. Phoebe came down in her school uniform.

"It's your first exam today and jolly good luck, I know you're going to blitz it!" said Tate.

Claudia felt a fresh wave of rage. She sat there, having helped herself to a cup of coffee. She was determined not to move.

"Was there anything you wanted in particular?" asked David.

"I just thought I'd come around and see how you are?" said Claudia airily, feeling like an utter fool, about to be dismissed from this essentially family affair. She sat there stolidly until she could bear it no longer and got up and flounced out. No-one said a word. Phoebe ate a little then got up and left. Only then did Tate turn to David.

"Grace asked me to take Phoebe back as soon as she finishes her exams. Apparently, there are things that she needs to do at Kiss Wood."

"I can't imagine what," said David frowning a little.

"Well she's coming of age, and the solicitors want her to sign some papers."

"Yes, that's right, I had forgotten all about that," said David, wondering whether he might be able to ask Phoebe to lend him some funds, lend on a very long-term basis. Both the girls were to be given substantial sums on their eighteenth birthdays, but the bulk of the fortune remained in the family trust and couldn't be touched by any errant or disgruntled future husbands.

"I'll talk to her about it tonight," said Tate. "Don't worry. I'm sure that Claudia will keep you company while she's away."

"But when are they all coming back?" asked David plaintively, doubt like ugly worms nibbled at the edge of his consciousness. When he thought about it - Grace had been gone for months, and all he had heard was one airy excuse after another, people were beginning to talk in the office.

"I have no idea I guess they'll be back for Christmas, then you can all go to the beach and have a lovely family celebration, perhaps a barbecue." Tate smiled at her inane suggestion. She couldn't imagine either Aunt Grace, nor Uncle David revelling in a barbecue.

"Yes, I suppose so," said David.

"I must go up and dress," said Tate. "I assume that I'll find the phone number for Melilla Polo Club on the internet."

"You'll be lucky to get anyone before lunchtime. The riding school seems to operate late in the afternoon and the evening," said David. "I must get off to work." He knew that he had to do some smoothing over of Claudia, but thought he might wait until she calmed down. Tate would come and go, and then Phoebe would be off, and if he told Greta to go and stay with her daughter for a week, then he would have the apartment to himself. That would make Claudia happy, give her the feeling that she had a proper place in his life. He would wait until Grace came back, she was always good at getting rid of mistresses who had done their dash.

Tate took herself off to the riding school late that afternoon. She had a lesson with Facundo, who was overcome with lust when he saw her. He liked awkward situations, and the complication of David and Claudia made this new fresh meat as he thought of her, all the more attractive. Tate played along, but she didn't like him at all, her taste ran in quite another direction.

Phoebe flew through her exam as if she was powered by wings of angels. The questions were perfect for her, and she wrote and wrote and wrote and finished with five minutes to spare to check her work. She promised herself when she finished her exams. She would go once more to see Rafael. Perhaps he would decide to come with her after all. But she certainly wasn't going to beg.

Tate came back that evening.

"Oh, that Facundo at the riding school, he is a sleazy, venomous little toad!" she said.

"Yes, Claudia's daughter, Marianela and he are an item, but I think that they're both as bad as each other. Although it's very odd, Marianela has disappeared. She's flown up to her father's in Columbia, just before the exams. No-one knows why. Perhaps I should have asked Claudia this morning, but I really can't bear to talk to her."

"I've been thinking about your young man. You know I think it is a good thing that he wants to work, not just rely on your money. It shows that he's a decent person. And you say he speaks perfect English - how very odd.

Perhaps later he'll come to England when he's proved himself over here. Are there prospects with this job?"

"Yes, I suppose there are. As many prospects as an Uruguayan could have anyway."

"So, don't despair just yet. Everything doesn't have to be decided immediately. Even with a baby, you are still so young. How old is he?"

"He is a few years older than me, but not much."

Tate was determined to deliver Phoebe safely back to England. She idled the week away. This was really the most boring country. There was simply nothing to do. The lotus-eaters, such as they were, would be at Punta del'Este, but she was determined not to leave Phoebe alone in Montevideo.

Phoebe wanted to for one last good-bye visit to Rafael, and she had suggested that she accompany her for moral support. When the exams were finished, they got in the car and drove to Atlantida. They arrived early in the morning and found Rafael mucking out the loose boxes. Florencia was riding, and Pablo and Valentino were watching her.

Phoebe felt horribly awkward. She wished she hadn't come. She didn't know what to say. She introduced Tate to Rafael, and they eyed each other warily. Tate was determined to be friendly, but Rafael seemed very suspicious. He glowered a little and wouldn't speak to them. Phoebe knew that bringing Tate had been a mistake.

"Come on, let's go," she said suddenly after three minutes. "This was a mistake. Rafael, here is my address in England if you ever want to come and visit. Good-bye." She couldn't bear to even try and kiss him farewell. It was all too painful. She stalked away, and Tate loped along behind her.

They went back to the apartment and Phoebe was going to pack the last of her things, and they would take a taxi to the airport. Greta was watching the news on the little television in the kitchen when they returned. There was a news flash. It was the distinctive dome-shaped indoor riding school that caught her attention - Melilla Polo Club. Then there was an image of a garage with pools of blood and a chair with broken chains. They were jabbering on about a torture scene and gruesome murder of two young men.

110

"Oh, my God! It's Facundo and Tomas!" gasped Phoebe. She stared at the screen in utter horror; the dismemberment was being described in horrific detail. The announcer was talking about the length of time for which they were tortured before they were murdered. Phoebe's mind was racing; she felt as if there were a band of iron around her chest. She had hated them, Rafael had hated them, they had imagined all sorts of horrible punishments for these two, but the reality . . the blood . . the chains. She sat down before she fainted.

"That ees where young Poppy went," said Greta. Phoebe could see the enthrallment of evil in Greta's small black eyes. "It ees good she is not here," said Greta.

"It's good that we are leaving," said Phoebe, then shot a glance at Greta. The old woman nodded. She had divined their departure long before Phoebe had known.

"Only a week ago he was giving me a riding lesson," said Tate, who had turned white with shock.

Phoebe felt as if she were going to retch. A wave of huge guilt was washing over her as if her hatred of these two had somehow summoned up the evil that had befallen them. Then it struck her like a thunderbolt. Rafael was much closer to Montevideo now, Melilla was just two bus rides away, could he have been involved in this?

"Oh my God!" exclaimed Phoebe, putting her hand to her mouth, feeling like she was going to throw up. She couldn't believe it. How on earth had this happened?

She turned away from the television; the images were being flashed repeatedly. She felt utterly sick. She just wanted to go up to her room and lay on the bed, curled into a foetal position. She felt as if she didn't have the strength to do anything; she was utterly drained. She didn't dare even frame the words. She had to go to the airport with Tate. In a way, it helped, this tragedy overtook the dragging pain she felt at leaving Uruguay and probably never seeing Rafael again.

Chapter Ten

Grace and her black Labrador, Sooty, drove to Heathrow to meet Phoebe and Tate. She was watching the Arrivals door intently as each group of people emerged pushing their luggage trolleys. She saw Tate first and almost didn't recognise the slimmed-down Phoebe. Although she had been told that she had lost weight, it was as if Phoebe had been transformed into another person. She was almost gaunt, and her face was pale. Of course, air travel did terrible things to one in terms of dehydration and disruption to one's circadian rhythms, but Phoebe was so altered, something must have happened. Grace felt that she had been derelict in her duty. Surely this couldn't simply be a reaction to the news that her parents were going to divorce? She felt a sharp stab of guilt that she had left her elder daughter without support, while she and Poppy had been swanning along in their happy horsey dream, building up their stables, recapturing her youthful dreams of pony bliss.

Now Phoebe was back she would make her move on David. They say that revenge is a dish best eaten cold. She was about to find out. She had left Uruguay without a single regret. When she had walked into her family's house, Kiss Wood, it was as if it had opened its arms and was holding her in a warm embrace. Although it was a cruel, cold end of a harsh winter, she didn't care. The ineffable crisp, cold air was so evocative of her childhood foxhunting days – the cry of the horn, thundering hoofs, a view halloa, the camaraderie of like-minded people intent on only one thing, a good run. She was back home and immersed in her rediscovered enthusiasm. All those stultifying years of being an errant diplomat's wife were merely a background to the delightful contrast of her present happy position.

Officially, she was not home permanently, so she had managed to dodge the inevitable round of Women's Institute meetings, the local Conservative committee, the Parish Council and even the Women's Guild at the local church. She was not going to slip back into the life of her own mother in a rarefied olde-worlde atmosphere. She had a vision. She was going to have an equestrian establishment right at the top of the competitive tree. She would do her exams to become a dressage judge, and she was happy to officiate at some of the local horse events. She might even get involved in the administration of horse trials or show jumping, but everything would be focused on horses and Poppy's future career as a showjumper.

Now, Grace was about to face the drama of her divorce. Before the solicitors contacted David, she thought she might give him a foretaste of just how uncomfortable life would be without 'good old Grace's lovely old money'. After giving Phoebe a cup of tea and sending her upstairs to have a shower and unpack, she went into her study and onto the internet. She had even written herself a schedule, and she worked her way through the various sites, user names, passwords and transfers. First, she paid off the joint credit cards one by one and cancelled them. Then all the money left in the joint accounts was transferred to her own accounts in England. David was now officially penniless, or peso-less. She wondered how long it would take before he rang, perhaps today, tonight but definitely by tomorrow morning. She felt the heady joy of vindication. It had taken her a long time to balance the scales of justice, and she could never claim back the last twenty years, but now it was over. She had her children safe at home and David was way out on a limb, about to go crashing down to a very hard and uncomfortable landing.

He rang within two hours, ostensibly to see if Phoebe had arrived safely but with a casual enquiry as to the state of their credit cards which had both been declined when he had tried to pay for his lunch. He asked if perhaps she had forgotten to pay them. She smiled into the phone, what she imagined was an 'evil grin'. He sounded his usual smooth and charming self, he hadn't worked it out yet! His arrogance was realistically based on the fact that he had had it easy for far too long. She decided to leave him hanging and told him she would look into it.

In Montevideo, Claudia had barged her way into the apartment, pushing past the indignant Greta, just minutes after Phoebe and Tate had left for Carasco airport. By the time David got home from work, his demanding mistress was firmly ensconced. Not only had she brought her entire collection of clothes that was now crammed into his wardrobe, but also a large collection of ornaments and several tea chests stacked in the hall.

"But Daveed darling, you know that Marianela is in Columbia. I am rattling around that apartment, so I thought I would move in with you."

David was aghast. He was expecting Grace and Poppy back by Christmas. It looked like he was going to have to move Claudia and all her chattels out rather quickly as soon as he knew when they were due to fly back. He didn't know that Claudia was about to be evicted. The rent hadn't been paid for months, and now all child support payments had ceased.

"Tell me, darling, why did Marianela go to Columbia, just before her exams, it is rather odd," he asked.

Claudia's face closed over, looking like thunder. She turned on her heel without replying to his question and stalked down the passage to the master bedroom.

David didn't like Claudia bulldozing into his life at all. He began to wish that Grace would come back. Grace had always been so useful for sorting out other women when he got into a mess. She had been away for months, and he was suddenly a little suspicious. He decided to go down the road and buy something and check again to see if the credit cards would work. They were declined again, so he went to an ATM and tried to withdraw some cash. All three accounts showed a zero balance. At this point, he felt discomfited. This could not simply be a coincidence, all three banks and two credit cards. Horrid furtive worries were darting into his brain, like little mice nibbling at a dried-out piece of cheese. He pulled out his mobile and rang Grace again.

"Oh, David, darling, how strange. I have no idea why your funds are suddenly drying up," said Grace with a distinct gloating note.

"Grace, this isn't funny," he retorted, fully aware that Grace never called him 'darling'.

"Well, sweetheart," and Grace had never called him 'sweetheart' ever before, "I don't know what you mean."

"What are you talking about?" he asked, squashing down those awkward little fears. He took a deep breath and mustered all the charm he could find, "darling, when are you coming back, I am at home quite alone, now that all my girls are back in the old country."

"Oh, are you missing me?" asked Grace, her voice deliberately soft, perhaps even teasing. She watched herself in the mirror, mouthing these ridiculous words. Perhaps her marriage had always been this insincere dance of platitudes.

"Of course, I am," said David, for once telling the truth. He desperately wanted Grace to come back and magic away the increasingly annoying Claudia.

"But I'm sure you've made friends there, you can enjoy yourself, go out, socialise, you know you were always so much better at that than me," replied Grace.

"Yes, but Grace, it's just not on. You know to leave a chap like this, people will begin to wonder." He laughed heartily. Grace was silent. She didn't reply. Whoever speaks first loses, she thought.

"Grace, are you there?"

"Yes," she replied unhelpfully. "Oh, I must go, can't talk now, Poppy needs help with her homework." She put the phone down with a gentle click and smiled. She was enjoying this cat and mouse game, and she would string him along for as long as it took, then she would strike the final death blow. She already knew that Claudia had moved in, she had rung Greta to chat, and the old woman was happy to make her complaints. In fact, if Greta was unhappy, then it really wasn't fair to expect her to wait on Claudia, she would give her three months wages and insist that she walk out and not go back. Perhaps Claudia could demonstrate her housekeeping skills!

David was puzzled by Grace's behaviour. Perhaps she was going through the change in life. It was unlike her not to attend to the practical matters, that was after all her forté. Slowly the wheels began to crank. If Poppy were in school in England that indicated that perhaps they were there for longer than they had planned. He tried to think what the plan had been, but he couldn't remember. Grace had simply said she would return home for a while to attend to some estate matters. Slowly the pieces began to shift into a very unwelcome picture, but then his mobile rang, and he saw that it was Claudia. Reluctantly he picked it up.

"Daveeed!" She was beginning to shriek, and her irritating accent came out. He hated women shrieking. Grace never shrieked.

"It's Greta. She took a telephone call, and I tried to listen in, but she was speaking in her odd English. Then I asked her to make me a drink, and she laughed in my face and hissed some rude words and walked away into her room. You have to talk to her. She cannot treat me like this!"

115

"Oh darling, you know she is a bit temperamental, I'm sure she didn't mean it," said David. He spent another five minutes whispering compliments and words of assurance and hung up. He had to go back to the apartment and comfort Claudia and smooth down Greta. He walked down the pavement past people who were lounging around, looking in shop windows at shoddy goods that were ridiculously over-priced.

He would ring Phoebe. She was such an artless creature. She would tell him the truth. She must have some inkling of her mother's plans. He rang Phoebe's mobile, and it rang and rang. Perhaps she was asleep and turned it onto silent.

In Phoebe's bedroom, Grace was holding the phone, looking at it ringing with an unknown number. Phoebe was helping Poppy with her homework. She knew it was David, she knew that he would try and pump poor Phoebe for information and Phoebe was not a dissembler. She was transparent, sweet, and always loving more than she was loved.

Grace would have liked to toy with David for longer, but unless she actually took a hammer to Phoebe's phone so he couldn't ring her, this wouldn't work. He would simply ring on the home phone until one of the girls picked up. She had already persuaded Poppy not to tell her father about their plans for the horses, that was just too obvious. It had all been, 'when he comes back at Christmas time what a tremendous surprise it would be.' He might fly back, and that would be worse, she would have him in the house upsetting the girls. He could get an emergency flight booked by the Consulate. She would just have to tell him, outright. Revenge was rather fun but really not her style. She would tell him he was on his own, cut off without a penny and Greta was gone, and now Claudia could do the housework!

Quietly she took Phoebe's phone and answered it.

"This is Grace."

"Why are you answering Phoebe's phone?" he asked.

"I imagine you were trying to ring her and find out what is happening."

"Well, yes, I wanted to know when you're coming back. But it's alright I'll come back for Christmas. I'm due some home leave."

"No."

"What do you mean 'no'?" he replied irritably. "I'll come back at Christmas."

"No, we don't want you here. In fact, I'm rather determined that you never set foot in Kiss Wood ever again."

David was struck dumb. This was a totally unknown Grace.

"Grace, darling, what on earth are you talking about?"

"David, you really don't think you have the right to ever call me darling again. You can spend Christmas with Claudia in that God-forsaken hole Montevideo, but you will have to pay for it out of your own salary."

David now began to understand. The awful knowledge spilt across his mind like a deluge of putrid liquid. He pushed back the realisation, continuing on with his line of denial, he reasoned that Grace was upset about Claudia. He would have to smooth her over.

"Claudia is just a friend, a harmless flirtation. You know she doesn't mean anything to me."

"Just like all the others who didn't mean anything. Perhaps just like I meant nothing. But no, I'm not worthless at all. I'm your cash cow, aren't I?"

"Grace I've never heard you speak like this before. Tell me, are you going through menopause?" His tone was unctuous, patronising as if chiding a recalcitrant child.

"Oh David, you're killing, absolutely killing. Menopause! Is that what you think this is? Perhaps you're right. It's a change of life. A huge change of life. Life at Kiss Wood with my daughters and without you. I'm divorcing you. I've got more than enough evidence of infidelity. I'm not paying you another penny, you can sing for your own supper now."

"Grace, you don't mean that," said David unbelievingly. But deep down, in the pit of his gut, he had a cold, hard feeling. He'd had a good run. He'd done whatever he wanted for the last twenty years. Now it seemed that his short-changed wife had drawn a line in the sand, and basically, he was washed up on an ugly beach tied to the increasingly unsexy and demanding

Claudia. The first thing he had to do was get rid of her. If he was ever going to win back Grace then he needed to see Claudia on her way, then he would fly back to Kiss Wood and use Poppy and Phoebe to get back into Grace's good books.

The days ticked by after this defining phone call. Christmas was coming up. Grace turned back to her equestrian pursuits. Poppy and her other pony friends were weaving tinsel into the manes of their mounts for the December events. Phoebe went for long walks with Sooty, the black Labrador. She picked at her food unhappily, but Grace thought that perhaps she just needed to adjust to British life. She wasn't paying attention, and she was entirely unaware of Phoebe's pregnancy.

Phoebe confided in no-one. She might have talked to Tate if she had been around, but she was away partying in New York, or Miami or wherever it was that the lotus-eaters clustered. It was surprisingly easy to hide her condition. She stopped eating, feeling utterly love-sick and alone. Continuing to wear her usual baggy clothing, her pregnancy bump was not visible. It had not taken long for her to admit to herself that Rafael had never really loved her. She had helped him out, and he had moved on. By Christmas, she was at least four months pregnant, possibly five months.

She promised herself that she would go to a doctor, not the family doctor, perhaps a woman at a health centre in Oxford. She knew she had to confide in her mother, but she kept putting it off. Grace and Poppy were entirely preoccupied with buying horses, saddlery, refurbishing the stables, and training. This equestrian obsession cut Phoebe like a knife, if only Rafael had returned with her, he would have fitted in so well. She was sure that her mother would have overlooked his lower-class origins when she had seen his riding ability.

Sometimes, Phoebe allowed herself to daydream. Perhaps Rafael would write to her and tell her that he missed her so much and wanted them to be together. He would be a father to his child and live at Kiss Wood and help train the horses. Then they would all live happily ever after – a perfect storybook ending! Then her dream would evaporate in the cold winter mist.

Even though it was increasingly clear that Grace didn't want him at Kiss Wood, David was determined to fly back to England. He had smiled winsomely at the woman who arranged the travel at the Consulate and persuaded her to book him a flight one week before Christmas. He had slipped away, leaving Claudia a scrawled note while she was at the hairdressers and had jumped in the car of a colleague who dropped him at the airport. He didn't have enough money for a taxi. He arrived in the early hours of the morning and had taken a train to Oxford. He was all geared up to be his most attractive and persuasive, his whole future depended on persuading Grace to come back to him.

It was grey and dull and very dark. He felt better once he was walking on British ground, a feeling of relief swept over him. He became confident that he could press the switch and reset his life, go back just eleven months before he had met Claudia and she had got her claws into him. He had been infatuated by her heavy sexuality, but now he found her cloying, almost disgusting.

England was so familiar. He couldn't believe that Grace would let him down. She was just making sure that he learnt his lesson. Perhaps he could resign from his job and stay here. It would be a relief never to return to Uruguay, and stay out of reach of the loan sharks, who had been paying for Claudia's expensive lifestyle in the last few weeks. He had not had the courage to tell her that he was penniless, that Grace had cut off his usual supply of funds. She would not have taken the news well, there would have been screams and accusations, and there was nothing worse than suffering through an exhausting emotional excess. He would settle down, wear tweed and play the master of the house for Grace. She could finally have the life she had been born to, the chatelaine of Kiss Wood, and he was happy to be her loyal husband.

He caught the bus from Oxford, feeling utterly demeaned, reduced to catching buses. He looked around at his fellow travellers. They were old, overweight, dressed in baggy grey and brown, pale faces staring vacantly out of smeary windows. He caught a glimpse of his own reflection in the window, and he looked haggard. He suffered a moment of panic that twisted his guts and left him breathless. He was losing his looks. He had always traded on his looks and his charm.

The bus stop was in the village, and he was hoping that no-one would catch a glimpse of him. The bush telegraph here was very efficient. Grace would be alerted to his arrival before he passed through the impressive gateposts that marked the entrance of Kiss Wood. There was no-one around the village street. It was all so familiar. He couldn't believe that he didn't still have a place here. The windows of the local pub, the Goat, were glowing and golden, decorated with tinsel and beckoned him in for some Dutch courage but he resisted. It wouldn't be good to arrive with the smell of alcohol on his breath.

He took the public footpath that led across a field and found himself on the road that led to Kiss Wood. The grass was wet, and his smart leather shoes were soon muddied and squelching. Greyish-pink light lit up the west as the sun sunk down to the horizon. There were rooks cawing and circling around the chimney pots of their neighbour's house, and he could smell wood smoke. The air felt damp, and as he passed the cow field, there was the rank smell of rotten mud.

Kiss Wood looked different in the half-light. For a moment, he wondered if he'd come the wrong way. There was the bulky outline of a huge shed off to the left of the house, near the stables. For an awful moment, he wondered if he were hallucinating. Obviously, there had been some building work. Foreboding then flooded his mind. Grace was, in her usual efficient way, making changes but without the courtesy of informing him, as she was used to, in her dry, clipped succinct manner.

His feet crunched loudly on the gravel, and he felt as if there were a hundred eyes staring at him from the dark, cloudy windows. He could see a light glimmering in the depths of the house, on the ground floor. Probably the housekeeper was preparing the dinner. There were no lights on in the master bedroom.

He decided to go around to the side door that was never locked and let himself in. The gravel was crunching very loudly now, but he couldn't bring himself to step silently on the wet grass, like a thief sneaking around. He was, ostensibly, still the master of the house. Usually, he would have a key to the large double front doors, but somehow it was missing off his key ring. The side door was locked. Perhaps Grace had stepped up security in his absence. He continued on around the house, now thankfully walking on a concrete path, so his footsteps didn't echo in his ears.

The kitchen was lit up. Looking through the window, he could see Grace sitting at the kitchen table. She had a mug of tea and was reading from a sheaf of papers, frowning a little in concentration. He noticed the thin vertical line that creased her forehead, making her look angry. She really did need to get some work done, he would suggest it as her Christmas present.

He tried the door, but it was also locked. He tapped on it discreetly. He heard her chair scraping as she got up. She probably thought he was one of the members of staff. The door opened inwards, and she was standing in the door frame, the light behind her. Her body was exactly the same, thin, almost gaunt, upright.

"Hello Grace," he said in his most urbane and gentlemanly voice.

She did not reply. He felt her eyes boring into him. She was blocking the doorway, and for a moment he thought she might deny him entrance. If that happened, he had no idea where to go next. Then after a very long minute, she stepped aside, and he was over the threshold. He was in. For a moment, he felt filled with hope. He looked at her face in the kitchen light and thought he could see happiness hovering around her impassive features. She must be pleased to see him.

Grace was indeed experiencing an unusual feeling. She searched for a name for it. Exaltation. How strange to feel so positive at such a moment, when she was going to end a marriage that had persisted for more than twenty years. Freedom, to say exactly what she thought. Revenge was indeed a dish best eaten cold.

"Sit down, dear," she said in a deceptively soft and sweet voice.

David felt flooded with relief. Grace could see his face relax. He thought he had been forgiven. For the first time she realised just how stupid he was, but perhaps it was the same with all men, ego far outweighing intelligence. All the slights and humiliations she had experienced over the years because of this pathetic human being!

She made him a cup of tea. It was the last gesture. Something so mundane, and utterly final, a tribute to their miserable domestic life of twenty years. She enjoyed the slow pace of this moment. It was something she would remember until she died. Her moment of pathetic triumph over this exceedingly pathetic man.

"Why did you come back?" she asked, leading him on.

"For Christmas, to be with my family."

She smiled at him wryly. He smiled back boyishly. He always used the 'boyish' look thought Grace, and it was wearing very thin.

"How is Claudia?" she asked.

"Claudia. Oh, darling, I don't know what I was thinking. She's frightful and completely erased from my life."

Grace smiled at him. Even though Greta had left, she was still friendly with other staff who worked in the next-door apartment, and she kept her former mistress informed. Ever since David had left, Claudia had been screaming and throwing things around. David really must think she was a fool, but she couldn't blame him, she *had* been a fool. She dwelt on this thought for several minutes. The silence stretched uncomfortably between them.

"What have we planned for Christmas, the usual large turkey I suppose, with all the trimmings," he said. Even to himself, this sounded inane.

"David, I told you I didn't want you back for Christmas. In fact, I'm sure that I told you our marriage was over. However, your arrival is fortuitous." She got up and called for Mrs Hopkins, the housekeeper. "I'm afraid I can't do this personally."

Mrs Hopkins walked in and looked at David in surprise.

"Hello, Mrs Hopkins," said David. She ignored him and turned to Grace.

"Would you kindly serve these documents on Mr Lester-Blyth," said Grace.

Mrs Hopkins did as she was told. David sat there, looking at the divorce papers. He couldn't believe it. The hard evidence was in front of him. Slowly he began to realise that this was more serious than he had thought. This was real.

"Grace, darling," he said in his most persuasive voice.

He expected tears, accusations but she was smiling at him and then she began to laugh out loud, a big jolly belly laugh, not her normal dry cackle.

"David, you really do think that your charm will get your anything. Well, let me tell you your future. You will walk out of this house, you will make your way back to Montevideo, and the money lenders will come knocking on your door and then they will turn up at the Consulate. But don't worry that you've lost this family you have another. Has Claudia given you the good news? She's pregnant, you know."

David blanched, and his dismay was writ large upon his once-charming face.

"You will have the buxom Claudia. She'll stick to you like shit on a blanket."

Grace had surprised herself. She wasn't even aware that she knew this phrase, and she had certainly never used it before. She smiled at his appalled expression.

"David, I know that I've allowed you your own way for a very long time, but really did you think I would put up with it forever."

"Yes," he snarled. "After all, you're no beauty."

She looked at him consideringly.

"Well, you've got your beauty, you can live with her! Now get out of this house before I call the men to throw you out."

"But I want to see Poppy and Phoebe!"

"You only have my word for it that they're your children, you know?" she said with a sly smile. It was worth it just to pull the rug from under his feet to see his face, the sudden discomfiture. "But of course, they are," she said wearily. "But you're not seeing them now, not yet. I will email you when it is convenient for you to resume contact with them after the divorce. Those papers might make rather interesting reading for you."

He got up, prepared to stalk out and tempted to leave the papers behind. Perhaps, she hadn't been as harsh as she had intimated. Perhaps, she would give him a settlement payment. He took the papers with him and walked out the door, clutching his travelling bag. He had no idea where he should go. He couldn't afford a hotel. He even wondered if he should go into the woods and camp out in the gamekeeper's hut but decided to leave the estate. He had a former mistress who lived in Oxford. She would probably put him up. He had to think. He had to read these papers.

He caught the last bus to Oxford and walked through the warren of streets to the home of one of his former mistresses. She answered the door, wearing her dressing gown, but she wasn't welcoming. She did allow him in but announced that she was now re-married to a rather good-looking young fellow who looked at David with mild shock. She agreed that he might stay one night, but, after that, he would have to go. They were expecting guests. He went upstairs and sat on the bed and got the papers out of the envelope.

At first, he couldn't focus. He thought he must have got it wrong. Grace was suing him for child support. He couldn't believe it. She wanted one-third of his wage for the upkeep of Poppy. As his salary was from the British Government, she would be able to make an application through the Court. He considered just walking away. Not returning to Uruguay, the money lenders, and now, apparently, a pregnant Claudia. He had no idea how Grace even knew this. Perhaps it wasn't true, and she'd thrown it in for good measure.

He began to ponder where he might go. He had two weeks to decide before his return flight to Montevideo was booked. He'd turned off his mobile so Claudia couldn't ring him. He would have to think through his options. Could he simply walk away and pick up a new identity? He had no family of his own that would be of any help. He had cut them off without a backward glance when he had hooked up with Grace. He had to make a plan.

Grace was sitting in the kitchen, thrumming her fingers on the table thoughtfully. She had enjoyed that. She had enjoyed it immensely. She felt vindicated. David's future was looking extremely uncomfortable, and she would be relentless in pushing for child support. She also wanted to ensure that he didn't contact Phoebe and Poppy. Phoebe had come into some of her own money on her eighteenth birthday, and he might persuade her to help him out. She would have to talk to her elder daughter.

The next morning, she took a cup of tea up to Phoebe and sat in the armchair beside the bed. Phoebe looked uncomfortable. She hauled herself up and leaned back against the pillows and sipped her tea.

"Phoebe there's something I have to talk to you about. Your father has just come back, and he is trying to wheedle his way back into my affections. I won't have it, and I must ask you not to give him any money. Apparently, that Claudia is now pregnant and he's going to be rather short, but I don't want you contributing when he approaches you with some sob story."

"Oh," said Phoebe. Claudia was pregnant. Her father's first grandchild would be born before this other child, this half-sibling. For some reason, this seemed important, although in the grand scheme of things it really made no difference.

"Phoebe, what are you thinking?" asked Grace, impatiently waiting for Phoebe to agree to what she was saying.

"Mummy, I have to tell you something," she began.

"Oh no, don't tell me you've already given him money?"

"No, it's not that. It's nothing to do with that. I'm pregnant," she blurted out. Grace looked at her in astonishment. She thought she must have misheard.

"No, Claudia is pregnant, not you."

Phoebe gulped. "I'm pregnant, about five months pregnant, the baby is due in April, in the spring," she added as if the season of arrival was important.

"But how?" asked Grace, which was obviously inane. "I mean, … who is the father?"

"I had a boyfriend in Uruguay, and then he got a job and had to go away, and I've only just realised."

"A boyfriend, but how? I mean, surely I would have heard about it?" Grace was suddenly struck by a thunderbolt of guilt. She had swanned off, leaving poor Phoebe without support or guidance. Of course, David wouldn't have noticed. He was too enthralled in his own extra-curricular sex life.

"What about an abortion? Or is it too late?" asked Grace. She had no idea at which point an abortion was feasible.

"I'm not getting rid of it. I loved Rafael like I will never love anyone else, and even if I can't have him, I can have his child."

"Are you thinking that when he knows about the child, he'll want to marry you?" asked Grace. "Because that would be no sort of marriage at all."

"I'm not in contact with him anymore," said Phoebe and began to cry. She could never tell anyone about her fears that the father of her baby was not just a murderer but a cruel, sadistic murderer.

Even in this extreme circumstance, Grace couldn't bring herself to put her arm around Phoebe's shaking, despairing shoulders. Physical displays of emotion were impossible for her.

"Never mind dear," she said kindly. "We will live here; me, you, Poppy and the baby and we will be happy and safe. . . . But does your father know?"

"No," said Phoebe in bewilderment.

"Well, he won't know about this. For the moment, it will be just us. It doesn't matter what other people think. We will love the baby."

"Yes," said Phoebe, rubbing her hand across her eyes. "We will love him. I'm sure it is a boy, a boy who will look just like his father, Rafael." Somehow just saying Rafael's name out loud made it seem better.

Chapter Eleven

Half a world away, Rafael was revelling in his new life with boundless hope, but tentative joy. Last time he had been employed by Valentino, he had thought that nothing could go wrong and it had fallen into dust and ashes. Rapture was installed in a splendid loose box, with a thick bed of rice husks and fresh alfalfa every day. There was one small field where the horses could be let out for a few hours a day so they could run free, or wander at will. But Rapture didn't seem to relish this opportunity as the other horses did. The gelding didn't seem to understand how to run free. Rafael would lean on the fence and watch him standing in the corner of the small field, his head hanging down. Rafael would have preferred that his horse would throw his head up to snuff the wind, mane blowing, and floating across the ground with a long, proud stride.

Rafael loved the opportunity to train over show jumps every day. There was no more leaping over piles of rocks at low tide. Florencia mainly rode her and Pablo's horses, but now and again Pablo asked him to jump one of them, and he and Florencia would watch. Rafael found that Florencia was a good horse trainer, which had somewhat surprised him, she was so uncompromising and prickly with the clients that he had imagined she was like that with the horses. All the horses seemed to adore her as if her straight up and down style was reassuring for them, they always knew where they stood.

Usually, Rafael rode Valentino's horses, sometimes under the older man's direction and sometimes unsupervised. Often Valentino, Pablo, Florencia and himself rode down to the beach and stood the horses in the swirling foam of the waves. It was at these moments that he remembered his time at Punta del Diablo with Phoebe, and he wondered what she might be doing all the way over the other side of the world. He was certain that she wouldn't give him a thought, she had been kind, but now she had gone on to her own life in her own country. He was determined that one day he would pay her back at least a portion of the money that she had spent on him. It irked him that he had been an object of charity.

He worked long hours, but he didn't care, this was all that he wanted to do with his life. The startling news of Facundo and Tomas's murders had flooded the television broadcasts. They all talked about it a lot, speculating endlessly, but no-one had any idea how this could have happened. The killings had the hallmark of cartel violence, but in Uruguay this was so unlikely. The police seemed to have no clue, and the killings remained unsolved.

The clients from Melilla came to them now that there was no-one to teach at the Polo Club, so Rafael was finally given the chance to be an instructor. The Polo Club girls loved his dark good looks; they fluttered their eyelashes, flicked their hair around and twittered like sparrows. Not one of them recognised him as the stable boy who had worked at Melilla, where he had effectively been invisible. He immediately began to work to undo the awful habits many of the girls had picked up. Teaching them not to lean forward as they approached a jump and to sit square and straight in the saddle and not imitate the slouching style that Facundo had used.

There were not enough riding school horses to go around, and some of the better riders were put up on the show jumping horses. Florencia wasn't keen on this at all, and she was not one to hold back when she was displeased. She stood by the fence watching the riding class scowling at whichever rider was on one of her precious horses.

Pablo had extra cash now, but he was loath to buy more riding school horses when at any moment Melilla could employ replacement riding instructors, and they would lose their newfound clients as easily as they had acquired them. He asked Rafael if he would mind if some of the more advanced students could ride Rapture, and Rafael would be paid 200 pesos per lesson. Rafael agreed as long as he was instructing, he wanted to keep a close eye on his own horse.

At first, the students assigned to Rapture complained that they didn't want to ride such an ugly horse. However, one boy called Jorge, twelve-years-old but very tall and lanky for his age, had been persuaded to give him a go. It was a jumping lesson, and Rafael had organised a small competition to make it more interesting. The jumps began at 60 cm, but with a tight twisting course, that tested the riders' ability to keep in balance and steer the horse. Jorge and Rapture had jumped clear as the jumps rose as high as a metre, and then they made it against time, and he came out miles faster than the others. After that, he clamoured to be given Rapture every lesson. Other students heard about Rapture's ability to twist and turn and clear every jump put before him, and they also asked for him. Rafael was pleased that others seemed to appreciate Rapture's good points, but he was worried that so many novice riders would ruin all his careful training. But somehow Rapture didn't pick up bad habits. He seemed to adapt to whatever type of rider was put on him and carried them carefully. It was as if he were so grateful for his wonderful new life that he put himself out to do the right thing.

Florencia grudgingly began to accept Rafael. She was uncompromising, but she did recognise his exceptional abilities when it came to horses. He earned her respect. He was a little wary that she might expect some sort of flirtatious relationship with him, but she was as utterly devoted to Pablo as she was to their horses. Rafael would watch them as a couple and felt a yearning then for Phoebe. She had been such a good woman and friend to him, steadfast in her goodness and the only thing she had asked of him he had obstinately refused to even consider. If he had been another type of person, he would readily have agreed to go to England with her and take advantage of all the opportunities that such an offer represented, but his male pride couldn't accept it.

Sometimes Rafael would casually ask about Estrella and Georgina, but no-one had any news. As far as they knew she was still at Melilla. Her father was on the committee of the Polo Club, and he wouldn't think of moving over to Pablo and Florencia's. Rafael yearned to see the big black mare, after Rapture she was his favourite animal.

Florencia, Pablo and Valentino were planning to go up to Brazil to a big show jumping event. They asked Rafael if he would like to bring Rapture and he was very keen. Finally, this was a chance for him to compete, and on his own horse. The only issue was that he would need a passport for Rapture and that would entail getting a vet's certificate. It would take nearly all the money he had saved from his wages, but on balance, he decided it was a worthwhile investment. And he needed some proper riding clothes. He asked Pablo what he thought, and Pablo very kindly found some old breeches he could borrow, but they were rather short as Pablo was not tall - suave, good-looking but not tall. If only he could get some long leather boots, then this would not be noticeable. He would also need a white shirt, a tie and a riding coat. If Phoebe had been here, she would have said, 'no problem,' taken him to the shop and bought it all for him. He found himself longing for her to reappear. He had been surly and unfriendly when she had come to say good-bye. He hated himself for the way he had treated her, but he had felt so embarrassed when she had brought that woman who was elegant, stylish and high-class and they had caught him in the middle of shovelling horse manure.

In the end, it was Valentino who tipped off by Pablo, had produced a jacket, shirt, tie and even a pair of old boots that miraculously fitted. Rafael dressed up in his new outfit. He didn't look flash, or glamorous, but it was all correct and would suffice for his first show jumping event. He was beside himself with excitement and nervousness. He had never in his life left Uruguay, even crossing the border into Brazil was a first for him.

He trained Rapture every morning very early before he was due to begin his mucking out tasks. He had jumped as high as 140 cm on him but hadn't quite wanted to push him to try 160 cm. Over the medium-sized jumps he was amazing, jumping cleanly and well and twisting and turning on the spot but Rafael wasn't sure that he was up to the highest jumps. It was a lot to ask of a horse that hadn't been bred to it. Finally, he decided he had to try it, and he put the jumps up, two at 140 cm and then the third at 160 cm. He rode Rapture wondering if this was the right thing to do, intuitively he felt that his horse wouldn't be up to it. He looked down between his gelding's funny loppy ears and felt so much love for this horse who had a huge heart and spirit.

Rafael felt all his hopes plummet to the ground when Rapture's front legs pushed the pole out of the cups. He just didn't have the scope. It was too much to ask, and Rafael hated himself for testing him in this way. All horses could clear a metre, and the good ones were fine up to 130 cm but to jump a whole course at 160 cm was for the élite of superb athletes and Rapture's heart was huge, but he just did not have the ability. Rafael could go to Brazil, and he could compete in the 130 cm, or he could leave Rapture at home. Finally, he decided not to take him, it wasn't fair, and the last thing he wanted was for his darling horse to be scorned and made a fool of.

Valentino was keen for him to begin competing on his horses, and, this way, Rafael felt that he would be able to focus more effectively on his job, which was to ride for Valentino. He felt a tremendous responsibility to do the right thing for Valentino who had believed in him and given him this chance.

Valentino was deciding which horses to take. The truck held ten horses. Pablo and Florencia had four between them; this left six more places for

Valentino. In the end, he selected four which were old hands, experienced Grand Prix jumpers who had performed well over many years. These were Pedro, a rather plain brown gelding who was renown for his reliability; Arturo, a good-looking flea-bitten grey that was very tall with thick legs and a magnificent Roman nose; Carlomagna a spritely old gentleman, chestnut with a large white blaze; Alano a temperamental bay gelding who on his good days was wondrous but on his bad days very quick to buck his rider off and gallop out of the ring. The two novices who had never competed at a competition were Shakira, a temperamental chestnut mare who moved like quicksilver and a skewbald gelding called Pancho who was stocky and only 15.3 hh but who seemed to have a rather huge jump in him.

Rafael rode each of the horses every day, forty minutes in the arena with mainly flatwork and jumping three times a week. He got to know them and began to form relationships with them - but it was hard work. Too many horses and not enough time. He knew in his heart; he had been right to decide not to take Rapture.

If Rafael had agonised over whether or not to take his own horse to Brazil, the next decision he was asked to make was a classic "between the cross and the sword" which is a Spanish expression for a dilemma which has no favourable outcome, in English – between a rock and a hard place. Jorge's father had finally agreed to buy him a horse, and the young boy was utterly determined that he wanted only Rapture. He had never forgotten that first wonderful show jumping experience when he had won the informal competition against the much older riders. Jorge's father first approached Pablo, who insisted that it was up to Rafael; it was his horse.

So, Jorge's father spoke to Rafael, whose first instinct was to say no. It would be like selling his own child. However, Jorge's father was a wily businessman, and he was sure that everyone had a price. He put pressure on Rafael, offering him more money on each occasion. What had begun at $10,000 went up to $15,000 which to Rafael was an almost unimaginable sum. He had to say yes, he had to pay back Phoebe and then he could afford to buy himself some decent riding clothes so that when he rode Valentino's horses, he would look professional. He grudgingly agreed, feeling as if he were cutting out his own heart. But it was a good home, and he knew that Jorge would love the horse and not ride him to death. Now, he could pay back Phoebe and then he would be a free man. He had no idea how much he owed her. He hadn't kept a tally as he had been so ashamed. Perhaps, if he offered $10,000 that would cover the initial cost of Rapture and the rent and the food and the equipment.

He had kept the address she had thrust upon him before she rushed off, and he sat down to write to her. He explained that he had been able to sell Rapture and he wished to send her the money that she had spent on him and asked if she could reply with some bank details. He said he was unsure of the exact amount but thought perhaps that $10,000 would cover it. He also thanked her for all the help she had given him, she had quite literally saved his life and he would never forget it. He took the letter down to DHL, as the Uruguayan postal service was notoriously slow and it would be a miracle if anything actually made it out of the country as the post office workers were continually on strike (usually about something as ridiculous as whether they had a choice of beef or chicken for their lunch).

The next day they spent hours packing up all the equipment to go to Brazil. Rafael hadn't had to go through a heart-wrenching good-bye to Rapture as the horse was to be kept on livery at the stables. Rafael went into Atlantida and deposited most of the money into his Santander bank account holding back just enough to buy himself new clothes in Brazil. There would surely be some retail outlets at the show, and hopefully the prices would be cheaper than those imported to the equestrian shop in Uruguay.

It was organised that he would travel in the truck with Joaquina, one of the girls from the riding school who had been asked to come along and help. Valentino, Florencia and Pablo were to follow them in the car. They were not going to unload the horses until they arrived at the showground. It was decided that it was too risky to unload them along the road. It would be a long trip, at least ten hours of driving, not to mention a wait at Immigration and Customs.

The truck was loaded with ten horses and all their gear and trundled out the gate very early in the morning. The trip across the border went smoothly, and they arrived in the middle of the hot Brazilian afternoon. Rafael was in awe of the enormous showground. The grass was like green velvet, so carefully tended and clipped that no weed dared show its raggedy head. There was a glittery, crisp quality to the air, luminous sunshine glimmering from a cyan sky, and multi-coloured flags and bunting that flew between flagpoles. The grandstands were large and well-built, and everywhere beautifully-dressed Brazilians jabbering away in Portuguese. He felt shabby in his second-hand clothes, dusty and dishevelled from the journey. He was ill at ease amongst this strange foreign crowd.

Florencia was jack-booting around finding out where their pre-booked stables were. She spoke Portuguese as well as Spanish, and her ugly rasping voice seemed twice as loud as anyone else's. She was complaining that their stables were so far from the collecting ring, just because they were Uruguayan they were treated as if they were at the bottom of the ladder. Pablo was his usual charming self, smiling graciously and chatting away with the other men in a manly sort of way. He called Rafael over and introduced him to some of his cronies. He treated the young man as if he were an equal, and Rafael felt grateful but completely out of his depth, he didn't know how to talk to these people. He stood there listening to them gossiping about the newest up-and-coming Bolivian show jumper who had brought a horse that had been imported from the States. He was reputed to have paid more than a million dollars for it, and it was meant to be unbeatable.

They pointed him out, and Rafael watched a slim young man with hands that jabbed at the reins attached to a malicious looking bit that seemed all metal and cruel leverage. He was riding a most magnificent grey stallion with a long black tail and mane. It didn't look natural, and Rafael wondered if they dyed it to give the horse that unusual appearance. He was cantering around the exercise arena, and the grooms were holding a pole up as a makeshift jump, no ground line and even worse, every time the stallion jumped they raised it, so it hit him on the forelegs with a distinct clunk that made Rafael wince. The purpose of this dubious training method was to encourage the horse to jump higher than was necessary, making it feel uncertain, unable to trust its own judgement eyeing up the height of a jump.

Rafael decided that he would go and attend to Valentino's horses, they had got hot and dusty on the journey. He thought he would take each of them to the luxurious wash bays and wash them and comb out their manes and tails. He felt like he needed to keep busy, so his nerves stayed under control. This was his big chance, if he messed it up, then Valentino might not ask him to jump his horses in competition again.

The competitions were due to begin on the following afternoon, just a couple of 130 cm events for novice horses and Valentino had suggested that Rafael ride Shakira and also Pancho in this competition. It was not an important event, and it would help him to get used to jumping in the ring.

Rafael decided to lead Shakira around. She needed to become accustomed to her new surroundings. She started, snorted, spooked and tit-tupped, swivelling her small curved ears; twice she trod on his feet, her light iron hoofs were sharp and painful. He hoped that she would settle tomorrow or his début in the show jumping ring would be ignominious. He led her back to the stable and put her inside. She still wouldn't settle, swinging around in circles, stirring up the bedding, splashing the water out of her bucket. He didn't know what to do with her. Perhaps it was best to leave her alone and hope that she settled herself. This did not bode well for the morrow.

He walked back over to the ringside and watched the workers putting up the jumps. The ring was huge, and the distances between the jumps were enormous, it would advantage the big long-striding horses. Shakira, the little chestnut mare would have to fly between the fences to make up the time, and Pancho who was overweight and rather stocky was not going to be at an advantage either. Valentino had found Pancho tethered to the side of the motorway and had had a feeling that he might be able to jump. He purchased him from his rather surprised owner, and they had been training him for several months now. He certainly did have a tremendous jump in him, but was very short-striding and not fleet of foot.

Rafael went back to the stables and went around and skipped out the loose boxes, keeping them clean so that the flies would not cluster around the horses. Joaquina came over and stood there first on one leg, then the other, hopping hopefully.

"Will you come with me to get something to eat, I feel too nervous to go by myself," she asked.

He looked at her in surprise. He had hardly noticed her on the trip up. He had been too busy with his own thoughts, preoccupied with how he was going to ride. She was sweet, not rampantly beautiful or sexy like Marianela. Her parents weren't rich, and that was why Florencia had asked her to act as a groom for token wages, and she had been more than happy to come along on what was probably the first big adventure of her life.

"Sure, why not?" he said casually. She smiled shyly at him. It suddenly occurred to him that she liked him. Liked him in *that* way. Such a thing was very far from his mind, but perhaps, here in another country, he was almost like another person, perhaps he should step into the role of a swaggering young showjumper, who was up for it.

He looked at her a little while they were walking along. She was cute, slim, athletic, with the ubiquitous long, brown hair and nice brown eyes. He had seen her riding, and she was good, very quiet with the horses, perhaps not strong enough to push them on but certainly kind and considerate, not a bad rider. He supposed he should talk to her, chat, make conversation, get to know her. The concept seemed so alien to his nature. With horses, it was so much easier, they just sensed you, and there was no need for lots of words to fill the gaps.

Joaquina said that she quite liked Brazilian food, so they went to the take-away and ordered *feijoada,* which is the national dish, a tasty mixture of beans, pork and beef. Rafael felt like an adventurous world traveller as he chewed on this unfamiliar dish; Joaquina was right, it was rather delicious, spicier and tastier than the average bland Uruguayan fare. They went back to the stables and took Shakira out again, and this time they took Pedro as well, the rather plain brown gelding, who Shakira liked very much. He was old and experienced, and they hoped that Shakira might settle in his company.

It was going to be dark soon, and Shakira seemed to cling to Pedro for protection. Rafael felt the spicy food burning its way down his gullet. He hoped that it wouldn't disagree with him. He had to be at peak condition tomorrow. They took the horses back and went along the line. Each of the horses had been fed by Florencia who insisted that she was the only one capable of making sure they each got their correct rations. After checking the hay nets and water buckets Joaquina and Rafael went back to the truck where they were to sleep in the back on makeshift camp beds, hessian stretched across metal frames and sleeping bags.

Joaquina was looking at him questioningly. He was embarrassed. The last thing he felt like was making love to a young girl who was essentially a stranger. He didn't want to hurt her feelings, but he just wanted to lie down and go into himself and prepare for the following day.

"Buenos noches," he said, and wriggled down into his sleeping bag. He lay there in the dark, listening to her breathing, very lightly and sweetly

and for a moment he wondered if he shouldn't have made a move. But not tonight, perhaps later if everything went well.

The next morning was his first-ever show jumping round. It was the defining moment of his life. He was desperate to prove himself not just to Valentino, to the world, but also to himself. Did he really have what it took to become a top rider? His mouth was dry with fear, and he could hear his own heart thumping. He rode Pancho around the exercise area. His hands were sweating and slipping along the reins. In English, 'Pancho' would have been called 'hot dog' which was just about right, the tubby horse looked like he'd eaten his way through the whole hot dog cart. Rafael felt as if they were both the same, uncivilised peasants from the wrong side of the tracks, skulking around, total outsiders in the milling crowd of the élite of the show jumping world in South America.

Joaquina was holding Shakira for him and watching; her soft, spaniel-brown eyes followed him adoringly. It gave him some encouragement, and he knew that Valentino believed in him, and surely Valentino was a wise old man with good judgement. The ground crew were going around with a measuring stick checking that the heights were correct for the first novice class and he watched carefully, so that he could learn the course, so there was no risk that he would lose his way when he was riding it. The ground crew were all wearing matching navy-blue polo shirts with the sponsor's name embroidered across their backs. The course was officially going to be 130 cm which was less than what he had jumped during practice sessions.

They called for the riders to walk the course and he handed Shakira's reins to Joaquina and walked into the ring. It was a large arena, much bigger than the modest indoor arena at Melilla. It seemed like a mile-long hike between fences. He walked alone but listened to the comments of the other riders as they strode out distances between the combination fences and laughed and joked and engaged in good-hearted banter. He stood with his back to each fence and imagined what the course would look like when he was riding it. He would land from this jump and then look towards the next fence, memorising the order of the jumps.

He walked back to the collecting ring and decided to give Pancho some practice jumps. The chunky, little gelding was straight-shouldered with a short, uncomfortable stride, but he was good at twisting and turning, and if they managed to get through to the jump-off and the course allowed for it, they could take some shortcuts between the jumps.

They called his number. He rode into the ring, saluted the judges and cantered in small circles near the start. Pancho felt very small compared to the other horses, and Rafael didn't feel like it was going to go well. Perhaps he jinxed it with his negative thoughts, but the determined little Pancho hit five of the fences, not just flicked but clunked, and the poles clattered. The little gelding seemed to be communicating to the world that he did not want to be a show jumper, he had been happy, tethered to the side of the motorway! Rafael left the ring feeling utterly humiliated, in comparison to Pancho who was cocky, perhaps he didn't understand that he was meant to clear the fences, and the object was to score as many knockdowns as possible.

"Bad luck," said Joaquina, as she took Pancho's reins and he checked Shakira's girth before mounting. All his hopes now rested on her slim shoulders, at least she was quick and lively. She hated hitting fences and sometimes turned herself inside out to clear them, but she was so inexperienced he didn't hold out much hope.

He rode her around, and she stepped out quickly, but surely, she didn't shy or leap about with nervousness. Perhaps she wanted to make it up to him; she was sensitive. She would know how devastated he felt. She was the opposite of Pancho, as fine as spun gold, like a shooting star. They called him in, and Shakira sped around the course, responding to the lightest of touches and they jumped clear.

"A clear round for Shakira!" said the loudspeaker and they played the music that announced that it was a clear round.

"You sweet, sweet darling," he crooned to her. His spirits shot sky-high, from the depths to the heavens and he felt as if he were the champion of the world as if he had drunk from the heady elixir of the golden goblet.

"*Muy bien,*" said Valentino who had materialised in the collecting ring.

He jumped down to the ground, and Valentino put his arms around his shoulders. Joaquina darted in and kissed him, her lips felt so soft, like butterfly wings. Florencia and Pablo shouted encouraging words to him. He felt as if he were not alone. He belonged in this group of fellow riders.

137

He walked Shakira around for the next hour, taking her out to the green sward and letting her graze a little. He tried to keep himself centred. He didn't want to watch the other competitors. Assuredly there would be plenty to learn from watching the others, but he would do that later in the competitions when he was not competing. They announced the competitors for the jump-off, and there were five of them, this meant he might not be placed. He went over to the ring and Valentino, and he discussed the jump-off. There was one shortcut which he could attempt, but it would mean presenting Shakira at a difficult straight fence now standing at 140 cm, with just two strides before take-off. He told Valentino that he didn't think it was a good idea, better to go clear and slow. It wasn't right to ask that of the young mare. Valentino agreed with him, smiling his approbation at this wise decision.

Rafael mounted and rode Shakira around, cantered her in a large circle, fast and then gradually pulling her back together, leapt just once over the practice fence that had been put up to 150 cm, she cleared it carefully, and he felt a rush of confidence. He knew that he was in with a chance if only he could hold it together. His nerves were jittery, his mouth dry, he could hardly swallow, his stomach was twisted into knots, darts, pleats and tucks. He rode over to Joaquina, who seemed to understand him without words. She handed him a bottle of water. He felt the fizzy liquid sliding over his tongue and down his throat. She put her hand on his thigh. He looked down, such a small, sweet, soft hand, such a timid gesture, but it comforted him. She was on his side.

He was called in, and he cantered swiftly over to bow to the judges and then back towards the start, listening carefully for the bell. For a second, he felt the warm sun on his back and then all his concentration went to the five enormous fences in the jump-off. He cantered towards the first and just for a split-second he felt a moment of hesitation from the little mare, but he urged her on with his voice, telling her she could do it, and they flew over and then another five strides and a slight curve to the left and over the red wall that looked extremely imposing. There was a long gallop around the arena. This was the place where he might have cut across to save time. Instead, he pushed her on to a gallop and at the last minute, pulled her back to a more balanced speed, four strides before the fence, and then one stride to the next element. He heard a click as she must have flicked the rail, but he didn't know whether it had fallen or not, and he didn't want to risk turning around to look. He urged her on to tackle the wide triple bar, knowing that speed here was called for so she could stretch over the widened jump, and then they were galloping towards the final fence which was a straight one, it needed careful jumping, it would be too easy to hit it in his haste to get across the finish line. They cleared it by miles, and he leaned forward to urge her on over the finish line. His happiness was as high and wide as the final jump. He pulled her up and looked back to make sure. There was no ground staff dashing in to fix the jump he had heard the knock. They had jumped clear!

"Did I go clear, what was our time?" he asked.

"You went clear," said Florencia in her loud, strident voice.

"Not a bad time, you're standing second at the moment," said Valentino smiling at him.

"Oh Shakira, you are such a darling," said Joaquina, putting her slim brown arms around the chestnut mare's neck. Rafael looked down and imagined those slim arms encircling his body, perhaps tonight they would.

Now he felt he could watch the other competitors. There were three more to jump, all Brazilians, all older than him. He was radiant with confidence, even if they all went clear and faster than him, he felt like a conquering hero. The first to go was riding a very tall but thin grey gelding, he leapt around, and his long stride ate up the ground, but he knocked the last jump, and the pole fell. Rafael breathed in relief. They were still second, just two more to go. The next a rather evil-looking black stallion called Diablo jumped, and he was clear and fast until he hit the second element of the double. Now, they were at least third! A rosette and prize winnings! And still the chance to get a second. The last horse to jump was a good-looking bay, with the most breathtakingly beautiful head, a dished face with a muzzle small enough to fit into a teacup. This divine animal went steadily, not too fast, obviously aiming for a clear but not the fastest time. They achieved clear, and their time was just one second faster than Rafael and Shakira's. This meant he was third. He was elated. It was more than he had expected. Everyone in their group clapped him on the back and congratulated him. He had to ride into the ring to receive his rosette and envelope of winnings. Florencia and Joaquina were holding up their phones recording this glorious moment. If only Facundo and Tomas had lived to see it! Then he banished this ignoble thought. He needed to focus on the positives and the future. He was alive and now in the winners' circle!

He galloped around the ring, respectfully behind the first and second prize winners. It was his first victory gallop. He was determined to remember this for the whole of his life. He rode back to the stables and untacked Shakira. She was in an upbeat mood and seemed to have swallowed a bucketload of fresh confidence.

"You and me, darling, we're going to storm the world," he crooned to her.

"We have to get the two horses for Valentino ready, for the next class," said Joaquina.

"Of course," said Rafael, finding it easy to slip back into stable boy mode. He saddled Pedro, the plain brown gelding, who had been Valentino's horse for years. Pedro and Valentino were like one being when they entered the ring, and although the horse no longer had the edge, they were rarely unplaced. Joaquina was tending to Arturo with the magnificent Roman nose. They led the horses over to the side of the ring and Valentino mounted Arturo.

"There's a small speed class tomorrow morning," he said to Rafael. "I want you to enter Shakira. The jumps will only be 120 cm, and you don't have to push her too fast, but it is a class that should suit her."

Rafael nodded in agreement. This was another chance for him, and he was pleased.

"What about Pancho?" he asked.

"I think we'll take Pancho home and give him to Pablo for the students. He is very reliable, and he can jump, but I think he lacks scope and the will to exert himself too much," replied Valentino wryly.

Rafael offered to ride Pedro around to warm him up, and Valentino nodded in agreement. He was jumping Arturo. First, he had already walked the course. It was a Grand Prix, and to Rafael, the jumps looked absolutely enormous. He sat quietly on Arturo, wanting to warm him up gradually and gently, to give him the best chance in the competition. Joaquina stood next to the practice jump, ready to put the pole back up if it was knocked. One of the Brazilian grooms came over and began chatting. She smiled and laughed, and suddenly Rafael felt a rush of annoyance. He felt possessive about her. He felt like he had a claim. She came over and took the reins and suggested he might want to watch the class.

"Thank you," he said gratefully, it was as if she had read his mind, he wanted to learn as much as he could while he was here. He stood next to the rails and watched Valentino and Arturo. He saw just how well Valentino rode. The older man was knowledgeable, and had a swift, sure touch and nursed Arturo round to a clear round. In comparison, the Brazilian riders often rode with a sort of flashy style that reminded him a little of Facundo. They did clock up clear rounds, but it was nearly always slapdash, and he could see that it was only chance whether they went clear or knocked the poles. He watched Valentino jump round on Pedro about an hour later and again their performance was impeccable. He knew that he could learn so much from Valentino, and he felt humble and grateful for this chance that he had been given.

He went back to the collecting ring and suggested that he hold the horses so that Joaquina could go and watch and get herself a drink. He watched her call to her new Brazilian boyfriend, and they went over to the food stalls together. He was amazed to feel a stab of jealousy. It was not what he had expected of himself. He turned back to Valentino, who was riding both horses in the jump-off. He held Pedro while Valentino went into the ring on Arturo. They hit one of the jumps, which probably put them out of the running, then Pedro, who went clear but was not fast, so they came third.

"I've been thinking, you might take Alano in that speed class tomorrow, as well," said Valentino. "If he messes up, don't worry I won't blame you, but he is experienced, and you won't have to nurse him around, ride him flat out to win."

Rafael smiled at him. Alano was a challenge, on the days he was good he was very, very good but when he was bad, he was a nightmare. After today's success, he felt he was up to it.

"You know *chico*, it is the mistakes from which we learn, more than the successes," said Valentino as if he could read his thoughts.

That night Joaquina was looking at him again, in *that* particular way. He took her in his arms and kissed her, and they made love on one of the camp beds. It wasn't comfortable, but he didn't care, he was riding a wave of victory, and she was one of his prizes. She murmured sweet, breathless words of love as he entered her, so tight and wet, but she wasn't a virgin. Compared to Phoebe, she was tiny, but he didn't like to make comparisons, it wasn't fair on either of them. Anyway, Phoebe was gone, and he doubted that he would ever see her again.

He rose early on the following day and left Joaquina sleeping peacefully. She looked like a beautiful angel, her lashes thick and brown, her small, pointy chin, smooth skin and tousled hair. He went over to the stables and began mucking out the loose boxes. He felt that he needed to use up some excess energy. His whole body and mind were zinging with excitement at the prospects of success today. He spent some time with Alano, trying to forge a stronger bond with the temperamental little gelding. Would today be one of his good days or his bad days? Rafael thought of leading him out to graze, in an effort to kid him along and get in his good books, but he thought the smart bay gelding would see through him and divine his motives.

He led Carlomagna out instead, no matter that he was old he was still magnificent, a strong chestnut with a dominant white blaze running down the front of his noble head. He and Arturo were due to compete in the big class with Valentino today. Pablo and Florencia had entered all four of their horses. It was the high point of the show. Everyone wanted to win. The prize was the most substantial and the competition fierce. Florencia was going to ride one of her mares in the speed class this morning as well. She insisted that the mare always jumped better if she competed in two classes in one day. This last day of the show was going to be exciting for them all.

Joaquina came down, her hair mussed up, smiling as if the doors of heaven had been opened for her. He smiled back but felt a stab of concern. He hoped she hadn't read too much into last night. She looked like she believed she was in love with him. She was looking at him in the same way that Phoebe had used to look at him. He felt a rush of guilt and treated her abruptly. The look of hurt on her face was like a knife in his guts.

Florencia, Pablo and Valentino arrived, and they all set to work on the horses. As it was the last day of the show, Florencia was insisting that all the horses be plaited up. He had never plaited in his life, and so he groomed them and got out the tack and hung it over the doors, ready to go.

The speed class was first, so Rafael rode Shakira over to the practice arena. He wanted to give her the best chance, and he worked her in circles and over the practice jump for thirty minutes. She felt wonderful today as if she were two feet taller with more confidence. He was hopeful for their future together. She was the sort of horse with whom he could forge a strong bond. The jumps looked so much easier than yesterday, but there were some tricky distances and sharp twists and turns. It was the sort of course at which Shakira should excel.

They were all called in to walk the course, and he gave Shakira's reins to Joaquina who was holding Florencia's mare and Alano. Rafael marched into the ring and strode around, frowning in concentration and counting strides between fences. Valentino walked with him, occasionally making a suggestion, getting him to look back and see the lines that he would be riding. There were some tricky distances and with them all going as fast as possible, he didn't imagine there would be a huge number of clear rounds.

Rafael was to ride Shakira first. Although she was much less experienced than Alano, Rafael felt that he knew her much better after their success yesterday. The little mare felt sure of herself. They cantered around the practice ring and jumped the post-and-rails set up at the same height as the jumps in the ring. She was quick and light on her feet. They bowed to the judges and then galloped around and through the start just one second after the bell rang. Rafael didn't push her on, nor try and steady her, he just willed her to do everything he wanted, and she responded. They were going so fast, much faster than was desirable for a novice horse jumping in the ring but somehow, they pulled it off. They went clear and had the quickest time so far. They galloped out of the ring, and Rafael flung himself to the ground and put his arms around her neck. There were tears in his eyes. He felt so emotional.

Joaquina came over and shyly kissed him on the mouth. Florencia and Pablo were watching and grinned at each other. They had a wager on whether or not these two would get together. Rafael barely noticed, he was elated. Now, he felt that he would be able to ride Alano to the best of his ability. He mounted the temperamental bay gelding, he was just 16 hh, and very narrow. He was strange to ride; it felt as if there was barely anything beneath him, like sitting on the edge of a knife. He wrapped his legs around the body of the horse to the best of his ability and pushed him into a canter. The little gelding sprang forward obediently and then tried to gallop off.

143

Rafael sat down in the saddle and drew him into a tight circle, rather than pulling on his mouth and starting a one-on-one battle. Alano slowed his pace and Rafael chose to disregard this show of defiance. He pushed him into a canter again and this time turned him sharply to the left, straight ahead, and then sharply to the right, then around in a tight curve and over the practice jump. He was going to push him very hard today. He wanted so much to have two clear rounds.

He got his wish. Alano galloped around as if the devil were on his heels and they skimmed every jump. The horse seemed to know just how close to judge it, to clear the jump but not spend extra time in the air. They were half a second faster than Shakira had been. There was to be no jump-off, the places would be awarded on the basis of the fastest clear rounds. There had been five other clear rounds, but they had all been slower. Then Florencia galloped into the ring. She grinned at Rafael and saluted him. He smiled and half-waved his hand. He knew Florencia; she would be determined to beat him, no matter what.

The mare Florencia was riding was her favourite, a sharp little bay, no flashy white markings and not particularly well-put together but she and Florencia understood each other. They meant business and no mistake. Florencia leaned a little too far forward, but the mare went with her and jumped and galloped at greyhound speed. They beat Rafael's time by a fraction of a second, which put her in first place.

No-one else came close. Florencia was first and Rafael second and third. Valentino, Pablo and Joaquina sent up a huge cheer as they galloped around the ring. Rafael was grinning. He felt as if his mouth was stretched so wide it would never go back to normal. Joaquina was dancing up and down on her toes, waving her arms around like a little marionette on a string.

"Rafael! Rafael!" she squeaked at him.

He dismounted, and they embraced, their arms wound around each other. Shakira nudged Rafael in the back as if to say, 'what about me?' He felt as if he were flying on top of the world. As if every wish had come true.

The rest of the day passed him by as if he were in a dream. Neither Florencia, Pablo nor Valentino were placed in the important event. They were outclassed by the well-bred and expensive Brazilian horses, and some were even imported from the States. Florencia looked put out, but Pablo was gracious, he clapped and congratulated the winners and smiled charmingly. Valentino wasn't surprised. He wondered if he was getting too old to excel at this game anymore. He would leave it to the young ones, Rafael would do well, he was sure of it.

Chapter Twelve

Rafael returned to Uruguay, feeling one foot taller. His successes in the ring had given him such confidence in himself and his ambitions. Florencia, Pablo, Valentino, Joaquina and himself had seemed to coalesce into a group, perhaps a family he imagined if that was what a family was like. Joaquina was like a sweet, admiring little sister, although one didn't have sex with one's sister, he felt towards her as if she were that, a girl he had to protect. She wasn't like Phoebe, who had always seemed to have the upper hand when they had been together. And Joaquina was Uruguayan. She was one of his own kind.

Pablo's sister had been looking after the horses in their absence and alerted to their imminent arrival. She ran out to greet them.

"Rafael, Rafael!" she called. "There is a letter for you. It came by courier. It's from England!"

Rafael looked at her in astonishment. As if he had received a missive from Mars. The only person he knew in England was Phoebe, perhaps she had written to him about the money. Then that would be settled, and he would go on with his life in Uruguay that had taken on all the dimensions of a dream come true.

He didn't open it immediately, so sure was he that it would just give him bank instructions. He helped unload the horses, and as soon as they were settled, he went to see Rapture. For a moment, he forgot that the loppy-eared grey gelding no longer belonged to him.

Later, after the horses were unloaded and settled, and the gear unpacked, he sat down and opened the letter. He stared at it, written in large letters and signed by Grace; "Come to England immediately, Phoebe is in hospital and needs you! Someone will meet you at the airport. Please advise of your flight. Use some of the money you wish to give to Phoebe." There was a mobile phone number. He stared at it. It was the last thing he had expected. Perhaps Phoebe was dying of an incurable disease? There was no mistaking the urgency of the message, nor the tone which was commanding, to say the very least. He could see no way forward but to obey. He went in to talk to Valentino and breaking his usual rule of 'keeping himself to himself' he showed him the letter. Valentino read it and looked thoughtful.

"There's no other way *chico,*" he said, "you must go. Don't worry about the horses. We will be fine without you for a while. You must go! Get on the internet and book the next flight."

Rafael knew that Valentino was right, but he feared to lose his newly found tiny patch of heaven. What if he went away and Valentino found another rider, then there would be no place for him to come back to. He felt as if his life were no longer his own. Again he was being tossed by forces other than himself, helpless on a sea of other people's desires and wishes. It was as if a phantom of destiny, which he could no longer escape, had claimed him.

Phoebe had insisted that he investigated his Italian grandfather months before and had paid for him to get a passport, so within twenty-four hours he was sitting in the belly of an aeroplane. Inexperienced as a traveller, he had been placed in the centre of the centre aisle, and he was crushed between an overweight woman on his left, and a fat man snoring on his right. He had to choose which to climb over to get to the toilet. He sat there, trying to shrink down into himself and felt as if this were a metaphor for his life, squeezed between people bigger and more powerful than himself. He began to worry about Phoebe. Even if she were dying, he couldn't quite see why his presence was demanded. Did she want some comfort from her first boyfriend as she slipped away into the next world?

The minutes ticked by so slowly. He put his little monitor in front of him to the world map and watched the plane inch its way across the screen. He was able to change it to a view as if he were sitting by a window. Eventually, he could bear the close contact of his neighbours no longer, and he crawled over the bulky woman and went down to stand in a recess near the exit door. He could glimpse the earth below in a tiny window. He stretched his limbs and then ventured further down the aisle to the kitchen and took a glass of orange juice from a tray left out for the passengers.

He thought about Phoebe now, as there was nothing else to do. How did he really feel about her? He found it hard to understand. She had rescued him, and he had been grateful and also resentful of the fact that she had paid for everything. Selling Rapture had been his great sacrifice to buy back his pride and independence. Nothing could repay the way she had stepped in to save him, but he did feel resentful, as the objects of charity do towards their benefactors. If he were to be very harsh, and he didn't like to think like this, she had picked him up from the ground and dusted

147

him off, buying herself a boyfriend because there was no other way she could find one. He compared her to Joaquina whose divine, lithe body had twisted with passion beneath him. Joaquina was the sort of girlfriend that suited him, sweet, subservient, and above all *Uruguayan!*

He would do his bit, stand by the bedside, hold her hand and wish her well into the next world and then finally his debt of gratitude would be paid, and he could go back to his charmed new life at Pablo and Florencia's place.

He got sick of standing up and wished that he could lie down on the floor and stretch out and sleep. If he were rich, he could have reclined in those gorgeous seats in first class, but he was destined for cattle class all his life. Although really, how many long-haul flights would he ever take – it wasn't as if he was going to become a jetsetter. Being good on a horse didn't automatically shoot one to the stars!

Finally, they announced that passengers needed to return to their seats and fasten their seat belts as they were landing at Heathrow. London, England – the very heart of the western world - the aspiration of nearly every Uruguayan and ironically, he had come here under duress. Then he remembered how Phoebe had almost begged him to go with her to England. His mind filled with dark suspicions, perhaps this was part of her plan, she had sent the message, she was not in hospital at all. They would pick him up like white slave traders, in this case, olive-skinned slave traders, take away his passport and he would be trapped forever in a world of plump white people who thought they were better than everyone else.

He got through immigration with some rather searching questions about how he was to fund himself and where he was staying. He had a return ticket and gave them Phoebe's address which seemed to mollify them a little, but it didn't make him feel welcome. He carried his bag out of the gates and was faced with a barrage of people waiting at the barriers searching for their loved ones. He had texted ahead to say when he was arriving, and he was amazed to see his name on a large placard, held by a tubby man in a chauffeur's uniform.

He went over to him, and the man looked him up and down rather superciliously and led the way out of the airport. They seemed to walk for miles, and, finally, they found the car that was something silver with leather seats. Rafael slid into the backseat. He had no idea where they were going, presumably to the hospital. He looked out the window at the scenery flashing by as they rolled down the motorway. This was the land from where Carina had come, the place from which she had run and never returned. He wondered idly whether there was any point in trying to find her brother, Edward Broughton, he could do a google search. He found it easier to brood about Carina than contemplate what he was going to find at the end of this journey.

"Where are we going?" he asked the driver.

"The Radcliffe."

He sat there thinking whether he should ask him what was the 'Radcliffe', presumably it was a hospital. He was loath to show just how ignorant he was. He decided to simply wait and see, he had no idea where the Radcliffe was, but he knew that Phoebe's home was in Oxfordshire. They didn't drive into London but travelled smoothly along a motorway chock full of other cars, streaming in long rows, cutting in and out of lanes. He shut his eyes and went to sleep.

Finally, they came to a halt, and he jerked awake. For a moment, he didn't remember where he was, and then it came back. They were parked outside the entrance to a hospital – obviously the Radcliffe.

"We're here, out you get," said the man. Rafael reluctantly climbed out of the back door. He thought that probably the man would be expecting a tip, but he had no British pounds, just American dollar notes, so he thanked him and walked off into the hospital feeling the man's eyes boring resentfully into his back. He decided to go to reception and ask for Phoebe. They directed him to the Horton Ward in the Women's Services. He set off down labyrinthine corridors with confusing coloured Ward numbers and letters. Twice he got hopelessly lost and had to backtrack. Eventually, he got to the Ward that he had been told, Women's Services and then he realised, and he was amazed that it had taken him so long to get it. It was a maternity ward, obviously Phoebe was pregnant. This news was so overwhelming that he stood there his mouth open. People were bustling to and fro, and they flowed around him as if he were a traffic island.

He made his way to the bed in the ward, and there was Phoebe, lying as if she were dead with a huge distended pregnant belly. Her face was washed-white, and her eyes shut. He approached quietly, like a cat creeping towards a big sleeping dog.

"Phoebe," he said very quietly, whispering. If she were asleep, he didn't want to wake her. She opened her eyes and saw him looking down on her.

"Rafael, have I died?" she asked.

"No, you're in hospital, and I've come to see you, you are not well."

"Yes, I have high blood pressure, pre-eclampsia they call it, they're going to give me a caesarean but, they were waiting for a while, they want the baby to develop a bit more.

"Is it our baby?" he had to ask.

"Yes," she said smiling. "Who else?"

He believed her. They had never discussed taking precautions, he had presumed that she would have been doing that, although now he came to think of it, Phoebe was so innocent, and she had been a virgin, he should have asked, he should have checked.

"Are you going to be alright? Is the baby going to be alright?" he asked, wondering whether the note from Grace had been exaggerated.

"Apparently, it was touch and go for a while, but they think that my blood pressure has now stabilised. The baby seems fine. But how did you know, did you decide to come to England to find me?" she asked, her eyes full of hope. He saw then that she hadn't forgotten him, she loved him, and now her fairytale had come true. She thought he had come because he loved her.

"Something like that," he said wryly. "Why didn't you tell me you were pregnant."

"I didn't want to use it to make you stay with me. I wanted you to love me for myself, not just for the baby."

He didn't know what to say. He didn't know how he felt. He didn't know what was the truth.

"I sold Rapture for $15,000, so I've brought you back the money that I owe you," he said.

"Oh Rafael, but you loved him so much, why did you sell him?"

"Because I loved you more," he said, knowing that in truth he had loved the idea of not being beholden to her. No matter what, it was of paramount importance that he didn't hurt Phoebe. He felt very protective towards her. She might be rich and privileged, but she was so emotionally vulnerable, sometimes he thought she needed rescuing more than he did.

Grace came striding into the room. He had seen her before at Melilla, but he'd never spoken to her.

"Can I speak to you for a moment?" he said and walked out of the room.

"Phoebe thinks that I've come because I love her, I don't want you to tell her that you sent me the message, it would be too cruel, let her think that I've come of my own volition," he said.

Grace looked at him hawkishly. She wasn't in the mood to trust him, to trust any man; but he was right Phoebe might not thank her for having interfered in the way that she had.

"I told her that I've brought the money back to her that I owed her. She thinks that I love her," he explained.

"Do you love her?" she asked abruptly.

"I care about her and the baby. It makes the difference," he said.

Grace frowned at him.

"Just for the moment, we need to think of Phoebe, make sure she is not stressed, think of Phoebe, not me or you," repeated Rafael. Grace smiled tightly.

"As you say, it is Phoebe who is important." They went back into the room.

"When are they operating?" asked Rafael.

"Tomorrow," said Grace, "first thing in the morning, see the 'nil by mouth' sign there."

151

"Do we know if it is a boy or a girl?" he asked.

"It's a boy," Phoebe said. "I always knew he was a boy, a boy just like you."

If Rafael had had any doubts, they were gone with this announcement. He had to stand by his son. There was no choice.

"I will stay here with you tonight Phoebe. I want to be with you until the operation," he said.

Grace frowned but could think of no reasonable objection. She agreed to come back in the morning so that she would be there when Phoebe came out of theatre. Rafael pulled up a chair and sat down. He was utterly exhausted and disorientated. There was so much to think about but he knew that his place was here at Phoebe's side. She was to be the mother of his son.

Rafael fell asleep in the chair, and Phoebe woke in the night and turning on her side she watched him sleep. He was so beautiful, those long black lashes and his glossy hair. She thought that she would never see him again, and it seemed a most unlikely miracle. He really did love her. He had come all this way to England to find her. She was assured now, the operation would go well, the baby would thrive and he would have a mother and a father. She sighed and drifted back to sleep.

Grace returned the next morning, and she confirmed it with Rafael, that neither of them would tell Phoebe that she had contacted him. The story was that he had come to England to seek her out, pay her back the money and found her about to have his child. Uppermost in Rafael's mind was the imminent birth of his son. He felt a rush of pure love like a torrent gushing from a hole in the cliff. But there was an undercurrent, a grinding rumbling feeling that he was being swept along on a tide in which he had no choices. He would face this issue later, what mattered was the birth of his son.

He and Grace sat in the family room. They didn't speak. She flicked through magazines, turning the pages sightlessly. He sat perfectly still and watched out the window; a smooth lawn spreading across a park with the trees dressed in petticoats of pale green, silvery young leaves shaking in the early summer breeze. His glimpses of pastoral England had been just as he had imagined, much neater than Uruguay that was tattered, untidy and dusty in comparison.

Finally, a young, pretty nurse came in to say that the child had been born and was on a machine in the Neonatal Unit, merely as a precaution. He was doing well, and he would probably be transferred to his mother's room within twenty-four hours. Phoebe had not come around yet. The nurse took them down to see the baby.

Rafael and Grace followed the nurse. Neither of them spoke. For both, it was momentous. The baby would be a focal point in all their lives, symbolic of so many things. They gazed down at the scrap of humanity lying in the crib, connected to machines. He was quite dark-skinned with curly black hair sitting on top of his head like a parrot's crest. His eyes were shut, but Rafael knew that his son would be a mirror of himself, like gazing into his own soul. Grace was grateful that the child was healthy, but she was more concerned for Phoebe, her first-born. She felt uncomfortable with Rafael. He did not slot into any of the neat social categories into which she normally shuffled new acquaintances. She was careful not to show her natural disregard for a man who she thought had taken advantage of her elder daughter, but this was a measure of her own guilt for abandoning Phoebe while she pursued her own dream of freedom.

The baby thrived, and Phoebe slowly recovered. She was weak, and the hospital insisted that she not be released until they were assured that she was well. Rafael insisted on remaining at the hospital all day and night, and only grudgingly agreed to go back to Kiss Wood for a shower, a proper meal and a change of clothes on the third day after the baby's birth.

They drove through the Oxfordshire countryside with low stone farmhouses and fields bounded by grey walls. Rafael glimpsed country lanes and little old cottages with hollyhocks in their gardens.

"This is it," said Grace as she drove him up the driveway of Kiss Wood. Rafael stared at the huge mansion that was looming out of the faint-blue dusk. He had always imagined Phoebe's home as something rather grand, but nothing had prepared him for this magnificence. It was a dream-palace, the colours softly smudged like a French watercolour. There were long marble steps, pillared façades and sweeping terraces. Grace leapt out of the car and hurried inside, passing the statues of horses and warriors in marble and bronze, without seeing them. Rafael felt as if the statues were frowning at him disapprovingly, telling him he had no right to be here.

"I'm not sure where we'll put you, perhaps in the west wing where Phoebe lives, you can have the bedroom next to the nanny's room, which is next to the nursery."

"But why a nanny? Surely Phoebe and I can look after the baby?" asked Rafael, not understanding the traditions of the British upper classes. Grace looked at him and realised the yawning gap that he was going to have to leap to fit in at Kiss Wood. She hoped that she had done the right thing, summoning him in the way she had. Perhaps Phoebe would have been better off getting on with her own life and finding a husband from their own sort.

"Come with me," she said, her tone softened. It wasn't the poor boy's fault. It would appear that Phoebe had swept him off when she rescued him, and he had fallen in with her romantic notions to please her. But this was going to be a rocky foundation for a lifelong relationship, co-parenting the baby, whether they married or not. She couldn't foresee the future. She shrugged her shoulders. She would deal with it as it came. She led him through the endless twisting corridors, and he felt his head swimming, wondering if he would ever be able to find his way back.

"There is a separate entrance to the west wing as well as through the house. It is entirely self-contained with its bathrooms, and a kitchen as well. In the future, it could be used as its own house and the connecting doors with the main house could be shut off," she said to him in an attempt to reassure him that if he and Phoebe stuck it out as a family, he wouldn't have a dragon of a mother-in-law tramping at will through his own domain.

She left him alone to gather his wits, adjust to his surroundings and have a shower. He must be utterly physically and emotionally exhausted. She hoped he would feel comfortable, or at least tired enough, to lie down and rest before he went back to the hospital.

Rafael went into the bathroom and locked the door. Finally, he had some privacy. He sat on the edge of the bath. He had never had a bath in his life, only showers. He decided to try it. The thought of floating in warm suds letting the kinks in his body stretch out was too tempting to resist. He left his clothes in a smelly heap and slid slowly down into the warm water. He had never experienced anything so luxurious, the sensuous lap of the warm foam soothed his skin and his soul. He couldn't imagine doing this every day of his life, just as he couldn't imagine living in a mansion so huge. If he were to marry Phoebe, he would suggest that they moved to a small cottage. Undoubtedly, there were cottages scattered all over the estate. He was just never going to fit in with these people. But then he thought of his son. He would do it for his son. Although, when it came to it, he wanted his son to grow up Uruguayan in his own country. He sighed and let himself sink down under the water, wishing that he could drift away in a cloud of warm and caressing gentle water and never have to face the real world again.

The water cooled, and he hauled himself out and went through his bag, finding his only change of clothing. His *bombachas* were old and faded and confirmed his status as a peasant. He lay down on the bed, trying to gather the strength to tramp through the corridors and find Grace. His eyes shut, and he slept.

Grace peeped in at him later that night, as a parent checks a child. She stood in the doorway and watched him sleeping, his face was angelic in repose and boded well for the beauty of the child. Like many of her kind, Grace had been brought up on the notion of bloodlines and breeding, and she believed that every now and again the aristocracy needed to outcross to strong peasant stock, and in that way, Phoebe had chosen well.

In the morning she took him in a cup of tea. She gently pushed his shoulder, and he opened his eyes to find an older woman staring down at him. He shut his eyes again, thinking perhaps it was a dream and then gradually he remembered he was at Phoebe's home with her mother and Phoebe was in hospital with his newly born son. He sat up and thanked Grace gravely for the cup of tea.

"Breakfast is in ten minutes. I'll come back and take you down," she announced crisply, in a voice that didn't brook any arguments. "Before we go back to the hospital, I'll take you over to the stables."

He shrugged. There was no point arguing that he wished to return to the hospital immediately. The lure of the stables was strong. There he might feel more at home, and he was curious to see the set up that Phoebe had talked of so often. He was amazed at the array of breakfast foods set out on the sideboard in the vast dining-room. He was ravenously hungry - airport food and hospital takeout were not real food at all. He piled his plate with what they called bacon, which he called *pancetta*, and some bright-yellow fluffy scrambled egg and then a strange concoction that

155

Grace told him was kedgeree which looked divine with smoked fish, golden rice, hard-boiled eggs, onions, and laced with cream.

He sat down and began to eat. He remembered to keep his elbows by his side and his mouth shut as he chewed. He tried not to shovel, but he felt as if he were eating heavenly manna. If for no other reason, he would live in England to feast like this every morning. Grace watched him eating. He had an amazingly plum pudding accent and good table manners to boot. She wondered how he had picked up these graces, but she didn't wish to question him. She would ask Phoebe later; she didn't wish to appear vulgarly curious.

He went back for second helpings, and when he had finally finished, Grace rose and suggested that they go to the stables. He followed her obediently, like a well-trained dog. Not a friendly Labrador, rather a Whippet, lean, elegant and mysterious. She sensed his change in mood when the stable yard came into sight. She always felt like this herself, when she entered her own private fantasy land. There were more than twenty loose boxes arranged in a three-sided yard and in the centre of the yard was a beautiful statue of a girl jumping a pony. She had had it specially commissioned, modelled on a photo she had of herself as a child. She loved to look at it as if it represented her very soul, the child who had loved ponies and horses above all else. Now Poppy was growing up in her image.

"Do you think our boy will ride?" she asked in a sudden rash moment, revealing her secret desires to this strange, dark, silent young man.

"*Si,*" he replied, and then he smiled at her, and she saw beyond the sadness in his dark eyes to the passion that burned for horses. He was the same as her and Poppy, and now the boy-child. She smiled, and her face cracked a little, she didn't normally smile. She would have to take care that Phoebe was not excluded from their exclusive club.

At that moment, Poppy clattered into the yard on a skewbald gelding. She and Loppy had had a passion for skewbalds for several years now, and she had found a half-brother to Loppy's gelding, and she and Loppy enjoyed a friendly, but deadly rivalry in the junior show jumping classes. Her pony was called Harlequin, Harley for short, and he had a strange pattern of brown and white patches, that looked like continents across a map of the world. She liked to think that he was a descendant of The Pie who had won the Grand National with Velvet. Of course, these days Velvet could quite

156

legitimately have won the Grand National and not been disqualified for being a girl.

"He's being naughty today, ducking and diving around, but it's just his sense of fun," she said. Then she caught sight of Rafael. She stared at him in amazement, and he could see her brain ticking over. She couldn't remember exactly how she knew him, then her face cleared.

"You're from the Polo Club," she cried. "It was you they accused of stealing the necklace and then Phoebe produced it like a rabbit out of a hat."

He smiled at her. "You used to ride Tibbet. This pony is perhaps rather more handsome."

"I liked Tibbet!" objected Poppy, "but you are right, he was not exactly good looking! But what are you doing here?"

"He is the father of Phoebe's baby," announced Grace. Poppy sat there with her mouth wide open then she laughed out loud.

"But that is absolutely marvelous. Are you going to live with us as well?"

Rafael stood there, dumbfounded. She certainly cut straight to the chase. She spoke out loud the question that had been hovering like a mirage between himself and Grace.

"I thought we might put Rafael up on Tinpot," said Grace, with a small tight smile.

"Tinpot!" exclaimed Poppy. "Well I'm sure he'll manage him, but no one else has."

Grace had rung ahead, and one of the groom's had saddled up the stallion. He was a magnificent animal, with the best bloodlines but only just broken and something had gone awry. So far, he had thrown every one of the stable's riders, and Grace had thought that she was going to have to send him away to get him re-trained. It would be a baptism of fire for Rafael. She was setting him a test. If he fell off and broke his neck, then Phoebe might never forgive her, but she was anxious to ascertain the mettle of this young man.

Tinpot was truly magnificent, a top Royal Dutch sport horse, registered with the KWPN. Grace had gone to the Select Sale which was always held as a finale of the KWPN Stallion Show in Hertogenbosch with Oliver Soames, her neighbour and long-time friend. She had seen the stallion, then three years old, an unusual golden colour with black points, a dun like a Moorland pony but there was nothing ponyish about him. If he had a silver mane and tail, he would have been a palomino, but this was a rare and unusual colour. She had been enchanted, and Oliver had smiled at her enthusiasm.

"You should have him if you want him, Gracie," he had laughed. He had offered to be a half-owner as the stallion was sure to be expensive. As a girl, she never would have thought it possible that she might one day be in partnership with Oliver Soames. He had been the modern-day version of the 'deb's delight' in the early 1990s when she had been a girl, and he had never once selected her for special attention. He had married the most beautiful young woman of that season, Elvira and they had been the golden couple until she had died of breast cancer a few years later. Now Oliver's only kin was his son, Hector, who lived with him at Tall Chimneys, the estate that bordered Kiss Wood.

Grace had bid on the young stallion, and as the price climbed, she felt as if she were the one scaling the heights for the privilege of paying the highest price of the day. Now she and Oliver owned the stallion together. In a carefree, happy gesture, she had nicknamed him with the modest name – Tinpot. Of course, she could have paid Oliver for his share and kept the stallion for herself, but she was entranced with the notion of being in partnership with the wondrous Oliver Soames.

Then something had gone wrong, and she was responsible for the failed attempt at breaking in the stallion. This disturbed her deeply, and she was ashamed. He was the most magnificent horse that she had ever owned. She had not told Oliver, and she had prayed that no whispers had travelled from Kiss Wood to Tall Chimneys, telling him of her failure. Now Rafael had arrived and would perhaps redeem her, make good the mistake so she would not be humiliated in front of Oliver.

Rafael watched as the stallion was lunged in circles. He thought that it might take a lot of work with that big stride to get him to engage behind and achieve balance, that would match his natural athleticism. The groom got him to stand up so he could be admired; he had a long neck, a good

158

sloping shoulder and an uphill and balanced frame. But Rafael sensed that something was wrong. The horse did not stand there with natural confidence. There was something wrong in his spirit, something convoluted and untrue, hopefully only a temporary twisting of the psyche.

Rafael examined the big stallion carefully and tried to tune in to read his spirit. He was restless. and his back was up, as if he were barely broken, which was probably the case. He thought that Grace was setting him a test, and he had to prove himself. He was glad that the test was of his horsemanship, rather than throwing him in to drown at a cocktail party. He had found it hard enough to engage in conversation with the showjumpers when Pablo had introduced him in Brazil: how much harder would it be to talk to the British gentry. The saddle was a synthetic dressage saddle with a deep seat and pads within which his legs would fit neatly. He measured the length of his stirrup leathers running them from his armpit to fingertips. Grace noted his long legs and nodded approvingly. He could wrap those legs around a horse and ride more effectively. He was glad to see that the horse was wearing a running martingale which would give him at least a measure of control, he shortened it to its tightest hole.

"What is his name?" he asked.

"We call him Tinpot, that's his stable name," said Grace. "He has a much longer registered name."

Rafael was handed a crash cap which he buckled under his chin. They asked if he wanted an inflatable jacket and he declined, such things were almost unheard of in Uruguay. They walked in a group to a small outdoor arena which was circular in shape, with a thick, soft surface of rubber particles, and rubber wound around the tightly spaced rails. Rafael had never seen such a well-padded arena, and, certainly, it would make a fall less uncomfortable. He gathered up the reins and Tinpot's back hunched. He was going to buck. The groom held the stallion's head while Rafael vaulted into the saddle and settled himself with his feet in the stirrups. The groom let go of the bridle and took a few steps backwards, quite quickly - as if she didn't want to be caught up in the fireworks. She turned and climbed over the rails to stand with the other spectators.

Rafael sat still waiting. He knew that the minute he asked the young stallion for something he would react, explode like gunpowder which had been lit. Rafael waited and waited and finally, he closed his legs and tightened the reins, it was the signal for the big horse to bound forward, and he tried to thrust his head between his legs and bucked, twisting in the air before he landed. Rafael knew then that something had gone very wrong with this horse's training. He had learned to buck in such a way that he would be able to dislodge a rider. This was no light-hearted excess of good spirits, this was vicious, a fight to the finish. If he fell, then Tinpot would probably take delight in grinding him into the strips of rubber. Whatever had happened with this horse shouldn't have been permitted. Perhaps the person who Grace had employed to break in horses was not as experienced or clever as he or she should have been.

Rafael stayed with him, his long legs wrapped around the body of the headstrong stallion, who stopped and stood stock-still, every muscle trembling. Rafael knew that this was not a good sign. It meant that he was thinking of another trick to play on the rider and get him off his back. Undoubtedly this horse had cost an absolute bomb, how had he been so mishandled? Then the stallion threw himself against the fence of the arena intending to crush his rider between the fence and himself. Agile as a cat, Rafael stepped off on the other side, waiting for the stallion to recover his feet and then leapt back on and gave him a kick in the flanks, a short, sharp sign that this behaviour was unacceptable. Then, he knew that it would be a fight to the death and if he didn't win this time, then the horse would be unrideable for life. And he was such a magnificent animal!

He squeezed with his calves, wondering how much the horse had been taught about aids. The stallion took a few hesitant steps forward. He wouldn't risk leaning forward and patting him, just shifting his weight forward would mean another bucking frenzy, also patting a horse after massive disobedience at the first sign of good behaviour wasn't merited. They managed to walk around the arena, and he tried verbal commands. Often a horse was taught the verbal commands in the initial stages of his training. He tried the aid to halt, but the stallion seemed to have no awareness of how to react to the bit, perhaps he hadn't been mouthed.

Rafael was now intrigued. He loved a puzzle, working out what the horse was understanding, what was ill-temper or fear. This young stallion didn't seem afraid, but it was possible that it was bravado after a very bad experience. This problem wasn't going to be solved in one session, and even if he succeeded in mastering the horse in this instance, there would be a string of battles. They managed to walk around once more, and then he dismounted and spoke gently to the big animal who was now dripping

160

with sweat. He ran his fingers lightly down the centre of his face. Grace was watching carefully and trying to hide her elation.

"What has happened to him?" asked Rafael.

She grimaced then. "We put one of the grooms up on him, and there was no supervision, and it was a disaster. He's gone now, the groom, but the damage has been done. I blame myself, it was very bad management; I was caught up in," she paused for a moment, "a family situation."

"He will need a lot of retraining, and he might never be reliable and safe," said Rafael.

"Will you retrain him for me?" she asked. He looked at her solemnly.

"While I'm here, I will do whatever I can to help you."

"I'll stipulate that only you can ride him, see how you manage. Yes, it is muddy water, in which we find ourselves. Your situation with Phoebe is," she pushed back her hair from her forehead wearily, "unusual."

"I want to be with my son," said Rafael.

"Yes, but what about Phoebe?" she asked.

"I don't know, at Punta del Diablo it wasn't like real life, it was a dream, untested by reality."

"You are very wise for one so young," she said and smiled. "I believe that one way or the other it will work out for the best, for everyone."

He nodded.

"Now let's get back to the hospital," she smiled at him faintly.

She trusted him now. He was a miracle when it came to horses; he was honest; he was good and true. Undoubtedly, he would not only stand by his son but also Phoebe, but was that a desirable basis for a relationship. She shrugged, she had no experience of a good marital relationship, who was she to judge. On the face of it, Rafael was not at all suitable, but the mystery of human relationships was beyond her; she much preferred horses, and if it didn't work out then the horse could be sent to a sale.

161

On the drive to the hospital, she told him of her dreams. Tinpot's first progeny would be on the ground in the summer. Last year he had been bred to three of Grace's mares. She was longing to see what he produced and had had the mares brought in to the park where she could watch them from the living room, and also her bedroom window. If he was going to be good, then Grace wanted him to be linked exclusively to her stable, which she had recently named Blythe Star Stables.

She had dropped the 'Lester' out of her name which was David's original surname and returned to her family name Blythe. She had spent long hours trying to think of a name for her equestrian enterprise, and Star seemed a cliché, but it had a pleasant ring. She had thought of Kiss Wood but had decided that it should be separate, her own creation, not what she had inherited. She had contracted a company to build her website, and when they had asked her for a copy of the content she had begun to structure her dream; breeding show jumpers, clinics with the top trainers and coaches, a cross-country course where people could come and practise and her home would become a centre for the great and the good, and the young and the aspiring – the equestrian élite. It was strange how a website could represent a dream, made of words and images and clicks and links. She loved the idea of being at the centre of things, for so long she had been living on the margins of communities, ex-pats in foreign countries. Now she wanted to belong, and make her mark. And quite secretly, almost a secret from herself, she imagined herself standing by Oliver in the centre of their world.

Chapter Thirteen

Phoebe wasn't recovering as quickly as she should have been. The doctors insisted that she stay in hospital. They looked very grave when they were speaking to Grace. The baby was thriving, off the machines and looking around wide-eyed in his crib next to Phoebe's bedside. Rafael sat with Phoebe, holding her hand. No-one told him exactly what was her condition, but to him, it seemed that she was fading. What if she were to die? He couldn't face that. He cared so much for her. He didn't think he was in love, but he did love her, as much as he could love another human. Thinking that she might die put it into perspective.

Eventually, she began to regain a little colour in her cheeks. She was trying to feed the baby herself, but it was a struggle, and she gave up, and he was given bottle feeds. Rafael loved feeding his son. It gave him the warmest, surest feeling of love that he had ever experienced. Finally, here was a human being that was a part of him. He knew that his emotions were universal, that this bond was a part of the human condition but like every movie star interviewed about the experience of parenthood, totally irrationally, he chose to believe it was unique to himself. He would do anything for his son, that included living at Kiss Wood, marrying Phoebe, complying with Grace's every wish, even if that entailed riding a bucking bronco every day.

In a storybook, he and Phoebe would have married and lived happily ever after, had more children, moved into their own home and he would have gone on to an illustrious career in show jumping. But real life has a habit of winding and kinking knots in people's lives, throwing the unexpected at them in the cruellest way. To live happily ever after, is always an unrealistic expectation.

Rafael made no move to get physically close to Phoebe. He held her hand, but it was a gesture of care and affection, not passion as if she were a suffering elderly relative. They were quiet and gentle with each other. They both doted on the child. Surprisingly, Phoebe found that the tremendous all-consuming love that she had felt for Rafael had been transferred - in a single moment - to the baby. Now she was fond of Rafael, but that childish infatuation seemed to have disappeared. She knew that he loved the baby equally, and that was now the bond between them.

Eventually, she was released from hospital, and they all returned to Kiss Wood. Phoebe and Rafael lived quite happily in their respective rooms along the passageway, the baby, and even the nanny between them. Rafael had not been happy about the nanny, but he had no right to object. They had agreed on a name without a single disagreement, the child was to be called Marco Edward Pisano, which could easily be anglicised to 'Mark', or he could choose to be called 'Eddie' if he wished, and Phoebe readily agreed that he be called by Rafael's surname. Her mother having reverted to Grace Blythe left Phoebe in some doubt about whether she was Lester-Blythe, or whether she should also be just Blythe. She had despised her father's behaviour, but she still loved him and felt it would be too cruel and rejecting to stop using his name, even though double-barreled names were cumbersome and pretentious. Rafael was on the birth certificate as the father. There had been no quibbles over this. Now if Phoebe were to die, he would have rights.

Grace had suggested that Rafael be employed by herself, legitimately paying taxation and superannuation. In the unlikely event of Brexit actually happening he would then have a record of legitimate employment that might stand him in good stead if all Europeans were evicted from England. So, all possible 't's were crossed, and the 'i's were dotted.

Rafael didn't relish the prospect of being employed by Grace. It made him feel undermined, a mere employee, although Grace showed respect to all her staff, she never took advantage, she was a true Lady of the Manor, who looked after her people.

Having their relationship sanctioned, legitimised, somehow rendered it far less exciting. The romance and passion were effectively cancelled. Rafael threw himself into his new employment and worked far more hours than he was paid for. He continued to train Tinpot every day, also spending time with him in his box, taking him out for hand-grazing, sometimes free lungeing him over high jumps in the school, marveling at his tremendous scope over jumps of 160 cm. Rafael admired the big golden stallion, but he didn't feel the closeness with him, that he had had with Estrella and Rapture. There was a hard edge to the stallion's character that prevented Rafael from establishing a psychic bond with him.

There were no other horses for Rafael to compete on at this point. Grace had put all her efforts into acquiring show jumping ponies for Poppy. Now, that she had bagged herself such a treasure as Rafael, she would be happy to buy him some horses on which to compete. The more successes on the board for Blythe Star Stables, the quicker they would become a recognised establishment.

She took him with her around the country, and they looked at horses from deepest, darkest Cornwall to the tip of Scotland. Certainly, there were good horses, promising horses, and plenty of average horses which he might make something of. But he didn't find anything that he recognised with *that* quality, that special something that promised great things. He held in his mind an image of Estrella, the black mare who belonged to Georgina at Melilla Polo Club. She was the standard by which he judged all others. He wanted something as special as her. Grace was happy to stand by his judgement. She didn't push him to say yes to the others, some of which she thought were very good, but she was waiting for him to recognise that special one. There was plenty of time and money. There was no need to work a dozen horses a day to buy and sell and keep the stable going. They had the luxury of choice ,and at first, she was happy to go along with Rafael's quest.

Poppy was doing well. She didn't have that same psychic communication with her ponies as Rafael, but she was devoted to them and she was rampantly ambitious. She rode every morning before school and then again in the evening. The indoor arena allowed her to train no matter what the weather. Nearly every weekend she was away competing, and often Rafael and Grace went with her, as well as the two grooms, Angela and Ruby. When competing on numerous ponies, one needed many hands to help, holding ponies during classes, changing tack, making entries, putting up practice jumps and doing all the multitude of tasks that competing involved. Phoebe considered taking Marco and spending the weekend with them, but the horsebox, although quite luxurious, was small for all of them and she stayed home with her son, lying around reading novels and thinking about writing, but not actually doing it. She felt as if she had to live a bit of life before she could write about it.

The fruitless search for that 'special' horse for Rafael continued for several months without result. Poppy was competing every weekend, sometimes travelling from one show or competition on Saturday, to the next on Sunday. Finally, Grace decided that they were wasting time. It was now mid-summer, and Rafael needed to gain experience at events, real experience, not just hanging around the edges as a spectator. She went out and purchased two experienced A grade show jumpers. She thought that such horses would teach Rafael, and this would give him valuable experience.

One was called Micky a bay sixteen-year-old 16.2 hh gelding who was consistently placed, with plenty of scope but not enough speed to win often in the jump-offs; the other called Gunner a seventeen-year-old 16.3 hh gelding who had been competing for many years and had seen his best days, but was very reliable and an old hand at judging the distances: what is called 'seeing a stride' in show jumping circles. Both horses had been chosen not for their prospects, but as schoolmasters for Rafael. He still found it hard to take in his luck in landing a job with such a generous benefactor as Grace, not to mention a handsome, healthy son. Working for Valentino at Atlantida had been within his realm of aspiration, but this transportation to the very hub of the show jumping world and being given every opportunity to jump to the top still felt distinctly unreal. He hated himself for not revelling in his new life. It was as if he had been cursed with a disposition for sullenness at birth, and no amount of good luck would lighten his spirits.

Grace, on the other hand, was riding high in a new fantasy world of her own creation. She was waiting for Tinpot's first progeny to be born. The three broodmares were in the park, and she could watch them from the house. She would go out and visit them several times a day, taking them handfuls of stud cubes, and sliced apples, letting them feed from her hands with their velvety lips. They were all heavily in foal, and she stared anxiously at their teats, looking for the signs that would indicate they were about to give birth.

She would run her hands over the mares' swollen flanks; feeling the movements of the foals inside the mares' bellies. She loved the unborn foals with a devout religious fervour. Blythe Star's future would ride on their backs. She purchased three more good broodmares, this time selecting different bloodlines and Tinpot covered them immediately, that gave her a chance of six foals next year. At night she would lie in bed and imagine long lines of Tinpot foals, growing year by year, stretching into the future. Her breeding programme would be the most famous in the world. She would keep control of her own bloodlines. All colts except the very best would be gelded, and she would keep the best, and they would be part of the pedigrees that would stretch across generations.

The performance of Tinpot's progeny would be more important than the performance of the stallion himself. But, still, she hoped that Rafael would manage to train him and they could storm around the world and prove themselves in international competitions. Such was her obsession that she began to consider another stallion; to breed with the Tinpot fillies. There was a huge emptiness inside her, and she felt that the only thing to fill it were more and more horses. There was no-one to say, 'enough' or 'perhaps slow down'. She was the master of her own little world, and there were no checks and balances. Poppy was tied up in her show jumping ponies and crazy enough about horses to think that there could never be enough. Phoebe was still in her post-baby haze, and most of her thoughts were on Marco and what was left were on Rafael.

Grace wished that Rafael and Phoebe would declare themselves and then they could marry. If they weren't married, there could be no christening for the baby. The local vicar always stood firm on this, parents should be married, and to each other. Otherwise, it would be a 'naming ceremony'. Just the title 'naming ceremony' set Grace's teeth on edge, she felt uneasy in this brave new modern world, but she knew she had to accept it, there was no pushing back the waves of multi-media politically-correct modernity.

She told herself that this was one of the reasons why her thoughts seemed to circle so often around to Oliver Soames, the owner of Tall Chimneys and the half-owner of Tinpot. He was part of her girlhood, her life before her disastrous marriage, and it was as if she could press rewind. She counted the days between his visits to see Tinpot. Sometimes he brought his son, Hector. She liked to look at the son. He was as handsome as his father had been when he was young, and she would find herself transported back in time to her youth when she, like the other young women, had adored Oliver Soames with his arctic blue eyes that had crinkled so seductively at the corners.

Oliver had cut a fine dash as a young man. She remembered him before he was married as if it were just yesterday; young, dashing, handsome and winning point-to-points all around the country. He had been a consummate horseman. They had all adored him, and he had chosen the fair Elvira, a young woman same age as Grace. Their wedding had been the grandest event in the county with Elvira swathed in diaphanous white crepe with a simple circlet of fresh flowers in her flowing blonde hair. She had been

167

exquisite with an elfin grace that far surpassed the conventional beauties of the day.

It had been at that wedding that Grace had met David Lester. She had worn a stylish suit of red and white check and a small pillar-box hat, set at a jaunty angle with a veil. The excitement and the romance of the wedding had inspired her, and she had 'fallen in love', whatever that means. She remembered the day that David had proposed, several weeks later. They had gone out walking across the fields of thick, waving golden wheat, a peerless blue sky arced above them, a black crow circling and cawing. At the stile, David had held her hand as if to help her climb over, and then he had gone down on one knee below her, his laughing face smiling up at her; and he had proposed. She had been enchanted, and soon afterwards, they had married. Their wedding had not been a grand society event. David's people had been thin on the ground and not presentable so it had been a small wedding in the local church and then they had gone off on their honeymoon to Vienna.

Her relatives in the Foreign Office had secured David's first appointment, and they had travelled from Vienna to Berlin. She had enjoyed that time together, swept away on a wave of romance in an exciting city. She had felt that she was living on the edge of things. Then she had fallen pregnant with Phoebe. When she had been big and ungainly with the fat baby in her belly, she had witnessed David's charm as he practised it on other women and she had known then that marriage was never going to be a romantic dream for her.

So long ago, she felt as if it had happened to another person, not the woman that she had become. She had thought that she loved David, but she had known nothing. But now, she felt those same feelings towards Oliver, but she dared not show him, nor anyone else. Oliver's Elvira had died when Phoebe was five years old, and Hector was four. It had been a tragedy. She had faded away, struck down by breast cancer before treatments had advanced to the stage at which they were now. Oliver had never remarried, and as far as Grace knew he had not even dated other women. He had devoted himself to Hector and the estate and lived quietly. He no longer competed in point-to-points but he had encouraged Hector to ride, and his son had grown into a rather splendid polo player. Oliver lavished everything upon him, and he had at least a dozen top-class ponies and competed every weekend, and travelled overseas to play in Argentina and also the States.

168

Grace nursed this newfound fledgling passion for Oliver in secret. She had lavished her love and attention on Tinpot. He was theirs. They owned him together. She had to believe that this meant something. She hoped that the bad behaviour of the stallion didn't foreshadow the nature of her relationship with Oliver. It was true he often invited her to tea. But afternoon tea was not being wined and dined at stylish restaurants. It was the mark of a friendly neighbour. He had offered to go halves with her in Tinpot and so far, he had not availed himself of the opportunity to put the stallion over any of his mares. Perhaps he wanted to look at the first crop of foals before he risked breeding any of his own.

She wasn't sure that Tinpot would be a suitable sire for polo ponies, except that they weren't really ponies, they were Thoroughbreds, with a dash of Quarter Horse or Criollo. They all stood at least 15.3 hh, and most at 16 hh. She had never heard of a KWPN stallion siring polo ponies - but it was not impossible.

Whenever she saw Oliver, she made sure to wear her most stylish clothes, shifting subtly, but not too obviously away from the ubiquitous tweed. She would apply more makeup than she usually bothered with. She felt girlish flutters when he offered her his arm, she would take it, but she could not flirt. She had never flirted, and she had watched David flirting so often in their marriage that the whole exercise made her feel nauseous. She had dreamed of the possibility of putting together their estates. Tall Chimneys was a very pleasant property, not as grandiose at Kiss Wood but a thousand acres of land and a substantial house. She was impatient for Tinpot to start competing, not only would their names be joined as 'owners' but presumably he would come with her to the shows.

Chapter Fourteen

Rafael's first opportunity to compete in a British show jumping competition was a big event in Staffordshire. They were travelling there on Friday afternoon; Poppy, Grace, Rafael and the two grooms, Angela and Ruby. The stables were booked, and Grace had also reserved two hotel rooms. There were four single bunk beds in the horsebox, and also a kitchenette with a hob, oven and microwave. Grace liked to be organised, and she always made sure that there was a stack of ready meals in the fridge, cold drinks and the makings of endless cups of tea and reviving cups of coffee. Phoebe had said that she would travel up in her own car with Marco early on Saturday morning.

The horsebox rolled into the showground late in the afternoon. It was beautiful mid-summer weather with golden sunshine and a warm wind that caressed the skin, like a lover with a sensuous touch. Grace wished that Phoebe had come with them in the horsebox, perhaps she and Rafael could have wandered off into the evening and felt the stirrings of their first true love.

They unloaded the four ponies and the two big horses and led them to their designated stable block. Angela trundled the wheelbarrow stacked with buckets and sacks of prepared evening feeds. Ruby walked beside her making sure the load didn't slip. There were lots of other competitors milling around. Grace nodded to right and left and stopped to exchange pleasantries. Loppy Wade, Poppy's best friend, rushed over full of the latest gossip about which junior rider was riding which pony, and which horse had been sold to whom. Rafael walked alone. He didn't know anyone, and although he was an outsider, he did feel that this was his world and he knew that with time he would also be saying hello here and there.

Angela and Ruby took the wheelbarrow back and reloaded it with more equipment. Rafael opened the big packets of sawdust supplied by the show at an extraordinarily exorbitant price and began to make up the beds for the horses. He loved the smell of the fresh sawdust. Grace came in and raked over the surface. She liked to be seen as hands-on; she thought it gave her more credibility.

When the horses and ponies were settled, Rafael walked off to look around by himself. There was a big indoor arena with tiered seating, and a huge grass ring, and three other smaller arenas with the latest in surfacing material. There were competitors riding around the designated exercise areas. They all looked so professional and self-assured.

He remembered the last time he had competed, the only time he had ever jumped in a competition in Brazil before he had rushed off to England. He remembered Joaquina, he had never even said good-bye to her, and he had had no contact with any of them since he had arrived. It suddenly occurred to him that Joaquina might be pregnant, in the same way, that he had unwittingly impregnated Phoebe, perhaps the same had happened with her. He shook himself. He was being ridiculous. He took out his mobile phone. He would ring Valentino and make sure, set his mind at rest, and then he would concentrate on this competition. It wasn't that everything was riding on it, it was just a first step in terms of gaining experience, but still, for him, it was a big deal.

He pressed the numbers for Valentino's mobile. It would be the afternoon in Uruguay. Valentino answered, and Rafael asked him how he was and then told him that he was about to jump in his first British competition. He asked Valentino how things were going there. Eventually, he casually asked after Joaquina and Valentino told him she was working there at the weekends and she missed him, but she was now going out with one of the students. Rafael breathed a huge sigh of relief. He told Valentino to send his love to Pablo, Florencia and Joaquina and rang off. Somehow, this contact with Uruguay helped him to feel more settled. He did have somewhere to go back to, if everything here fell apart. He even had a few thousand dollars in an Uruguayan bank account. If he did have to return, he wouldn't be penniless. His heart felt lighter, and he whistled as he walked back to the horsebox. He was hungry and had grown very partial to the chicken korma and rice. Such spicy food, albeit extremely mild-spicy, was rarely available in Uruguay.

Angela and Ruby were in the horse box watching Emmerdale, and Angela was insisting that they watch in silence. She was a huge soap opera fan. He sidled around them and put his meal in the microwave and then went outside to eat it. He didn't understand the English predilection for soap operas. It was the same in Uruguay - people loved the Brazilian soap operas there.

Phoebe rang him on his mobile to ask if everything had gone according to plan. She wanted to make sure that they hadn't forgotten anything that she could bring up the next morning. She told him that Marco had finally settled, he had been tetchy for days with teething. She said she was looking forward to watching him the next day. Finally, he would get his chance in England. He thanked her gravely for her good wishes, and they hung up.

He couldn't really fathom the restraint between them, but he did understand that it was on both sides. He just couldn't feel like a man with a woman whose family was so rich, and he was the object of charity. If it wasn't for Marco, he knew that he would return to Uruguay immediately, back to what was familiar where he felt he had a legitimate place in society. He thought that Phoebe didn't want to take up their past relationship, perhaps she was embarrassed because he was so far below her in terms of social station.

He walked back over to the stables to check the ponies, and in particular to make sure his two competition mounts had settled in satisfactorily. Poppy was there by herself.

"Are you nervous about tomorrow, you are entered in the Grade A competition on both the horses?" she asked.

"No, not more than normal. They're both so experienced, and there's nothing riding on it, do or die, or anything."

"At least Phoebe is coming up to watch you," said Poppy, looking at him sideways. His face was impassive.

"Why don't you two get together, properly. I know that you both love each other," she said in a rush. She knew that Rafael hated talking about personal issues, but it seemed so ridiculous that neither of them could make the first move.

"She's the mother of my child, I love her for that, but she's not interested. We were stuck in a strange situation in Punta. There was no-one else for either of us. Now it is different," he replied. Then he walked away. Poppy sighed, as far as she could see grown-ups were hopeless at relationships.

Grace was probably more excited about Rafael's début in the UK show jumping ring than he was. On Saturday morning she chose to wear her best Fairfax and Favor outfit, a very smart suit of a tailored skirt with a matching jacket and a natty hat that matched the long brown leather boots and a satchel shoulder bag. She felt that Rafael would be the key for her entry into the mainstream show jumping scene. Watching Poppy compete brought on an almost spiritual excitement; there was something magical about horse shows and winning. Her intense preoccupation with her own Blythe Star Stables was such a wonderful contrast to the dull world of diplomatic conversation that she had endured for so many years. It was as if she had found the key to a mystical existence that she had known in her youth and then lost.

Two hours before the A grade competition was due to start, Grace saddled up Micky and Gunner. She sent Rafael into the horsebox to try on the new outfit that she had purchased for him. A tailored riding jacket, breeches and the most beautiful hand-made leather black boots and the very latest in crash caps.

Micky and Gunner were kitted out in beautifully-crafted, soft leather show jumping saddles with matching bridles. Grace bent down to put on open-front show jumping boots on their forelegs. She had recently put Gunner on a course of vitamins that would perhaps bring him back a vestige of his youth when he had been up there with the stars. She was hoping that Rafael's magic touch might inspire the horses to jump beyond all their previous abilities.

"Angela, come with me, I want you to lead Micky, I'll lead Gunner, and then we'll go up to the exercise arena. I want you to hold them while Rafael and I walk the course," Grace said.

"Yes, Grace," said Angela, who had been plaiting up Harley, struggling with his unruly thick mane, half brown and half white. "Ruby, can you finish this for me," she called thankfully handing over the cotton reels and thick needle.

"He's got this trick that at that exact moment when you need to secure the plait, he shakes his head," complained Ruby.

"He is rather clever like that," said Poppy, patting the smug, little skewbald's face.

Rafael walked over, looking resplendent in his new outfit. He would have liked to examine himself in a long mirror, but there was only a small mirror in the horse box, and he had to judge his appearance reflected in the expressions of those who looked at him.

"You do look flash," said Poppy with a big grin, looking Rafael up and down. He smiled at her wryly.

"I'm the soul of nonchalance," he quipped, attempting a casualness of air and stance.

"You're taking my staff, what with Mummy and Angela, poor me and Ruby are going to have to manage three ponies," went on Poppy.

"Come on, Rafael, which one do you want to warm up first? We need to get over there so you'll be ready to walk the course," said Grace peevishly.

"I'll ride Gunner first, just warm him up slowly, see how the old fellow is feeling today," said Rafael.

He checked the girth, tightened it a hole, mounted and rode off with loose reins. Gunner stretched downward with his neck, and Rafael patted him. He liked these old horses. They were unbelievably well-trained and such honest, old gentlemen.

He walked, then trotted around the exercise arena. Gunner had a lovely, long low stride, but he needed a fair amount of holding together when asking for shorter strides and quick turns. Rafael jumped him over the practice jump standing at over a metre, and he cleared it easily.

"They're calling for competitors to walk the course now," said Grace. He dismounted and handed the reins to Angela. He walked beside Grace, matching his long stride to her shorter steps. They followed the track, and Grace insisted on pacing out the strides with him and discussing every approach and every angle. He didn't mind, she knew a lot, and he was sure that he could learn something from her. Other riders had coaches and members of their entourage with them.

Thirteen obstacles in total. There were a couple of international riders, one from Germany, another from Ireland, which was good for the show as it was the height of the international season and there were any number of top competitions being held in Europe at this time. Grace was already talking about going on tour around Europe before the end of the year.

The time allowed was set at 375 metres per minute, so he would have to be careful not to get any time faults. There was one-time fault for every four seconds over the set limit. The last jump was a combination of three obstacles; the first two were two strides apart, then only one stride and over the third element. There were several fences that were perhaps seven or eight strides apart, curving around bends, this was called a 'related distance', and Grace suggested that they pace them out twice. He judged the most difficult part of the course was the wide triple bars and then just three very short strides to a combination of two upright verticals with planks as the top rail. For some reason horses often hit planks. He would have to put on a bit of speed towards the triple and then bring Gunner back for the short strides. However, in all, the course was fairly straightforward, with no real twists or difficult fences that presented real problems.

Rafael was due to jump on Gunner first and then he would warm up Micky. He suddenly felt nervous, the adrenalin flowed through him with a rush, it was all too real, and the fences looked enormous. He hoped the horses, not to mention himself, were up to it. He cantered around the arena several times, half-halting every five strides, trying to collect Gunner with a short, bouncy stride, waking him up sufficiently so that he knew that this round was important and he had to try his very hardest.

He rode over to the collecting ring, where the riders and horses were gathered together, waiting for the steward to call them to go into the ring. He watched the two competitors before him jumping, and he counted under his breath the number of strides they took on the related distances, 'one .. two .. three .. four .. five .. six .. seven,'. The steward called.

"Rafelle Pishano on Gunner, number 56," He winced at the mispronunciation of his name and cantered in and bowed to the judges, then they cantered in a wide arc towards the start, waiting for the bell. Up close the fences looked even more enormous. He felt his heart thudding, and his mouth had gone dry.

None of the previous competitors had had clear rounds. He wanted so much to do well, to justify Grace's faith in him and to please Phoebe. He could see her standing over at the side of the ring near the grandstand. She was holding Marco up so he could see his father, although it was obvious that the baby would never take in what was happening, at least they would be able to tell him that he had been there. Rafael knew he had to prove himself for his son.

Finally, he heard the bell, and he urged Gunner through the start. He had to make sure he kept up the pace, so he got no time faults. They cleared the first jump, and he felt a sense of certainty flow through him; he had a frame of mind that seemed to help him to maintain rhythm and pace, over the second and the third. He might have panicked. Thinking he couldn't remember the course, but he breathed deeply and maintained his concentration, knowledge filled his mind. The course was laid out before him, and he rode with confidence and technical accuracy and as he galloped through the finish, he heard the loudspeaker announce that this was the first clear round. He smiled, a wide smile like the sun coming out from behind thick grey clouds.

"Yay Rafael!" He heard Phoebe's voice ring out from the crowd, and he felt proud. This was his first clear round in England, and his family were supporting him. He turned that word 'family' over in his mind – he had never had a family before – it still didn't seem real. He felt as if he had fallen amongst strangers. He had been much more at home with Valentino, Florencia, Pablo and Joaquina. He wished that he could embrace this British family, but it felt too awkward. He was probably going to always be a black sheep with a chip on his shoulder. He sighed if only he could find it in his spirit to be bigger than that.

He did smile shyly at Grace as he left the ring. She was jubilant. She knew now that she hadn't over-estimated Rafael's skill. It was not the greatest test, he had been riding an experienced horse, but the course was a big one at a sizeable show, and he had not succumbed to the pressure. His ability was not a flash in the pan. He was a true horseman, and with more experience, he would go from strength to strength.

He dismounted, and Grace offered Gunner a slice of fresh apple which he crunched up, with a casual face, as if 'well what's all the fuss about!' Rafael checked Micky's girth and mounted. He needed to work him before his next round, which was about fifteen riders away. He was going to have to hunt Micky around today, there were some long distances, and he wanted to make sure he didn't clock up any time faults.

He walked him around on a loose rein letting him stretch down, then he trotted on a long rein and gradually brought him together. He graduated then to a 'coffin canter' stride, very slow and bouncy. Rafael felt relatively confident, after his perfect round on Gunner and perhaps that was why he was not careful enough. He brought down the plank fence and then he misjudged the curving related distance and brought Mickey in too close and hit that fence as well. Eight faults. Grace pinned a brave smile on her face and made excuses for him.

"That's the way that show jumping goes. Nothing is ever certain," she told him as if she had been show jumping all her life.

He had to concentrate on the jump-off now. Angela led Micky back to the stables, and he remounted Gunner, who should have been bouncing around on the glucosamine and vitamin additives that Grace had been stuffing into him, but seemed very calm and sedate. Rafael wanted to be by himself for a while. He needed to focus, so he rode to the far edge of the collecting ring, away from Grace.

They announced the jump-off course and the horse and rider combinations, who would be performing. Rafael and Gunner were to jump first. He rode back to Grace, who was quickly drawing him a diagram so he could memorise the shorter jump-off course. He stared at the piece of paper and then looked into the ring, imagining the way in which he would ride it. He could see several corners that might have been cut if he had been riding a quicker horse that could turn on a sixpence, but that wasn't Gunner. He would have to simply push the old horse on to gallop down the long side to gain as much time as possible.

He rode in, and he felt more nervous than he had, perhaps, ever been in his life. Taking a deep breath, he felt again a semblance of the sensation of certainty that had inspired him in his first round. He ran his fingers lightly down Gunner's neck. They were galloping towards the first jump. He didn't interfere, didn't try to balance the old horse, nor push him on or steady him, he just left it to him, and they jumped. He trusted this horse, which had jumped his way around showrings countless times. Rafael only gave the aids so that they followed the correct course and down the long side he leant forward a little and Gunner automatically increased his speed. They jumped clean and their time was good, perhaps not going to be the fastest, but it would put pressure on the others to beat it.

"Well done!" said Grace, smiling at him.

There were nine more competitors and Rafael dismounted and stood next to Grace to watch. He overcame the temptation to ride away and put his head in the sand. He felt like he had to behave like a professional competitor. The next combination galloped around at a tremendous rate, spinning half-turns dramatically but had the last fence down. Grace flashed a secret smile at him, just for a moment, she didn't want to appear a bad sport.

The next competitor, a tall thin man on an angular black horse with its ribs and hip bones showing went very, very carefully and clear, but he was a full three seconds slower than Rafael and Gunner's time. The third was a very professional Dutch rider on a majestic chestnut stallion with a bright shimmering coat. Rafael was sure that there was no way that he would be able to beat this magnificent combination. He watched in awe as the big horse leapt the first obstacle, touching the ground lightly, racing on to the next jump, making sharp turns and jumping the last fence at an impossible angle. The crowd gasped, and they were clear and two seconds faster than Rafael's time. So now, he was standing second, and there were still six combinations to jump.

The next combination had three fences down, then the following went clear but slowly, followed by another who had a refusal. Rafael was counting on his fingers now, just three more to go, and he was standing second. He almost screwed up his eyes so he didn't have to watch, but he didn't want Grace to see how tightly wound he was. He watched a hard-faced woman, her hair encased in a hairnet ride in on a flashy grey mare. They went fast and professionally, cutting corners but just tipped the rail on the second last fence. Rafael had been holding his breath. Slowly he exhaled. The next went clear and fast, a whole second faster so they were in first place, the Dutch rider on the chestnut second and he was third. Third would be fine if only this last rider had one down, or went tremendously slowly. He tried to remind himself that this was his chosen career, that this suspense and excitement was part of the thrill and he should be enjoying it! He suddenly wondered if he might be able to train horses, and even give lessons, and leave the competing to others.

The last rider galloped into the ring with a great flourish. It was an Irish man wearing a shamrock-green coat on a bright bay horse with a perfectly-shaped, white star in the middle of its forehead. They looked extremely professional and set off very fast, spinning around the short-cuts and then to the crowd's surprise his horse refused the penultimate jump. There was a collective groan from the spectators, and Rafael almost clapped, he was third. It was his first British rosette, and it was the dream of every Uruguayan rider to win in Europe, and he had done it! He could now die happy. Phoebe waved at him and made her way over.

"Well done, you're a hero!" she said and self-consciously kissed him on the cheek. For just a second, he remembered Joaquina kissing him at the show in Brazil, but that had been in another life. Now, his son Marco gurgled happily, and Rafael felt like life was finally beginning to take shape.

Poppy hadn't been there to cheer him on. She was over in one of the smaller arenas, warming up three ponies while Ruby juggled with reins. It was only a relatively minor competition, but to Poppy every competition was important. Her drive to win was indomitable. She was to jump Harley, Fleet and Sark. Harley was always erratic, but today seemed to be one of his good days. He flew over the practice jump half a dozen times with a confident, almost arrogant flick of his hind feet. He was dancing with the joy of life, and Poppy felt sure that she could trust him to jump like a bird. Fleet was a strong, bright chestnut gelding with no white markings and he was probably her most promising, although least experienced pony. She had been training him for two months now, and, he had performed so well that he was out of novice classes and ready to step up. Unlike Harley, he was always the same, reliable and honest. She liked him enormously and felt that with his scope, he had a great future. He was still a little clumsy and not quick on the turns in a jump-off, but she didn't want to push him on too fast in case he lost his confidence. Sark, was a little smaller than the others, only just reaching 14 hh, a light bay with a pretty white star. He had been mistreated in his previous homes and was extremely head-shy. Poppy had spent long hours trying to cure him, and Rafael had helped her. Rafael had the magic touch when it came to nervous and unsure horses. Sometimes Sark seemed better, then he would be back where he had been when he had arrived, 'never forgive, never forget' was the mantra learnt by horses from the moment of their birth. Once he was bridled and saddled, he would be confident, and lifted his hoofs over the jumps in an extravagant gesture, as if he had also been rapped as well as beaten around the head.

Poppy had timed it well and when all three ponies were well-warmed up the loudspeaker called for the competitors to walk the course. Usually, Grace went with Poppy, and they discussed angles and strides, but this morning all the others were watching Rafael. She didn't mind. He needed support, and she hoped with all her heart that he would do well. She paced out the distances between the elements and considered the course from the perspective of each of her ponies; they all needed riding in slightly different ways.

Ruby led the ponies around in a bunch and then tightened Harley's girth, he would be the first to jump. Poppy mounted and rode into the ring. She was the first competitor. She bowed at the judge and then cantered through the start as the bell went. Harley was such a jolly little pony when he was in a good mood, he flicked his heels, tossed his head and responded to the very lightest of aids. A clear round. Then Fleet who was more sober and serious and conscientious. Poppy had to make it very clear to him exactly what she wanted, she needed to help him judge his stride, and he obeyed readily. Another clear round. Sark was nervy, it was such a big event, and he swerved this way and that. He didn't like the brightly-painted flower tubs, and when the hooter signalled the beginning of his round, he leapt in the air. Poppy sat on him and tried to instill her own sense of purpose and confidence into the gelding. She felt as if she were holding him together between her hands and legs. Twice he panicked at the last minute and took off too early and brought down a pole with his hind legs.

"That's two in the jump-off," said Ruby. "You hold both of them, and I'll take Sark back."

"Are you sure you'll be ok taking his bridle off and putting on the headcollar?" said Poppy anxiously.

"I'll be ever so careful, I will take off his saddle and then slide off the bridle and leave him in the stable, he should be fine," said Ruby. "I think he trusts me now."

Poppy watched the rest of the competitors. She knew many of them at least by sight. She called out congratulations to those who went clear. One of the other girls came over to talk to her.

"You're without your supporters today?" she queried.

"We've a new rider, Rafael and they're watching him in the big arena. These two went clear. You're in the jump-off with two of yours as well, aren't you?"

"Yes, that's right," said the other competitor. "This afternoon's competition is the big one. I've got my best pony, Jigsaw, for that one."

"Yes, I'm entering Harley, this chestnut and also Bosley, he's a lively little grey, very pretty," said Poppy.

"Yes, I saw him at that agricultural show when he took exception to the merry-go-round," said the other competitor.

"Yes, he didn't quite cover himself in glory on that day. He's not keen on distractions, but he should be fine this afternoon, it's in the indoor arena," replied Poppy.

Ruby returned, and Poppy mounted Harley who was scheduled to jump first in the jump-off. She had carefully memorised the course and had decided to take a risk and attempt one turn, which left only two strides to the triple, which was wide and high. She knew that Harley was capable of this and she hoped that together they could pull it off. If she failed, then she would nurse Fleet around with a safe but much slower round.

Harley was still full of good spirits, and they bowed to the judges and then galloped through the start. Over the first three jumps, then in mid-air, she positioned herself for the sharp turn upon landing, then two bounding strides, and she felt Harley launch himself over the wide jump. They seemed almost suspended in mid-air, and, then they landed, and she heard no pole fall behind her, but she dared not risk a backwards glance to check. She pushed him on relentlessly, and they flew at full speed over the last of the jumps. Her time was very fast, and they were clear. She breathed out slowly and patted him gently. She hated those boisterous slappy pats that some of the competitors indulged in. Ruby produced some sliced apple, and he took it gently from her open palm and chewed it delicately.

"You are the best boy in the world, today," she said.

Poppy mounted Fleet. He felt so different from Harley. She was determined not to take risks, to ride around quickly but not desperately fast. She didn't want to encourage Fleet to begin to flatten as then he would hit the poles. The other competitors were going all out to beat her time on Harley, and they were crashing around recklessly. She rode clear and fast on Fleet. She won first and second. She rode Harley and led Fleet into the presentation, and the rosettes were fastened on their bridles. Ruby clapped and cheered from the ringside, and the other competitors congratulated her as she rode out of the ring.

She dismounted and loosened the girths, and she and Ruby led the two ponies back to the stables. The big class in which Rafael was riding was still in progress and Poppy thought of going over to watch with the others but decided that she would know the outcome soon enough and sat on a bucket in Sark's stable, feeding him grains of oats quietly from her hand, and gently stroking his face. She hoped that eventually, Sark would calm down and begin to feel more confident. If he didn't, then he would never make a show jumper, perhaps he could try dressage, less excitement and risk, and he did have lovely paces and a good head carriage.

She decided to take Bosley out for a walk. He had been cooped up in the stable all morning. She would take him over to the far side of the grounds and give him a chance to crop some grass; it would be good to stretch his legs. He was a lively little firecracker, probably the prettiest of all her ponies and he moved like quicksilver whether spinning in an arc to take the shortest route, or shying away from something he deemed terrifying. She hoped he would settle better if he had walked around a bit and had a good look at the other horses and ponies, the trucks, and the crowds. They stopped at one of the small arenas and watched younger children on small ponies bucketing around the course, running out, hitting poles and galloping between jumps.

They got to the other side of the showground away from the crowds and the noise. Bosley put his head down to crop the grass. They were next to a small deep wood, the cuckoos and nightingales were singing at their quintessential best. Poppy savoured her success this morning – first and second – it felt good. Then she scrolled through her phone and saw that Phoebe had put up a photo of Rafael with a third rosette on Gunner's bridle. She felt a surge of joy for him. He would be so pleased. He had come a long way from being a stable boy at Melilla Polo Club.

She led Bosley back to the stables, and everyone was there, milling around patting Gunner and congratulating Rafael and clapping him on the back. He looked embarrassed as if he wished he were not the centre of attention. She stood there, holding Bosley, letting the pony get caught up in the swirl of humanity, hoping that it would serve to further desensitise him.

"Are you jumping this afternoon, Rafael?" she asked quietly.

"I don't think so. I have to see what Grace says," he replied.

"Have you had enough excitement for one day?" she asked.

"And you, how did you go this morning?" he asked.

"First on Harley and second on Fleet," she said grinning.

"That is marvellous!" he exclaimed and gave her a swift kiss.

"Don't mention it now, I don't want to steal your thunder," she said.

"Thunder?" he asked.

"Congratulations," she replied, smiling at him.

"You know I don't like that," he said.

"I know," she replied.

The horses and ponies were settled in their stables, and Grace swept them all off for a celebration lunch at the most upmarket of the eateries on the showground. Rafael looked increasingly uncomfortable. Marco was getting tetchy and started whingeing. Ruby and Angela tucked into the delicious food with great gusto. They were enjoying being included in the circle of 'the blessed'. Phoebe was pleased for Rafael, but somehow every success he enjoyed with the horses seemed to sweep him further away from her. Grace was unaware of the undercurrents; she was riding high on her horse dream and just wishing that Oliver was here to see her in her moment of glory. She felt as if she had a shining halo above her head.

In the end, Poppy couldn't bear the fact that she had been pushed into the sidelines.

"I'm taking Bosley, Fleet and Harley in the big competition in the indoor arena this afternoon. You haven't forgotten have you Mummy?" she said loudly and plaintively.

"Of course not, darling. How did you go this morning?" asked Grace as an afterthought.

"First and second," said Poppy grimly.

"But that's wonderful!" exclaimed Grace, still distracted and didn't ask which pony had come first and which second.

183

"I'll be there cheering you on, Poppy," said Rafael.

"Thank you, Rafael, I'm glad someone cares," she retorted. She was tempted to get up and stalk away, but she wanted dessert.

After lunch, they walked in a mob back to the stables. At last, Grace seemed to remember the big competition this afternoon and then began to issue instructions. This infuriated Poppy even more.

"First, she forgets I exist. Then, she starts bossing me round like a five-year-old!"

"Don't worry. Can I walk the course with you?" asked Rafael. "To give me some more experience, to learn."

Poppy smiled at him radiantly. At least he understood!

"Angela, I want you to re-do Harley's plaits, that thick mane of his is impossibly bristly," said Grace with a note of haughty authority in her voice.

"No!" said Poppy. "He hates being fussed over, he looks fine. Leave him alone. He jumped very well this morning, and I want him to relax before the big event."

There was quite a crowd in the indoor arena, and the air was buzzing with excited conversations and laughter and the pinging of mobile phones. The surface of the arena was freshly raked and watered, and they were setting up the jumps. Phoebe sat on the bench with Marco minding the places of the others while they fussed over the horses. She was thankful to get a little time for herself. Memories of when she had sat in that ghastly arena at Melilla, the one that looked like a misshapen, space ship, swept through her mind. The sand had not been watered, she had been so fat, and the sweat had run down over her ripples of flesh. Claudia had been there in her cloud of stinking perfume sleazing up to her father. She shook her head as if to clear it of these unpleasant memories. Now it was a different arena with the newest and most modern of comfortable seating, controlled temperatures, and she was thin! Also, a mother and if only she and Rafael could somehow recapture that 'being in love' then life would be perfect.

They had finished building the jumps, and the competitors came in to walk the course. Poppy was flanked by Grace and Rafael, and they all had their heads together pointing out 'lines' and discussing 'strides'. Eventually, Rafael made his way over and sat beside Phoebe. Grace was determined to continue to direct the action from the collecting ring.

Poppy rode in on Harley. She was the fifth rider to go and so far, there were no clears. Rafael was watching intently as if he were jumping every obstacle with her. Phoebe felt as if she were outside the magic bubble, watching everything from a distance. Poppy jumped clear, and Rafael stood up and cheered and then was loping down to the exit to congratulate her. Phoebe clapped automatically.

There were endless rounds to go before Poppy came in again, this time on Bosley. Phoebe knew enough about the ponies to know that this was important. Bosley had to prove himself after some disastrous mistakes when he had freaked out over the noise from the sideshows some weeks ago. He came dancing in. He certainly was a beautiful animal, thought Phoebe. Rafael had suggested that they dye his mane and tail black, which gave him a very dramatic appearance.

They cantered over to bow in front of the judges. Then Poppy cantered him on a short rein in a wide arc, heading for the start. They were through, and he was not moving correctly, dashing a bit sideways here and there, and Poppy's face was red with the effort of trying to keep him straight. He could jump alright, there seemed no chance that he would hit a pole, but going so high in the air over the jumps and not going in straight lines would count against them. Somehow, they made it round, but they had one-time fault, and as there were already eight clear rounds, it meant they wouldn't make the jump-off.

Phoebe could see Rafael and Grace standing by the exit as Poppy galloped out, her face grim with disappointment. She and Rafael were talking together, and Grace was fussing around the pony. Phoebe felt more out of it than ever. She just couldn't find the necessary enthusiasm for this activity. She saw her life stretching before her, soon Marco would grow up, and then he would be competing, and she would be sitting on the sidelines watching them all follow their obsessions. She sighed. Why did humans always want more? She should be content with what she had.

Poppy rode Fleet in soon afterwards, but somehow her spirit seemed dampened, and this affected the chestnut gelding who ran out at the third jump. Phoebe sighed. She knew this was a very bad error and thought that Poppy and Grace would be carrying out a post-mortem for days to come.

In the jump-off Poppy galloped in on the crazily-marked Harley and they bucketed around at the speed of light. This made Harley careless, and they had a pole down, so Poppy was relegated to third. She wouldn't be pleased, only winning made her happy. Phoebe sighed for her little sister.

Chapter Fifteen

They returned to Kiss Wood with their rosettes festooned across the windscreen, although Grace had muttered that this was in bad taste, Poppy had prevailed. Then they would be pinned up in the 'recreation room' in the stables that was next to the tack room. This room was specially designed for the comfort of the stable staff. There was an inner circle of squashy leather sofas, draped with warm rugs and soft cushions. A wood stove burned in the centre of the room throughout the winter, - the warm heart of the stable yard.

It was here that the stable staff took their breaks, and stayed through the nights when there were sick horses that needed continual twenty-four-hour care. The young grooms gossiped, argued, exchanged banter, and confided in each other. There was always cake in the tin, to be carved up in hunks and eaten with the endless cups of tea and coffee.

The day after the show Rafael had risen early and ridden Tinpot alone in the school. The stallion was as rebellious and recalcitrant as always, even more so perhaps as he had had two days without work snorting and cavorting around the field, calling out to the mares that were heavy with his foals in the park. Rafael preferred to fight his battles with the golden stallion in private, especially since he had sensed that Jamie Landon resented his presence. Jamie had originally been employed not only as the stable manager, but also to train, and later compete on Tinpot when he was ready, and Grace had also promised him the chance to break in and train Tinpot's progeny. By sheer bad luck, he had commenced his employment one day after Rafael had first ridden Tinpot, so he had lost his chance with the stallion. He had been usurped by Rafael.

Jamie had thought that he might be able to scrape the money together to buy himself his own horse and Grace had agreed that he should have the keep of one horse that he could take to the shows. Everything had gone wrong with the drama of Rafael's arrival, and Jamie in a fit of pique had returned to his past bad habit of gambling, not on horse races, as one might have expected, but on the currency markets. He had lost his savings, and now he was sunk in a dismal state of despair. He could not believe he had been so stupid again, and he wildly resented Rafael and felt that Grace had betrayed him. The latest ignominy was that when the others went off to the shows, he was forced to stay behind as if he were the least important of the stable's employees.

Grace had done nothing but publicly defer to Rafael and then she had bought him the showjumpers to give him experience. Jamie had bucketfuls of experience competing in shows, but he had had no fairy mother-in-law to shower horses upon him to keep him sweet.

Rafael's position in the stable was not clear cut. As the father of Grace's grandson, he was obviously family and he lived in the big house, but he was officially employed on a groom's wage. Jamie saw that Phoebe and Rafael were not a real couple; there was an unmistakable distance between them. He had wondered for just one minute if he could romance Phoebe away from Rafael and marry her himself, and then he might be the golden boy, but he was not the romantic kind, and she was far too young for him. Jamie kept his cards close to his chest. He was not one to display his feelings to the world. He had learnt that lesson during his harsh childhood. He was now forty years old, and he knew that he was good with horses, but he had never had his chance to shine. He was not malevolent like Facundo, nor a mindless follower like Tomas, but he was no friend to Rafael. He stood back and wished the young man would fall on his elegant bottom and go back to where he came from. Jamie was not malicious or treacherous, but he had a very large chip on his shoulder, and his negativity turned inwards on himself and led to thick, black depression, from which he could not escape, it was as if he were wading through treacle.

Rafael was probably the only person who took a moment to understand Jamie's feelings. He wished he could befriend him, assure him that he might still have his chance, but he had no facility for friendship, and he felt that his own position at Kiss Wood was tenuous and unsure. It had not been so long since he had been in a worse position than Jamie, his talent totally unrecognised when he had worked as a stable boy at Melilla. Thus, it was on the day after they had arrived back from the show after he had survived another training session with tempestuous Tinpot, he went into the recreation room and cut himself a big slice of cake and made a cup of coffee. He sat down on the couch so he could view his single rosette pinned to the wall and began to brood. He was getting nowhere fast with Tinpot, and he had begun to dread every training session. He wished that he could somehow arrange for Jamie to get an opportunity to ride the stallion, but he didn't have much confidence in himself being able to persuade Grace to give the older man a chance.

Then he heard Grace's voice outside.

"Jamie! Jamie! Come quickly!"

Rafael went to the doorway and looked out. Something must have happened.

"The chestnut mare, she has foaled! The alarm didn't go off. It's the middle of the day, and she's done it herself!" she called.

Jamie laughed, "Perhaps she knew better than us!"

Rafael watched from the door of the recreation room. It was the first time he had heard Jamie Landon laugh. It was a low-pitched, dry laugh, similar to Grace's.

"What is it?" asked Jamie.

"I don't know, I didn't look, it is big, and it is golden."

"Come on, let's go!" said Jamie moving quickly across the stable yard and towards the park.

They strode together. Grace matched his stride. Rafael followed behind. He was curious to see Tinpot's first foal.

It was a colt, tall, standing up proud and shining in the afternoon light that streamed through the green leaves of the oak trees. His coat was pure gold and shone like a sculpture made of gilt.

As the small phalanx of humans approached, he looked at them boldly, then took off at a gallop around the park, leaping into the air like a young gazelle. His mane and tail were almost the same golden colour of his coat, perhaps a shade or two darker.

"He is beautiful," breathed Grace, staring at him as if she were bewitched.

"He is a good, strong, healthy chap," agreed Jamie.

Grace walked up to the big chestnut mare and went behind her and lifted her tail.

"We should bring her in, and clean her up and then perhaps the vet can come and make sure she has got rid of the afterbirth. We will put Tinpot

189

back over her in a few days," said Grace. "This is the beginning. You do understand Jamie."

He nodded to her gravely. Once the chestnut mare and her son were safely installed in the foaling box, they stood and watched the colt suckling.

"Look at that rump, those shoulders, those strong legs," said Grace.

Rafael came over to watch as well, standing back a few paces.

"Would you mind bringing the other mares in, they will probably foal tonight," said Grace.

"Of course," said Rafael, turning on his heel to collect the headcollars and walk back to the park.

"What shall we call him?" asked Grace.

"He will have the prefix Blythe Star?" asked Jamie.

"Yes perhaps, or just Blythe, perhaps Blythe Bliss," said Grace.

Phoebe had joined them now.

"Suitably alliterative," she murmured, but no-one listened.

The other two mares, one chestnut, the other brown both gave birth that night. They had fillies, pretty, good-looking, with almost faultless conformation, but not splendid like Bliss. Nor were they golden, one was a light chestnut with flaxen mane and tail, the other brown with no white markings. There was only one golden foal, Bliss - the only son of Tinpot. He was destined to be the ruler of Blythe Star kingdom.

"There will be no mistakes with Bliss, not this time," said Grace in a determined voice.

The staff were now overworked. There were Poppy's six show jumping ponies, the A grade horses Gunner and Mickey, three mares and three capricious and demanding foals, and the arrogant, rebellious Tinpot. Grace insisted that the mares come in every night and they would be put out during the day. There was a cold tang in the air now, and winter was coming. The leaves were russet and yellow and came drifting down and swirled around the stable yard. One member of staff was always wielding a broom.

Jamie and Rafael worked hard, as did Angela and Ruby but Grace knew that at least one more member of staff was needed. She contacted an agency, and they sent her a clutch of resumés. She looked through them and couldn't make up her mind. She thought perhaps another man, and, finally, she picked one, a young chap who had done some eventing, and wanted to bring his own horse as part of the deal. He came to be interviewed, and she and Jamie talked to him. His accent was definitely working class, and he had worked at a local riding school in the north and gained experience, rescued an ex-racehorse that had been left abandoned in a field full of ragwort and only puddles for water, and trained him up.

The riding school where he had worked had closed. Now, he needed a new place to take his horse. He promised to work all hours and asked for the opportunity to study for his BHS (British Horse Society) qualifications. His name was Jerome Bradley, and he was nineteen-years-old. He was not a handsome man, rather plain and ordinary with a freckled face, but he was well-built and strong.

Ruby and Angela were rather interested in this new member of staff. They took him in hand and initiated him into the ways of the stable, laughing and mocking him, flirting and frolicking around. He took it with stolid equanimity, but he had no real sense of humour, and the girls soon stopped flirting with him. He was very serious, and he took himself very seriously. Grace was pleased with him. He was a hard-worker, extremely conscientious and strong as an ox.

Jamie liked the young man because he was hard-working and wanted to learn. He was a good rider, perhaps not extraordinarily gifted in the same way as Rafael, but what he lacked in flair he made up for with honesty, and he had no propensity for gossiping or trouble-making.

Rafael neither liked, nor disliked Jerome. It was the thought of Jamie that preyed on his mind. He knew that the older man watched him when he was riding Tinpot. Rafael had a finely developed sense of natural justice and knew what he had to do. The next day Rafael led Tinpot into the indoor arena and seeing Jamie's shadow by the tiered seating he called out.

"Hi Jamie! Come here! I want you to ride him today. I want to watch. I think we need a new strategy."

"Yes," said Jamie brusquely striding forward.

"Would you ride Tinpot this morning?" asked Rafael again. He knew that he had sounded like he was giving orders, but he was on shaky ground and had tried a display of bravado to carry it off.

"Alright," Jamie replied. "But what about Grace, what does she say?"

"I'll tell her when we see how he goes for you," said Rafael prepared to take all the responsibility if this didn't work out.

Jamie had watched Rafael with his horse-whispering tactics, and he knew that such methods worked with many horses, but it was never really going to master this stallion, who thought he was the king of the world. He needed to be taught a few sharp lessons, and then perhaps he would submit his indomitable will to the humans that owned him.

Rafael hung back, and Jamie led the stallion into the centre of the arena. He checked the girth and adjusted the stirrup leathers. Then he vaulted into the saddle and slid his feet straight into the stirrup irons. Tinpot still liked to begin his training sessions with a savage buck or two, just to make things more interesting and this afternoon was no exception. As Tinpot went to put his head between his legs and hunched his back, Jamie put the shortened reins in one hand, and with the other, he gave him an almighty whack down the flanks with the training whip. Tinpot threw his head in the air and snorted in disgust. This was not the sort of behaviour that he was used to! Rafael smiled at this, perhaps Jamie was right, someone did have to tell Tinpot in no uncertain terms who was the boss. Horses' social relationships are organised in a vertical hierarchy, be the boss or be bossed.

Jamie sat still for a minute and then gave a very clear, firm leg aid with a verbal, 'walk on'. Tinpot dropped his head subserviently and walked forward, but he was not relaxed. He swished his tail, and his ears were laid back. He looked malevolent. Jamie didn't wait for another negative reaction. He gave him an indisputable, firm aid to canter. Tinpot leaped forward and began to career around the arena, dropping his shoulder, cutting corners and trying to duck his head down between his knees again. Jamie didn't tighten or loosen his reins but drove him on with his seat and steered him in a circle with the strength of his legs. Tinpot obviously wasn't happy. This wasn't going the way he wanted at all. Usually, Rafael would cajole him and persuade him to go where he wanted, but this man was different, he was indisputably the boss.

Tinpot began to falter a little, he had been bucketing around for at least ten minutes, and the sweat was dripping off him. Half a dozen times he had attempted evasive manoeuvres but Jamie was implacable. Now, that the big horse wanted to slow down Jamie drove him on and taking up the reins he began to twist him one way then the other, making him halt, rein back and then go forward again into the canter. After that, he pushed him into a strong sitting trot and made him do 15-metre circles. He was asking a lot of a horse that was barely trained in the basics, but it seemed to work. Tinpot was now accepting the discipline and half-heartedly trying to perform as his rider was asking. Jamie made him halt and stand for two full minutes and then jumped off.

"Bravo! Bravo!" said Rafael. "You did very well. Now he knows who is the boss!"

Jamie looked at him and thought, 'well I've done the work now you can take the credit'. But he misjudged Rafael's sense of honour and innate honesty.

"Don't worry I will tell Grace that it is you who cracked the nut, as the English say," he said and flashed a quick smile. They led the stallion back together and washed him down, scraped him dry and put a light sweat rug on him and walked him around quietly for ten minutes before putting him back in his stable.

"I will suggest to Grace that you ride him every day, and I will watch and learn," said Rafael. "He'll be jumping very soon now at the rate you train him." He hoped he wasn't laying on the flattery too thick. Jamie smiled at him disbelievingly, he didn't know whether to trust him or not. He would wait and see before he started to believe that this might be the chance that he needed.

Chapter Sixteen

The day after Jamie had ridden Tinpot, Phoebe received a distraught phone call from Tate.

"Oh, Phoebe darling, I'm in a fix. I've just lost my purse with all my credit and debit cards, I'm afraid I was out partying last night, and they somehow disappeared. I'm due to fly out from Heathrow early this afternoon, and I don't have a bean. I was wondering if you could lend me a wedge of cash to take with me, I am in such a fix. I'm due in Miami tomorrow for a photoshoot."

"That's fine," said Phoebe. "You have reported them all missing, haven't you?" she asked anxiously.

"Yes, yes, I'm about to do it, but how can you get me the cash. Could you possibly drive to London and then take me on to the airport. I can't even catch a cab with no funds, and there's no-one I know in London who gets up before mid-afternoon."

"Of course, no problem. And better than that I can lend you US dollars, I've oodles of them, in a plastic bag in the bottom of my wardrobe."

"Really! But why?" asked Tate. "Never mind, I'll jump in the shower you drive down here and pick me up."

"Of course, darling," said Phoebe. She always found herself imitating Tate's extravagant showbiz-type language, and it made her wince. She never normally talked like this, just with Tate.

"I'll text through your number plate and make sure you can park in the residential parking outside my flat," said Tate.

"It's fortunate you didn't lose your phone," said Phoebe laughing.

She grabbed the plastic bag at the bottom of her wardrobe that was full of dollars that Rafael had thrust upon her on the day when she had returned to Kiss Wood from the hospital. She went in to see the nanny and told her that she had to dash to London. Dragging a brush through her hair, shrugging on a light jacket, thrusting her feet into a pair of flat shoes she ran down the stairs and out the front door to her car which was parked in the driveway.

The drive down to London was not too bad. The worst of the commuter traffic had dispersed. She parked outside Tate's flat, wondering what it must be like to live in London, in the midst of so much humanity packed into the busy streets and houses and flats standing like sentinels side by side. Tate flung open the front door, "Phoebe, my saviour!" she cried dramatically.

Phoebe smiled up at her and held up the plastic bag.

"Oodles of yank cash!"

"Come in, come in," said Tate. "Coffee is on the hob."

Phoebe handed her the plastic bag in exchange for a mug of hot coffee, just the way she liked it. Tate was good like that she remembered the small details, even if she was somewhat lax about the big things. Tate tipped the contents of the bag on the floor and sat down to arrange the bundles in neat piles.

"Darling, where did you get this?" she asked.

"When Rafael came to find me, he brought it with him, to pay me back for his rent and stuff like that, and of course the horse. He actually sold his horse to pay me back, doesn't that show he loves me?" she asked, wincing at the way she sounded pleading and pathetic.

"What is this?" asked Tate, holding up a sheet of much folded paper, hidden amongst the dollars. She opened it out and read it aloud.

"Dear Phoebe, I have the money that I owe you, please can you send me bank details and I will send it to you."

"What is that?" asked Phoebe. She could hear the distant clang of truth, and she suddenly felt very afraid.

"It is signed by Rafael, and there's another one here." Tate opened it out and scanned it. "It's from Grace. This seems to be an exchange of notes from Rafael to you, and then your mother has replied. Did you not get the first letter? It is dated back in April."

195

"I must have been in hospital," said Phoebe very slowly. "Let me see it," she scanned the note. "It is from Rafael just wanting my bank details. Obviously, he didn't know I was pregnant. The note from my mother, give it to me.

"Come to England immediately, Phoebe is in hospital and needs you! Someone will meet you at the airport. Please advise of your flight. Use some of the money you wish to give to Phoebe."

Phoebe stared into the distance. This was the truth, the cold, harsh, bitter truth. Grace had summoned Rafael, and that was why he had come to England, not because he couldn't live without her. He had arrived and then Marco was born, and of course he couldn't leave, he had a son, who he loved above all else. He didn't love her at all. It had started out as need, not having any alternative, and now it was because of the child. He had never loved her; he would never love her. Certainly, he was fond of her, but suddenly that wasn't enough, if he didn't love her then she didn't want to be with him. She stared into the distance. Her world was fragmenting into cold, harsh pieces that could never be put back together in any sort of satisfactory pattern again.

"Tate," she cried, looking so tragic that Tate threw her arms around her.

"My darling, it's not that bad. He didn't have to come. He came because he cared for you."

"But neither of them told me. They colluded in the myth that he had come because he loved me. They lied, they both lied, they deceived me."

"But Phoebe you were so ill and then it must have seemed the best solution, to make you happy, so that you and Rafael could be together."

"But we're not together. He lives down the passageway. He is polite, he is respectful, he is even kind, but he doesn't love me. I knew there was something amiss. I knew it. I knew it." Then Phoebe broke down into heart-breaking sobs, wracking sobs that seemed to shake her to the core.

"Oh, darling. You're such a dreamer. True life isn't like that. There really is no true love, believe me, I know," said Tate. "Lovers come and go, and come and go, but at the very core of things, we are always alone. Perhaps having children is different, I don't know."

196

This was an unfortunate idea as it had been her mother who had betrayed Phoebe as badly as if she had thrown her to the wolves. Deceiving her that Rafael loved her when really it had only been duty, never desire.

She flung herself on Tate's sofa and began to rock herself. She remembered now when she had lain in the dust outside the cottage at Punta and had wished that Rafael would come outside to fetch her. But he hadn't come. She had been utterly alone.

"I won't go, I'll ring and say I can't come. I can't leave you like this," said Tate.

"Oh no, Tate, you mustn't. I'll drive you to Heathrow. Take all the money I don't want any of it. I didn't even count it. Perhaps it is $10,000 minus the airfare," she said bitterly.

"Phoebe, darling, he's a good man. He didn't have to pay you back. He came all the way to England. He's stayed with you. Do you mean that you and he haven't resumed your relationship since he has come back?"

"No, first I was sick, and then after having a baby, and then he didn't make a move, nor did I. There's been this sort of restraint between us. Then I began to think that perhaps he had been responsible for the murder of those horrid men, but he told me he knew nothing about it, beyond what was on the news. The fear was growing in my mind. I thought that this was the thing between us. Now I know that it was all based on my mother manipulating the situation."

"But your mother has welcomed him into the house. She's given him a job, a quite brilliant job."

"Yes," said Phoebe, "but she hasn't just done it for me, or even for him, it's her obsession, horses, horses, horses she wants him because he is such a good rider. I'm just the convenient broodmare and no doubt she loves Marco because he will grow up to be a brilliant rider. It's all for the love of the horses. I hate horses!"

Tate was silent. She was thinking it over. They had one hour before she had to leave for her plane. She really needed to do this job, it was important, it was for a top-selling cosmetic firm, and she was hoping that she might be chosen as one of their minor models. She wasn't famous or old enough to be the 'face', but it was an important step up. Besides, she

197

had a rather divine lover waiting for her in Miami with the best cocaine that money could buy. Miami was the place to be!

"Phoebe, darling, I hate to do this to you. But I must go. I can call a cab, and you can stay here as long as you like, until you're ready to go back to Kiss Wood. Come and live with me if you want." Then she paused. "I'm not sure about darling Marco, of course, I love him to bits, but I don't think I could cope with a baby as well."

"Thanks, Tate, but no, life doesn't end, I'll drive you to Heathrow, and then I'll go home, I'll pull myself together. I'm not that pathetic," said Phoebe in a quavery voice that belied her words.

They drove to the airport. The traffic was heavy. Tate kept up a flow of inconsequential chatter, filling the empty silence that emanated from Phoebe. When they finally arrived, she hated to say good-bye.

"Why don't you park and come in we can have another coffee, you can talk about it if you want," she suggested.

"No Tate, I'll be fine, it's just confirmed what I was feeling all the time, I will get used to it. It was just the shock, at realising that they had both lied," said Phoebe, staring ahead stonily.

"You need distraction darling, as soon as I'm back I'll ring you, and you must come to London and stay with me for a few days, I'll organise some entertainment that will quite take your mind off it," said Tate, with a wave of her hand as she hurried across to the airport entrance.

As soon as Phoebe dropped Tate off, she would drive until she came to a layby and then she would quietly collapse and cry, and it wouldn't count because no-one would know about it. The memory of that night in Punta when she had gone outside and wept, wanting to sink into the ground and slip away into oblivion was now haunting her. It was her own fault; she had put Rafael in such a position that he had no alternative but to play the part of her boyfriend; now she was upset that he didn't love her genuinely. How could she have been so stupid?

Tate flew off to Miami, with some lovely cocaine lined up ready for her when she arrived. She had a gorgeous friend there who supplied her with the very best from Bolivia, flown over by private plane. She loved Miami with its Latino culture, bright colours, huge fragrant blooms and the pristine sands and blue-green waves. Usually, she was one to live in the present, luxuriating in the sensual pleasures of the moment, but Phoebe was on her mind. She was very fond of poor old Pheebs, who she had known all her life. She was one of the good guys, and she didn't deserve this playing around with her emotions. As soon as she got back to London, she would insist that the poor darling come and stay with her and she'd jazz her up and initiate her into the joys of the nightlife of London, rather than let her fester alone and heartbroken in the boring Oxfordshire countryside.

A few days later, as soon as the plane landed at Heathrow, she switched her mobile on and rang Phoebe.

"I'm going to dress you up and take you out tonight and then you can experience what it really means to be young, single and carefree with the world at your feet."

Phoebe sniffed and looked at her bedroom walls where she had been skulking for the last few days. In her heart, she knew that Tate was right. She had hardly experienced life, transformed from school girl into mother, with scarcely a moment in between. Why not, Tate was everything she was not, she would take her into fairy worlds she had hardly ever dreamed of. Besides she knew Tate, it would be easier to simply give in and be swept along.

She threw some of her favourite black items of clothing into a bag. Always wearing black, as if she were in mourning for the lost days of her youth, she thought grimly. She told the nanny that she was going away for a few days and left a note for her mother and ran lightly down the curving staircase to the side door that led to the garage. When she got to London, she parked in front of Tate's flat and went inside.

"We're off shopping, darling, going to get you glammed up a bit," said Tate.

"But I've got some very cool gear," said Phoebe, "my black outfit."

"Oh, how terribly Emma Peel," laughed Tate.

"Who is Emma Peel?" asked Phoebe.

"Don't worry, classic, coolest woman in the world, off The Avengers, originally a black and white TV programme."

They sashayed from one boutique to another and Tate picked articles of clothing at random, held them up against Phoebe and insisted that it 'was just the thing'. The retail assistants seemed to bow and scrape, and they all knew Tate. In fact, Phoebe was beginning to realise that Tate was rather a celebrity. As they walked down the street, people stared at her companion as if they recognised her, and other impossibly glamorous people waved and nodded, sometimes stopping to embrace her and air-kiss.

They walked on, and Phoebe was led into a salon that was so opulent with gilt-and-rose painted columns, mirrors framed in curlicues and striped pastel wallpaper that for a moment she baulked. Still, Tate firmly swept her along and organised an immediate appointment with an utterly gorgeous, handsome, young man, wearing far too much makeup. He began to chop at Phoebe's hair in a bizarre blunt cut of different lengths and then dyed it two different colours.

"We'll stop short of a tattoo," said Tate, "just in case you find a fella from the county set and really fall in love."

"I was *really* in love," said Phoebe plaintively. "I still am, but I can't show it, especially now that I know that he was tricked into coming back. He just wanted to pay back the money, but my mother twisted him up, and now he's got a son he can't leave him."

"I can't fault your logic," said Tate, "but love can be strange, twisted, mixed up with all sorts of motives, perhaps you shouldn't give up on him. But in the meantime . . ." she gave her a cheeky grin. "There's nothing wrong with going out and enjoying yourself and meeting new people. If nothing else it will help you realise how lovely you are, he should have to fight for you, and then you can be persuaded that he really loves you. Come on, do it for me, enjoy yourself, darling!"

Two hours later, weighed down with shopping bags of wonderful clothes, they staggered back to Tate's flat.

"Now before we begin to get dressed up to go 'out out' we're going to jazz ourselves up a bit. She took out a smart leather pouch from which she produced a razor and a mirror and cut up some cocaine into two rather sizeable lines.

200

"One for you, one for me," she said. She picked up the elegant silver tube and snorted hers. "Now the other one is for you."

"No Tate, really, haircuts, dressing up is one thing but drugs that is appalling, what sort of mother would I be?"

"You will do as you're told, and by the way, you're a fantastic mother, and when Marco goes out partying you'll be empathic," said Tate, smiling to herself at producing such a convincing argument. "Don't worry. I'm not going to force you to have sex with anyone. But just for one night you're going to go wild, and this will make you feel utterly divine, I promise you."

"What if I become addicted?" asked Phoebe.

"No-one gets addicted on one line, and certainly not you!" said Tate.

Phoebe tried sniffing. It wasn't that hard. She blocked off one nostril and sniffed with the other, just like they did in the movies.

"Now lick your finger and wipe it over the crumbs and rub them on your gums," said Tate.

"I've seen them do that in the movies too. Why do you do that?" asked Phoebe.

"You don't want to waste it, part of the great dance of fun," said Tate laughing.

Phoebe sat back and monitored how she felt. At first nothing, then she did experience a rather thrilling feeling of exaltation as if she were light and funny, and she felt like chattering on.

"Well that seems to be working well," said Tate, preparing a couple more lines. "I have probably got a bit of a tolerance. I just need a little bit more."

They went upstairs, and Tate helped Phoebe to undress, she put a plastic shower cap on her newly-styled hair and pushed her into the shower. When she emerged with a big fluffy towel wrapped firmly and modestly around her body, Tate had set out her outfit on the bed.

"I think for you navy blue in all its inky understated glamour is the thing. Black is far too draining, too *passé,*" said Tate.

"Yes, I like darker colours," said Phoebe, all too well aware that she liked to fade into the background, not to be noticed.

"I do understand, you know, you need to dress in a way that gives you confidence, that helps to enhance your identity," said Tate.

"But what is my 'identity'," said Phoebe. "I have a child, and I *don't* ride horses."

"Well that's not strictly true, you have spent your youth travelling the world, you have a beautiful home and a family that cares about you. Don't be so annoyingly self-deprecating, live large Phoebe. You know you only get one life, one performance, one chance to make a story, make sure it is a good one!"

Tate dressed her as if she were a doll, slithering a dark blue dress over her head. It clung to her curves and Phoebe instinctively felt fat.

"You're not fat anymore, you know," said Tate.

"I know, but I always feel like I'm fat," said Phoebe starting to gabble confidingly as the cocaine took effect, lowering her inhibitions and inspiring her to reveal her inner fears that seemed to be diminishing by the minute. She began to understand why so many people used cocaine; it did have an extremely beneficial and liberating effect.

"You look positively slinky," said Tate, standing back to admire her work. "Now we need to add a dash of glittering glamour. She turned to her own jewel box that was overflowing with all sorts of pieces, from impossibly expensive glittering diamonds to artistic tat."

"I just love Butler and Wilson. No-one can miss it!!"

She hung a pair of earrings onto Phoebe's ears.

"They look like chandeliers," said Phoebe wonderingly.

"Look at yourself in the mirror," said Tate, smugly.

"I do look entirely different," said Phoebe hesitantly.

More cocaine, half a bottle of champagne each and they went back out into the road, and Tate effortlessly whistled up a taxi.

"Now we're going out out," said Tate, as if it were a magic mantra.

"What do you mean, 'out out'?" asked Phoebe, looking at herself in the darkened taxi window, shaking her head back and forth so she could see the effect of the earrings.

"Oh, but darling, going out out, is a thing you know, it's an open mind, spontaneity, getting glammed up with no plan, and it is such fun! And it happens on Wednesday or Thursday."

Phoebe couldn't think of a single remark to make about this. She vaguely remembered that the truly trendy people didn't go to clubs on Friday or Saturday.

"Going out relieves collective social distress," said Tate airily. "We can dress up, or dress down. It's about pride in your identity."

"Collective social distress, is that something to do with Jungian ideas?" asked Phoebe, mystified and trying desperately to find something vaguely related to say. "Identity, I always find that word hard to explain. I know everyone uses it, but what does it really mean?"

"Feeling connected in a fragmented society, it's sociological you know, dancing is rejuvenating," said Tate, smiling mischievously.

Phoebe couldn't help thinking that with Tate's wit and obvious intellect, it was a shame she couldn't aim for a more serious goal in her life. Hedonism seemed pointless to Phoebe, but perhaps it was her that had got it all wrong. Possibly going out and living in the moment, *carpe diem*, 'seizing the day' was what it was really about.

"So are we dressing down or glamming up," she asked, trying to get a handle on these concepts that seemed so vague they were like threads of silver clouds drifting by, enticing her with a vision of belonging to the glamorous people, rather than dressing in clothes that made her look like a clone of her mother.

"This is going to be such fun, positively Bacchanalian, debauched, think Gatsby," said Tate.

Phoebe remembered how badly it had all turned out for Gatsby who had so loved the illusion of Daisy, rather than the trite and thoughtless reality of a selfish and vapid society beauty. She remembered how she had herself fallen hopelessly in love with the mirage of Rafael, but in those heady days she had lived life recklessly, driving to Punta, making love on the beach, it had all been such fun. Perhaps Tate was right. She had lived her life to the full then, the trick was to sustain the illusions and not expect them to turn into 'happily ever after'.

Now her mind opened under the influence of the magic white powder, and she dared to think of a future, with - Rafael. She had always imagined that if she could get truly thin, then Rafael would love her, well at this moment she was not only slim but enormously glamorous, how could he resist? Suddenly the brittle hopeless future dissolved like an unwanted reflection and she could see something so much more hopeful glittering on the horizon. At the very least, going out with the in-crowd made her feel as if she were living with melodrama, not suffering silently and alone in her bedroom at Kiss Wood.

"You will look after me, won't you Tate, don't let anything bad happen to me!" said Phoebe in a stage whisper.

"Of course darling, just think of me as your big sister. We're going to make you feel wonderful."

The cab took them to one of the backstreets of Soho, and they ducked into a tiny little dark bar and sat at a counter. Tate ordered them some fancy-sounding banana cocktails.

"Yum, these are delicious. Are you sure it is alright to mix you know that other stuff and these," said Phoebe holding up her glass of thick, creamy, yellow liquid garnished with coloured glacé cherries on sticks.

"I do it all the time," said Tate smiling, "banana is very good for you, a health food!"

"Well, that means it's all fine!" retorted Phoebe, suddenly feeling more spirited and less hopeless.

Some young men came over, and as far as Phoebe could tell Tate knew them. They seemed to be chattering on about other people that they all knew. Everything seemed to be happening quite far away, but she felt warm and happy and part of it, not talking, just smiling and nodding. She watched Tate, and how she behaved, her friend seemed to have the power

204

to enslave, inspire, but most of all, torment men. She had an extraordinary allure, and at the same time, she seemed contemptuous of the passions that she aroused in the men who gathered around her. Phoebe vaguely wondered what it might be like to wield that sort of power, but she giggled helplessly at the thought that she might do the same, it was a ridiculous fancy.

Phoebe wondered then if she could feel like this all the time; floaty, happy, carefree and full of love. She smiled at them all, feeling surrounded by love, not in love, that had just brought pain but warm, carefree affection radiating towards the whole world. Suddenly she understood why people took drugs. They made everything better.

"Come on!" said Tate, "this is getting dull. Let's go somewhere else."

"Always impatient," said Phoebe, floating along beside her, her high heels which had made her stumble and trip, now made her feel ten feet tall, high above the universe.

Tate took her by the hand, and they got through the maze of tiny streets onto a bigger road and caught a taxi. Tate gave the instructions, and they were deposited outside the front of a coffee shop. Inside was fitted out like a Middle Eastern harem, with long low couches and bright ethnic-coloured cushions. The dazzling oranges, rusty browns and putrid purples seemed to be vibrating with unearthly hues and tones.

"Come on, let's go through to the back," said Tate.

The air was thick with the haze of a strange smelling smoke.

"Is that marijuana?" asked Phoebe in surprise. "How can it be? I thought that was illegal." Perhaps she had been transported by magic carpet to the Netherlands or Morocco. Perhaps, they were to be lured into white slavery. She tried to reason with herself; she was becoming ridiculously imaginative. But Tate was dragging her on, no time to sit in front of a laptop, tap-tap-tapping out a wondrous story that would make her into another Virginia Woolf.

"Here, have a little puff on this," said Tate, sprawled elegantly across the cushions, holding out what looked, rather comically, like an enormous spliff.

"I hate the thought of smoking," said Phoebe, laughing at how prim she sounded.

"I know it's a drag," said Tate. The others around her laughed uproariously. Phoebe didn't get the joke. "Just try it once, darling, material for the novel, you know."

Phoebe felt as if Tate had the power of reading magic thoughts or had she been talking out loud. How embarrassing! Delicately she took the spliff and put it to her lips. She felt the warm wet mouths that had sucked on it before. Normally this would have repulsed her but tonight she felt as if she were joined together with the others, a community of caring and affection. She sucked in. She managed to take some into her lungs but then began to hack at the acrid taste.

"No, darling, try again," insisted Tate.

Phoebe took a sip of water and bravely tried again, just once. She couldn't go through life without having ever tried certain things. This time, she managed to take a decent breath and hold it down in her lungs for all of two seconds before she exhaled. She quickly drank some water and suppressed the urge to cough.

"It will take at least ten minutes before you feel anything," said Tate.

Phoebe in a fug of an altered state of consciousness wasn't sure that her present state left her in any condition to analyse different sensations. She sat there and smiled inanely. Focus then shifted to a newcomer who had just made a rather exhibitionistic entrance, standing in the doorway for just a second or two, then striding towards the table.

"Oh, Tate darling, you're back, we've missed you so much!" he declared.

Phoebe looked at him with interest. He was the prettiest boy she had ever seen. Limpid blue eyes, blonde curls, full rosy lips and the most divine cheekbones.

"Sebastian!" said Tate in a casual drawl. They air-kissed, and Phoebe thought that there was a tension between them. Perhaps it was just the instinctual competition between the two most attractive people in the room. She wondered whether good looks were sometimes actually a burden. It was much easier to fade into the wallpaper and observe.

Phoebe did begin to feel tremendously hungry, and she gratefully accepted some chocolate brownies with her coffee. Tate smiled at her.

"They're hash brownies, Phoebe, don't eat too many."

The evening rippled along. Phoebe felt as if she were floating on a gentle foamy sea, tossing here and there. Eventually, she fell into a sleepy daze, still half-conscious of the music and the voices around her. She was roused when Tate gently shook her.

"Come on darling. We're off to a nightclub to dance the night away. Come into the toilets and have a couple of lines, that will wake you up."

Phoebe followed her obediently. It was as if she had lost the use of her own will. She was Tate, or rather Tate was her. But she didn't like the nightclub, there were lights flashing and booming music that seemed to vibrate through the whole of her body. Tate had somehow come alive and was jerking around like a marionette on a string. Phoebe lost sight of her as she was swallowed up by the crowd. For a moment, Phoebe felt utterly lost, as if she was only surviving through a spiritual umbilical cord attached to Tate. She was too scared to push her way through the crowd around the bar and scurried off to search for the toilets. When she found them, she put her head down to the tap and gulped water. It was most inelegant and uncool, but it was the best that she could manage.

She splashed water on her face and then took a paper towel to wipe it, beginning to feel rather ragged around the edges. This seemed to be the signal her body was crying out for more drugs; it needed topping up to keep floating on that wonderful high experienced a few hours ago. It wasn't cold hard logic, but her mind seemed filled with a more dangerous knowledge, the highs weren't permanent, they swooped up and down and voraciously demanded more drugs. She had mixed it all up, the cocktails, cocaine and hash, and had not been able to experience the purity of any of them. She should have experimented, with one at a time, or she could return to her dreary normal loveless life. That wasn't true, she loved Marco with every atom of her being, and she still loved Rafael. She imagined that he would not approve of her behaviour tonight, but he had no right, if she hadn't felt so woozy she would have tossed her head in defiance.

She didn't like it here, hating the boom, boom reverberating through her body, and worst of all the flashing lights that could all too easily bring on a full-scale migraine. She would go and find Tate, get the keys to the flat and go back to sleep. She found some stairs and climbed up to a balcony so she could look down on the room. There was Tate swaying in the centre of the crowd. She had to get down to the stairs and reach Tate before she moved, or the crowd crushed her underfoot.

"Tate! I want to go home!" She had to shout to be heard, sounding plaintive and moany. Tate nodded and fished a key out of her pocket.

"Leave the door on the latch so I can come in later," she said. "You will take a taxi, not a night bus."

Phoebe nodded. The thought of a meandering night bus going around half of London was terrifying. She only just remembered the name of Tate's street, and the front door was painted green. She would jump in a taxi.

The traffic was light at this time of night, and they sped through prettily-lit streets, that hid the rimy greyness of London and transformed it into a fairy landscape, or so it seemed to Phoebe's still-addled brain. The taxi cruised down the street, and she spotted the doorway, it had a strange trellis plant growing beside it. Undoubtedly her mother would have known the name of it. She let herself in. She was a little afraid to leave the door on the latch, and she shut it behind her. Perhaps if she just lay down in the living room so that she could hear Tate calling and knocking, and surely she wouldn't be home until daybreak. She didn't like the idea of lying alone in an unlocked flat in central London, waiting for a rapacious stranger to burst through the door. Most attackers know their victim, was the thought that ran through her mind. The people that hurt you most are those that are closest to you. They have more opportunities. And wasn't that the truth!

She took her high shoes off and got changed into some track pants and a comfortable t-shirt, then lay down on the lounge with her duvet and pillow. She lay there, looking at the wall. The streetlights and the odd passing car threw up strange shadows, and it made her feel less alone to watch the dancing lights on the wall. This would be the advantage of living in London, in the midst of a mass of humanity, unlike the quiet country life. She began to drift into a dream, and she was back at Punta del Diablo by the sea, the waves crashing in a foaming swirl then receding out to sea. Rafael was there, but he was different, he was happy and laughing, carefree and running through the waves, swinging his arms in exhilaration.

A state in which she had never seen him. He was always so reserved and even sullen.

"Phoebe, Phoebe!" he was calling her. She woke up with a start; someone was thumping on the front door. She leapt to her feet. Pale half-light filled the room.

"Phoebe!" she could hear Tate calling.

She stumbled to the door and let her in.

"I'm so sorry I was afraid of burglars, so I didn't want to leave it on the latch," she apologised.

Tate laughed at her. Even after a night of heavy partying, she looked beautiful, her skin flawless, her lips plump and shaped like a bow. "Tell me, did you enjoy yourself?"

"Tremendously," Phoebe said, only half telling the truth. Certainly, it had been a fascinating experience, but she wasn't entirely sure she would like to repeat it.

"I knew that you just needed to be taken out of yourself," said Tate smugly. "I'm off to a party tonight, and I don't think you will like it, but I've got an idea to arrange something specially for you!"

"That is very kind of you. I'm pretty tired now, I think I need to sleep, I was having such a beautiful dream."

"Of course, darling, was Rafael in your dream? Don't worry you don't need to answer. You know this lifestyle means that we sleep til at least two or three in the afternoon."

Phoebe couldn't see that fitting in with Marco's schedule, but at the moment it would suit her just fine. She had a secret, vain hope that Rafael would notice her absence and wonder what she was doing. But he was so tied up with his son and the horses he probably wouldn't even notice. She stumbled into the guest bedroom and lay down, desperately wanting to get back to her dream. Rafael had been coming towards her. She wondered if he were dreaming of her.

Chapter Seventeen

But Phoebe slept peacefully and didn't dream again. At Kiss Wood, Rafael rose as usual. He had promised that he would tell Grace that Jamie was riding Tinpot now. He was determined to do so, but he wanted to find the most auspicious moment. He wanted to see how the stallion went for Jamie today. If all went well, then he would tell Grace.

He was whistling below his breath. He looked in at Marco who was lying quietly in his cot, coo-ing and playing with his own toes.

"*Chico Marco, Chico Marco*" Rafael crooned.

The nanny came in and lifted Marco out of the cot.

"The little master needs changing," she said and laid him on the changing table.

Rafael stroked the boy's forehead, wondering at the softness of his skin, and then left the room. He never imagined that his son would be called 'the little master'! He hadn't even noticed that Phoebe was away. He went down through the kitchen and picked up a mug of coffee and took some slices of bread with a hunk of cheese. He had not time to feast on the kedgeree on the sideboard.

In the tack room he took down Tinpot's saddle and bridle, he would tack him up for Jamie, as if their positions were reversed. They were still using a running martingale, and Grace had even considered a more severe bit, but Rafael didn't think more metal in his mouth was going to be the answer. He went over to the stallion box which was situated some distance from the other loose boxes.

Rafael wondered if it was a mistake to try and train the stallion at the same time as he had been covering mares. He had hesitantly mentioned this to Grace, but she wouldn't listen. She was becoming increasingly autocratic, as her dream was taking shape around her. Oliver had come over to see Bliss, and he had been impressed and had promised to send some mares next season, it was too late in the summer now.

Jamie followed Rafael and Tinpot into the arena and mounted the stallion. As usual, the big horse hunched his back and prepared himself to leap forward and attempt a bucking frenzy. Watching, Rafael felt dispirited. He did not like fighting with horses; that was not what he did. He loved them and wished to breathe the same air as them, infuse his spirit into theirs. Jamie yanked Tinpot's head around and brought his long whip down, on one side of the flank, then on the other. The stallion snorted and braced his four legs on the ground. He was rigid with anger.

"Walk on," said Jamie, quietly, in a neutral voice. Tinpot stepped forward, he wasn't happy, but he seemed confused about what to do next. Jamie took advantage of his confusion.

"Shall we tell Grace today, or would you rather work on him some more?" asked Rafael.

"Good morning Rafael, Jamie," said Grace, standing in the doorway. "I see there has been some alteration to the training plan," she said evenly, in a threateningly soft voice. They both looked at her startled. Tinpot took advantage of the moment and threw himself forward. For a split second, Jamie was caught off-balance, but he rode out the first few bucks and then took control and again he used the whip, down one flank with a resounding 'thwack' and then down the other. Grace and Rafael watched him. Rafael saw no point in explaining, the truth was self-evident.

"It was my idea," he said, trying not to sound defiant.

Tinpot was determined to show his wild spirit and didn't give up just because Grace was there. It was as if he were determined to show the mistress exactly what he was made of. Jamie sat him out, and after several minutes he mastered the big horse. This time, as before he rode him around and around the school at top speed until the big stallion was dripping with sweat.

Finally, Jamie called "Halt!" and blocked his hands. Tinpot staggered to a ragged halt and hung his head, breathing heavily. Grace stepped forward and took the reins, and Jamie dismounted. There was silence. No-one wanted to speak first.

"I'll take him and wash him down," said Grace. Jamie and Rafael stood there looking after her. They were not sure what to do. The hierarchy of authority was in question.

"I'll go with her to hose the horse down," said Jamie. Rafael nodded. Perhaps it was best if Jamie and Grace worked it out between themselves. He wished that he'd had a chance to tell her before she had discovered them as if they were naughty schoolchildren.

Phoebe slept the whole day and woke late in the afternoon when Tate had gently roused her.

"Darling Phoebe, there's something I have to do tonight. I hate to be mysterious, but it is nothing that would suit you at all. So, I've arranged for my divine friend, Tinker, to take you out to dinner."

"Like a date," said Phoebe, about to say 'no, no, no'. Not at all like that. Tinker isn't like that. He is a dear, sweet man and he is going to take you to a lovely restaurant that has just been opened by a friend of his, and he has promised to help his friend. The more people that dine there, the more popular it will become. It's south of the river in Northcote Rd, but south of the river is the new 'north of the river' so to speak. It's not far, and they say that the food is to die for."

"Alright," said Phoebe. "That is terribly kind of you, Tate. I'm not sure that I could cope with another night of drugs!"

"It's alright darling. I quite understand. But you see Tinker is a writer, and I told him you loved to read and had the odd aspiration yourself, and he is keen to sit and talk books, characters, plots, whatever it is that you literary types talk about," said Tate airily.

"He's a writer," said Phoebe. "Oh, that sounds wonderful Tate, I don't think I've ever actually met a real writer before."

"Well he's self-published which I know used to be vanity publishing, but everything has changed so much these days. I'm sure he'll tell you all about it. I've actually bought one of his books. You know we all like to try and help each other with our forays into the arts. I must admit I haven't read it. It does seem an awful lot of words. Here it is, rather a tome. Come into the sitting room, and I'll make you a cup of coffee and some toast, and then you can get ready."

"Tate, you're the best friend I've ever had," said Phoebe, like a spaniel dog looking up at its mistress. She pulled her dressing gown around her and hurried into the front room and began to read. She barely noticed the cup of coffee and the plate of buttered toast that Tate placed before her, so entranced was she with the book. Two hours later she looked up, and Tate told her that it was time to have a shower and get ready.

"I'm not sure that it's the most brilliant book I've ever read," said Phoebe a little hesitantly, "but I can see that the writing shows great promise."

"Well please do be kind to Tinker, he's rather sensitive about his creation, you know how writers are," said Tate.

"Of course," said Phoebe, "I would never mock someone like that, he's done it, he's written it, I've just as you say vague aspirations, but this is inspiring me. You couldn't have thought of a better plan, Tate, you're a genius."

"So, they say," said Tate wryly.

"I'm going to wear one of the new outfits that we bought yesterday," said Phoebe. "I was thinking this rather slinky fitted skirt, my high shoes again and my plain black jumper. I still do like black jumpers, you know," she said apologetically.

"Just right for a restaurant in Clapham with a writer chum," said Tate approvingly.

Phoebe carefully did her makeup, trying some of the new techniques that the girl on the makeup counter had suggested. She came out shyly, and Tate was busy on her mobile in the front room. She looked up.

"Oh well done, Phoebe, you look like yourself but a much more cheerful version of yourself. You'll have the world at your feet tonight!"

Tinker turned up. He was rather effeminate, and immediately Phoebe thought he must be gay, but she could never tell, there were a lot of straight metrosexuals around, so she believed. He had nice blonde curls and sweet round blue eyes and rather chubby cheeks. He was terribly posh and had gone to Eton, and he had the most lovely, gracious and polished manners. He kissed her hand and bowed to her and then swept open the taxi door and she climbed in as elegantly as she could, as usual, she felt like a lumbering elephant.

They crawled through the heavy London traffic.

213

"I don't know how you can bear driving around this city. It would test the patience of a saint," she said.

"I know, usually I take the bus, but I thought tonight it would be better to travel by taxi," he said.

"I've been reading your book, this afternoon, Tate lent it to me."

"Dear Tate bought it, but I don't suppose she's even opened the pages," said Tinker.

"I think it is fascinating, I've never met a real-life author before," said Phoebe shyly.

They spent the evening with their heads together, while Tinker imparted his worldly knowledge of the self-publishing industry.

"You just write the manuscript, design a cover and upload it. It's that simple."

"But I've got nothing to write about," said Phoebe. "I've hardly lived, I got pregnant while I was still at school and now, I have a baby and live with my mother and sister in the country."

"Well you've become a mother, I don't imagine that is nothing," said Tinker admiringly, and living in the country that could be very conducive to scribbling, the pastoral idyll and all that."

Phoebe laughed. By the end of the evening, she had invited Tinker to come and stay and enjoy the rural peace at Kiss Wood, suggesting that it might help him overcome his latest writer's block. He seemed very excited and accepted the invitation with alacrity. They decided that she would drive him there tomorrow morning. He took her to a bar nearby and they talked into the night. Phoebe believed that she had found her soul mate.

Tate smiled knowingly when Phoebe told her.

"Jolly good, at least that will be one non-horsey person for you at Kiss Wood."

Tate made no crass remarks about making Rafael jealous, upsetting the apple cart with Aunt Grace, or asserting herself. She was happy that she had helped Phoebe find a friend. Tinker was not exactly conventional boyfriend material. As far as she knew he had never had a girlfriend, but then he had never had a boyfriend either, he seemed an ideal companion for Phoebe at the moment, who was struggling to keep her head above water in a horse-crazed household.

The next day, Phoebe drove up the driveway to Kiss Wood, feeling like a different person. She still felt betrayed by Rafael and her mother, but she felt that she had taken a step in the right direction, she would make her way in her own life and stop hanging on the coattails of the stronger personalities around her. She knew now that she and Rafael would never be married. He was here for his son and the horses. Grace wanted him for Marco but most of all to ride her blessed horses. That was all now crystal clear. They hadn't used her. She was merely irrelevant, and somehow this made it even worse!

Grace was over at the stables when they arrived at Kiss Wood. Tinker was not intimidated by the grandeur of the house; he had many friends who also lived in grand houses. He would probably have been more entranced by a bohemian stone cottage hidden away in a fold of the desolate moorland hills. Phoebe took him upstairs and deposited him in a bedroom in the same corridor as her own, Marco's, the nanny's, and Rafael's.

"And Tinker makes five," she said to herself, grinning.

"Come down, and we'll see what Mrs Hopkins is up to, perhaps a cup of coffee," she suggested.

"And then you must show me around this gorgeous house, and we can choose somewhere to work together. You are going to help me with my writing, or perhaps you're going to start your own project," he suggested.

"Oh, yes, definitely," she said. "There is my favourite place on the wide landing of the curved stairs, which is set up like a room with some very comfy armchairs and two huge windows from floor to ceiling that look out on large expanses of sky. Also, the library is jolly nice, lots of old books and they've been read, they're not just first editions locked up in cages. My great-grandfather was a great reader, almost a man of letters. And there's a lovely big fireplace and comfortable chairs. Do you actually handwrite or tap into a laptop?"

"Oh, laptop, I'm afraid," trilled Tinker. "It's an extension of my personality. I go nowhere without it."

215

They went into the library with mugs of coffee, so that Tinker could test the ambience, to see if it was suitable for creativity. He pranced around like a show pony and Phoebe did think he was rather affected. But he appeared to genuinely love books and now ran his finger lightly across the spines of the volumes that lined the walls. They talked literature until lunchtime, then wandered down to the dining-room at the appointed hour. As they entered, there was a shocked silence.

"This is my friend, Tinker, don't worry, I told Mrs Hopkins that there was an extra for lunch," she said, not sure why everyone was staring at her.

"Your hair Phoebe," said Grace. Phoebe had entirely forgotten her new dramatic haircut and dyed two different colours, jet black and dark blue. She put her hand up self-consciously.

"It looks very nice," said Rafael stiffly. He knew he had no right to be jealous, but he looked a little darkly at Tinker. The man looked like a girl with his blonde curls and big, round blue eyes. And this wasn't the end of it, Tinker was enchanted by Marco and carried the chubby little baby off into the living-room to play with him after lunch. Rafael wanted to snatch his son away from this effeminate-looking man, but he knew that he had no right. He hoped that Phoebe kept her eye on them. What if the man was a pedophile? He was conscious that to make this accusation was to demean and distort a complex human being who seemed to make Phoebe happy. Who was he to deny her happiness? She deserved it. She was a decent person.

However, Tinker continued to be a thorn in Rafael's side, a stone in his shoe, a perceived threat to his son and Phoebe. He feared that he was losing her, and there was never going to be a way for them to be together properly, in a family unit. Rafael was never good in social situations and certainly not in any way equipped to make a stand. He watched helplessly from the sidelines as Phoebe tried to fashion herself into another person. She was determined to become 'social' and stop being a wallflower - sitting with her back to the wall in the great dancing hall of life.

Tinker stayed for days and as he was in a bedroom right next to Rafael's he could not ignore him. In the end, Rafael decided to sleep on the sofa in the stable's recreation room, whenever Tinker was staying. If he had to listen to Phoebe laughing at Tinker's inane witticisms for one more second, he would stride into the man's bedroom and punch his snub nose!

Chapter Eighteen

Grace and Poppy had no inkling of the undercurrents. They barely noticed that Phoebe was changing, beyond the haircut she seemed to be going about a bit more, but they were both too focused on the horses to pay much attention. They were planning a two-week trip around to various autumn shows in Europe. Rafael was told that he was to jump Mickey and Gunner at all the shows and Grace had organised for a show jumping coach to come to Kiss Wood for several days to give Poppy and Rafael some intensive coaching a week before they left. It was the most marvellous opportunity for Rafael and as he could do nothing about the Tinker situation, he shrugged his shoulders and applied himself to the task of learning as much as he could. Perhaps if he became a star rider then somehow it would work out with Phoebe. He would be a success in his own right, and then he could make a move. He was unsure how this would change the situation, but it seemed his only hope - the only thing that he was good at.

Poppy chose to ride Bosley and Rafael was mounted on Gunner for the first coaching session. As far as the coach Thomas Mortimer was concerned, one needed to go back to basics. He was an old-fashioned military man of a bygone age. In fact, he could remember Grace as a girl. She had been one of the most gifted young riders he could remember. All gone to waste as she had swanned off with that 'puff' as he thought of David Lester. Thomas was in his mid-seventies, with heavy jowls and mottled purple and crimson skin, and rather large yellow teeth. Grace had come across him at one of the district agricultural shows and asked him to come over and stay for a few days.

This morning he told Rafael and Poppy to cross their stirrups and rising trot around the arena. Poppy groaned a little, but did as she was told. Rafael was rather mystified he had never really come across this strange training practice, but he obediently crossed his stirrups. He had spent so many years riding bareback that he didn't find it particularly arduous. Gunner had a smooth, long stride, so it wasn't difficult to rise to the trot without the support of stirrups.

Jamie and Jerome had been told to stand by ready to carry out orders to build jumps as was required by Thomas. They stood at the side of the arena, both crossing their arms, their eyes narrowed. Thomas called them over.

"I want you to build a grid, six jumps, each three big human steps between them and all of them 50 cm high, except the last – that shall be 80cm. So the horses will bounce over one, then the next, with no intervening strides. Down the middle of the arena and some post-and-rails along the side, then we'll send them down one after the other."

Grace came in and watched them. When they were finished, she turned to Jerome.

"Would you like to have a go as well Jerome?" she asked. "You could go and get your horse."

Jerome nodded his thanks and dashed out.

"Tell Angela to come in, so she can help Jamie if there are any rails down," she called after him.

"Can we take our stirrups back?" asked Poppy, her voice high and shrill. She didn't like this trotting without stirrups; it was as if he were treating them like beginners.

"No, not at all, no stirrups. Perhaps it will be better if you take them off entirely, crossed they are uncomfortable beneath your upper thigh," said the gruff old man. He was rather curious about this young chap who looked foreign. Unless he was mistaken, he had the mark of a great rider on him.

"Now before we jump, I want you cantering around the arena, no stirrups and your reins knotted and dropped on the horses' necks. Canter down the long side and using your weight and your legs I want the horses to leg yield in until the half-way mark then leg yield to the outside, until you get to the corner."

Rafael was fascinated at these instructions. He could see the logic of steering the horse by one's weight and legs, and with an old hand like Gunner it was not a problem, it wouldn't have been much fun on Tinpot. Poppy was feeling incensed; this wasn't what her mother was paying this man for, silly exercises for babies! Her bad mood communicated itself to Bosley and he began to swerve this way and that.

"Perhaps you've come to rely on your reins too much," said Thomas, a little grimly. "It does no harm to go back to basics sometimes, little lady."

Poppy almost pulled a face at being called a 'little lady'. This old man was so patronising! And he looked ridiculous hurrumphing and shaking his jowls, as if he were a horse neighing deep in his throat, his large strawberry nose and ugly thick moustache were awful.

They cantered around a few times, and every time Bosley tried to duck into the centre of the arena.

"Use your legs, girl!" roared Thomas, his face flushing a deeper shade of crimson and purple with annoyance.

"Legs, legs, legs," muttered Poppy, "he sounds like a Colonel out of the Pullein-Thompson pony books back in the fifties."

Rafael looked at her frowning. He had no idea what she was talking about.

However, Poppy did use her legs as hard as she could and finally, she succeeded in steering Bosley, more or less, in a ragged form of a leg yield in and then out. Jerome rode in on his ex-racehorse, Joe.

"That's enough," called Thomas. "You'll strengthen your seat with those exercises, you're never so good that you don't need to go back to basics."

Poppy wasn't happy, but she could see the sense in it, and she resolved that she would practise the exercise with all the ponies, but in private, she didn't like being watched when she wasn't getting it right.

Jerome's horse was not a beautiful beast; he was tall and exceedingly thin, with just a hint of being herring-gutted. He was a plain brown with no white markings, and his mane and tail were rather skimpy. However, he could jump, and he was fast, and that was what mattered. Just as Jerome was a solid northern lad, he had a plain horse, but show jumping was not a beauty contest, and the winner was decided on whether the poles fell to the ground and on the time it took to gallop through the finish line.

"What is this one called?" asked Thomas.

"Joe," replied Jerome.

"So, we have Joe and Jerome," said Thomas and laughed to himself as if he had made a witty comment.

"Lad I want you to trot with no stirrups and then canter around to warm him up. You other two come in here," called Thomas. "The helpers will hold the horses. I want to see how supple you are. Now lean forward and touch your nose up on the horses' necks, and then back, so you're lying along their rumps."

Poppy and Rafael submitted to this exercise.

They bent forwards and backwards, and Poppy forgot her pride and began to giggle. They sat up and watched Jerome on his big gangly horse. He was not a bad rider, his long legs wrapped around the sides of the horse, his seat firm in the saddle, his back poker-straight.

"Now, each of you, one after the other, down the jumps, no stirrups and no reins, balance and legs that's how you do it."

Poppy rode forward first. It was not the most difficult exercise she had ever attempted, and Bosley had a light, quick jump. He went like a deer down the line of jumps, having to stretch a little to make it from one jump to the next. Gunner and Rafael went next. He was steady, and with his long stride, he achieved it easily. Joe was the wild card. No-one had seen him jump since he had arrived. Jerome schooled him on his own, late at night, in the indoor school and if he jumped then no-one knew as there were no jumps left standing and the school was cleaned and raked in the morning. Sometimes he simply rode off across the field, and no-one knew where he went. He would come back two or three hours later, his horse dried with sweat. Although it was thin, its ribs hardly covered with flesh, it was fit, its muscles bulging.

"Do you think he needs more condition?" Angela had asked him after he had been there a week.

"He doesn't put on weight," he had replied shortly, and certainly the horse ate well.

Grace had looked at the horse carefully and called in her vet. She asked him to endoscope him, and he had diagnosed ulcers. Now Joe received Omeprazole every day, and he had improved, he had even put on a little weight, but he still looked like a scarecrow. However, his coat was shiny, and his eyes bright.

Everyone was curious to see how Joe jumped, and Jerome rode him down the line. He leapt straight and true and evenly, and Jerome barely moved in the saddle, bending a little at the waist. There was a spontaneous burst of clapping from the spectators. Now, they recognised Jerome's talent, he was a good rider, and he had trained this horse well.

"I think you should bring him as well when we go on the show circuit," said Grace. Jamie stood there with his face closed, inside he was furious. He should have kept his money and bought himself a horse as well. He would stay back to look after the ponies that were left behind, the mares and foals and the proud, intractable stallion.

"Jamie, I wondered whether Thomas might give you a private session on Tinpot after lunch," said Grace. "I've invited Oliver to lunch, and then we will come over and watch, I think it is time that he learnt to jump. Thomas will also join us for lunch."

Jamie's heart leapt. He had not been forgotten. This was a gesture from Grace that seemed to ratify his right to be the stallion's trainer. He felt his heart opening to her in gratefulness, not an emotion that he experienced very often. Neither was she demonstrative, but he felt as if somewhere, beyond their respective positions, there was an accord, even if he wasn't invited to lunch. But he had no time for sitting around in a dining room making conversation. He had no taste for such activities.

Oliver arrived with his son Hector. Poppy heard their voices and dashed upstairs to change for lunch. She jumped under the shower and washed her hair that was flattened and greasy from wearing her helmet. She had golden curls, the only person in her family with curly hair and grey eyes with strange black lines around the outside of the irises. She took the hairdryer and fluffed up her hair, so it dried in big fat curls. Then she rubbed moisturiser into her skin. She looked at herself in the mirror and grabbing a tube of creamy blusher, she rubbed a little onto her cheekbones and just a swipe of mascara, to darken her light eyelashes.

Grace had asked Mrs Hopkins to use the second-best cutlery and crockery and the white linen tablecloth. She used the excuse that these items needed to be used, not left in the cupboard to moulder. There were to be eight at lunch; Grace, Oliver, Thomas, Rafael, Phoebe, Tinker, Hector and Poppy. Grace smiled ironically to see that for once, she had managed a meal with more men than women. It was the bane of all hostesses to find sufficient males to equal females. They were served cold lettuce soup, drizzled with fresh cream which was very refreshing and an excellent entrée, to be followed by a salad with three different types of lettuce, watercress from the garden, fetta cheese, hard-boiled eggs, fresh walnuts and cherry tomatoes. This was served with a variety of cold cuts, and followed by lemon mousse. Grace was rather pleased with the menu, not only healthy but also sufficiently light as not to render everyone sleepy for this afternoon's further training sessions in the arena.

She was particularly excited that Oliver had come to watch Tinpot with his first exercise over jumps. For several weeks now Jamie had been walking and trotting over poles on the ground. Now he was to try him over some low jumps supervised by Thomas.

"You're expecting great things from our stallion, I believe," said Oliver. Grace felt a frisson of delight at the word 'our'.

"Yes, I believe that he is very promising, and his three foals are all good types," she said, making sure not to babble on fatuously, like a silly woman. Oliver smiled at her, and she felt flutterings in her stomach.

Hector and Poppy were seated together at the end of the table and Poppy was cross-examining Hector about his newest acquisition, a champion polo pony that he felt would carry his team to victory.

"You two should come over and have a go," said Hector, smiling at her and including Rafael in the invitation. "Show jumping isn't the only equestrian sport, you know. You have to have a go, it's amazing."

"I've tried tennis," said Poppy, "but I'm not the best at hitting the ball, but I will come over and have a go. What do you call it, 'stick and balling'."

"Yes, my handicap is zero at the moment, but I'm hoping to get up to a one shortly."

"Zero doesn't sound brilliant?" said Poppy hesitantly.

"You start at minus two and then go up, the very best is ten, hardly anyone gets to ten."

Rafael was listening in to this conversation. He wasn't totally unaware of the sport of polo, having watched from the sidelines at Melilla. He wondered how he would fare, would he be able to hit the ball, he'd never played tennis or any other type of organised sport.

"I wouldn't mind having a go," he said shyly.

"I bet you'd be brilliant at it. I thought the best players are from South America," said Poppy.

Hector, smiled at Rafael, "I've heard how good you are with horses, Poppy has told me."

Thomas was chomping his way through the cold cuts. He wasn't overly fond of 'rabbit food' as he called salad. He was interested to see how this famous golden stallion was going to go this afternoon. By all accounts, he was something pretty special.

"Grace dear," he said between mouthfuls of cold chicken, "what about you? Which horses are you riding?"

"Oh, I don't ride anymore," said Grace dismissively.

"Damned shame, never saw such a good seat on a horse when you were a gel," hurrumphed Thomas, reaching for several thick slices of cold beef, with a liberal dollop of horseradish.

"You seem to have found one of your old admirers," said Oliver smoothly.

Thomas hurrumphed again. Of course, he remembered Oliver when he had been young and dashing. He wasn't such a slimy chap as that one that had married Grace, but he was altogether too smooth for his liking. Grace was a wonderful woman. She deserved better!

"You should ride again, shame to give it up now, why not try dressage?" suggested Thomas in a softer tone.

"Women of a certain age take up dressage," said Grace, a little acerbically.

"That sculpture in the stable yard, that was you jumping," chipped in Poppy. "Mummy why don't you try dressage, you wanted to start riding again, and we've got Gunner and Mickey, you could make a start on one of them, then if you like it, buy yourself a trained horse."

"Tinpot?" said Rafael questioningly.

223

"I'm not sure that that stallion is ever going to be a lady's ride," said Grace.

"It will be interesting to see how he goes this afternoon," said Oliver. "I think you're right. He needs a man to control him."

The pure sexism of this was not wasted on Grace, but she had prompted it with her comment 'a lady's ride' – what had she been thinking? They were right. She did want to ride again. Now everything was set up and running smoothly she would take Gunner out one day. She was only forty-seven! Although sometimes she felt about a hundred.

After lunch, they all trooped out to watch Tinpot's first proper jumping lesson. Jamie had him saddled and ready and was riding him around the arena. He didn't care that there was a crowd watching, he had been competing for many years, albeit without huge success. He'd always had second-class horses that he'd picked up cheap and trained himself. This stallion was something different. He had royal blood flowing through his veins and the spirit of a warrior, fashioned from fire and ice.

The big horse was stepping out today as if he knew that something was in the air. He had improved, and there was rarely a bucking exhibition, but his spirit was still flaring and rebellious. Jamie agreed with Rafael. It had been a mistake to be using him to cover mares and trained at the same time. Perhaps now he would settle down.

Jamie and Jerome re-arranged the jumping grid, the jumps were 40 cm high but they were spread out so that there were two strides between them, and each was given a solid groundline.

"First trot him over," said Thomas.

Jamie had shortened his stirrups a little, but he sat down deep in the saddle and guided the stallion over the jumps. Tinpot knew what a jump was, Rafael had free-jumped him over obstacles far bigger than this any number of times. Tinpot trotted up to the first jump, hopped over and on landing broke into a canter and rushed over the others.

"Trot!" said Thomas. "If you approach at a trot, then you expect him to trot on landing."

Jamie nodded and circled around the perimeter of the arena and back to the row of low jumps. This time he took a stronger contact with the reins, and when they landed after the first jump, he was ready and steadied Tinpot back to a trot. He flashed over each of the jumps.

"Not bad, not bad," said Thomas, "he's coming on well. Twice more at the trot and then canter, I think he's more than ready for this."

Tinpot performed very well. He was boisterous and leaping about, but Jamie contained him with his legs and his hands. He loved the feel of this horse, so much raw energy and spirit if only this could be harnessed and bent to the rider's will.

"Can we put that last jump up, give him something to think about," said Jamie.

"Right, good man, you're right. Put the last jump up to a metre. He'll get his striding established. Then, he'll be set up to jump it well."

Jamie cantered the golden stallion around the arena and Grace watched him, this was everything she had dreamed of, standing next to Oliver watching their horse. She was filled with a new resolve. She would start riding again. She would show these men that she was as good as them.

Tinpot was getting het up; the excitement was getting to him. Jamie turned him into the line of jumps with just two strides so he didn't get a chance to rush. He bounced over each of the lower jumps and then a perfect parabolic leap over the final jump.

A burst of spontaneous applause came from the small group of watchers.

"Oh Mummy, he is beautiful, do you think I might ride him one day," said Poppy.

"Perhaps in a few years," said Grace laughing out loud, she felt a rush of exaltation, like a girl again, full of hope and joy for the future.

"Another session with Poppy, Rafael and Jerome, I think," said Grace. "Thomas, come into our recreation room, and we can have a coffee or a cup of tea if you like."

Grace led the way, and Thomas entered the room he said, "What a wonderful room! Grooms weren't treated to this type of luxury in my time!"

Poppy giggled at this. Rafael thought of the facilities available for the staff at Melilla.

"You could join in," said Poppy to Hector, "you can have a pick of my ponies, or you could ride Mickey or Gunner, whichever Rafael is not riding."

"Why not?" said Hector, "I'll show you that polo players are up for anything."

Oliver smiled at him, dotingly. Since Elvira had died, his son was the light of his life.

They were mounted; Jerome on Joe, Rafael on Mickey, Hector on Gunner and Poppy riding Fleet. This time Thomas allowed them to jump a course of about one metre in height, with various difficult related distances, and curved approaches, to help them 'see a stride'. Hector was good, he had a strong seat, and he'd jumped at pony club as a junior. He was also rampantly ambitious, just like Poppy and they were competing against each other. They didn't listen to the technical directions issued by the bluff Thomas but rather raced around heedlessly, taking ridiculous risks, laughing and shouting at each other. They both had fences down, and Grace frowned, Poppy had to learn that all this was serious, no time for messing around, especially with such a promising pony like Fleet.

Rafael obeyed the instructions, and he and Mickey jumped impeccably. Jerome also performed well, his performance was perhaps not as polished as that of Rafael, his Thoroughbred had a long raking stride, but he was bold and fearless and had apparently been well-trained, although sometimes if he got excited his neck was likely to 'go upside down', harking back to his racing days.

When the coaching session was over Poppy and Hector rode back to the stables, giggling and whispering together like two errant children. Grace followed Rafael and Jerome. Her attention had been caught by the Thoroughbred horse, Joe, she was interested to see how he performed in dressage. She had been impressed with the way that Jerome rode, and she wondered if she might use him as a second-string jockey if Rafael or Jamie couldn't ride. She liked the idea of having a stable of not only handsome, well-bred horses, but also able horsemen, as well as Poppy, who would all ride in competitions. In fact, she was feeling rather pleased with herself. Everything was going well.

Rafael and Poppy drove over to Tall Chimneys some days later. They were to be introduced to the noble game of polo, and Hector was keen to show off his beautiful ponies. Rafael drove them in Grace's car. He had recently passed his driving test, and he was anxious to practise his driving.

"Are you looking forward to travelling around Europe and going to the horse shows over there?" asked Poppy casually.

"Yes, it should be good. I have never been to any of these countries," replied Rafael. He found it easier to talk when they were driving in the car. There was something about sitting together in a car, that created an atmosphere of intimacy that made the painful process of self-disclosure easier. He liked talking to Poppy, she seemed like a link to his past life in Uruguay, when he had known who he was.

"What do you think of that horse, Joe? You know the one that Jerome brought here?" she asked, chattering on.

"He's alright, needs more condition, but your mother is sorting that out."

"Yes, dear Mummy, she is a great sorter-outer," said Poppy laughing. She was excited. She had been thinking about Hector ever since that day when Thomas had taught them show jumping.

"Do you think it might be fun to play polo?" she asked.

"I suppose so, it never really appealed to me though, too much of a fracas, bouncing and bumping off each other. The ponies take it hard."

"I suppose so," said Poppy, "but I think they like it as well, galloping together, dashing here or there. I'm not sure how good I'll be at using the stick, I'm not particularly gifted when it comes to tennis."

"We're not going to be playing for real today," said Rafael, "surely not, just being shown around."

"I hope that I'm good at it, I do so want to impress Hector," said Poppy, her imagination running away with her. Hector was waiting for them in the stable yard. He had three of the ponies saddled.

227

"They're not really ponies," said Poppy "they're all well over 15 hh."

"They're just called ponies," said Hector in a slightly patronising voice.

"I like the bay," said Poppy.

"Then you shall ride the bay," said Hector, in an attempt at gallantry to make up for his previous remark.

"Which one for me?" asked Rafael.

"You can have the tallest, the chestnut, he can be hot, but I suppose you'll handle him," said Hector off-handedly.

He swung himself into the saddle of the bay mare. She was his favourite, she was called Dancer, and his father had paid a fortune for her.

"Jack!" he called to one of the grooms, "can you bring us each a stick, the ones in the blue bin in the tack room and then bring us out a bag of balls, we're going to have a hit around on the pitch."

They spent the next hour whooping up and down the field. Poppy was wild with her stick and rarely connected with the ball.

"Just don't hit the pony's legs," called Hector, suddenly wondering at the wisdom of letting her loose with what could be a lethal weapon.

He tried to explain the principles of a ride-off, "When a ball is hit, it creates its own right of way, and the player who hit it is entitled to hit it again. But if another player puts his horse's shoulder in front of that first player's horse's shoulder, and a good horse will feel the pressure and push the other horse off the line, then the second player takes up the right of way."

Poppy shook her head. She couldn't make any sense of it at all.

After they had finished, they trooped inside, and Mrs Beeston, the Tall Chimneys' housekeeper, served them afternoon tea.

"I don't think I've much of a future in polo," said Poppy. "I think I'll stick to show jumping."

"You could be good, you know, Rafael," said Hector. "You're welcome to come over any time you like. If the job with Grace doesn't work out, you could come and work for me."

"Don't you dare poach our Rafael," said Poppy indignantly. "We love him!"

"Really?" said Hector, wondering at the emotion in her voice.

"I promised I would stay working for Grace," said Rafael quickly. "But thank you for the offer, it is very kind of you."

"Not at all," said Hector, then changed the subject.

The day before they were due to leave for Europe, Grace decided that she would ride. She asked Jamie to saddle Mickey and Gunner and said that they would go out together, as Rafael was spending the day with Marco. They set off across the small field beside the stables and then letting themselves through the gate rode along a rough dirt lane, before turning off at a bridle path that wound its way down through the woods to the river.

Jamie had never seen Grace ride before. In actual fact, nobody had for many years. He didn't want to stare and be caught appraising her, so he kept his eyes to the front. Grace had felt self-conscious as she had mounted wearing a brand-new pair of jodhpurs, but now she was absolutely fine. Much better than fine, like she was doing what she was always meant to do. Looking through a horse's ears gave you the best world-view! She found herself grinning inanely. This was what she had been born to do. They had to trot through a small wood before they got to the river. The horses' hoofs were muffled by a thin layer of leaves that were falling in the early autumn. She looked surreptitiously at Jamie riding beside her on the wide track.

"Let's canter," she said as the ground rose temptingly before them, a gentle slope. On one side of the track, small log jumps had been built, and Grace set Gunner up the line of natural obstacles. It was many years since she had jumped, and she felt as if they were flying. One never lost it, the love of horses and moving through time and space as if on the wings of destiny.

Jamie kept pace beside her, not putting Mickey at the obstacles. They moved over the ground in perfect harmony, matching stride for stride. For a moment, Grace remembered hunting as a child, her pony galloping fast to keep up with her father, who had been known as a hard man to hounds. She had loved those days, she had adored her father and still missed him. She had been his precious little girl. No man had ever felt like that about her since.

They reached the top of the track, and the path narrowed and wound down and around the trees. Grace had to duck every now and again as the branches were level with her head. They came out on the banks of the river that flowed slowly and leisurely across the water meadows. The mechanical whir of wings broke the silence as the ducks flew away at the sight of the horses. Soon they would come to the end of the country that belonged to Kiss Wood, where Grace's fields adjoined those of Oliver's. They would be a perfect match, thought Grace wistfully, wondering if there was a chance that Oliver's thoughts might align with her secret wishes. If only she had been chosen by someone of her own class all those years ago. David had been a terrible mistake. She had imagined she was in love. Love was nothing but a projection of one's own need to be attached to another being, she thought cynically.

She told herself that her feelings for Oliver were entirely different, to the way she had felt about David. She and Oliver were of the same ilk, and the joining of the house of Blythe with the house of Soames would create a force for good in the area. Well, it would if they had been still living in medieval times. It would be like a fairy tale, the happy ever after she had long since given up on.

They trotted along the path that ran beside the river. She felt stronger on top of a horse. She couldn't remember why she had not ridden before. It was madness. She was several years off fifty, not that old, not too old to still compete, if she chose. She was invigorated, happy and smiled widely at her companion. His expression lightened in response, but he was too taciturn to grin back, that was beyond him. They returned to the stables, and Grace ignored the stares of Ruby and Angela.

"Is everything ready for tomorrow?" said Grace. "I'll go through the list with you now."

"Yes, Grace," said Angela bowing her head, as usual - another list.

Chapter Nineteen

The two-week trip around Europe worked out well. Rafael and Poppy both won small competitions and were placed in several big ones. Jerome did not win any rosettes, but he and Joe had not disgraced themselves. It gave them all a taste for life on the road, travelling from one show to another. On their days off, Grace escorted them around to see the sights, visiting museums and art galleries. This was meant to be educational and to make up for the fact that Poppy was missing school. Rafael quite liked the sight-seeing. It was so far from his childhood experiences; the sheer novelty enchanted him.

Christmas was a few weeks away, and the horses were to be rested until the end of February, let out to graze every day that it was not pouring with rain, wearing the very latest in waterproof rugs. Grace had finally mustered the courage to invite Oliver and Hector to join them on Christmas Day. Oliver had accepted without a moment's pause, it was as if he had been waiting for the invitation, and she was so filled with hope. She began to make plans for a festive Christmas that no-one could ever forget. Rafael watched the preparations from the sidelines. It was to be his first Christmas in a cold climate, and it snowed in the second week of December. The countryside was transformed; it looked like the land was covered with a thick layer of white frosted icing. He rubbed the cold, wet stuff between his hands and tasted it – so strange.

Rafael and Poppy took Marco out into the field, and he sat up in his pram and watched them build a snowman with stones for eyes, a bright red scarf around his neck and a large carrot for a nose. Phoebe was not there for the snowman making. She was away a lot these days, spending several nights a week in London. Lured with the promise of that lovely white powder and also Tinker's invitations to various book launches, poetry readings and just meeting up with his friends in cafés.

She continued to sport her blunt haircut of blue and black and began to paint her face in stronger colours. The shape of the haircut suited her round moon face, creating a vague illusion of planes and angles. It was impossible to be around Tate and not become aware of the new trend for 'having work done'. She hadn't a wrinkle in sight, but she did get some filler injected into the top of her cheeks to give her at least a hint of rounded high cheekbones. She told herself that she was almost over her disappointment that she and Rafael could not be a couple. She reasoned that he had never really been in love with her, and he had never pretended to be in love with her, so he had not betrayed her, nor broken his promises.

She had even begun 'scribbling' as she called it. Unlike Tinker, she didn't feel any particular empathy with a keyboard, so she bought herself a bound-notebook and began to jot down her thoughts on life; a description of a scene, an attempt at characterisation and various other jottings. She mainly wrote when under the influence of cocaine and she had to admit that when she read it over later, not under the influence, they were not the great thoughts that she had thought them when she had put them down.

She still thought about living in London and working in a job; creating a new life that belonged entirely to herself; where she was not merely an irrelevance in the world of horses at Kiss Wood. Tate took her along to lots of Christmas parties in London and during the day she shopped for glamorous clothes and elaborate Christmas gifts for her family.

"This will be our first proper Christmas together at Kiss Wood, and we will celebrate fittingly," said Grace. Phoebe thought that they had been at Kiss Wood last Christmas, but it had passed without much fanfare, as they had been so caught up in the drama of getting rid of her father. She thought about her father and wondered how things were going in Montevideo. He had written to tell her and Poppy that Claudia had given birth to a fat, healthy little baby boy called Pablo. They had a half-brother who they had never met. She understood why her mother didn't want to be married to him, but he was still her father, and she missed him.

She could fly out to Uruguay to see him, take Marco with her so that he could meet his grandfather and his uncle, the baby. But she couldn't quite bear to fly there on her own, she dithered and dallied and tried to decide what to do. Her life was wobbling along with no clear direction. She had to do something, either begin studying or get a job, looking after Marco just wasn't enough, not with all the staff and the nanny. She couldn't decide.

Grace's considerable energy was focused on Christmas. If Oliver had refused her invitation, her dreams would have been in tatters, and her very secret imaginary world where she and Oliver were married would have dissolved like morning mist in the sunlight. She had been swept away by a wave of elation when he had accepted, and this carried her along for days. She spent hours writing lists and ticking off items and supervising the girls from the village who were brought in to polish the house from top to bottom. Her vision of the perfect Christmas had enlarged; she would host a party on Christmas Eve, and then her family, along with Oliver and Hector would go to Midnight Mass in the village church. She decided that they would use the old ballroom in the east wing of the house for the party and employed a party planner who organised the decorations; bright, lavish green and red bows, strings of silver and blue tinsel, golden lights, coloured candles and a myriad of other decorations. There was also a large fresh green Christmas tree that Grace had had cut down in the wood.

"It's not very environmentally friendly, you know," said Poppy.

"What are you talking about?" asked Grace sharply.

"Cutting down a tree just for Christmas."

"It was due to be cut down anyway, thinning out those pine trees that were planted in the copse a few years ago," replied Grace tartly. She found it irksome when Poppy criticised her.

The large ballroom in the east wing had not been used for a social event in years, not since she had been a girl. She remembered those days when her parents had hosted the hunt ball, and she had been allowed to stay up to watch the dancing.

Phoebe had surveyed the list of guests to be invited to the Christmas Eve party, of course, there was Verena Wade and her new husband, Tate and Loppy. She asked her mother if she could also invite Tinker and her friend Panda and her husband. She had met Panda down at the Goat and found her rather sweet. She was only a few years older than Phoebe with bright shiny black hair cut in a geometric bob. She was married to a rather unassuming and plain husband called Teddy. He adored her, and she enjoyed all the attention. They had only bought their cottage in September, but already she seemed to have befriended a great many people in the area, although obviously not Grace. She said that she adored people and found them so interesting and Phoebe suspected that this amounted to a voracious desire for gossip, but it was all done in a spirit of good fun, and there seemed to be no malice in it.

Phoebe had a rather splendid choice of outfits to wear since she had been gadding about in London. After much deliberation she narrowed it down to two; a close-fitting silver sheath that flattered her figure with matching

233

high silver shoes, or a soft flouncy gold skirt with a tight sequined black bodice. She chose the gold and found some matching black high heels, with gold hoop earrings in her ears, she wanted to create a vaguely gipsy look.

Verena and her new husband arrived early. She had promised to help Grace greet the guests and introduce people to each other, in order to get the party going. Verena had been recently re-upholstered with a facelift, filler injected into her cheekbones, and every inch of her body had been tautened, fake-tanned and massaged. Her small, narrow aristocratic nose had always been one of her best features, but her generous full lips were like a loophole in a careful statement, that suggested that beneath her composed elegance there lurked a sensual and impetuous nature. Grace smiled with genuine warmth at her staunch friend.

"Verena, you're looking absolutely stunning, obviously marriage to," she paused for a split second as she tried to remember his name, "Justin is suiting you very well."

Justin smiled with a hint of oily charm that reminded Grace of David at his most ingratiating, but she banished this thought. Verena had been around the block a time or two; she wasn't an innocent young woman; she would know how to handle him.

Phoebe and Poppy were circulating with plates of savoury delicacies and making small talk with the people from the village. There were two waitresses kitted out in black and white who were carrying trays of drinks. Soft scented light flickered from the myriad of candles that were lit around the edges of the room, and melodic Christmas music wafted through from the other room, not loud enough to make it hard to converse, but sufficient to give the event an ambience.

Rafael felt uncomfortable. He couldn't imagine anything worse than this sort of party. Phoebe took him by the arm and led him over to Panda, who was such an easy, chatty person that she trusted her to help him to feel at ease. Rafael smiled as if his teeth were being drilled, shuffled his feet and answered her interested questions monosyllabically. Panda liked the look of this exotic young man who she knew was the father of Phoebe's child. She was desperate to find out the inside story, how did they come to get together. Rafael was not enlightening her in spite of her subtle questioning style.

234

All the members of the local Parish Council had been invited, and they were there in force, clustering in a coven talking about the latest council news and making plans to bring Grace into the fold, she was just the type of council member that they needed, high-born, influential and of an impeccable character, in spite of being divorced. The Vicar joined them. He was new to the area and very keen to get involved in the community. They looked at him with a little suspicion; he was known to be one of those 'born-agains'. He was clearly top-drawer with a public school drawl and bouncing with zeal and enthusiasm and clean-cut good intentions.

"Now do please introduce yourselves," he said with a wide, happy grin.

"I'm Mrs Raymond, Chairperson of the Parish Council, for my sins," she said, trying not to sound too portentous. Her double chin wobbled a little and her wrinkled hand with big carbuncle rings fluttered up to her neck self-consciously. "This is Gilbert Seymour, our Treasurer," she said with a small gesture towards the man standing at her side. He was short and portly with some self-conscious ginger stubble on his wobbling chin. He stuck his pallid hand out for a slightly damp handshake, but the Vicar, 'call-me-Rob', was extremely well-mannered and didn't give in to the temptation to wipe his hand down the side of his trousers.

"Let me introduce you to dear Pippa, my better half," he said heartily, gesturing to a no-nonsense woman in a voluminous violet and lemon printed dress with low-heeled court shoes and the ubiquitous string of pearls.

"How do you do? How do you do?" she said in matter of fact tones, shaking hands all round. "No doubt we'll be seeing you in St Michaels in the coming weeks," she said self-confidently. "And we'll be starting an Alpha course soon, and I expect you'll be fascinated to join in."

"An Alpha course?" asked Bertie Whistler, one of the councillors.

"Yes, it is to introduce interested people with questions about life to Jesus," said Pippa, as if stating the most obvious of facts. She was finally giving them the chance to meet Jesus, who could resist? The councillors looked at her with a collective quizzical glance.

"Fascinating," boomed Mrs Raymond, in mock enthusiastic tones. "Always questions," she said politely, hurrumphing and turning on her heel she moved across the room to talk to dear Oliver Soames.

"Oliver, that new Vicar, he and his wife are rather unusual," she said.

"Yes, they're from that strange church just down the road from Harrods. Full of enthusiasm, they sing in a chanting style that induces a sort of consciousness that makes people vulnerable to being persuaded," said Oliver smoothly.

"Oliver, speaking of persuasion, do you think you could persuade Grace to stand for the Parish Council, she is just the sort of member that we need," she suggested to him.

Oliver smiled. "I'm not sure that I've that much influence on dear Grace," he replied.

"But of course you do, she respects you inordinately," said Mrs Raymond, who was hawk-eyed when it came to possible couplings in the community.

Oliver changed the topic of conversation. "How is the budget balancing this year?" he asked.

"Gilbert has reined in the spending, and we should be coming out even," said Mrs Raymond.

"Glad to hear it," said Oliver in hearty tones.

"Hector! Hector!" said Loppy Wade, bouncing over to him, standing next to his father. "How's the gee-gees?"

"Good," said Hector and began to regale her with the latest exciting match in which he had scored the winning goal. Oliver listened in, thinking Hector was so young and enthusiastic, he had yet to learn to dissemble and behave with more modesty.

Poppy came over with a fresh plate of savouries and joined them. The three young people ate their way through the plate and were sipping spicy mulled wine that was rather going to their heads.

"Poppy darling, are you meant to be drinking that?" asked Phoebe, sweeping by in her gold flouncy dress.

"Mummy said I could, as it is Christmas," said Poppy taking a brazen gulp.

"It's more potent than you think," said Phoebe, "we don't want you getting squiffy."

The room filled with people. Some of Grace's friends had even come down from London, travelling together in several cars with designated drivers. In all, the evening was judged a success. A great deal of wine was drunk, and the people from the village staggered back down the drive at half-past ten. Grace marshalled Oliver, Hector, Rafael, Poppy and Phoebe to walk down into the village for Midnight Mass.

"It's that new Vicar, isn't it?" said Poppy. "what's he like?" she asked pirouetting drunkenly down the gravel drive.

"A little odd, perhaps," said Grace disinterestedly. She had absolutely no intention of getting mixed up in village politics. She had her sights set on conquering the equestrian world.

In spite of her dismissive attitude, Grace was disquieted by the service. She had previously enjoyed the essentially ritualistic, high-church leanings of the old Vicar. She had envisaged herself kneeling beside Oliver in a mutual act of worship. Instead, there was a happy-clappy music group at the front of the church, chanting with strange mannerisms of raised hands, which reminded her a little of the "Heil Hitler" salute.

They walked back to Kiss Wood, and it was a beautiful moonlit night, and the stark trees were etched against the velvet sky. She wished that she and Oliver could walk hand in hand, but he strode along swinging his arms in a manly fashion. This was not a moment for intimate tenderness. She sighed. She was going to have to wait to see if he was ever going to make a move.

Christmas Day was perfect. They woke and it was snowing, just a light drift of beautiful soft snow that covered the ground with a light-reflecting blanket of pure white.

"It's like a scene in a Christmas card," said Phoebe, clapping her hands with excitement after all those soulless Christmas days in Consulate houses, this is in our real home, where we are meant to be!"

Everyone congregated beside the Christmas tree in the drawing-room in the west wing. There were piles of presents, and Phoebe retrieved her present for Rafael and handed it to him. It was, a large parcel with three items wrapped in one bundle. He tore it open solemnly. She had wanted to give him his present first. She imagined that Carina would have bought him Christmas presents as a child, but perhaps this was his first real Christmas since she had died. He held up a pair of smart casual trousers, a light sand colour.

"Thank you, Phoebe, they are very smart," he said politely. Then he looked down at the two books. He ran his fingers over the cover of first one, then the other; "Twisted truths of modern dressage: A search for a classical alternative" by Philippe Karl and "The Art of Classical Dressage to High School" by Philippe Karl."

"You want the father of your son to not only show jump, but also do dressage," he said, smiling shyly at her.

"Dressage is only training," said Phoebe, who knew her equestrian facts well. "Besides you need to hold your own against young Jerome."

"Oh Phoebe, how clever of you to choose those books, I must read them," said Grace, who had already secretly organised an agent to show her several dressage horses in Utrecht in early January. She had yet to find the courage to ask Oliver to come with her, she didn't want him to think that she was angling to get him to help pay for another horse. She would tell him that she would value his opinion. Perhaps there might be an opportunity to mention it later.

Rafael gave Phoebe a small box wrapped in silver Christmas paper. For just one moment, she thought it might be an engagement ring, but, of course, it wasn't. It was a pair of diamond earrings, just tiny, but genuine diamonds, which had probably cost him a month's salary.

"Thank you so much," she said, leaning forward to kiss him but withdrawing. "I shall put them on straight away." Her fingers had fumbled as she pushed the earrings into her ear lobes. Then Rafael turned and gave an identically sized box to Poppy, who ripped it open quickly.

"Oh Rafael, they're lovely, just what I like," said Poppy, with no inhibitions she leant forward and kissed him on the cheek. She held up the little red enamelled earrings. "So Christmassy, totally perfect for my outfit today!"

This made Phoebe feel uncomfortable, but she couldn't quite pin down the reason for her flash of disquiet. Of course, Rafael had bought presents for everyone. He had given Grace a tasteful silk scarf in pale pink, specially chosen to match one of her favourite outfits.

Everyone had splurged on Marco who sat in a welter of Christmas paper, with a huge array of brightly coloured toys. He cooed and gurgled and tried to eat the paper and had to be restrained by Phoebe.

"He's always so happy," said Poppy, playing with one of the toys. "I wish there'd been this sort of thing when I was a baby."

"You make yourself sound so old," said Rafael, smiling at her.

Oliver presented Grace with a framed painting of Bliss, which he had commissioned from a local artist.

"Oh, Oliver! This is so wonderful, you knew just what I wanted!" said Grace warmly, smiling at him. She almost kissed him but couldn't quite bring herself to be so demonstrative. Phoebe smiled at this. She couldn't see what her mother had bought for Oliver, no doubt it had been a choice over which she had agonised for hours. There wasn't much spontaneity in Grace.

They all trooped over to the stables to help Jamie muck out, as Angela, Ruby and Jerome had gone home to celebrate with their own families. Hector and Poppy were skylarking and throwing things at each other. Oliver manfully pushed the wheelbarrow showing that he was still capable of manual labour. Jamie had been invited to lunch, and when they had finished the horses, he went off to his quarters to wash and change before he joined them at the big house.

Lunch was utterly splendid; a glorious golden turkey from a local farm where they were reared free-range, surrounded by four different types of home-made stuffing, two types of gravy, an endless variety of baked vegetables, tiny fried sausages, strips of bacon, and steamed greens. This was followed by a home-made Christmas pudding which was lit with brandy, served with a halo of translucent blue flames. When it was dished out, each person had a choice of thick cream and or delicious home-made custard.

239

Jamie ate a lot but didn't talk. He felt out of his depth in this company. He was too conscious of the fact that he was staff. There was a giant barrier between himself and the others. His glances darted surreptitiously towards Grace, who was sitting at the head of the table. There was no-one at the foot of the table, she had placed Oliver on her right and Hector on her left. Beside Hector was Poppy, and then Jamie, and beside Oliver was Phoebe and then Rafael, with Marco in his high chair between them. Everyone ate well and then they began to toast each other, then each of the horses. Poppy and Hector seemed to be giggling at their own silly jokes.

Finally, Christmas Day was over. At tea time Grace waved off Hector and Oliver, back to Tall Chimneys. She wondered if it were possible that next Christmas she and Oliver might be together. She felt helpless. There were only so many moves she could make, it was up to Oliver now. She had decided not to ask him to go to look at the Dutch dressage horses, she would take Jamie, he was probably a better judge of horseflesh anyway.

On Boxing Day she felt dreary again. In the days of her childhood, there would have been the Kiss Wood Boxing Day Meet. It had always seemed to be the best day of the season; somehow, there was always a good run on Boxing Day. She remembered when she had been seventeen, the same age as Poppy now. There had been no snow that year, and it was perfect weather for good scent. The hounds had drawn the first covert, and the horses and riders waited, some trembling with excitement, some calm and experienced. They had harkened to hounds opening, the music grew, swelling to a wild clamour as the pack found the line. "Gone away!" shouted the Master and broke into a gallop, the field pounded along behind him. They were over the first hedge that had been carefully trimmed by her father's orders to provide a good obstacle. Her horse had jumped next to her father's horse, and the rush of cold air against her cheeks and the feeling of flying was the most exhilarating experience she could remember. The field was pounding all around them, into the small wood and then out, and they were galloping across the river meadows that adjoined the fields of Tall Chimneys. She sighed as she remembered, political correctness had a lot to answer for!

Chapter Twenty

Grace had decided that she was going to become a dressage rider. She had asked Jerome if she could watch him training and he had warily, but politely agreed. She had studied the high-class performances of freestyle and Grand Prix on youtube; and had spent hours of careful deliberation over the amazing array of dressage horses offered for sale, like choosing two delicious chocolates from a whole box of favourites. Finally, she had decided that she would buy a Grand Prix schoolmaster and a promising young mare. There were two particular horses that she had selected from the list for sale.

The first was advertised as a Grand Prix schoolmaster who had 'been there, done that' and had achieved some good scores but didn't quite have the flair and personality to make it to the top. He was a beautiful black gelding. She had never had a black horse, not coal-black with no white markings, so she was attracted to this animal, as something novel. She had watched the video of him many times. He had a beautiful head with a kind eye. He was proficient at one-time changes, executing flying changes from one leading leg at the canter to the next. To the uninitiated, it looked like the horse were skipping elegantly across the arena. He also performed excellent piaffes, trotting on the spot. The description of him stated that he was good to hack and travel and was not sharp or spooky. She liked the look of him enormously.

The second was a chestnut mare with a lovely long neck which would afford a 'good length of rein'. She was working at advanced medium stage, and starting in-hand piaffe training. She had qualified for next summer's regional championships and had scored up to 72% in her tests. She was straightforward with a lovely temperament, a smaller horse with big paces.

Grace spoke to Jamie, and he had been totally surprised when she had told him that she wanted him to accompany her to the Netherlands. An agency representative would meet them at Utrecht airport and escort them to the different stables where the horses were for sale. Hotels would also be organised for them. It promised to be a dream tour. She had asked Jamie not to mention it to anyone else but didn't explain to him that this was because she was feeling shy about her new venture. She was afraid that the others would wonder if she was up to it. Finding herself a dressage coach

241

was put off until the horses were chosen and purchased. Jamie nodded agreement. She had no fears that he would gossip, if nothing else he was 'close as an oyster'.

In the week before their departure Grace rode Gunner and Mickey every day, they were meant to be resting for a couple of months, but she wanted to regain just a little of her 'riding fitness'. She did sitting trot around the arena, rising trot without stirrups and practised transitions as if her life depended on it. She woke every morning with that feeling that something exciting was happening and this state of exaltation was sustained throughout the day. The agency would be showing them at least a dozen horses, but Grace had set her heart on the black gelding, Darthvader, and the chestnut mare, Redwings.

Jamie watched Grace riding the old show jumpers from the sidelines and wondered that she had thought of inviting him to go to Holland. He felt heartened, perhaps she, unlike anyone else, had recognised his talents. Although, it might just be that she knew she could trust him to keep a secret.

On the morning of their departure, he and Grace had driven out the front gate. She had arranged for the car to stay parked overnight at the airport. There were both aware of a delicious sense of intrigue. As if they were off on a clandestine date, although buying wonderfully expensive horses had to be far more exciting than any boring, tawdry affair. This was the stuff of real life for both of them!

Rafael had watched them leave from the wide landing of the curved stairs. Jamie had said he was going away with Grace but had not told him where, and asked him to ride Tinpot. Rafael watched them go. He had no idea where they were going, but he was not particularly curious. He did not discuss it with anyone else. He went down to the stables and saw that Gunner and Mickey were already out in the field, wearing their handsome light and dark blue waterproof rugs. He was glad to see them having a rest, which had been the original plan before Grace had used them to train herself. He tacked up Tinpot. He hadn't ridden the stallion since Jamie had taken over his training and he was interested to see how he went now. He took him into the arena and trotted around several times. The big horse made no attempt to buck.

He moved freely with a long powerful stride, his hindquarters were engaged and his head in a good position, quite high and just slightly bent at the poll. Jamie had improved him a great deal. Rafael decided that he might try some trot work that was the foundation of extension. He had learned that true extension was impossible until collection had been mastered, but he attempted to give the stallion length of rein and some lengthening of his stride while he was in rising trot. This seemed to go well, so he tried something different; lateral work on two-tracks, shoulder-in and renvers and the horse bent well. Rafael had developed a new interest in dressage since Phoebe had given him the Philippe Karl books for Christmas and he was trying it out for himself. He found it difficult to follow written directions and often got confused, but sometimes, it came together, and he began to understand.

Phoebe drove into London that afternoon, leaving Marco in the charge of the nanny. She was to attend a book launch at Waterstones with Tinker. There was a bunch of them meeting up, 'the gang' as they described themselves. Phoebe was now a fully signed-up member, and there was talk of a weekend at Kiss Wood.

They were meeting at the pub down the road, and when Phoebe arrived, there were half a dozen of them drinking glasses of wine. Tinker, Nic, Maddie, David, Georgia, and Stiggy. Phoebe knew them all, and there was a general roar of welcome, and she was clasped and kissed by each of them. Everyone was in high spirits, expecting a fun party after the book launch, which was a very literary high-brow work written by one of Georgia's former school friends. They were a jolly band, and Phoebe felt happy and accepted.

Nic was a moody looking, rather lugubrious chap with a greasy curly topknot of dark hair with a long face and prominent jutting jaw. He wrote biographies and histories and was regularly working on one dull story of an old person or another, but it paid well, and he was in much demand as a hard worker who was very respectful and ingratiating with his various clients. Maddie was in her mid-thirties and had lived in China and taught English; she had thick, long hair draped around her pale Madonna-face with an impressive huge shelf of a bosom that jutted out in front of her like the prow of a galleon. David was a producer of musicals. He was very smart and likeable, a gifted musician who loved burlesque; he smiled widely at those around him, and his eyes were darting here and there, bulging out of his head in a quite distinctive manner. Georgia aspired to be a writer but up until now had only produced textbooks for a training organisation in the Middle East. She had very pale porcelain skin and rather watery blue eyes. Stiggy was a Romanian whose parents had brought him to England when he was twelve-years-old, he had soulful brown eyes and the physique of a rugby player, no neck and a barrel chest, but his aspiration belied his appearance and he proudly called himself a poet.

They were trooping out the door to go down to Waterstones when a tiny bird-like girl called Shea called out to them in a fluting, high-pitched voice. She was twenty but looked about twelve, and Tinker was teased a good deal as he professed himself in love with her. He hung back while the others kissed and embraced her; his round chubby face was crimson with embarrassment.

There was a decent crowd at the book launch, and Phoebe bought herself a copy of the book and stood in the ragged line waiting for it to be signed by the author, Annegret Rickman. She wondered how it must feel to be Annegret Rickman who was smiling and chatting to each person in turn as she scrawled her signature with a thick black pen. She was dressed in a severe, but extremely, well-cut black suit, with a fresh hairdo straight out of the hairdresser. She was looking a little glazed and out of it. Perhaps, she was so overcome she didn't feel as if it were real; or perhaps she had done this so often it was getting unutterably boring. Phoebe couldn't imagine signing her own books for buyers would ever get boring, but somehow it seemed an impossible dream.

Eventually, she reached Annegret and looked her in the eye and smiled sincerely. She felt as if she couldn't make contact. The 'gang' descended upon the nibbles as if they were a starving hoard – it was one of their 'things'. Phoebe suspected that her newfound 'gang' were just a tiny bit childish, but she quickly banished the thought, she'd never been one of a group before, and she was determined to savour the experience.

Maddie rounded them up at eight-thirty and announced that they were off to 'The Watering Hole', one of their favourite haunts, and they all trooped out. They seemed to have gathered up a few more members, and there was quite a swarm of them.

"Annegret said she would join us later," said Georgia self-importantly.

"Have you actually read the book?" asked Nic, who had been leafing through Phoebe's copy – he was too poor or stingy to buy one for himself.

"Yes, I was a beta-reader," said Georgia proudly, "and it's jolly good, very erudite!"

"But does it have sex in it?" asked Stiggy who had a one-track mind.

"There were sexual issues but no grotesque descriptions," said Georgia primly.

Stiggy pulled a face as if he wouldn't bother with it.

"Soon you'll have one of your books picked up by a wholesaler and then we'll be trooping to your do," said Phoebe to Tinker.

"I'm not sure that commercial success is my primary aim," said Tinker pretentiously.

"Perhaps no type of success is your future," said Maddie waspishly. Phoebe knew that Maddie had self-published, but she never appeared on any of the bestseller lists which were updated hourly on Amazon.

Once they were safely ensconced in one of the booths at 'The Watering Hole', they began to gossip seriously.

"She's an absolute prune!" shouted Shea.

"Well I love her breasts, beautiful big breasts like melons," said Stiggy lasciviously, in his affected thick Eastern European accent.

"Like melons, that is the most inane simile," said Tinker superciliously.

"How would you describe them then?" challenged Maddie.

"I prefer the small original detail than the obvious sexual dimension," said Tinker pompously.

Phoebe had a sudden revelation. These people were not glamorous and intellectual as she had thought, but rather pretentious and ugly. She still loved Tinker, but she had admitted to herself that his writing was not that good, nor probably ever going to be good. She felt extremely uncomfortable with this new and most unwelcome idea and said good-bye, making excuses and caught a taxi back to Tate's. She was afraid that this awful knowledge would show in her eyes, and they would know that she despised them. She hoped she could find some lovely little packets of white powder at Tate's. At least drugs were reliable.

Several days later, Grace arrived back from her trip to Holland glowing with radiance. Phoebe immediately noticed the difference in her mother's mien and wondered if she had fallen in love. She knew she had gone away with Jamie, surely not? Although she herself had fallen in love with a stable boy, so obviously it was not beyond the bounds of possibility; and Jamie was after all of higher station than that of a stable boy, and like her mother, he was obsessed with horses. But still, surely not!

At this stage, Phoebe didn't know that it was the purchase of two dressage horses that had caused this change in her mother's state of being. Grace had, in fact, purchased the two she had originally chosen although she had ridden at least half a dozen additional possibilities, and looked at many others. Unerringly she followed her instinct, and it was the black gelding with the kind eye that had drawn her. His movements had displayed harmony, elasticity and consistency, all qualities that were highly desirable; and he had technical ability in abundance. The chestnut mare was something else, although still at a more basic level of training she exhibited true self-carriage and her paces were divine, she showed enormous promise, and she might well be good enough to make it to the top. The horses were to arrive in a week, and Grace was floating on air. Now she set about finding herself a dressage coach. She made appointments with several, and they came to Blythe Star Stables to give lessons to herself on Gunner, Jamie on Tinpot, Rafael on Mickey and also Jerome on Joe.

Finally, after much discussion and deliberation, and checking the recordings that had been taken of each of the lessons Grace chose Uwe Blacklock. She liked the style of this austere, hard-faced woman who had been specialising in dressage for many years. Uwe had been born and raised in Germany and had had the best of classical training, then marrying a British rider had come to England and was regularly competing at Grand Prix level as well as bringing other horses up through the lower levels. She was the one whose explanations were the easiest for Grace to comprehend, she was almost the most expensive, but at this point, Grace paid no heed to cost, nothing must stand in her way to follow her dreams.

She told Jamie to re-arrange the horses, so her two new horses were placed in the best and most roomy of the loose boxes. She scrubbed them out herself with strong disinfectant, and when they had dried, she filled them with the highest quality dust-extracted sawdust. She made appointments with her favourite saddler, and he was to come and measure the horses and make her new dressage saddles, with matching snaffle bridles, and also double bridles. She had a special dressage coat made to measure and a pair of new riding boots. Nothing but the best would do.

Poppy watched these preparations with interest. The news was out now that her mother had bought two dressage horses. It would be somewhat of a relief that her mother would be otherwise occupied and not spend so much time watching her and giving orders. Although there was the distinct, and to her unwelcome possibility, that her mother might carry her along in the wake of this new enthusiasm and insist that she had to do dressage as well. Poppy had got to the point where she wanted to go her own way. Her 'rebellious' stage had been delayed with the return to England and the enchantment of becoming a young showjumper. Now she was beginning to flinch under the yoke of her mother's iron will. She wanted to make a stand, to do her own thing but as yet she wasn't quite sure what that would be.

Darthvader and Redwings arrived in a large horse transporter. Everyone had gathered to see them unloaded. Even Phoebe and Marco had come over from the big house. The horses were lightly rugged with huge padded travel bandages. The black gelding was more than a hand higher than the chestnut mare. Grace had them led to the indoor arena where they were stripped of their rugs and boots. Then they were trotted up and down, and she checked that they were not lame.

"They're absolutely gorgeous," said Ruby enthusiastically. She particularly liked dressage and was happy about this change in direction.

"I like that black gelding," said Angela.

Rafael watched them and nodded.

"You're a good judge of horseflesh," he affirmed smiling at first Grace and then Jamie.

"Can we see you riding them?" asked Phoebe.

247

"Tomorrow I'll ride them in the school. My coach, Uwe, is coming over to see what they look like. You can watch if you want," she replied. She was so happy, that she was finding it hard not to give in to the temptation to ride them immediately. But they had been travelling for many hours and needed to rest.

"Can they jump?" asked Poppy, with just a whisper of belligerence in her voice.

"No, Poppy, of course not," retorted her mother. "One doesn't risk top class dressage horses over poles. They might be injured."

Poppy snorted with derision. Grace ignored this. She was dreaming a most enticing vision. She would be dressed up in top hat and tails and dancing with her horse in the dressage arena, and Oliver would see her and then realise that he was in love.

"Are we going to have to employ more staff, two more horses in full work, perhaps we need another groom?" questioned Jamie.

"Yes, I see what you mean," said Grace. "I will think about it. Perhaps we might consider some working pupils."

The following day Uwe Blacklock arrived and was impressed with the horses.

"You have chosen well Grace, but we have a lot to do, in some ways you are starting at the bottom. But there is nothing like an experienced schoolmaster to teach you all you know. I never understand the school of thought that suggests that two novices will learn together. It is certainly not the German way."

Grace worked hard, every morning, schooling each horse for forty minutes. Schooling a dressage horse for forty minutes was not a hack through the park. It was utterly exhausting! She began to feel every one of her forty-seven years. She was determined to be the best that she could possibly be. She rode either Micky or Gunner in the afternoon, taking them out hacking, just quietly walking and trotting, just so she could spend more time in the saddle, building her fitness. She also went down to the leisure centre and began swimming laps. She found it relaxing and helped to soothe her aching muscles.

Sometimes Rafael rode out with her, other times it was Jamie or even Jerome. None of these men was a good conversationalist, but, usually, she was too fatigued from the morning's schooling to have the energy to sustain any type of dialogue.

Grace had previously made the arrangements for another show jumping trip to Belgium - for four days. She was loath to leave her dressage horses but in the end was persuaded by Jamie that it would do them no harm to have four days off, they had been schooled continuously since they had arrived.

There was a great deal to do with the show jumping ponies who all had to be brought back into work and trained and got fit. Grace began riding two ponies a day in the school, practising some of her new dressage techniques on them, hoping to improve them, although when she saw Poppy zooming around with them in her increasingly slapdash style, she thought that perhaps any improvements she was bringing about would be promptly undone. She asked Jerome if he would start riding one or two of the other ponies each day.

Then she began on her lists again, planning the trip. She even considered sending Jamie instead of herself, but there would not be enough people to stay at home to look after the other horses, and she had no desire to have to actually muck out stables herself. She also needed to keep an eye on Poppy who was becoming increasingly unruly. She would have to hire more staff, or cut down on the horses. With six mares in foal, Tinpot, six ponies, two show jumpers and two dressage horses, there was a great deal to do. She thought perhaps they should sell two of Poppy's show jumpers, six was a ridiculous number. She tried to talk to Poppy suggesting that perhaps they might sell Bosley, who still hadn't settled, and Harley who was unreliable. But Poppy became hysterical, screaming that she could not get rid of any of them.

"But darling, you'll be moving on to horses soon anyway, and you need to concentrate on your schoolwork, if we got rid of two of them now, then there won't be so many to sell in the near future."

Poppy protested and flounced out, and that was the end of that conversation. Grace began to think that perhaps she had created a monster. There were an alarming number of horses now, and the costs of keeping them all was skyrocketing. It looked like she would need to pay more wages. Her funds were not absolutely limitless, and her accountant looked increasingly grave every time they had a meeting.

Grace, Poppy, three ponies and the two show jumping horses, and Jerome's Joe, along with Rafael, Angela, Ruby and Jerome left early on a Thursday morning and would be back by Tuesday evening. Phoebe felt as if she had been deserted. She felt increasingly isolated as the horses continued to dominate every activity at Kiss Wood. But it was worse when they were all gone. She hated being at Kiss Wood without her mother, Rafael, or Poppy. The vast rooms echoed and it was like living in a ghost house. Most of all, she missed Rafael, it was not that they enjoyed any particular intimacy, but she felt comforted when he was around. They shared a bond through Marco, and it was a powerful connection. She had resigned herself now to the fact that he would never love her in the way that she wanted, but she had to be happy with crumbs as she was never going to enjoy the cake.

She would go to London; Tate was away, but Tinker was always around to go out and have some fun. She rang him, and he told her that he was meeting up with the gang at a pub near Leicester Square and they would go and have a Chinese meal afterwards.

"That sounds fun," said Phoebe half-heartedly. To be honest, she was not that keen to meet up with 'the gang' again. They tended to gossip endlessly about people she didn't know, and nothing is so dull as people talking about someone you have never met, and, in truth, she didn't much want to meet. She no longer loved the dressing up and becoming a 'different person', she was the same old dull Phoebe, and they were the same old gang.

She had finally mastered the art of being late, and tonight it was because she was not particularly looking forward to the event. The crew were all gathered like black crows, picking the eyes out of the carcasses of those who they slandered. She remembered this imperfectly, it was some line out of Michael Dransfield's poetry. They smiled at her when she entered, but she saw their eyes sliding around as if they had been caught out talking about her. Tinker came forward and kissed her, and she chose to believe that at least he was genuinely fond of her.

"Are you going to buy a round?" asked Georgia, as if mocking her because she was rich. She couldn't help being rich, and she had begun to understand what a burden wealth could be, trying to discern if people liked her for herself, or because of her financial resources.

"Of course," she said politely and feigned enthusiasm. She went to the bar, and Georgia went with her to detail the list of drinks.

"How are you going?" asked Phoebe, for want of anything more interesting to talk about.

"Fine," said Georgia defiantly, as if it were a trick question. Phoebe sighed. Posturing and posing was so exhausting. She thought longingly of Rafael He was not talkative but at least what he did say was genuine. She tried to imagine him here with her tonight, how would he get on with 'the group'. He wouldn't want to have any part of it. The bar person supplied them with two trays, and Phoebe carried one carefully back to the table. Everyone seemed thirsty tonight. Nic was looking rather pleased with himself.

"Did Georgia tell you I've got a new commission," he said proudly.

'No, of course, she didn't' thought Phoebe, 'the last thing she would do was impart good news about the achievement of someone else.'

"Do tell!" she said enthusiastically to Nic. He was at least a writer who actually wrote, if not his own creations then the stories of others.

"It's not an autobiography. It's a manuscript which needs editing and tidying up, which is something different and it's actually not bad, at least I can make something of it."

"Oh well done, what fun for you," said Phoebe.

"Well done," mimicked Maddie, and Phoebe's fears were confirmed. These people didn't like her, and they didn't even like each other. She would have more fun down at the Goat in the village giggling with Panda. Perhaps she should spend more time and effort with the people from the village.

"Remember you promised us a house party," said Tinker. Phoebe looked at him with dawning horror. She couldn't remember promising them a house party. Perhaps it had been on one of the nights when she had been riding high on the effects of cocaine. She suddenly became aware of the danger of drugs. All those strictures at school had not just been an attempt to stop people having fun. Reality had this horrible habit of jolting one out of a drug-induced dream.

"You said everyone was away until Tuesday so this weekend will be perfect. We'll all come down on Friday night and after Sunday lunch make our way back to London," said Tinker. "You'll all love it," he said warmly and expansively to the group. "It is the most fabulous house, and we shall have such fun."

"But where on earth is it?" asked Shea, her little bird-like eyes darting around, as if searching for some crumbs to peck at.

"Don't worry I'll take you on the train, I'll even pay your fare," said Tinker rather grandly, like a man of the world. Shea twittered in response.

"What's a house party?" asked Stiggy suspiciously, he had no previous experience of anything like this and had obviously never read Evelyn Waugh.

"Perhaps they don't have houses in Romania?" said Nic, bitchily.

"Pheebs darling will put us up, her people have a frightfully grand place and there's spare bedrooms, and then we party to our hearts' content all weekend," said Tinker.

"Brisk, country walks?" questioned Maddie cattily. Her family lived on a council estate in Reading, which she felt gave her enormous street credibility. In fact, she considered Phoebe to be half-baked, a 'rich bitch' who was trying to experience a slice of 'real life'.

"Can we bring some chums?" asked David, who knew the terminology because he *had* read Evelyn Waugh.

"Yes, well within reason," said Phoebe hesitantly, wondering what her mother would say. She would have to talk to Mrs Hopkins and perhaps they could put the breakable ornaments away. She hoped this brainwave of Tinker's wasn't going to get out of hand. What if her mother returned and found a hoard of squatters had moved in?

She wrote down the address of Kiss Wood, and a rough map with directions and her mobile phone number on half a dozen beermats and these were distributed among the members of the gang. She was hoping that no-one would turn up. She was almost tempted to mislead them with false directions, but Tinker knew where Kiss Wood was, and he would rumble her. She reasoned that if they left on Sunday afternoon and her mother wasn't back until Tuesday there would be time to make good anything broken or ruined. She made her excuses and left, assuring everyone she was looking forward to seeing them tomorrow night. She would drive back to Oxfordshire early tomorrow morning to make the preparations for a horde of hungry and careless strangers to descend on her home.

Chapter Twenty-One

Phoebe was thankful that she had less than twenty-four hours to prepare for the house party. Days of dread would have been horrible, anticipating all sorts of nightmare scenarios that she could do nothing to prevent. She thought that they would use the ballroom in the east wing as the venue, she didn't want her guests raiding her mother's supplies of alcohol in the west wing drawing-room. There was a small conservatory adjoining the ballroom, and she would use gas heaters in there. If more guests than anticipated arrived then the crowd could spill into the ballroom. There was a music system there, and guests could also dance, if they wished. She would have to organise some music, but had no idea what would be suitable. She would ring Panda and ask her to come and help. Panda was such a dear, and this event would not be beyond her capabilities.

She arrived back at Kiss Wood at mid-morning and immediately went to Mrs Hopkins to tell her that a number of house guests were expected that night and they would need feeding. She suggested that a list of provisions be prepared and she would drive immediately down to Sainsburys to buy the food that would be needed. Mrs Hopkins hurrumphed a little but then seemed to get into the spirit of things.

"Don't be silly dear, I'll order on the internet and ask for an immediate delivery," she reassured her.

"Oh, Mrs Hopkins, you're an absolute treasure. Thank you so much. You know it wasn't really my idea, and now they're all coming, I don't even know how many," said Phoebe, wringing her hands, distraught.

"That's all right, dear, now, I'll just ring the girls from the village to come up and help set the place to rights. All the spare bedrooms need to have the beds made up."

"Yes, and not the best linen," said Phoebe. "These guests are perhaps not the most careful of people.

A frown flashed across Mrs Hopkins' face. "Then we shall lock up the valuables," she said as if it were a joke, but they both knew it was not a joke.

"Now don't you fuss, why don't you go and arrange the furniture, set it up in the way that you think best."

"Yes, yes, that's what I'll do. I must just ring Panda and ask her to come and help," said Phoebe reaching for her mobile in the depths of her handbag and hurrying away.

Panda was thrilled to be summoned by Phoebe, she adored being a part of things, and an impromptu house party at Kiss Wood with a crowd from London sounded like great fun. She was hugely supportive and listened avidly to Phoebe's disjointed account of what was to happen.

"The music, that's what matters, why don't you ring Tinker and ask his advice, perhaps he can bring something." Tinker promised to bring an eclectic selection, and he said he would be arriving on the 6 pm train and would be bringing a bunch of them.

"Pheebs, darling, don't stress, we're all very casual, we'll just go along with whatever is happening."

"Sure," said Phoebe, not believing a word of it. She knew the crew. They would be picking faults and moaning from beginning to end. Never, ever again! She swore to herself.

"We've three hours before we have to pick up the first bunch from Oxford train station," she told Panda.

Phoebe was freaking out at the thought of cigarette burns in the wooden floor, drink rings on tables. She suggested that the first thing they do was to carry various antique items to be hidden in one of the lockable rooms that adjoined the kitchen. Whatever was left needed to be arranged. She felt helpless, she had no eye for these things, when she and Panda had finished the little tables and chairs looked like shrubs dotted randomly around a desert.

She was rather hoping that the party crowd might congregate in the conservatory that ran down the length of the drawing-room, looking out over an expanse of lawn to the fields below. A line of ragged elms raised their bare branches to the sky on the horizon, as if in supplication. She also raised her eyes to heaven and asked that this weekend would pass without disaster and she promised she would never again host a weekend house party.

"Phoebe, if you want to drive into Oxford, you really need to leave now," said Panda, like a mother hen.

"I'll just text Tinker, so we know how many people will be at the station," said Phoebe.

She waited anxiously for his text in reply.

"Good heavens, twenty people, they have gathered together a bunch," she said in faint tones

"Would you mind coming too, driving one of the other cars? But there still won't be enough room," she asked Panda

"Wouldn't it be easier to hire taxis for all of them, I know it will cost a bit, but it will give us time for a glass of wine to fortify ourselves before they arrive."

"Yes, yes, of course," said Phoebe. "I should have thought of that."

"I'll ring up the taxi firm and get them to meet them off the train," said Panda, happy to take charge.

"Now darling, let's head up to your bedroom and get dressed and made up, we'll take a bottle with us, just text Tinker and tell him to look out for the taxis. Let's have fun. You never know you might actually enjoy yourself this weekend," laughed Panda cheerily.

They ran like schoolgirls up the curved staircase. Panda was giggling as if it were some jolly jape. They scuttled along the passageway to Phoebe's room. Panda had brought an outfit in her overnight bag and some makeup. Phoebe was spoilt for choice for dressing up these days. She took out the slinky dark blue dress that she had worn on the first night that Tate had taken her out. The first night she had tried cocaine. It seemed aeons ago. She sighed, never had she felt more in need of a couple of lines. She hadn't thought to bring some with her when she had rushed back to Kiss Wood this morning. Perhaps Tinker might have some, but it was not likely. She realised then how she had become dependent on the drug, this was the beginning of the slippery slope, and it had crept up on her without her realising it.

They had drunk half a bottle of wine each by the time they went downstairs to wait for their guests. The smell of hot savouries was wafting past them as Mrs Hopkins sent the village girls with platters to set out on the big table in the conservatory. The gardener had already been requisitioned to

256

put the beer and cheap white wine on ice in large buckets, and there were glasses set out on trays. Soft music, albeit Grace's choice, floated through the house from the sound system in the ballroom. Phoebe knew that this was a 'moment' her first hosting of a house party and she only wished for a more sophisticated and intellectual group, rather than this crowd of try-hards and pretentious artistes. Perhaps she was being ridiculously idealistic, trying to find that 'group' which she longed for, she should just make do with imperfect people like herself.

The convoy of taxis swept up the drive, all driving too fast, spattering gravel onto the smooth lawns. Grace hated it when people drove too fast on her carefully raked gravel. Phoebe sighed that was another job she would have to supervise before her mother returned. A raucous chorus floated across the early evening air, the crew were excited, chattering, laughing, whooping at the sight of the big house. Phoebe handed out bundles of cash to each driver and made a show of cheerful welcome.

There were the usual crowd, Tinker, his cheeks bright pink with his hand ever so casually on the arm of the tiny Shea; Nic looking more sullen and lugubrious than ever, probably harking back to some long-forgotten socialist principles; Maddie's face screwed up with the effort of trying not to look impressed by the grandeur of the surroundings; David was goggled eyed with genuine appreciation of this glorious house thinking of it as a backdrop to a musical; Georgia's eyes were very watery today but Phoebe doubted it was from any positive softer emotion; Stiggy looking brutish and macho, perhaps to cover any nervousness at finding himself in unfamiliar surroundings; and there was a gaggle of other people that Phoebe couldn't place. Some looked vaguely familiar, but her attention was caught by the twins, 'the heavenly twins' – they must be! She had heard them being spoken of but had never seen them before. They were both over six foot, with gorgeous shiny, clean wavy dark hair but very white skin, providing a splendid contrast with their eyes which were a strange golden colour, flecked with hazel, they were smiling, utterly identical smiles and they were divine, a double vision of heaven indeed!

Everyone was carrying bags with changes of clothes, and there was even an odd bottle to contribute to the party. Stiggy had brought a big bag of crisps. The only bunch of flowers was presented to Phoebe by one of the twins.

"Thank you so much!" she exclaimed and felt herself going an unbecoming shade of tomato red, like a silly schoolgirl. She buried her face in the bunch of various coloured roses – bright yellow, deep red, yellow-pink and pale violet. At least, the vision of the heavenly twins had for several minutes completely banished the nagging worries that had besieged her for the last twenty-four hours.

"Let's all go inside, have a drink, get warm," she called out, amazed to hear her voice so authoritative and positive.

Panda herded the group like a sheepdog, and they trooped into the hall where the bronze statues of horses and warriors in gleaming marble looked down on them disapprovingly.

"Come through this way," said Phoebe leading the way into the east wing, no matter what they should be kept away from the main section of the house. The ballroom looked bare and desolate. There were no Christmas decorations or soft lights. The group seemed to coalesce into a pack, drawing together in the large room beneath the vaulted ceiling.

"Come through and have some wine and food!" called Phoebe, striding across the wooden floor, her footsteps echoing loudly. The conservatory was decorated with glossy-green leaved plants. The exotic orchids had been taken away to safety; the gas fires burned brightly, and the group began to relax and tossed back bottles of beer and glasses of wine, hoovering up the savoury snacks as if they had not eaten in days.

The heavenly twins homed in on Phoebe and Panda.

"Tell us your names?" said Panda roguishly, shaking back her shining black cap of hair, flashing her long green eyes at them.

"I'm Maddox, and this is my younger brother, Mason," said one of them.

"But how can we tell the difference? Are you totally identical?" asked Panda.

"Well, there is one tiny difference, but you'll have to have us naked to see it," said the one called Maddox.

"Such a tempting prospect," said Panda, flicking her hair around.

"I must go and introduce myself to our guests that I have not met," said Phoebe, with a trace of dutiful disappointment in her voice.

"I will come with you, and do the introductions," said the one called Mason.

Phoebe felt her head reeling not from the string of introductions but rather the fact that Mason had encircled her waist with his arm and introduced her as if she were the most important person in the world. She smiled shyly and welcomed the string of strangers; Brandon, Ariadne, Jordie (of indeterminate gender), Felix, Emmaline, Lolly, Flint, Jonathon, Laura, Toby, etc, etc; Phoebe couldn't remember any except Jordie as this was a 'transgender' person she assumed, transiting from female to male or male to female, she couldn't work it out and suspected that it would not be *de rigeur* to ask.

She smilingly welcomed them all and didn't dare to add up how many beds they were going to need. They would just have to bunk up together or sleep on the floor. The party seemed to be going well; the air buzzed with inane conversations, the drinks was sliding down gullets, savouries were crunched and people were smiling and even a couple of the girls, perhaps Emmaline and Lolly were gyrating to the music that Tinker had brought with him.

She reluctantly disengaged herself from the arm of Mason, and floated between her guests, offering a fresh platter of cheese straws. It had been brought over by Mrs Hopkins who was curious about Phoebe's new London friends.

"Make sure you keep the west wing locked up," Phoebe had murmured. Mrs Hopkins nodded, she knew how fearsome was Grace's wrath once roused and this crowd seemed rather raucous and reckless.

Soon the conservatory was filled with the fug of marijuana smoke. Reefers were being passed around. Phoebe had finally learnt the art of smoking without coughing. She felt that wonderful wave of happiness, the dopamine released by the magic weed and looked at Mason, she thought it was Mason, it could have been Maddox and dreamt what it might be like to be wrapped in his arms and legs. She had only ever slept with Rafael, perhaps now was the time to give up on him entirely and find another man.

Her dream was not to come true that evening. Mason and Maddox oozed their way around the room, flirting with all the girls, seemingly indiscriminately. Phoebe spent several hours swaying around the dancefloor, sipping white wine, and then eating to assuage the pang of the 'munchies' that assailed her as her blood sugar levels dropped.

More food was brought in by two of the girls from the village, it was an informal buffet but with enough for everyone. Finally, people wandered up to the bedrooms. Phoebe longed to slip over to the west wing to sleep in her own bed and kiss Marco goodnight, but she knew her duty as the hostess, and she needed to be around to make sure that the house wasn't burnt to the ground.

The next morning everyone woke late and wandered down to the ballroom that was empty and desolate. The soft lights and the music had stopped, and the clear winter sunlight lit the scene with harsh reality. The conservatory was littered with empty bottles, dirty glasses and plates. Phoebe began to clear away, piling the dirty plates and glasses onto trays and carrying them through to the kitchen. Mrs Hopkins was making sandwiches for lunch. Plates and plates of triangles of brown and white bread with every imaginable filling.

"Mrs Hopkins you are a wonder, thank you so much for this," said Phoebe genuinely grateful.

"I've got the girls coming up from the village this afternoon, and they'll go through and clean up a bit. I assume that tonight will be more of the same."

"I thought we might walk down to the village and visit the Goat, give the locals something to talk about," said Phoebe.

"I'm sure that will be enjoyable," said Mrs Hopkins with her mouth in a prim line. She hated to think what Grace would say if she were to see this rabble let loose in her precious house.

Panda turned up in the afternoon, looking fresh and pretty as always. This time she had brought her dowdy husband, Charles with her.

"I thought we might muster the troops and take them for a brisk country walk," she said brightly.

"What a jolly idea," said Phoebe ironically. Only Panda would attempt to rally this bunch of desperates for a jolly country walk. The guests emerged sleepy-eyed from the bedrooms and drank cups of coffee to revive themselves.

"Are you going to give us a tour of the house?" asked Maddie when Phoebe came in with a plate of croissants.

"Not really, the west wing has been closed for renovation," said Phoebe glibly, conscious of how easily the lies tripped off her tongue.

"These smell delicious, all buttery," said Shea who seemed to have become surgically attached to Tinker who was gazing at her starry-eyed.

By two o'clock Panda had mustered a group of more than half the guests.

"Phoebe, you must come too," she insisted, "they want to see the horses, but I don't know my way around the stables."

Phoebe grimaced at the thought of Jamie Landon's face if this lot shipped up at the stables and started messing around with the horses.

"We need to try to steer them away from the stables," she muttered out of the corner of her mouth, "my mother would have a fit." They set out down the gravel drive in the direction of the village.

"I think the Goat would be a lot more fun than the woods," said Phoebe, utterly determined that come what may, they would go nowhere near the horses.

They got to the village without losing any of the stragglers and Phoebe spoke to the landlord and put £150 behind the bar, for anyone who wanted a drink. Panda was nothing if not adaptable, her brisk country walk had been hijacked, but she didn't care, she felt as if she were at the very centre of things, the hub of life. Everyone began to drink, and Phoebe slipped away back to the house, she wanted to keep an eye on things and make sure the mess was cleaned up before tonight which promised to be more raucous than last night. She staggered around the conservatory, picking cigarette butts out of the pot plants, finding beer bottles dropped all over the place. Then she went back to the kitchen.

261

"Mrs Hopkins, I'm so sorry that you've had all this foisted upon you, I promise you I'll make it up to you somehow," she said pleadingly.

"It's alright dear, I don't suppose you're going to make a habit of it," said the housekeeper who often felt sorry for Phoebe who always seemed to be left on the margin of her family. "I can't imagine what your mother would think."

"I'm making a huge effort not to imagine that," said Phoebe. She made her way up to the west wing where Marco and the nanny were locked in seclusion.

"My darling little boy," she said, "your mother has been behaving very foolishly, but I promise you never again."

"I'm just going to lie down and have a little rest before tonight," she told the nanny and went back to the east wing to sleep in her guest bedroom. She could hear some people in the next-door bedroom who seemed to be in the throes of sexual passion, and she shuddered. What might seem perfectly normal somewhere else, was somehow sacrilegious here at Kiss Wood.

She felt utterly exhausted and lay like a limp rag on the bed, but she couldn't sleep, her mind was still racing. Now she was alone she thought again of Mason, or was it Maddox, surely Mason. Could she possibly have sex with another man? For some reason, this seemed totally wrong, or perhaps because it was in her family home, it seemed impossible. If she were ever to move on with her life, she needed to take the next step, and that seemed to involve a sexual adventure with another man.

Another buffet dinner was served, this time on trestle tables that had been set up in the ballroom. Mrs Hopkins had excelled herself, and there was a splendid array of delicious food. Home-made pizza that included a luxurious vegetarian topping with all sorts of delicious Mediterranean char-grilled vegetables. There were tiny home-made meat pies with a choice of tomato or barbecue sauce, sausage rolls, tiny toastie sandwiches, and chicken kebabs.

"Oh, Mrs Hopkins, thank you so much for organising this, you're an absolute star," said Phoebe.

There was plenty of alcohol, and the guests did not hold back. Everyone, including Phoebe, was totally drunk by ten o'clock. She found herself swaying, and one of the twins caught her as she was about to fall. She giggled helplessly and wriggled in his arms.

"Shall we go upstairs and lie down for a while," he whispered in her ear, his hot breath tickling her and giving her goosebumps. She felt her stomach clutch in excitement, the way it had used to when Rafael had kissed her before they made love. She nodded mutely. It was all she was capable of. He encircled her waist with his arm, and even though she was drunk, she was still capable of being thankful that she was thin now.

They went up the stairs to her room, she felt terrified, which was ridiculous, men and women did this all the time, casual lustful couplings, it was a normal run of the mill Saturday night occurrence. She wished she had drunk more, she needed Dutch courage, but then she might vomit, that would be even worse, the utter depths of humiliation.

In the room Maddox turned on the bedside lamp, to give a soft romantic light. He pushed her gently on to the bed, and they began to kiss. She could feel his hard penis pressing against her. He seemed big. Gently he peeled her out of her dress and took her shoes off, kissing and caressing her with soft words as they went. She began to get into the mood and lose her self-consciousness. They worked their way up the bed and under the sheets, and he turned the light off. Now she found herself imagining that she was with Rafael again, but he was bigger, thicker than Rafael and used different techniques. Several more minutes, and she stopped thinking, she was immersed in a sensual experience.

As he entered her, she imagined herself riding a mighty stallion, strange that she should imagine a horse – the antithesis of everything she worshipped. Perhaps, she was eroticising that which she feared, but such philosophical meanderings came later in the aftermath, some hours later, before she drifted into sleep. She could not identify the moment when the other twin joined them. She gradually became aware of more hands, another body, the doubling of the sensual pleasure. She became aware of a pleasure so secret, so forbidden that she relished the notion of enjoying what was happening. Her will had dissolved into the two bodies that lay on either side of her. Very gently, and with some sort of lubricant, she felt one of the hard cocks pushing at the entrance of her anus. This was not entirely unknown, Rafael had used to sometimes insert his finger there to

263

give her extra pleasure. But she felt so full she might burst, and the pleasure set her screaming, no longer aware that she was in her mother's house full of strangers who might hear her.

Chapter Twenty-Two

Unfortunately, Phoebe had not known that Rafael would be returning early. Gunner had had a suspected case of colic, and after vet treatment, Rafael decided that the old horse needed to go home. Jerome was to ride Mickey in his classes, and Grace had organised that Rafael and Gunner hitch a lift with another rider who was heading back to Oxford. Thus, he arrived very early on Sunday morning. After settling Gunner in the stable and talking to Jamie, he headed up to the west wing to see Marco.

He popped his head into Phoebe's bedroom and saw that her bed had not been slept in.

"Is Phoebe in London?" he asked the nanny.

"She had a big party over the weekend, and they're all sleeping in the east wing. Mrs Hopkins has been moaning about all the extra work," said the nanny spitefully. As Rafael walked out to go and find Phoebe, she smiled to herself. She rather adored Rafael and disapproved of Phoebe's new friends who were, in her opinion, ridiculously pretentious. On the one occasion when she had come into contact with them, they had looked through her as if she were invisible.

Rafael made his way through the house. He didn't usually go into the east wing, which was reserved for guests and rarely used on a daily basis. However, it was the mirror image of the west wing, and he went upstairs to the passageway lined with doors to the various guest rooms. Maddie was wandering down the hall, her thick hair mussed and tangled like a bird's nest, her eyes bleary.

"Where is Phoebe?" asked Rafael politely.

"She's in the far room on the left," said Maddie and padded down to the kitchenette at the end of the hall where they could make coffee. They had had a serious night of partying, and she could barely remember her own name. She had not intended to put Phoebe in hot water; she wasn't thinking straight.

Rafael padded like a leopard down the hall, with the easy lithe grace of a young man in peak athletic condition. He came to the closed door and tapped once and then pushed it open. It had never occurred to him for one minute that Phoebe might not be alone.

He didn't see her at first. There were two young men, obviously identical twins, with thick thatched dark hair and smooth ivory-white skin, one on each side of the bed. Then he saw her, in the middle of the bed between them, just stirring, obviously awakened by the tap on the door. She opened her eyes and saw Rafael standing in the doorway, rooted to the spot. He was staring at her naked, tangled in the sheets, pressed in on both sides by the bodies of the young men. He felt like he was going to be sick. He turned on his heel, pulling the door shut and set off back down the passageway. His mind was churning with disbelief. This was not his Phoebe, so decent, so correct and shy. Perhaps if it had only been one man he could understand, after all, he had made no move on her, she was technically a free agent, but two men, this was the depths of decadence, and he felt himself drowning in black bile.

He walked swiftly down the hall and pushed past Maddie, who was tottering back with a hot mug of coffee. It slopped on the carpet, and she exclaimed in annoyance. He kept going. He couldn't bear it. Not his Phoebe, the young woman who he almost regarded as a Madonna, the sainted mother of his darling son.

He stumbled back into the front hall and looked around vaguely as if he had just awoken from an awful nightmare. He was confused; he didn't know what to do. He didn't want to go back to the stables. He needed to be alone. He had to think. He walked down the front gravelled drive and then headed for the footpath, climbing over the stile and into the neighbouring field. If he kept going, he would reach the village. Perhaps he should go to the Goat and have a drink? He had never before felt the need to reach for a drink when things went wrong, but perhaps that would help him to gather his scattered wits and calm down. He had felt so unutterably angry to see Phoebe there. He had wanted to drag the men out and punch them senseless. His brain wasn't functioning, and he forgot that it was early morning and the pub wouldn't be open.

Phoebe lifted herself up in bed and pondered how she might get up without waking the sleeping twins. She was feeling rather wretched. She had dreamt that Rafael had opened the door and seen her sleeping with two men. What had seemed like a most delightful, hedonistic adventure the night before, now seemed rather sordid and shame-making this morning.

She pulled on her clothes that were in a tangled heap beside the bed and scurried down the corridor. There was no-one else around. Then she thought she heard her mother's voice downstairs talking to Mrs Hopkins. They were all home! She almost panicked, she had thought she would have two days to clean up the mess and get them all out of the house. Perhaps she had imagined it?

She tottered down the stairs, across the entrance hall, beneath the solemn gaze of the horses and warriors and up the stairs towards her bedroom. She slid through her bedroom door and jumped into the shower in the adjoining bathroom. She washed her hair to get rid of the smell of not only cigarettes, but also the joints, then she stepped out and moisturised her skin and sprayed herself with a light perfume. Then she cleaned her teeth thoroughly. She dressed in her jeans and t-shirt and went back to start cleaning up the conservatory where they had been drinking and smoking.

The nanny saw her in the passageway.

"Did Rafael find you?" she asked with a sly smirk.

"Rafael?" echoed Phoebe.

"He came in to see Marco and then he went over to find you," said the nanny.

"Oh," said Phoebe, and suddenly she was dropping through the floor with embarrassment. Perhaps it hadn't been a dream, Rafael standing in the doorway, he had really been there.

"Oh no!" she said startled. The nanny smiled at her as if she were the cat who had got the cream.

Phoebe felt her stomach seize up. The last thing she had ever wanted was Rafael discovering her in bed with two men. It was so embarrassing, he would never, never want her again. She didn't know how she would ever face him. She went quietly down to the kitchen.

"Mrs Hopkins, are they all back?" she asked.

"No, just Rafael, the horse was ill, and he brought it back – apparently," said Mrs Hopkins, looking at Phoebe's face that was washed blank.

"You look very pale my dear, sit down and I'll make you a cup of tea, too many late nights," she said like a mother hen.

"Thank you," said Phoebe faintly. She had to rally herself, face Rafael and brazen it out. He had no right to tell her how to live, but still, she felt ashamed, as if she had betrayed him and Marco. She sat staring blankly out of the kitchen window that faced in the direction of the stables. She felt like running to Rafael and begging his forgiveness but knew that that would not be the right thing to do. She had to pretend that nothing had happened. She would go and clean up the ballroom and the conservatory, marshal the guests and put them in taxis and tell them never to return. She didn't want to see any of them again. The thought of facing the twins brought back memories of all the things that they had done to her last night. She felt as if she would retch.

After she had sipped the tea with two heaped teaspoonfuls of sugar, she took some black plastic garbage bags and went to pick up the debris from the party the night before. She hoped that action would help to banish her darkest feelings of despair. She needed to forge on as if cleaning would wipe out the shame of the weekend. She had collected all the rubbish and went back with a broom and a bucket and mop. She would scrub the floor herself, in the hope that this might wash away her guilt.

Two of the girls from the village turned up, and they helped her, wiping down the surfaces, opening the windows to let the cold fresh air blow in. The three of them scrubbed, washed and wiped and eventually there was no trace of the night before. Some of the guests came down and began to light cigarettes. Phoebe coldly asked them to go and smoke outside. She also suggested that they pack up their belongings as the taxis would be arriving soon to take them to the station. Phoebe felt her anxiety rising, soon or later, she was going to have to face the twins.

When there was nothing left to clean downstairs, she set one of the girls on guard, so no-one went in and messed it all up. She marched upstairs, bracing herself to face the twins. They started in the first bedroom, which was empty; threw open the windows, stripped the bed and put the dirty sheets in the hallway. Then they dusted and vacuumed and locked the door. Then the next bedroom, there were two bodies unconscious in the bed. The girl from the village, Maisie, strode in and shook them awake and then gathered up their belongings and dumped them in the hall.

"We're here to do the room," she announced and they sat on the bed wincing. "Up and outside, it's a lovely morning," she said in a voice that was louder than it needed to be. She threw open the window and began to strip the bed as the couple staggered out into the hall. Phoebe began to wipe surfaces and then vacuumed.

There were four more bedrooms before they reached the room where Phoebe had slept with the twins. She absolutely dreaded the sight of them emerging into the passageway. The next bedroom was empty, and they went through the cleaning routine, taking the scattered personal items that had been left behind and put them in a plastic bag. Maisie picked up a used condom that was lying on the floor and held it up at arm's length with her face screwed up in disgust. Then it struck Phoebe like a thunderbolt – contraception! It had not even occurred to her. She felt her face glowing like a bright-red tomato. Had she learned nothing? She was like a very stupid babe in the wood. She opened the window and leaned out, taking great gulps of fresh air. There were guests straggling across the back lawn beneath her, treading their cigarette butts into the lawn.

"Everywhere they go they leave a trail," she said in anguish.

She knocked loudly on Tinker's door and went in to find him and Shea entwined together.

"Tinker, I really have to clean this place up, I want you all on the train, can you get up and help organise everyone. There's a train at two o'clock. I'll order the taxis for one. Get up Tinker and do your stuff!" she said and banged the door as she went out to the passageway.

"I'll send the other girl up from guard duty to help you finish," she said to the Maisie, and I'll go and try and get the others to collect their belongings," said Phoebe.

"It's like herding cats," quipped Maisie.

Phoebe rushed downstairs, thinking she might just get away with it, avoiding the twins, feeling like she never wanted to go to London again. She would shut herself up here in the country and start writing the novel, or perhaps she could get a job in the village, anything but a repeat of what had happened this weekend. She was utterly humiliated.

She walked back and forth across the lawn, picking up cigarette butts. Her guests frowned at her, but she didn't care.

"Have you all got your things together?" she asked in a loud voice. The taxis will be here in thirty minutes. She couldn't wait to see the back of them. She saw the twins emerging from the side door and almost ran across the lawn to go in by the kitchen door. She didn't care about dignity or not showing her feelings. She just couldn't bear to look them in the face. She had jumped from the frying pan and into the fire. Rafael was sitting at the table with a mug of coffee, he looked up and they stared at each other. Mrs Hopkins didn't understand the deadly tension and bustled around talking about her day off on the morrow, she had left some food in the fridge, and they would have to fend for themselves.

"Of course, Mrs Hopkins, you deserve a month's holiday after putting up with that lot all weekend," said Phoebe. "Thank you so much for your help. I won't forget it."

"You might want to take those cans of air freshener out of the cleaning cupboard and go and spray all the bedrooms, or we're never going to get rid of the smell," replied Mrs Hopkins, but she smiled at Phoebe to soften the harshness of her voice.

Rafael got up and walked out without a backward glance. He can't bear to be in the same room as me, thought Phoebe and felt like melting into a pool of tears. But instead, she went to the cupboard in the utility room and made her way upstairs. The rooms were now all empty, but the smell of corruption still lingered; the rank odour of iniquity. She began to spray the fabrics, the carpets and the curtains. When she got to the twins' room, grotesque visions filled her mind, and even worse, she felt the overwhelming sexual excitement that she had experienced the night before. She couldn't bear it and sank down onto the carpet and wept silently and bitterly. Eventually, she sobbed herself to a standstill, got up went to the bathroom and splashed cold water on her face. Then having recovered her composure, she went downstairs and saw that they had all left. She had been derelict in her duty as a hostess, but she didn't care, she was just overwhelmingly relieved.

She went to the west wing to see Marco. He did not judge. He just loved her. She put her arms around him and cuddled him. He was her only comfort now. She knew she had to harden up, to live with her own mistakes, and really there was no crime committed, but she could not shake off the shame. She knew she had to move on, to carve out her own life.

When the others returned, she made an announcement when they all sat down to dinner.

"I've decided that we're having a naming day for Marco, on his first birthday."

Rafael looked uncomfortable. He would have liked her to have talked to him before this public announcement, but he said nothing. Phoebe had made it abundantly clear that he was not important in her life.

"And I absolutely insist that we invite Daddy. I want him to be properly introduced to his grandson," said Phoebe in a decisive voice. "Don't worry Mummy, we don't have to have it here, we'll have it at a hotel with a proper reception. I'm going to arrange it all."

After lunch, Grace went up to Phoebe.

"Do we have to have your father?" she asked peevishly. She knew that this was definitive. There was no prospect of a wedding for Phoebe and Rafael on the horizon. But David being invited?

"Yes, Mummy, I insist," replied Phoebe. "Don't worry, I'll organise it, so he doesn't come to Kiss Wood, and he'll have to promise to be on his best behaviour."

Grace shrugged and walked away. Perhaps it was time for Phoebe to begin asserting herself.

Chapter Twenty-Three

The naming day was set. Despite Grace's protestations Phoebe did not give in, she wanted her father there. She stood her ground and no-one could argue against her. Poppy had agreed with her, for all his faults, he was still their father.

One week before the baby-naming ceremony, Phoebe set out for Heathrow. She was to meet not only her father but also Claudia, Marianela and Pablo, the half-brother baby boy. She arrived in good time and saw that their flight was on schedule. Pacing up and down, she kept away from the crowds around the barriers. She felt extremely nervous. She really didn't want to have anything to do with Claudia and Marianela. She had not forgotten the way in which Marianela had taunted her at school, and the wicked way she had tried to send Rafael to prison. Phoebe had wanted her father to come alone, but it seemed that that hadn't been possible.

She moved closer to the barrier; it was fifteen minutes since their plane had landed. She saw them coming out of the swing doors. Marianela stood out from the crowd. She looked even more gorgeous than she had as a schoolgirl. Her tawny blonde hair still had a greenish tinge to it, making her look exotic and highlighting her strange light green eyes. Her eyebrows were perfectly etched, not in thick stripes like a lot of British women were doing at the moment, and her lips were full but not garishly lipsticked, unlike Claudia whose mouth was a crimson gash.

Claudia had blossomed in every sense of the word, to the point of looking unattractively blowsy. Her figure had thickened with having a baby in her late thirties. Her hair was blonde but with ugly dark roots, flat and greasy from the air travel. She was wearing clothes littered with sequins and flashy ribbons, that made her look like a tired carnival doll.

Phoebe then looked for her father and saw to her surprise just how much he had aged. He had always looked so vibrant and handsome and cool, especially next to her mother who had been almost determinedly frumpish, but now his hair had thinned and there was a distinctive widow's peak, his skin pallid and lines around his eyes. Claudia was struggling with a pushchair from which an unattractive squall was emanating. They say you should never marry your mistress as she knows you too well and this was certainly the case even though David had so far avoided marrying her. Nonetheless, Claudia kept him on a very short leash.

Phoebe stood back and looked at them as a family group and wondered that she might be related to them, an ill-assorted group of strangers. Her father seemed like an altogether different person. He had traded in their family for this clutch of Latino-types. She wondered what the baby would be like when he grew up. He was only a little younger than Marco, but he would be her son's uncle. Extended families were tied in knots and always unravelling, she thought.

She took a deep breath and stepped forward, a polite smile stretched across her face.

"Phoebe, my darling child, you are so thin, so svelte, amazing!" said her father.

"Yes, I'm not that big chubby teenager any longer," she replied lightly.

"Claudia, Marianela." She kissed the air as far away from them as possible as if she were avoiding poisonous mushrooms.

"And the little one, Pablo, how sweet," she said looking into the pram to see a squashed angry face.

She led the way marching ahead, across the concourse of the airport, weaving between other arrivals, pushing trollies piled high with luggage. She felt strange seeing them again. The sight of Marianela especially. She had had a vision of Facundo and Tomas smiling evilly, cruelly as they had plotted the downfall of Rafael. But now they were dead, not just murdered but tortured before they had died. She felt enveloped in the thick, cloying combination of both Claudia and Marianela's perfumes, a miasma of unappealing sexuality. She couldn't imagine what the other guests at the naming day would make of these strange *nouveau* relatives, although *riche* they certainly weren't. Her father hadn't a bean, and she wondered how Claudia had taken this unpalatable fact when it had finally come to light. He certainly wouldn't have been the golden goose she had set her sights on. Perhaps she was underestimating the woman's feelings for her father, perhaps she loved him for himself.

"It won't take too long to get up to Oxfordshire. I've brought the Range Rover, and there shouldn't be too much traffic at this time of night."

"I can't wait to meet your lovely little Marco," said her father affably.

"He's absolutely gorgeous, the happiest child in the world."

"You and the father, are you getting married?" asked her father.

"I doubt it, it's complicated," she said, trying to laugh it off, the last thing she wanted to do was discuss this in front of Claudia and Marianela.

"That sounds like a Facebook status," said Claudia trilling in the background, eaves-dropping unashamedly on their conversation.

Phoebe felt as if she were an entirely different person since she had said good-bye to her father when she had left Uruguay. She'd had a baby and grown up fast. She was also thin, and her face was angular and carefully made-up. Today she had chosen to look like a mini-me of her mother, dull as dishwater. But it was a safe persona, and she adopted it whenever she felt anxious.

They reached the shiny black car, this year's model with all the luxury trimmings, presumably the South Americans would appreciate this. The luggage was piled in the back, a suitable baby seat produced for Pablo. Phoebe had a chance to look at him as her father strapped him in. He was not an attractive child, which was strange as both Claudia and her father were good-looking, but he was her half-brother so they must embrace him and include him in the family, he couldn't help the circumstances under which he had been conceived. When they were all strapped in, she drove off.

"I guess you're all pretty tired after your flight," she said, then tried to think of something more interesting to say, but it was safer to stick with polite nothingness.

"Well, it might have helped if we had been able to fly first class," said Claudia and Phoebe could hear the carping, sniping tone in her voice.

"Yes, I guess first class is better," agreed Phoebe, resisting the urge to say that Grace always insisted that they fly first class. She just wasn't that sort of bitch, too kind-hearted. Her mother had always schooled her to have impeccable manners, like a well-trained dog. Her father began to chat then. Asking her questions about her home life. He was very curious about Rafael, and also keen to find out whether Grace was seeing anyone else. He was still hoping that she might have him back, although at this stage it seemed unlikely.

Phoebe was vague in her replies. She suspected that there was some sort of understanding between Oliver and her mother, but it was only suspicion and certainly nothing that she would report to her father. Oliver had very kindly agreed to have David and his new family to stay at Tall Chimneys as Grace was adamant that they weren't coming to Kiss Wood. Even the reception after the child-naming ceremony was in a local hotel so that David had no excuse to go back to Kiss Wood and Claudia and Marianela would have no chance to poke around. Grace suspected that they might steal the ornaments.

Certainly, they would be comfortable at Tall Chimneys although not as grand as Kiss Wood, there were ten bedrooms each with its own bathroom, and a lovely paved terrace out the back looking over the fields. Phoebe described the place to them, and she could feel the prickliness of the two women in the back. Undoubtedly, there would be resentment that David was not the owner of such a lovely big house with extensive lands. Claudia should have done her research before she had targeted him.

"It is very kind of Oliver to allow us to stay at his place," said David

"Oh yes, he's a most agreeable man," said Phoebe.

"I remember that I met your mother at his wedding," said David. "He was rather dashing and handsome, and Elvira was to die for."

In due course Phoebe turned into the gates of Tall Chimneys, the large stone griffins sitting atop the pillars watched the car slide by. She had often visited this house, but today she saw it through the eyes of Claudia and Marianela. Compared to the rather scrappy estancias that the Uruguayans had as weekenders, it would look palatial.

Oliver came down the front steps to welcome them. He was a tall man with a rather hawkish thin nose and slit-like nostrils, a trim figure and hair that was grey but not yet thinning and the most attractive arctic-blue eyes. He looked rather like Charles Dance, and like the actor, he had exceptionally charming manners. David adopted a hearty tone and held his hand out for a firm clasping handshake. Oliver smiled his thin-lipped smile. Then David ushered forth Claudia looking blousy and sleepy with the child clinging to her ample breasts. Marianela lurked in the background, she was hating every minute of this, but anything was better than being locked up in her father's apartment in Bogota. Then David turned to her and taking

275

her arm, gently introduced her to Oliver. Phoebe was watching with interest one moment, and the next she felt distinctly uneasy. Oliver was staring at Marianela as if she were an alien, then his face creased into an unctuous smile, and he almost bowed to her. He took her hand and looked as if he wanted to press it to his lips. Marianela barely acknowledged him.

The housekeeper, Mrs Beeston, bustled up and helped to carry suitcases up the curved staircase to the first floor. There were family portraits lining the wall; generations of austere Soames. Marianela was looking around, her green eyes wide, this was far more splendid than she had ever envisaged. She was used to a degree of wealth and luxury at her father's penthouse apartment, but this was something else entirely, with all the hallmarks of old money and tradition.

Phoebe was feeling exhausted. The stress of meeting her father's family was telling on her. She made her excuses and went home. Oliver could take over from here, and her father was very good at smoothing out everyone's feelings. He was after all a diplomat. She had an overwhelming desire to be away from all of them and to go home to Marco at Kiss Wood.

She drove up the circular gravel driveway and parked carelessly by the front steps. Locking the car, she went inside the quiet house. The housekeeper had left a few low lights burning. Her mother, Rafael and Poppy were away at a show for the weekend. Marco would be asleep upstairs with his nanny in the next room.

Phoebe was relieved that she didn't have to describe her day's activities, talking about her father's arrival with his concubine, and the ghastly Marianela was upsetting. She found herself disturbed by tumultuous memories of her last few months in Uruguay. It was as if she had dropped through a hole in the bottom of the floor and was back there – an awkward, chubby teenager. She had managed to save Rafael from prison, and she was now the mother of his most beautiful baby boy, and miraculously he was living here at Kiss Wood but even this was not enough for her.

"We're never content with our lot," she murmured to herself.

She was dreading Marianela's first confrontation with Rafael, and the snide remarks that might be made about him being a stable boy. Now the whole story would come out. Not that Phoebe was ashamed of how she had behaved, if anything Marianela should be embarrassed by her part in it. She wondered then if Marianela knew what had happened to Tomas and Facundo. Rafael had denied all knowledge, and Phoebe believed him, well almost, it still nagged at her, that horrid thought that perhaps Rafael had exacted his revenge.

She felt unsettled by Oliver's reaction to Marianela. She knew that if her mother had seen it, she would have been hurt. Phoebe shrugged, it would be easy to pass it off with an observation about the inevitability of men's lust. She edged away from this thought, thinking where her own lust had landed her – in bed with the twins. Now she and Rafael maintained the status quo with mutual polite and respectful behaviour, and this seemed to be working for both of them.

She trudged up the stairs and walked down to the bedrooms in the west wing. She didn't even bother to take off her discreet, pale makeup and crawled into bed. She pulled the covers over her head and slept. She refused to think about how she had once felt about Rafael, that all-consuming hot passion and love.

She rang Tall Chimneys in the morning and talked to her father. She suggested that she bring Marco over to meet him. She was to go for morning tea. She lingered over her breakfast cup of coffee, while the nanny took Marco upstairs to bathe him and prepare him to meet his grandfather for the first time. Inevitably, her father would give her the third degree and sooner or later they were going to twig that the father of the baby, had, in fact, been Rafael from the Polo Club.

Just as she had divined, they arrived at Tall Chimneys, and Claudia and Marianela were in the drawing-room. It was almost as if they were determined not to leave Phoebe and her father alone. The truth about Marco's paternity came out before the cups of coffee were passed around.

"Marianela! Marianela!" screeched Claudia, "You will not believe it, Phoebe's baby – the father!"

Marianela looked annoyed. She couldn't care less about Phoebe's illegitimate child.

"Who cares?" she snapped.

"His name is Rafael, and I believe he was the stable boy at Melilla Polo Club."

This pronouncement caught Marianela's attention.

"Rafael! The stable boy! That nasty little snake in the grass brought up in the gutter!" she exclaimed spitefully.

David looked distressed at this. He had been hoping that they were all going to behave with at least the minimum of good manners. Already Claudia was showing herself up. He smiled at them with a strained look. Phoebe was flustered and upset, wondering why on earth David had brought Marianela and Claudia to England with him. Probably Claudia had insisted that he didn't go alone. Now the mother and daughter began to talk about Rafael, calling him a 'snivelling little stable boy', a 'cunning thief' and various other descriptions that were not flattering. This was too much for Phoebe.

"You set him up, you nasty piece of garbage, and now you have the temerity to label him a thief. The whole thing was a ruse on your part with those ghastly young men, Facundo and Tomas. How dare you even pretend that it was Rafael who stole your necklace. I saw you plant it in his bedroom, I went in and took it back. How could you have anything to do with these women Daddy? You're unbelievable!"

She snatched up Marco, who had been happily crawling around Oliver's priceless Persian rug and stormed out with a parting shot.

"You are not to bring those sluts to the naming day!"

David sighed. He had never heard Phoebe speak like this; she was more like her mother than he had thought. He supposed it had all been entirely predictable. He would not have brought Claudia except that she had thrown such a tantrum when he had wanted to come by himself. Claudia also wanted an excuse to get Marianela away from her father's place, and Marianela had been happy to leave her confined existence in Bogota. Her father's eagle eye was always upon her, and he never let her go out on her own, there was always two bodyguards and also this old crone, who was her designated 'companion'. Now Marianela understood exactly what had happened at Melilla. It had been Phoebe who had foiled their plan. In fact, that and everything else that had happened was down to Phoebe. She hissed with fury. How she hated that pale slug of an English girl.

David took refuge in the one comforting thought that at least Oliver had not witnessed this extremely disagreeable quarrel. He had been out with his estate manager looking at the mares in the water meadows. Two of them had just been mated with Tinpot, and he liked to check them every day.

He came in for lunch and was a little surprised that Phoebe and Marco had left. He accepted the excuse that she had things to organise at Kiss Wood. He spruced himself up and prepared to play the urbane host. It was his duty to make his house guests feel at home. He was particularly struck by Marianela. the girl was extraordinarily attractive, those green eyes had quite mesmerised him. And her body was a gift from the gods. He wondered how David Lester-Blythe managed to live with it. Then he remembered that she usually stayed with her own father in Bogota.

He offered to show them around his estate that afternoon. Marianela was looking sulky. She probably wanted to go into town or even London. Her first trip to England and she was stuck in the backwoods of Oxfordshire. After they had driven over field after field, with lots of fat cattle grazing everywhere, Marianela's eyes were glazing over.

"How many acres have you got?" asked David in interested tones.

"There's one thousand overall," replied Oliver.

"The farm has been in your family for several generations?" asked David.

"Yes, my great-grandfather farmed it many years ago," said Oliver proudly.

"Have you ever worked as anything but as a farmer?" asked Marianela.

Oliver beamed at her interest. I went to college and studied agriculture, and I spent a year in Australia working as a jackaroo in one of the big stations in the Northern Territory."

"That sounds interesting," said Claudia who was nursing the baby who seemed to enjoy the bouncing around in the Land Rover more than any of the rest of them.

"I would love to do something like that," said Marianela. Her mother shot her a sharp look. The idea of Marianela working on a huge, dusty, isolated farm in the middle of nowhere was laughable. But Marianela had decided that she may as well entertain herself by flirting with Oliver. She resented

279

the way that Phoebe and Grace were enjoying their pots of money, and their grand friends and huge houses. Well, she could play that game too!

It would serve the stupid bitches right if she enchanted him. From what she could gather, he and Grace were 'special friends'. She decided that she would steal the old man from that dried-up nightmare in tweed. It seemed that at least he was independently wealthy. She couldn't believe her mother had been so stupid as to get knocked up by David and then find out he was utterly penniless. They drove down to the river, and Oliver stopped the Land Rover, and they all got out. The glittering water slid around in curves, and circles and gurgled through reeds on the banks.

"We've got a little boat, and you can go out on the river and fish," said Oliver.

"Oh, how delightful!" enthused Marianela. Oliver beamed. David sighed. He could see trouble ahead. Marianela was a little minx. He had to work overtime to keep up his own avuncular attitude towards her. Marianela had started flicking her hair around, a sure sign that she had gone into flirtation overdrive. She was standing just a little too close to Oliver. David looked at Claudia, but she was occupied with the child, and he had no doubt that Claudia would be more than pleased if Marianela could bag herself a rich husband. Eventually, they drove back to the house, and David felt as if he were dying of boredom. The county set was not his cup of tea.

"I might take Pablo up for his nap," said Claudia. She was feeling rather flat herself. Jet lag was taking its toll.

"Perhaps you all might like to have a rest," said Oliver. "I have to go into town and attend to some business."

"I could come with you," said Marianela brightly.

"Of course," said Oliver, his face lighting up, hoping that David would stay back at the house. David knew that he should go as well, but he felt very weary. He could see troubled waters ahead, and he was now dreading seeing Grace again. She had been relentless in her manoeuvring over the divorce and good as her word she had made sure that he got nothing. She had even managed to claim child support. They were supposed to deduct it from his salary, but the system hadn't kicked in yet. He went upstairs and sat on a chair at the end of the corridor overlooking the driveway.

280

Marianela was tip-tupping down the steps, flashing herself around. Oliver, believing he was unobserved, was looking at her in blatant admiration.

David's mobile rang, and he saw that it was Grace's number.

"Hello David, how are you?" Of course, she didn't care how he was; it was mere politeness.

"How are you, Grace?" he replied.

"I hear that Phoebe left Tall Chimneys this morning very upset. Have you no control over those ghastly women with whom you consort?" Her voice was a wave of icy water. He didn't reply. He was assuming it was a rhetorical question. There was an uncomfortable silence between them.

"It was very kind of Oliver to offer to put you up, do you think you could at least behave like civilised human beings," she snapped and hung up.

David was unhappy. He wondered at what point had his charmed life sunk into this swamp of unmitigated horror. He had had it all, and then in one fell swoop, he had lost it. He sighed. He probably deserved it. He often daydreamed that somehow, he could come into enough money to run away and start again as another person – Brazil, Spain, wherever exiles ran to for a happy life. He didn't want another rich wife. He'd had enough of that. He wondered if there was some easy way of making money, something criminal, fraud was probably what he was best suited to. He would set his mind to it. A fraud would be easier to perpetrate here in the UK. He could see no opportunities in Uruguay.

"Daveeed!" called Claudia from their room.

"What?" he said impatiently.

"Who were you talking to?"

"Grace."

"What did she want?" she asked a harping, jealous note in her voice.

"She said that Phoebe was upset this morning. I'm going down to get a drink. Do you want one?" he asked.

"Oh yes please, a screwdriver." This meant vodka and orange juice; he hated it when she used that word, it sounded so cheap and American, as if she were a hostess in a Japanese night club.

He carried two tumblers back up the stairs. He swallowed his down and then got up.

"I'm off for a walk, I need some fresh air," he said. Claudia frowned but before she could voice an objection, he had walked out and run down the stairs and out the front door. He breathed in the country air - freedom, so alluring, so sweet, he had to find a way.

Chapter Twenty-Four

Dusk had fallen, and the countryside was black. There were the first hints of the summer to come, some gentle, sweet fragrances from the spring flowers. At Tall Chimneys there were lights blazing from every window, lit up like a Christmas tree. Usually, the frugal Oliver patrolled the house switching off lights, but tonight he was feeling the temptation of extravagance, of old dreams suddenly awakened.

Phoebe had pulled herself together and driven back, hoping to see her father alone. She had had enough of his new family to last a lifetime, but she wanted to see her father and talk to him seriously. She wanted to explain about Rafael. Perhaps he might have some words of wisdom, to help her sort out her confused feelings. Emotions weren't really her mother's forté. She could hear music coming from the drawing-room. It was the Bee Gees. How truly bizarre!

Then she heard Panda's high-pitched laugh. Dear Panda, she would cheer everyone up. Phoebe stood in the doorway. The room seemed filled with people. There were Panda and her husband, Charles in the centre of the room which was aglow with light and music. They were dancing, and Oliver and Marianela were cavorting beside them. Oliver was hopping around awkwardly. Phoebe stared in amazement. She had never seen Oliver making himself look so ridiculous. Usually, he was suave and debonair, the epitome of class and elegance.

Marianela was wearing a flouncy midi skirt that swirled around her legs, emphasising her slim ankles. She twirled around and over to Panda, and then the two of them were holding hands and laughing at each other. Oliver hopped awkwardly to one side. One of his friends who lived in the village was standing in the background watching the dancing girls with a glass in his hand. The fire was blazing strongly and throwing strange black shadows against the walls, grotesque dancing shapes like a Bacchanalian debauched scene. Andy Gibb's high-pitched falsetto voice wailed around the room.

Phoebe felt as if she had slipped into an alternative universe. Woken up on the wrong side of the wardrobe. Marianela was the centre of attention, and she was smiling in a dreamy, sweet way as if she were high on drugs. No-one could deny that she was unutterably beautiful. For a moment, Phoebe experienced a tremendous longing to be as beautiful. No-one noticed her standing in the doorway, poised on the edge of this strange gathering. She sidled into the room and slid along the wall. Nothing on this earth would have tempted her into this dancing frenzy. She had spotted her father over in the far corner, tapping his feet and vaguely smiling.

The song came to an end. Oliver called to them that dinner was served and they all trooped into the dining room, which was lit up with a hundred candles. The best china was in use with shining, gleaming silver cutlery. Oliver circled the table filling everyone's glasses. Phoebe was suddenly conscious that she hadn't been invited. There was no place set for her.

"Phoebe!" called Oliver. He turned to one of the serving staff. "Another place please. Next to Mr Lester-Blythe."

The dinner was delicious and tasted remarkably like the food served in the best French restaurant in the county. Perhaps Mrs Beeston had had it driven over, as a very upmarket type of take-away. Phoebe had never known Oliver to take such trouble over a meal. Every mouthful was heaven, and the wine flowed generously. Phoebe sat next to her father, and they bent their heads together, and she swore him first to secrecy and then she told him the whole story of what had happened to Rafael. He listened, looking grave.

I let you down, didn't I?" he said, and for once he sounded as if he genuinely cared.

"Daddy, are you happy with these women? And a baby? Is it what you always wanted?" she asked.

He smiled at her. "I didn't do the right thing by your mother, nor you and I suppose if I had gone on, I would have also let Poppy down."

"But this!" she gestured up the table to Claudia who was competing with Marianela to flirt with Oliver.

He grinned at her wryly. "I guess I just have to make the most of it. I do rather wish that we could go back in time to when we first arrived in Uruguay. I would not have got involved with Claudia."

"I don't think Mummy would want to go back. She has been transformed, she seems set on a goal, it's all to do with her love of horses," said Phoebe.

"So how do you manage in a house full of horse-addicts?" he asked.

Phoebe sighed. He did seem to understand.

"I have carved out a little life for myself. I have Panda, she is great fun and not at all interested in horses, and Tinker and a group of friends in London. You'll meet Tinker at the ceremony. He's a writer, you know."

"But what about you and Rafael? Why have you not got together properly?" he asked. "What is holding the two of you back?"

She sighed again and told him how Rafael had been manipulated to come to England, and she knew that he didn't really love her. He felt beholden to her, and then there was his son. Nothing on earth would have dragged a confession about the twins out of her.

"But do *you* love him?" he asked gently.

"I don't know. I was in a dream in Uruguay. Everything seemed different over there. It's not like England."

"Why don't you and Rafael go back to Uruguay, with Marco, away from Kiss Wood and the weight of wealth that seems to be crushing him?" asked her father. "I'd be there, not that I'm much good for you."

"Not when you're ring-fenced by those ghastly women," said Phoebe.

"Marianela won't come back with us. She'll be back to Bogota, to her father. Claudia is manageable. I can escape on the odd occasion."

"But what would I do there?" asked Phoebe.

"What are you doing here?" he asked.

She stared into the distance. He was right. She was stagnating. There was Marco, but she was only a part-time mother. She had no plans to go on and study, and then there was that nebulous dream of 'writing', but she hadn't actually written a word that she wanted anyone else to read.

Before dessert arrived, Phoebe decided to leave. She went and spoke to Oliver, thanked him for the meal and made her excuses. He barely seemed to hear her. He was bedazzled by the witch Marianela. Phoebe hoped he would get over it before he saw her mother again.

Grace was waiting for her when she returned.

"How did it go?" she asked.

"It was very odd," said Phoebe. "I don't really know what got into Oliver, but he hosted a wonderful dinner, and he had his best wine from the cellars, and it was food from Le Dauphin, I think, you know the French restaurant. He was actually playing the Bee Gees when I arrived, and Panda and Marianela were dancing in the middle of the drawing-room."

"Oh, dear," said Grace, "how embarrassing."

"I know it was the height of uncool, can you imagine what Tate would have said if she'd walked in on it," said Phoebe giggling.

"I've been making a list of things that we need to do before the naming day," said Grace. "Tate is arriving the day before. I've told your father categorically that Marianela and Claudia are not to attend the event."

"It will be good to have Tate here. She will certainly add to the glamour of the gathering," said Phoebe. "Panda made a huge effort and was very friendly with Marianela last night. I'm sure she did it for me. She knew how difficult I was finding Claudia and Marianela, and somehow, she worked her magic and managed to get along with them."

"I think it might take a little more than Panda's guileless befriending techniques," said Grace sarcastically. "Anyway, I'm off over to the stables."

"Good-oh," said Phoebe, running her eye down the list. "Thank goodness, you're so organised, what a wonderful mother you are!"

The days passed in a flurry of arrangements for the event which was to be held on Friday. Grace had sent out a number of invitations to the great and the good in the county. She wanted to make absolutely certain that her first grandson was accepted in polite society. She wanted no sneers and innuendoes to spoil his childhood.

On Thursday morning, Phoebe made a fresh effort to go over and see her father. She took Marco with her. The day was cold and grey, and the forecast was not favourable for the following day, but perhaps by Sunday, it might warm up.

Hesitantly, Phoebe made her way up the front steps. She hated the thought of having to face Claudia or Marianela again. The front door was unlocked. She stepped into the hallway. It was very high-ceilinged, and there were two staircases curving up on either side. The white and black flags on the floor looked like they needed a wash. Perhaps Oliver needed a wife to take Mrs Beeston in hand. She walked down the hall to the drawing-room. She thought she could hear Claudia's voice. She entered and caught the tail end of a conversation.

"The stupid, stupid man!" said her father.

"Who is a stupid man?" asked Phoebe.

"Oh no, my darling girl, something has happened," said David. "He has done something unbelievably foolish. I can't believe it."

Well coming from you that has to be an understatement, thought Phoebe to herself.

"Please tell me what has happened!"

"Oliver has run away with my Marianela. They've gone to Las Vegas to get married." Claudia's face looked almost ugly with spite. Phoebe laughed out loud.

"That's hilarious!" she said. Her father walked towards her, and his expression was grave.

"I'm afraid it's true."

"Oliver and . . . Marianela," said Phoebe. "Why on earth would she be interested in Oliver?"

"His money, of course," said Claudia. "At least she will have a husband with money."

This was obviously aimed at David. He was appalled at what had happened. Grace was never going to forgive him now for this latest debacle, and for once it wasn't his fault.

"But why would he do such a thing?" asked Phoebe, she knew that this was going to hit her mother hard, it seemed an awful betrayal.

"She is very beautiful," said Claudia triumphantly, as if she had finally won a prize.

"I thought everything was weird the other night, you know with the Bee Gees," said Phoebe, "but I would never have imagined in a thousand years. . . But are you sure?" she asked disbelievingly.

"Marianela texted from the airport. Oliver left a letter in his study for Hector, who will be back this afternoon. I'm afraid I opened it and read it. Just to make sure it wasn't some ridiculous prank."

"Fancy being wooed by the Bee Gees, how utterly bizarre," Phoebe laughed hysterically.

"See what you and your poisonous daughter have done!" shouted David at Claudia.

"My Marianela is a true beauty compared to your daughter," replied Claudia maliciously.

"I can't stand this. I don't know how you could ever have hooked up with that woman! And her daughter!" Phoebe's hysterical mirth dissolved and now she was spitting with outrage. David stood there aghast. This was a worse disaster than he could have imagined. He had rather hoped that Grace might soften in her attitude towards him. Now she was going to see this as the very, very last straw.

"I'll drive you back to Kiss Wood," he said. "You need to break the news to your mother."

He drove her in her car, and then he left and trudged back down the driveway. He would have to return to Tall Chimneys before nightfall, but in the meantime, Phoebe had given him some cash, so he had enough money to get blind drunk at the Goat. Phoebe stumbled inside the front door. She stood in the hallway, looking around in bewilderment.

"Pheebs darling! I haven't seen you in an age! But what on earth is wrong. You're looking completely drug-fucked! You haven't started taking pills, have you!" said Tate, sauntering towards her in impossibly tight torn denim jeans, with a sloppy olive-green jumper. Her hair was slicked back against her head, and she was wearing huge sparkling diamond earrings, undoubtedly two real carats apiece.

"Oh Tate!" said Phoebe, "thank goodness you've come early, you have to help me break this news to Mummy. She's going to be absolutely furious, devastated, I'm not sure, but it's not going to be great!"

"It's alright, darling. Nothing can be that bad."

"It's Oliver he's run off with Marianela, they've gone to Las Vegas to be married."

"Marianela?" said Tate. "Oh, I remember the ghastly Claudia's daughter, I never actually met her. You say she's run off with Oliver, is that old Oliver Soames? The old dog obviously still has some life in him."

"I can't believe Oliver would do such a thing, there must be a mistake," said Grace, walking in from the hallway and overhearing what they had been saying.

"This is all Daddy's doing, how could he have brought those two women here!" exclaimed Phoebe. "I know it is terribly upsetting Mummy, but I hear that lots of men go through this stage as they're entering their dotage. Perhaps she reminded him of Elvira, and he had some bizarre time shift and got manipulated. Marianela is a very knowing type."

"Did you say Las Vegas? How terribly common!" said Grace, feeling like a stunned mullet. She went into the drawing-room and poured herself a brandy and drank it down in one gulp. "I've got some things to do out at the stables," she said crisply and walked out with a straight back and a steady gait.

"Poor Mummy," said Phoebe, "I think she thought that she and Oliver might get together. This is going to be a terrible blow. First Daddy and Claudia and now Oliver with Marianela. Really you have to wonder what goes on in men's minds?"

"More likely their trousers," said Tate.

289

"In all these years Oliver has never got involved with another woman, and now someone as unsuitable as Marianela. Unbelievable!" said Phoebe, still not really taking it in.

"So, she's going to be your new neighbour," said Tate smiling at Phoebe.

"All the more reason to move back to Uruguay," said Phoebe.

"What did you say? It's the first I've heard of that. Are you and Rafael going back to Uruguay?" asked Tate.

"No, no, no. It was Daddy's suggestion. I was telling him how it was so different when we were there. The magic just hasn't transferred to here, I don't exactly understand why," said Phoebe.

"What does Rafael think?" asked Tate.

"Goodness! I haven't said anything to him. We don't talk about things like that. We never really talk about anything important, except Marco. It was just Daddy last night. There's no way I would talk to Rafael about it. We're just not - like that. He talks to Mummy about the horses. I'm not sure what he talks to Poppy about, but I guess it's the ponies."

Tate shrugged. It wasn't her business. She had hardly spoken to Rafael. They circled each other suspiciously, and that was it.

The naming day was an anti-climax after the revelations of Oliver and Marianela's elopement. Hector arrived back on the following day. He didn't object to the fact that David had opened his letter. He looked shocked. He had never thought of his father getting involved with another woman. He was used to his friends' mothers flirting outrageously with his father, but he had assumed that Oliver would remain a widower until he died. Poppy had wanted to go over and talk to him, but Grace had forbidden it.

"After this, Tall Chimneys and Kiss Wood are no longer going to have any contact," she announced.

"But what about Tinpot?" asked Poppy.

"I'll sort that out, but I don't want us to have anything to do with Oliver or Hector ever again. I am not going to socialise with that awful woman's daughter. We're cutting them off totally," she said in a voice harsh with hurt and steel-edged determination. I will sort something out with Tinpot. I will buy Oliver out, or he buys me out, and if neither solution is satisfactory, he'll go to auction."

"But Mummy all your hopes were in Tinpot!" said Poppy, genuinely shocked.

"Bliss will probably be better than him. That stallion has been a thorn in my flesh ever since those mistakes were made with his breaking in. I'm going to think again. Breeding horses might not be the 'be all and end all'. Perhaps buying young horses and bringing them on to competition would be better. I've got a first-class trainer and rider in Jamie Landan, and of course Rafael, Jerome and you too Poppy, we don't need to breed. It takes too long, and it's expensive."

Poppy looked at her mother askance. It was the first time her mother had ever mentioned money. She had actually said 'it's expensive'.

"Are we running short of money?" she asked in bewildered tones.

"No, but I've been spending too much, we're going to cut back now. If Oliver doesn't want to buy Tinpot, we'll send him to auction."

Chapter Twenty-Five

News flashed around the district two weeks later when Oliver limped back into the country and slunk in through the back gates of Tall Chimneys. Mrs Beeston was beside herself with excitement and had carolled the news far and wide. David had already flown back to Uruguay, but Claudia had insisted on staying at Tall Chimneys. She had declared that she had to be near her daughter at this important moment of her life and had had a lovely couple of weeks swanning around Tall Chimneys as if she were the lady of the house. Now Oliver found himself confronted by this nightmare mother-in-law, trying to explain what had happened to his new bride and why she had not returned with him.

"Where ees my Marianela?" she screamed at him.

"I don't know," he said, looking down at his shoes.

"What do you mean? What have you done to her?" asked Claudia.

"Absolutely nothing!" retorted Oliver and stalked over to the drinks tray to pour himself a hefty Scotch.

"You must tell me, or I'm calling the police," screeched Claudia, playing the part of an outraged mother with every decibel of her high-pitched rasping voice.

"Why are you still here?" he asked helplessly.

"To make sure you treat my daughter well," hissed Claudia. No matter what, she would stand her ground. She liked it at Tall Chimneys. David had turned out to be such a disappointment. This was the sort of life she had envisaged for herself and her new-born son.

"Your daughter," said Oliver, roused for a moment from his apathy, "ran off before the wedding night, and she stole all my cards, my passport and cash. It took days to get replacements. I'm thousands out of pocket, and I've been made to look like an utter fool. I'll be seeking an annulment on the basis that the marriage was never consummated. My lawyers are onto it already."

Claudia looked at him with narrowed eyes.

"How can you prove there was no consummation?" she asked.

He looked at her, and for the first time, began to understand what sort of hornets' nest into which he had stumbled. The apple had not fallen far from the tree. Losing Marianela was upsetting, but acquiring her mother and the ugly little red-faced brat was utterly humiliating and embarrassing. He would be the talk of the county.

"Marianela looked just fine as I watched her disappearing across the casino floor," he said. "I'm sure she can look after herself. If she's so precious to you then presumably she would have contacted you."

Claudia laughed. A loud, unpleasant laugh. Oliver shuddered at the discordant sound. This was to be Greek chorus to the tragedy of his old age. He suddenly thought of Grace. Dear Grace, so predictable, so very 'right' and she always knew how to behave. He decided to go and see her. Kiss Wood was one place where Claudia would not be able to follow him.

He went out to the garage and started up his Range Rover. He would have to remember to lock up the keys so 'that woman' as he thought of Claudia, wouldn't be able to drive his cars. As he drove, the sight of the familiar countryside should have been a balm to his soul, but he felt utterly wrecked. He couldn't believe he had been so stupid.

'Nothing like an old fool,' he muttered to himself.

Grace would be sympathetic. She would understand. This had happened to her with David. She would be a great support.

She wasn't at the house. They told him to go over to the stable yard. No doubt she was fussing over the wonderful golden stallion that they jointly owned. Tinpot was being washed in the wash bay. Grace and Jamie were working on him together. He was sidling around restlessly, and Jamie growled at him to stand up.

"He's looking good," said Oliver in a jolly rousing voice.

Grace looked up and stared at him in astonishment.

"I heard that you were back, without your young bride, it seems," she said acidly.

"Yes, Marianela and I didn't work out," said Oliver ruefully.

293

Grace didn't reply.

"How is the stallion going?" asked Oliver.

"He's behaving well now. I'm dissolving our partnership. I don't want him, either you buy my half off me, or I'll send him to a suitable sale," she said evenly.

"What!" exclaimed Oliver. "Surely that's not necessary!"

"I don't want anything to do with you, your wife and most of all, your mother-in-law who I understand is now living with you. I want no more contact with any of you. No-one from Kiss Wood will have anything to do with anyone at Tall Chimneys."

"Grace, I don't understand. I've been a fool. I thought you would be the one person who understood."

"Oh! Yes, I understand alright. I also understand that I don't want anything to do with you. Please email if you wish to buy the stallion otherwise, I will make arrangements for him to be sent to a sale, and I'll get my solicitor to transfer your half of the proceeds to you. I'll be deducting the cost of half his expenses since we bought him."

Oliver beat a swift retreat. All this had been said in front of that stable manager, which meant that the gossip would be circulating instantaneously. This was a worse blow than Marianela running off. That he was a silly old fool who had been momentarily infatuated with a beautiful young woman, was bad enough, but Grace shunning him, that was different, that was part of his real-world crumbling beneath his feet. He felt absolutely awful. He went back to Tall Chimneys. He had to get rid of Claudia, but he didn't have the strength right now. He told Mrs Beeston that he didn't want anything to eat, took himself upstairs and locked himself in his bedroom.

Claudia dug herself in at Tall Chimneys, and she had no intention of leaving. She moved into the largest and most luxurious of the guest rooms, with Pablo next door. She settled into a routine. Oliver had made sure she couldn't get her hands on any of the car keys, but she wasn't keen to leave the house anyway. As long as she was inside the house, it was going to be hard to dislodge her.

She had heard the servants talking about the way that Grace had told Oliver she never wanted anything to do with him again and smiled a smug, secret smile. She didn't miss David. There was nothing that he could offer her that she wanted. Now, Oliver, he was a different kettle of fish. He had money, undoubtedly, although, at this point, she wasn't sure how she might get her hands on actual cash. She had roamed through every room in the place, but Mrs Beeston had been given strict instructions to lock up anything valuable, and Oliver carried the key to the strong room around his neck. They lived in a state of suspended hostilities. She continued to refuse to leave until Marianela returned.

"What if she never comes back?" asked Oliver.

"Of course, she will come back. You are her husband. Anyway, she has nowhere else to go," retorted Claudia. Although she wondered. Now Marianela was free from her father's control and had undoubtedly managed to withdraw cash on the cards before Oliver cancelled them, she could easily hook up with another lover and be away for months.

At Kiss Wood, there was also an atmosphere of uneasiness. Poppy was looking more unhappy every day. She flounced around and answered back when Grace said something to her.

"It's just a stage, she's a teenager," said Grace shrugging it off. However, Poppy was now seventeen, not really the troublesome fourteen-year-old stage of sulking and rebellion due to hormones running madly through her system.

Phoebe felt very uneasy; there was an undercurrent in the house that was dark and mysterious. Secrets were swirling around, and she was sure that there was something between Poppy and Rafael. Every time she turned around, they seemed, to be whispering in corners. She had gone right up to them once and asked.

"What is it that you two are whispering about?"

They had looked guilty, but told her nothing. Both shaking their heads in outright denial.

Summer was coming, not clear sunny days with blue skies, but an ominous sultry humidity. Phoebe escaped from the escalating tensions at Kiss

Wood and went to London. Tate was bursting with the good news that she had been booked for a series of prestigious photo shoots in New York.

"Once you make it in New York, you've made it in the world!" she pronounced.

Phoebe made a mental note. She absolutely must start writing her novel. She hated to think that she might be one of those people who were always talking about writing, but never actually doing it. She wished she could fly off to New York and become a different person. Perhaps she could understand Marianela who took her chance to escape.

Phoebe finally admitted to herself what was making her feel so uneasy. She felt suspicious of Poppy and Rafael. Finally, she let herself consider the absolute worst; they had fallen in love with each other, and it was too awkward to announce it.

If it were true that her little sister and Rafael had got it together, then she had to find some evidence. Otherwise, she would go absolutely doo-lally with awful thoughts and dark jealousy that was eating away at her soul. She went up to Poppy's bedroom, looking for a clue, perhaps an idle doodle with the letters RP, or his name written inside a love heart, anything that would confirm the very worst. Poppy's bedroom was a shrine to the horse. She had a huge collection of china horses and other types of models, some expensive Royal Doulton and Beswick, and others were anonymous curious designs from antique shops. There were posters on the wall of famous showjumpers. Phoebe looked around and wondered what it must feel like to care more about horses than other humans, or ideas.

She cast her eye along Poppy's horse books. Many were children's pony books, and there were also some sizeable tomes about riding and training techniques, and horse care. Would she hide a love note in a book? No, of course not. It would be a love-text, or even a sextext. She shuddered at the sordid reality; the thought of her sister having sex with Rafael made her feel positively ill.

She automatically scanned the spines of the books, and perhaps it was her inherent good taste in literature, but she picked out "Foal's Bread", which was a strange title. Not about rosettes, ponies, gymkhanas or with 'riding' in the title. She sat on Poppy's bed and began to read. The book had won literary awards and was set in Australia in the 1920s. Thankfully her mind slid off into this fictional world, her favourite refuge from the horrors and tribulations of real life. Then the horror dawned, this was no innocent book of wishing for ponies and wanting to win rosettes. The girl brought on a miscarriage, and when the child was born alive, she put it in a butter box to float down the river to its death. Later she found that the young girl had been impregnated by a horrid old man – her uncle - really old! This was Marianela and the suave, but ancient, Oliver! She shuddered, there was no escapist fantasy in this book! How often fiction layered over reality in her private world.

She went back to her room, shut the door for privacy and paced. Up and down. Up and down. Then as she was the sort of person who tended to blame everything on herself and not on other people, she decided it was all her own fault. She had never asked anything of Rafael, but just given up and left him free to look for love with someone else. She should have taken her courage in her hands and gone after what she wanted, and now it was too late because finally, she understood that what she wanted was Rafael.

She decided she couldn't bear to be one more minute in this house. She would go and stay at Tate's tonight, and hopefully, Tinker would be around. Tate had given her a key and assured her that she could visit whenever she wanted. She knew that Tate would be away, but at least in London, she could lose that appalling sense of isolation that she suffered here. Being surrounded by hordes of humanity was comforting, compared to the bleak loneliness of the rural landscape.

She told the nanny, and her bag was already packed. She jumped in her car and drove down to Chelsea. It was cold and dark, but this did not serve to empty the streets, there was always a throng of people walking here and there, crossing roads, looking into shop windows. She wondered what it might be like to live here, to go to work every day, perhaps a job at a publishing house. It was the traditional route for girls of her class to move into genteel employment. She didn't like the idea of leaving Marco for so long, but he would be fine, with the nanny and also Rafael. Working at a publishers, could be rationalised as a move towards the literary world, surely it was what writers did, before they began to scribble their masterpieces?

She went inside and rang Tinker. He picked up after three rings.

"Hello, Pheebs darling, how are you?" he asked.

"I'm at Tate's all alone. I wondered if you would like to go out to dinner. My treat."

"Oh darling, I would love that. Where shall we go? Le Gavroche?"

"Perhaps not, there is a lovely little brasserie around the corner, and then we can come back here for coffee," said Phoebe.

She was sitting on Tate's big squashy sofa, with ethnic-coloured cushions. She saw Tate's fancy little brown leather wallet which contained the razor blade, mirror and silver tube sitting on the coffee table. She picked it up idly, and there was a packet inside. A whole gram. Lovely! Just what she needed to cheer herself up. She prepared herself a good-sized line and snorted it up. She felt rather glamorous, so insouciant when it came to this. Nothing like the schoolgirl Phoebe who had blundered around like a baby elephant. In a few minutes, her mood lifted. She floated down the passageway to the spare room where she kept some of her going out clothes and got changed into something relatively suave and elegant, Prada, which was one of her favourite designers and then went into the bathroom to apply her makeup. She wanted to trade in her boring old personality and become an interesting person. Perhaps then Rafael would love her. Although truth to be told, Rafael didn't show much interest in such people. He was a conservative person, with much more in common with the Phoebe-who-lived-at-Kiss-Wood, than the Phoebe-who-stayed-in-Chelsea.

Tinker rang the bell and she opened the door. They kissed each other and he told her she was looking beautiful. She grabbed her bag and her phone and she and Tinker walked around the corner to the brasserie. The waitress found them a table in the corner. The cocaine had lowered Phoebe's inhibitions, and she poured out her worst fears, the reasons why she thought Rafael was in a relationship with her kid sister. Tinker listened attentively. He was enthralled.

"Really darling, it's not a bad story, bit of a clichéd plot, but I can't see it. Rafael seems too straight up and down for that. I mean it's all a bit close to home, isn't it?"

"But they have so much in common, and they're always whispering together. The other day Rafael took Marco out, and when they came back,

I saw that Poppy had gone with them. They're going out and about like a family, without me!" Tears ran down her cheeks.

"Phoebe darling, please don't cry. You'll make me feel so bad. Have you thought that Rafael might not be the man for you? Perhaps there is someone much better out there for you?"

"I want Rafael. He was my first love, my only love. He is the father of my darling Marco, and I want to have more children, all by Rafael."

"Well, then there's only one thing for it. You know you have to tell him," said Tinker, forking up his delicious salmon and pasta.

"I can't," wailed Phoebe. "I know he's going to say no. Then when it comes out about him and Poppy, I'll have made an absolute fool of myself."

"Then you seemed to have reached an impasse," said Tinker. "Have you thought about trying to make him jealous. I know that it's the most boring tactic in the world, but I believe that it does work."

Phoebe remembered Rafael standing in the doorway of the room while she lay between the twins.

"No, no, that won't work, that's why it will never work, he saw me, with another man." She couldn't admit, even to Tinker, that it had been two men, it was just too embarrassing. Tinker looked uncomfortable. He probably knew about the twins. They would all know, the whole horrible crew! They left the brasserie and went back to Tate's flat for coffee.

"But tell, tell, what was it like when you first got together with Rafael?" asked Tinker.

Phoebe launched into the whole story. The way they had foiled the evil plan of Facundo, Tomas and Marianela. Tinker's round blue eyes opened wide.

"This is the same Marianela who ran off with Oliver Soames, stole his credit cards, cash and passport and disappeared?" he asked.

"Yes, that's right," replied Phoebe.

"But how bizarre that that girl swings back into your life," said Tinker.

"Well not really, she is the daughter of Claudia, the ghastly woman who my father was having an affair with, and now they have this awful squealing child, Pablo, and they all came over for the naming day, but by then Marianela had run off with Oliver, and Mummy had forbidden Claudia to attend."

"Oh, that's right. Things seemed a little awkward at the time," said Tinker.

"My mother went absolutely ballistic. You see, I believe that she had some designs on Oliver herself. So, when Marianela ran off with him, it was twice as insulting. Now that Claudia has refused to leave Tall Chimneys, my mother has absolutely forbidden anyone from Kiss Wood to fraternise with the enemies from Tall Chimneys."

"That sounds rather extreme, for your mother, I mean she's not exactly emotional, is she?" said Tinker.

"Yes, but it was just too much. She left my father and Uruguay, and has made a new life for herself. Then he brings those two sluts over, and the daughter runs off with her best friend, and now the one that was with her husband is living next door."

"Yes, I do see, it was rather heaping insult upon injury, wasn't it," said Tinker. "But never mind about that, tell me the whole story of you and Rafael and let us try and work out where it went so wrong."

"It was wrong from the offset," said Phoebe sadly, "I rescued him but he lost his life, and he had to rely on me for money, and he couldn't go back, well not until later when Tomas and Facundo were murdered."

"What!?" said Tinker. "Murdered? You never told me about that."

"Well, it's complicated. When Rafael was living at Punta del Diablo, I would go up there every weekend. Daddy didn't even notice. He was too busy cavorting with the awful Claudia. Mummy and Poppy had gone back to England. I didn't even know that Mummy wasn't coming back. I guess we were all too caught up in our various personal dramas to realise that that was strange in itself. We were so in love, no . . . that's not right, I was so in love. It was as if the universe was full of bright colours, music vibrating in the air."

"Go on," breathed Tinker.

"Then we bought Rapture for Rafael. He was this horse that was so badly treated and Rafael felt an absolute conviction that he had to rescue him, and he only cost $400, US that is. Then I suggested that Rafael come back to England with me and he said he couldn't leave Rapture. That nearly finished me off. I realised what a mistake I'd made buying him a horse. Of course, he was going to choose the horse over me," said Phoebe, looking sorrowful.

"Poor Phoebe," said Tinker, "that must have hurt, to be second to a horse."

"I guess it's better than being second to another woman," said Phoebe, the tears running slowly down her cheeks. She couldn't even say the words again, that perhaps now he loved Poppy.

"So, tell me, you're in Uruguay in the lovely little fishing village, and you're due to return to England," said Tinker, pushing her on with her story, to try to make sense of what had happened.

"I had this idea that perhaps he could live with Florencia and Pablo, they were a couple, a rather odd couple he was at least 30 years older than her. They were showjumpers, and they had moved to Atlantida. We went there to see if Rafael could work there, or at least stay there and work for his keep. And Valentino, the man who had originally given him a job was there then, and they took him on. I went back to the apartment, and Tate had arrived, with the news that Mummy was divorcing Daddy and she was charged with bringing me home."

Phoebe gulped and cut herself another line of coke. She would leave some money for Tate to pay for all the product she seemed to be consuming in increasingly large amounts. She sat back with her eyes closed and waited for the rush. At least, it took the edge off her pain.

"Keep going Phoebe, at least it might be a little cathartic to tell me the story," said Tinker, laying his small, soft white hand on her arm.

"Tate arrived, and Claudia was upset, and Tate deliberately wound her up, playing it all sexy, and for some weird reason, Marianela had gone to her father in Columbia, just before the exams. And I went one last time to see Rafael, but he was sulky, glowering, he wouldn't talk to me, perhaps he was embarrassed that I was there in front of his Uruguayan show jumping friends."

"You flew home with Tate," prompted Tinker.

The memory of that last awful day in Uruguay when she had felt utterly humiliated and crushed by Rafael's cold farewell swept over her.

"It got even worse," she said. "Before we went to the airport it came on the news. Facundo and Tomas, you know the evil boys who had tried to set up Rafael, they had been murdered, tortured and murdered, they showed a few pictures on the television, but, of course, didn't go into details. It was odd, very strange, that was the last thing that happened to me in Uruguay getting that news. I was glad to get away in the end, to come back to familiar old England. At least I belong here."

"And you came back pregnant with Rafael's baby," said Tinker, trying to find the good side to the story, he hated to see Phoebe so upset.

"Did you think perhaps that Rafael had had something to do with what happened to those boys, some sort of revenge?"

"No, of course not," said Phoebe, but there was a hint of doubt in her voice.

"But," persisted Tinker, "he was very angry at what they'd done. Perhaps that's why he didn't want anything to do with you, he had just executed his justice, and he wanted to protect you."

"Tinker! Why are you saying this?" asked Phoebe, hurt and exasperated. It was as if he was trying to make everything even worse.

"I guess I'm looking for the drama, divining the plot," he replied. "Rafael came to you in England, he came to pay you the money back, so why haven't you got back together?"

"I don't know. I was ill in hospital when he arrived. I had just had a baby, I wasn't thinking like that. Of course, I was amazed to see him, but it's as if there is this yawning gap between us, that neither of us is prepared to leap across," she replied.

"Neither of you seems brimful of self-confidence," he said. "He may be one of the most handsome men in England, but he's not high in self-esteem."

"I found the note in the bag of money. Mummy had tricked him. He had written to ask for bank details to pay back the money and she had written back that I was ill and needed him. She made it sound like I was dying. When he arrived, Marco was born, and Mummy arranged it all so that he would work for her. You see he is a miracle with the horses and of course he wanted to be with his son. None of it was of his own volition. He came, and he was a father and Mummy bulldozed him in every direction. He's been backed into a corner, and there doesn't seem any way out."

"I see that. It's all been arranged by dear Grace. She is quite a powerful person. It's hard to see how you two could break free. I guess you could go and live somewhere else, but he's into the horses, isn't he? He could get a job with someone else, but equestrian wages are not high, and you're still the one with the money, and he's a good person, he would always want to be with his son."

"It's like we're trapped in a gilded cage," said Phoebe. "Think how many people would love to be in my position, and I'm utterly miserable."

"But you said you suspected something between Rafael and Poppy?" asked Tinker, then regretted it. Phoebe's eyes clouded over with pain again. "That is going to be very awkward if they get together. It seems to squeeze you out of the equation altogether," said Tinker thoughtfully.

"It's the horses, it all for the love of horses, perhaps if I loved horses as well then it would be alright, but you see I just don't see the point."

"I agree with you there, I don't see the point at all, they kick you, need constant cleaning up, and there's always the strong possibility of falling off. It is a rather strange obsession," said Tinker. So much talking, but, still, the problems seemed insoluble.

Tinker left to catch a bus home, and Phoebe went along the passageway to the spare room. But she couldn't sleep, she felt as if she were floating up near the ceiling, on a soft cocaine-induced wave of consciousness. It was like in the films when someone died, and the camera was up in the sky looking down from the perspective of a spirit which had left its body below. A thought kept recurring to her: Was it Rafael who had tortured and murdered Facundo and Tomas? At the time of the murder, he had been living in Atlantida, not far from the outskirts of Montevideo and if he'd borrowed a car, he could have gone around the ring road and been at Melilla in less than an hour. He had the means, the motive, but was he that ruthless? They had talked endlessly of their hatred of those two, had she encouraged him in his hatred? He was the father of her son, a murderer? Then the prospect of him getting together with Poppy was even worse. She couldn't see her younger sister married to such a cold-hearted killer.

It went around and around in her head. Then, she remembered Marianela. She had mysteriously disappeared to Columbia a short time before the murder. Would Rafael have murdered her as well if she had been with Facundo and Tomas? It was different to kill a woman, although she had been just as malicious as Facundo and Tomas, and she had been one of the main people to have devised the plot.

Chapter Twenty-Six

Back at Kiss Wood on the following day, Phoebe was standing on the wide landing of the curved stairs. She saw Grace's car slide up the driveway and out climbed Poppy and Rafael, no Marco this time. They were deep in conversation, and as they talked beside the car, their heads were close together. This confirmed her worst fears. She could think of no innocent reason for them to go out together. She had to find out. She would confront them. She would ask Poppy, not Rafael. She didn't have the courage to question him and perhaps ruin forever even their rather formal, cold relationship.

She was determined, she would corner Poppy and ask her outright. Well, perhaps not outright-outright, she would ask her where she had been this afternoon for a start. Any type of guilty reaction would be a give-away. She watched Rafael and Poppy. They were both wearing their jodhpurs and boots and were heading around the side of the house, to the stables. She wondered where Marco was, presumably with his nanny. Then, she heard him at the bottom of the stairs, squeaking and chirruping, and she went down to find him with the nanny. They had been out for a walk.

"I'll take him upstairs to change him," said Phoebe.

"I'll prepare his tea, in the kitchen," said the nanny.

Marco was at the stage where he had just started walking, pulling himself up on the furniture, and walking around holding on.

"You're such a clever boy!" said Phoebe as she peeled him out of his clothing, the bath running. He laughed and gurgled and laced his chubby fingers around her hair, trying to poke her in the eye.

She had no chance to talk to Poppy yet. She must still be over at the stables. Mrs Hopkins had mentioned that they were all off to a show the next day. They would be over at the stables with her mother and one of her endless lists. Life with horses reflected Phoebe, meant endless packing, unpacking, cleaning, distributing and gathering back up again. She was feeling so frustrated that she wanted to kick out against someone.

Tate and Verena arrived. They had not been expected.

"I have to talk to your mother," said Verena.

"Phoebe darling, come down to the Goat with me. Let's have a drink," said Tate.

Phoebe had wanted to talk to Poppy, but there would be no time now, not with visitors.

"What's up with your mother?" asked Phoebe.

"I'll tell you later, but first, Tinker told me how unhappy you've been," said Tate as they drove down to the village. "You know if you love Rafael, then you'll have to make a move, declare yourself, or kiss him, or whatever it is that people do when they're declaring their passion."

Phoebe laughed out loud. "Tate, you sound as if you have never been in love!" she exclaimed.

"But darling, I thought you knew that about me, I'm a cold fish and I have never been 'in love' as they say. I'm not claiming to be a virgin of course, but sex is just something one does occasionally. I have no idea what it feels like to be in love."

"Oh, Tate! You poor thing. I may be a sad specimen, but at least I know what it is like to be in love."

"Come on, let's go into the Goat. It's ages since I've had a drink in the village, no doubt there is lots of juicy gossip to catch up with," said Tate cheerfully. "Then we can get in a huddle, and you can tell all, and we can make a plan on how to make you happy again."

"Oh, if only," said Phoebe in a sad little voice. They parked out the back and walked in through the pub garden.

"Phoebe!" called a voice. They looked over. It was Panda, and with her was a woman with her back to them. Phoebe instantly recognised Marianela's long thick mane of strange greenish-blonde hair. She waved and then went to walk on.

"Phoebe, you must come over. I absolutely insist, this silly ill-feeling between you and dear Marianela must stop, I say so, and you know I always get my way," said Panda rogueishly. Phoebe instinctively went to walk on, but Tate steered her over to the wooden table where the two women were sitting.

Panda stood up and kissed Phoebe on both cheeks with a bossy air as if she were the judge of who was friends with whom in the village. Phoebe was beginning to wonder why she had ever liked Panda. No friend of Marianela's was ever going to be a friend of hers. She looked at Marianela. She had lost weight, but she didn't look gaunt, she was even more beautiful – if that were possible - her cheekbones were more prominent, and this made her green cat's eyes wider.

"Tate, do you know Panda?" said Phoebe, automatically fulfilling her social obligations.

"I know of you, but I don't think we've actually met," said Tate.

"Then let me introduce you to Marianela," said Panda proudly, as if Marianela was her latest prize acquisition.

Phoebe was feeling totally cornered. She still hated Marianela. This woman had caused so much trouble. Then she remembered Facundo and Tomas. Perhaps Marianela knew something about that. Why had she run off to Columbia? Then marrying ancient Oliver, how bizarre was that? There was a story here, and just for a moment, she thought about a complicated plot for a novel. Then it was as if she were watching a movie on the big screen. It was Hollywood in the garden of the Goat and she and Panda were relegated to audience status. One could almost hear the music of angels in heaven playing on violins, cupids flying back and forth with cherubic limbs, harps, flutes and the clash of cymbals.

Tate was staring at Marianela as if she were a vision from outer space. Tate's divine sculpted features were etched on her face in an expression of wonder. Marianela looked at her, as if expecting the usual hostile reaction from one of Phoebe's friends, but then she smiled, and Phoebe saw at that moment the true beauty of Marianela. Her long tawny green-blond hair flowed around her shoulders, her green eyes sparkled, and her full, red lips stretched into an enticing smile.

"Are you Marianela?" asked Tate. "I had no idea, I've heard such things about you."

"I'm sure you have," said Marianela in a soft, breathless voice.

They stared at each other, and the world tilted and twirled around them. The feelings between them were palpable, like a perfectly shared stream of consciousness. Phoebe felt that she could reach out and touch the energy that flowed between them. They smiled into each other's eyes.

"I think we should go and buy some drinks, Panda!" said Phoebe, trying to edge away as quickly as impossible. She felt as if she were intruding on a very private moment.

"Panda!" she said again, adopting the commanding tone that she had heard her mother use so often. Panda scurried after her.

"When did Marianela return?" asked Phoebe.

"She turned up yesterday. There was quite a scene between her and her mother and poor old Oliver."

"Poor old Oliver, phooey!" exclaimed Phoebe. "He should have had more sense at his age."

"Well it looks like Marianela has worked her magic again – this time - on Tate," said Panda plaintively.

"Are you jealous?" asked Phoebe, surprised. "It sounds like you are jealous. You're happily married to Charles, what difference does it make to you?"

"I know, of course, I am, it's just Marianela is rather entrancing, exotic, you know and she has this weird sort of power, and I did so want her as my special friend."

"Tate also has a rather entrancing beauty, not like us plain Janes," said Phoebe, determined to rub it in. She had decided that she didn't trust Panda anymore.

"If we all end up living in the village, then it's no good feuding like something out of Romeo and Juliet," said Panda plaintively.

"I don't suppose Tate is ever going to live in the village, she lives in Chelsea, and perhaps now Marianela and Oliver's marriage will be dissolved, and Marianela will go and live with Tate."

"Gosh, that's a huge leap. All they did was look at each other," said Panda.

"It was more than that. Surely you can see that. Did it remind you of when you and Charles first met?" said Phoebe, surprising herself with her own cattiness. "It was strange, only today Tate told me she's never fallen in love, talk about tumbling over the brink, it was like something in a movie."

Panda was upset. She felt ridiculously side-lined. She had thought that the glamorous Marianela would enhance her social cachet. She loved being the spider in the middle of a web of social intrigue. She had relished the idea of watching the twisted conflict between Tall Chimneys and Kiss Wood. Now it looked like Tate would magic Marianela off to her racy life in London. Phoebe might have an open invitation to visit Tate, but Panda hardly knew Tate. She had never been deemed interesting enough.

"I think we should leave them alone," said Phoebe. "It's not really our business."

Panda bridled at this. She hated the idea of it not being any of her business. As far as she was concerned, everything that happened in the village was most definitely her business. There were several local people propping up the bar, discussing the return of Oliver's bride. They were chortling over it. Nothing this dramatic and shocking had happened in the village for some time. They had no idea that an even more exciting melodrama was being enacted several metres away!

Phoebe ordered two glasses of red wine and a couple of packets of crisps. She felt as if she needed sustenance. Her own small drama, a planned confrontation with Poppy had been entirely forgotten. It was rather satisfying to have her relatively tedious worries washed away by witnessing a tidal wave of love that was going to sweep through all their lives. Tate and Marianela! Never had she considered such an eventuality. She hoped that she and Tate could continue to be close. She did depend on her when she needed to escape Kiss Wood.

It never occurred to Phoebe that Marianela and Tate would not become an item. The feelings that had fizzed between them were tangible. If you thought about it, they were a perfect match, both of them flawlessly beautiful in a very different style. Perhaps that was why Tate had never fallen in love; she had never found her equal when it came to beauty. Phoebe could have begrudged Marianela this chance of true love after the way that she had played with Rafael's life so spitefully, but she didn't. Marianela had an undeniable allure, and now it would flourish. Probably, with Tate's contacts she would have a career as a model, although she wasn't thin as a rake there had to be openings for someone so beautiful, perhaps her hair might feature in a shampoo advertisement?

She remembered then that Verena had turned up at Kiss Wood, needing to speak to her mother. Probably they had heard the news of Marianela's return, and she had come to warn her. Now someone was going to have to tell Verena about Tate and Marianela. That would certainly upset the apple cart! How would poor Verena cope with being the 'mother-in-law' of Marianela - in a lesbian relationship with her daughter.

Phoebe sipped on her wine, her mind running through all the permutations of this situation. She was relieved that never confided in Panda with her deepest fears and secrets; undoubtedly, they would have spread around the village.

"I think I'm going to walk home," she said peremptorily to Panda and jumped up and left. Panda decided that she wasn't going to be left out of the action for another moment and went back outside to the garden to sit with Tate and Marianela.

Grace smiled grimly at her when she went into the drawing-room. Verena looked up brightly, "Where's Tate and my car?" she asked.

"She's down at the Goat with Marianela," said Phoebe.

"Really, well perhaps she'll be able to tell us the inside story," said Verena, displaying a salacious desire for juicy gossip.

"I think I should explain what I've just seen," said Phoebe slowly. She wondered why she felt that she had to do this. Perhaps, she should have just walked away and let Verena learn the truth from Tate herself. She took a deep breath. "Tate and Marianela just looked at each other, and I think they've fallen in love."

"Don't be so ridiculous," said Verena laughing out loud.

"I'm not, it's true, they looked at each other, and it was," for a moment Phoebe searched for the words, "very obvious."

Grace looked at her old friend Verena and shook her head. David obviously had more to answer for than all that had gone before. Verena might have married a younger man, but this was way beyond the limits of her ability to flout social conventions.

Chapter Twenty-Seven

Life went on at Kiss Wood without much change. The day after the Tate and Marianela meeting, Grace took Rafael, Poppy, Jerome, Ruby and Angela off to a show. They were away for three days. Phoebe felt restless. She had been all wound up to confront Poppy. Now, she had to wait until they returned. She hadn't contacted Tate. She thought it best to wait for a few days, undoubtedly Tate and Marianela were going to be so tied up in each other they would have no thought for anyone else.

She was restless and annoyed. She went back up to Poppy's room to see if there was any evidence that Poppy and Rafael were involved. That's when she found the contraceptive pills.

"Oh no," she exclaimed in horror. She felt physically ill and clutching her stomach she doubled up. All along, she had hoped that she was merely paranoid. But here, this little blister pack of not-so-innocent pills were the tangible proof. She felt shell-shocked and blundered out of the room and down the passageway. Poppy was in a sexual relationship, and it was blindingly obvious that it must be with Rafael. She began to wonder when they had first got together. There were surely not that many opportunities. The place was always teeming with other people. They must have been sneaking around for ages.

Phoebe felt as if her heart would break in two, it was bad enough to lose Rafael forever to another woman, but for it to be her younger sister was the death blow. She stumbled over to the west wing and lay down on her bed and covered her face with a pillow. If only she could suffocate herself, she just wanted to die. There seemed no reason to go on living. Everyone would be much happier without her. After a couple of hours, she sat up. She could hear Marco and the nanny in the room next door. She wondered if the nanny knew, she was always sharp-eyed, and Phoebe began to wonder if she was the person to have such unlimited access to her beloved child.

Several hours later, the horsebox rolled back up the drive. Phoebe was standing on the wide landing looking down on them. Rafael was driving, with Poppy next to him and Grace next to the window. Jerome, Ruby and Angela were on the back seat. How could they do it? Hide their feelings for each other to such an extent? It seemed incredible. She shook her head. She couldn't bear it. She had no idea what was going to happen now. This made the relationship between Tate and Marianela fade into insignificance.

She went down to the stable yard, unable to contain her impatience. She had to talk to Poppy, ask her outright. She walked in on a conversation with Jamie and her mother, who were standing in the small office in the stables.

"Why don't you geld him?" suggested Jamie. Surely, he couldn't be talking about Rafael? "He's always going to be unruly as a stallion but gelding him might take the fire out of him, then he could be a very successful show jumping horse, or eventing, or even dressage. You've still got Bliss, and we've made sure he's handled properly since the moment he was born."

Grace looked at Jamie. This had never occurred to her. They both looked towards Phoebe who was standing the doorway.

"Hello Phoebe dear," said her mother in a distractedly. She turned back to Jamie.

"We could collect enough semen to be frozen," she said. "Jamie, I think you might have come up with the perfect solution. You could ride him with Uwe, get some dressage training. You know he might be a very good eventer. He's certainly bold enough, pots of courage to tackle the cross-country."

"Fresh fields to conquer," said Jamie quietly smiling at her. She smiled back. Jamie seemed like the only person who did understand her.

"What are you talking about?" asked Phoebe in a high-pitched voice.

"It's Tinpot. Oliver has emailed me to tell me that he's giving me his half-share. Poor man has lost his spirit, seems as if he's given up on the world," said Grace crisply, without a trace of compassion, but also no bitterness. She had moved on.

"Oh, of course," said Phoebe, it had to be a horse. She looked around. Poppy came out of Harley's loose box.

313

"Hi Phoebe, we're back," she called.

"Obviously," retorted Phoebe. "Poppy, I *have* to talk to you now. Can we go somewhere by ourselves?"

"Of course," said Poppy, her eyes wide, "But I do have to settle in Bosley."

"Just for once can we leave the ponies and talk about something important to me," said Phoebe.

"Is there something wrong, Pheebs?" asked Poppy anxiously, as soon as they were out of earshot of the others. Rafael had watched them walking away and frowned.

"I went into your room and found the contraceptive pills," said Phoebe accusingly.

"Oh," said Poppy. "But what were you doing in my room? That's not like you at all."

"What is like me?" asked Phoebe bitterly. "How could you do this to me?"

"Do what? You mean have a sex life. I'm seventeen. I'm legal. But please Phoebe, don't tell Mummy, it's so jolly awkward, I don't think she'd take it very well."

"*She* wouldn't take it very well," said Phoebe exploding in a fury. "And how the fuck am I meant to take it?"

"Phoebe, it's not like you to swear. I thought you'd understand after what happened with you and Rafael, but at least I'm taking precautions, so I don't get pregnant," said Poppy, genuinely bewildered at her elder sister's attitude.

"You're having it off with Rafael, and you don't think I'll mind," said Phoebe, so angry she wanted to shake Poppy until her teeth rattled.

Poppy stared at her in astonishment.

"Rafael? You think I'm having it off with Rafael? Phoebe, how could you think that of me?"

"Well tell me it's not true then, deny it to my face."

314

Poppy burst out laughing. "Of course, I'll deny it. I do love him, but only because of you and Marco, not like *that*! Oh! Phoebe are you on drugs?"

This was awkward. Because for many months now Phoebe had been on drugs, but, of course, she wasn't going to admit that to Poppy.

"But you're taking the pill?" she spluttered.

"Yes, and I am in love, and he's in love with me, well he says he is, but who really knows. We would tell everyone except for this ridiculous feud. I was rather hoping that Mummy might calm down a bit and then we can come out in the open. I'm wishing I was you in love with Rafael, and only have to hide it from Daddy who was absent most of the time. You should try it with Mummy on the warpath."

"Who is he? This boyfriend?" said Phoebe, feeling really, really sick, but also there was a dawning of hope, perhaps, just perhaps it wasn't Rafael.

"Hector, of course!" said Poppy. "It's so good to tell you, I've wanted to tell you for ages, but we made a pact. I had to tell Rafael because he'd seen us and I swore him to secrecy."

"That's why you and he are always disappearing off together."

"Yes, he's helping us to see each other. He's not happy about it, but he understands."

Phoebe began to laugh hysterically.

"You didn't honestly think that Rafael and I had got together? You know he loves you to death, he just can't tell you, he hates us being rich."

Phoebe's head was dizzy with hope. The world had suddenly got brighter. She went from utter hopelessness and despair to bursting joy. Poppy told her that Rafael loved her, that didn't seem possible. But Poppy didn't know about the twins. Or did she? Did her confidences with Rafael extend to him telling her what had happened?

She wanted to run to him and fling her arms around him and declare herself. But she decided not to. As usual, the yard was teeming with people. It had to be a private moment. She only hoped that Poppy was right. Then she thought again, what if he were the murderer, but suddenly she didn't care. Those two young men were despicable excuses for human beings, better to have them banished from the earth. Sooner or later, she had to confront Rafael. It was do or die. If he really loved her, then they could get together, money or no money, she didn't care, she would give it all away to a cats' home.

A week dragged by and Phoebe made a resolve every morning, that this was the day she would declare her love to Rafael. But every day, she put it off, she just couldn't bring herself to do it. If only some calamitous event would bring them together, in the same way as the dastardly plan by those three at Melilla, then she would have to act, no more procrastination.

Phoebe wished that she could talk to Tate, but of course, Tate was off being in love, for the first time in her life. Grace had been in daily contact with Verena, who was off on another planet with disgust and fury. She didn't mind her elder daughter being a lesbian, that was rather fashionable at the moment, and it wasn't as if she were some look-alike man.

"What I can't work out is how these dykes say that they prefer women and then do their very best to look like men, can you understand it, Grace?"

Grace had shaken her head sympathetically. Phoebe may have had an illegitimate child, but at least she appeared to be heterosexual, and the father she had chosen to mate with was a horse person. It had all worked out rather well. She sympathised endlessly with Verena, and felt that it was somehow partly her fault. If only she had managed her husband a little better then he wouldn't have gone off with that ghastly Claudia and Marianela and Tate would never have met.

Finally, Phoebe decided she would ring Tate. Surely by now, Tate could spare an hour or two away from her new object of desire and listen to Phoebe's troubles. That was if Marianela hadn't succeeded in turning her against all her former friends. She waited until four in the afternoon, by which time Tate must surely be up and around, and rang her.

"Hello Pheebs darling," said Tate, picking up on the third ring.

"Tate, I've been dying to talk to you. How is it going? Or is that a silly question?"

"Oh, it is utterly marvellous. I can highly recommend falling in love. I don't know why I didn't do it before," trilled Tate lightly.

"Can I come up and speak to you? Can you spare me an hour, I'm desperately in need of some big sister advice?"

"Of course, you know I've always got time for you. And I've got some things to tell you, rather a story actually, the truth about the murders. Marianela has finally agreed that I tell you, but I have to swear you to absolute secrecy."

"More secrets!" exclaimed Phoebe.

"More? Why have you got some secrets to tell?"

"Nothing in the league of what you have, I imagine," said Phoebe dryly

In the course of her first great love affair, in between the most divine and sensual sex she had ever experienced, Tate had learnt the truth about the deaths of Facundo and Tomas. The truth was far worse than Phoebe's fears that it had been Rafael exacting such a gruesome and blood-thirsty revenge on them. It had taken many patient hours to persuade Marianela that Phoebe needed to know the truth, as she suspected it had been Rafael. Eventually, Marianela had given in, persuaded by Tate that Phoebe was not a monster, but a decent old stick, or rather a decent young stick, and she wouldn't use the knowledge to hurt Marianela. Tate desperately wanted to join the two ends of her nearest and dearest, and she hoped that Phoebe might be able to be friends with both of them.

Phoebe caught the train down to London. She had been missing her London sprees at Tate's place. She could always go down and visit Tinker, but he lived in a dinghy bedsit in Maida Vale, and it just wasn't the same. Tate was the sparkling presence that lit up the world around her, Phoebe and Tinker were the much duller satellites. Phoebe was hanging on tenterhooks, she wanted to see this transformed Tate, the Tate-in-love, but most of all she wanted an explanation about the murders, she just hoped that it wasn't an indictment of Rafael. Perhaps if she understood what had happened, she could move on, and she had to confront Rafael. After tonight there could be no more excuses.

They met up at a café, and Phoebe found herself immediately longing for a line of cocaine. She had come to associate Tate with the wonderful feeling that the drug gave her. She suppressed the desire; she was becoming aware of how much she was craving for the magic white powder. She was determined that she wouldn't use it again, not forever, but not for a while. It was starting to cloud her thinking. She had a lot at stake, and she needed to think clearly.

"Now, I'm here so you can tell me all about Marianela and the delightful person you've found inside that beautiful, but cruel shell," she said, hoping that Tate would not take offence at this comment.

"Yes, I know she told me all about the dastardly plot with Rafael. She admits he didn't deserve it, but what happened afterwards to her, was utterly cruel. Perhaps you and Rafael can find it in your hearts to forgive her," said Tate.

"Really! I didn't think you would ever be so mealy-mouthed," said Phoebe, shocked at this new Tate, preaching forgiveness and redemption.

"First, I'll give you a bit of background. She was only twelve years old when her mother prostituted her to a disgusting old man, as she couldn't pay the rent. Marianela was rewarded with strawberry ice-cream. You know she can't eat ice-cream these days without remembering the horror of it."

Phoebe was shocked. Her face went white. It might have been predictable that such a thing had happened, but somehow joking about it, then knowing that it actually had happened, made it worse.

"But she's the mother of my half-brother now!" she said. "Do you think she'll do it to him, make him a rent boy."

Tate shrugged her elegant bony shoulders.

"I wouldn't put anything past the old witch. Poor darling Marianela was raised to be a whore. You do know that Facundo was the first proper boyfriend she had ever had, of her own choosing. She was frightfully proud of it, showing off to her mother, which is what made it all the worse when he . . ," she paused, searching for words.

"What did Facundo do to her?" asked Phoebe. "I would have thought she was more than a match for that horrible young man."

"It was after the debacle with Rafael. He decided to blame Marianela, although I'm sure he was looking for any excuse. I don't think he liked women at all. He was a closet gay, him and that weak, lily-livered Tomas.

318

Rafael had guessed that Marianela wasn't a virgin as she had pretended and he was determined to punish her."

"Did he beat her?" asked Phoebe wide-eyed.

"If only it had been a bit of physical violence. He had it all planned and I don't think Marianela was the first. I think he had done it before. It's good that he will never do it again."

"Are you saying that what they did to Marianela was related to their deaths? Torture and everything? Surely not Marianela!"

"No, they did something unutterably foul to her, and she went to her father in Columbia and he arranged it."

"Oh, my God! That explains why she disappeared just before her exams, I thought it was weird, but there was so much going on. Do you think my father knows?" asked Phoebe.

"I have no idea. I don't suppose so. Marianela kind of blames you and Rafael. You see it was because he didn't succeed in hurting Rafael that he decided to hurt Marianela instead," explained Tate.

"Well, I don't think that is totally logical. But what exactly did they do to her?"

"She said I could tell you, but I don't think you really want to hear the details. They took her to a brothel, and she was subjected to stuff that you can barely imagine. A lot of men, beatings, and at one point they put a needle through her nipple, you can still see the scar. They forced her to lick their arseholes, and they came all over her face and inserted their clenched fists inside her. They made her do things that you would never have dreamt of. She was an absolute mess, and Facundo dropped her off at her mother's apartment and drove away while she was cowering in the gutter. Her mother wanted to hush it up, but then she realised that they needed to do something, and Marianela went to her father's, and he made her a prisoner, she was never allowed out alone, always with bodyguards. That was why she wanted to come to England, and she was so desperate to escape that Oliver seemed the answer. But when it came to sleeping with him, she panicked, she just couldn't do it. She ran away."

Phoebe shuddered. For the first time, she considered Marianela as a victim. All that swanning around and being nasty, it was the way she had kept hold of her self-respect. She couldn't imagine a mother prostituting her daughter, and such a beautiful daughter. Poor Marianela. But now she had found love and Tate was a good person, a strong person and she would look after her. Then finally, it came to her, Rafael was not a murderer, he was not involved. He would no more have done that than she would have. Now the worst thing she had to face was him telling her that he didn't want to ever marry her.

"Thank you for telling me this Tate. It makes a difference in all sorts of ways. Do you think Marianela can bear to see me, so we can still be friends, or does she really imagine that I was somehow involved?"

"She acknowledges that you had nothing to do with it. She knows what they tried to do to Rafael was wrong. She says she was spiteful. She wants to be a different person."

"Can I tell Rafael, explain to him what happened?" asked Phoebe.

"Yes, but only so we can resolve this all for once and for all, then we can move on. She's still so young, and I've promised her we're going to have a wonderful life."

They talked for several hours, and Phoebe's kind heart cried out for the girl who had tried to make her life hell. She was so beautiful. It was as if she had to pay the dues for such beauty. In the end, it was very late, and Tate insisted that they go back to her flat.

"Come home with me and stay the night, it's too late, and you shouldn't go to a hotel or anything. Perhaps you don't want to be alone."

"No, my head is full of horror."

Back at the flat Tate offered her cocaine, but she stuck to her resolution. She went to bed and lay on her back, staring at the ceiling. She had been so upset at the thought that Poppy and Rafael loved each other. That was nothing to the cruelty in Marianela's world, just loving the wrong person wasn't so bad. But he didn't love Poppy. She was certain now. She would go home, and she would talk to him, no more procrastination. And perhaps there would be a happy ever after for them.

She got up the next morning full of resolution. She went into the kitchen to make coffee and came face to face with Marianela. They looked at each other. Everything in their respective worlds had changed.

"I'm so sorry to hear what happened to you," said Phoebe.

For a moment Marianela looked like she wanted to scratch her eyes out.

"I don't want your pity," she hissed.

"No, of course not. Let's start again. We both love Tate. For her sake, there is no reason why we should hate each other."

Marianela looked at the floor and nodded.

"Can I have a cup of coffee?" asked Phoebe, as if bowing to the fact that Marianela lived here, and she was only a visitor. "I'm really happy for you and Tate, you should be so happy together."

"What about you and that stable . . , Rafael, are you going to get married?" asked Marianela.

"I don't know. But we'll be connected in all sorts of ways. Do you think your mother will go back to my father?" asked Phoebe. "She seems pretty happy at Tall Chimneys."

"I'm not my mother's keeper," snapped Marianela. Then Phoebe remembered that this poor girl had been prostituted by her mother all those years ago and probably ever since. What a family! She was thankful to have her mother. Grace might not be overtly affectionate, but she did care about her daughters in her own way, and that was what was important.

Phoebe jumped in her car after coffee and drove back to Oxfordshire. Sitting in traffic she felt like screaming in frustration; on the other hand, it helped her to put off the defining moment. If Rafael shunned her now, that would be the bitter end. At home, she gave Marco a big hug and took him down to the stables. Rafael was watching Jamie riding Tinpot.

"Hi Rafael, I've been to London. Marianela was at Tate's place, you know they're together."

"Yes, the gossip has been buzzing around," he said in a disinterested voice. "Do you think that your mother will resume contact with Tall Chimneys now?"

She stared at him. Why did he care? Of course, because he wanted Poppy to be able to be open about her relationship. The silence yawned between them.

"I found out last night how Facundo and Tomas died, who had them killed. It was Marianela's father who organised it. He's friends with some of the narcotrafficking cartels."

"Why would he do that?" he asked incredulously.

"They did unspeakable things to Marianela."

"But why, she was in it with them?" he asked, genuinely bewildered.

"Facundo was a very nasty person, and he subjected her to some awful abuse, other men raping her, you don't want to know," Phoebe said.

"It's good that those two are dead. They were bad men," said Rafael. "Thank you for rescuing me from them."

"That's the problem, isn't it!" burst out Phoebe. Her voice high-pitched and desperate. "I rescued you, and you're grateful. You never really loved me, not the way I loved you." She had no pride anymore; she just said it. The bleak truth.

"No, that's not exactly true. I am not a schoolgirl, but then neither are you, anymore. We have Marco. We belong together. I do want us to be a family, but it just doesn't seem possible."

Phoebe was listening intently. What she really wanted to hear was 'I love you.' But that wasn't happening. She would have to make a fool of herself and say it first.

"I love you, and I want to marry you," she said.

The silence reverberated between them.

"You can't say it, can you!" she said in utter despair.

"Yes, I can. I love you," he said quietly, and then he looked at her, and she felt herself melting in his beautiful dark eyes. She began to laugh, laughing out loud, her mouth wide open.

"But I have nothing to offer you," he replied.

"What if we go back and live in Uruguay. We can have a riding school and more children, brothers and sisters for Marco. We can live a simple life, give riding lessons, go up to Brazil to do show jumping," she suggested.

"But what is there in Uruguay for you?" asked Rafael.

"I want you to be happy, and I know that you love your country, you love horses, we can have a riding school, and you will be the master. I guess I can be a writer in my own time, in between looking after the children. They will all be as beautiful as Marco."

"Can we really go back to Uruguay?" said Rafael, as his face lit up with happiness. Phoebe had never seen him look so happy, happier than when he had a rosette on Gunner at the Staffordshire show. "Perhaps we could take some of Tinpot's frozen semen, and Estrella could have a foal by him. You remember that black mare at Melilla. I know I'm just thinking of spending your money, but I did so love that mare. And we could have competitions with proper courses, different types of competitions, top score, puissance." He was building golden castles in the air, his black eyes shining with joy, his mind buzzing with plans. Phoebe laughed with delight; this was the Rafael that she had always imagined.

"I guess we could, and as far as I'm concerned it's not *my* money, it's *our* money!" said Phoebe, laughing out loud. She could never compete with his love for horses. She would accept it and go with the flow.

"Hopefully Claudia will stay here with Oliver, and then my father can come and visit and get to know his grandchildren. He won't be alone."

"What about Poppy and Hector?" asked Rafael.

"They're so young. I imagine my mother will relent and perhaps their love won't last."

"Our love with last," said Rafael, taking her in his arms.

323

Epilogue

Grace smiled when they told her.

"There is only one condition I am going to impose," she said. "That you learn how to shoe horses before you return Rafael, I cannot bear to think of those poor Uruguayan horses with their hoofs at all different angles."

Rafael and Phoebe laughed out loud.

"So - we have your blessing Mummy," pealed Phoebe.

"Yes, of course, you do. I will be over to visit and inspect those horses' hoofs," said Grace, and she laughed too. A dry, hard little laugh. "Anyway, I imagine after a few years you'll come back. The standard of horsemanship is absolutely dire over there, and it's going to take more than your expertise Rafael to change that!"

"There's just one more thing, and it's not my secret to tell, but Poppy and Hector are in love."

"Hector Soames! Well, that has to be a good match," said Grace and laughed again.

The sun shone on the countryside of Oxfordshire. All was right with the world, just for a moment, not forever and ever. Oliver perhaps was to suffer more than he deserved as Claudia refused to leave Tall Chimneys. Grace and Jamie gelded Tinpot, after they had his semen collected and frozen for posterity and Jamie was to compete on him. Rafael learned to shoe horses, and he and Phoebe and Marco returned to Uruguay to find a suitable property, an estate with houses, stables and fields on the outskirts of Carasco. Tate and Marianela travelled the world and became the most famous and beautiful couple in the world. Hector and Poppy began dating openly but decided that they weren't really in love after all. The dance of love and the search for rapture and revenge flowed on through the years.